The Lebensborn Experiment

Scott Grant

Visit actionthrillers.net to view other books by Scott Grant.

DEDICATION

This book is dedicated to the millions of innocent Jews who became victims of a eugenics plot to permanently alter the future of human civilization. Hitler's inconceivable plan involved a global scale genocide, not just of Jews, but everyone who didn't fit an Aryan fantasy profile in Hitler's demented mind. Hitler wanted to begin the design of a single Aryan race by using thousands of children who were born as a result of eugenic experiments within the Lebensborn project. Some of the children survived and live among us today in obscurity, but many were beaten to death, or starved in mental hospitals after the Nazis fled. The incredible evil involved in murdering millions of people to re-order the physiognomy of the planet is shocking enough but the audacity of using eugenics to create a capricious race according to skin, eye and hair color is insane. A central part of Hitler's delusions of grandeur was his attempt to use medical science to extend his own life by a few centuries. A sufficient number of documentaries and history books exist that deal with this subject matter. In this book an attempt has been made to revitalize this critical phase of history by combining accurate chronology with fictional characters and dramatic circumstances. Can another holocaust catch us again? We cling to the hope that mankind will never fall so low once more but as philosopher George Santayana warns us; "Those who cannot learn from history are doomed to repeat it."

SG

Thine are these orbs of light and shade,

Thou madest life in man and brute

Thou madest Death and Lo Thy foot

Is on the skull, that thou hast made.

Thou wilt not leave us in the dust,

Thou madest man he knows not why

He thinks he was not made to die

And Thou hast made him, Thou art just.

Sir Alfred Lord Tennyson
In Memoriam A. H. H.

The Lebensborn Experiment

Chapter One: Northern Lights

Aamu Tuuri perspired through the sheets. Her trembling body seemed to float on a lake of perspiration with each clinching spasm of a breached birth. Her country doctor worked feverishly to unbreach the fetus when he suddenly discovered there was another. Twins! He sadly let his mind drift to the fact that Finnish people are burdened with such strange names. Tuuri meant Mrs. Luck and her first name "Aamu" meant Morning in English. This Morning there would be no luck. In spite of his London education in medicine without special equipment and anesthesia he correctly surmised that her poor heart would not be able to endure the extra burden. He made the incision laterally above her pubic bone and pulled the infants from her womb. He reached them to his wife who served as his nurse assistant in emergencies, then immediately began to pound on Aamu's chest plate as he moved to give her artificial respiration. He himself was bathed in sweat as he worked frantically, but in vain to save her. Finally, Aamu's husband Ahti gently laid his large palm on the doctor's shoulder and pulled him away from the scene of life and death.

"You tried Dr. Turhala." The doctor had to constrain an urge to laugh insanely as he considered that Ahti didn't speak English and couldn't know that his name, Dr. Turhala translates into English as Dr. Useless. "What will you do with two children and no wife Ahti?" " I have a sister who married well in Norway. I will take the girl to her to care for. My son will remain here with me. I can teach him many things that I could never teach her." He replied. "Will you do this soon?

1

I suggest you delay this until the children at least get to know each other. Otherwise they will both grow up hating you for denying them a reasonable childhood together." Dr. Turhala explained. "I am full of sadness now Dr. Turhala. When I have slept on it I will contact my other sister in Helsinki and she can come here to stay with us until the children are a little older. Now I must keep my wits about me until Aamu is in the ground." Ahti stared across the lake nearby and the thick forest along the horizon as the mid September Aurorealis Borealis, Northern Lights pulsated across the sky.

"Winter will soon be here and the permafrost will deny Aamu a proper burial until spring if we wait too long for her funeral." "Yes, I understand Ahti. If you wish, until your sister from Helsinki arrives, my wife can care for the infants in our home to give you time to part with your wife." "I am deeply grateful Dr.Turhala."

While Mrs. Turhala bathed and swaddled the infants, the two men wrapped Aamu in layers of white sheets then placed her in a large wooden tool chest and locked her in the barn. Soon the Turhalas and the infants were in a coach pulled by large dapple grey horses headed for the doctor's country home near the village of Suomussalmi, Finland. As the coach swayed, Dr. Turhala wrote in his journal, "Twelve September, 1920. Twins, a boy and a girl, born to Ahti and Aamu Tuuri. Time of birth, 0400 hours. Aamu died of a massive cardiac arrest at 04:10 hours God save her soul." The coach slipped through the darkness with speed and purpose while the autumn morning fog suddenly opened across a large valley as the forests already sprinkled with snow came into view. The light rain now turned to frozen sleet and the driver availed himself of a long pull of vodka.

Across the valley a great herd of reindeer moved in an enormous circle which appeared to be a large miller's wheel grinding flour beneath its grating surface. Winter was arriving slightly early. Dr. Turhala had witnessed the miracle of life and the sad drudgery of death many times in his long life, but to comprehend that it had just occurred in the midst of this greater spectacle of life and natural harshness choked him up and brought mist to his eyes. He had seen so many successful operations performed in London, where antiseptics and anesthesia were available. Here he had only vodka and a scalpel. He struggled to blame her death on his lack of modern support but deep inside he knew his soul would be burdened with the nagging question of whether he might have done just one more thing to keep her alive.

He looked at the tiny bundles in his wife's arms and pondered what sort of lives they would live without a mother to protect them. The days grew shorter and the nights longer until there was only night. The infants remained with Mrs. Turhala because she refused to consider risking their health by transporting them home in such an unusually harsh winter. The babies grew at a rapid rate thanks to the robust diet of reindeer milk and when spring finally arrived, Ahti appeared with a coach and almost ungratefully demanded the return of the children. "Have you registered them with the church?" Mrs. Turhala asked. "We were winter bound and had no way of knowing what to call them besides Tweedle dee and Tweedle dum" she enjoined with a trace of sarcasm. " I shall call the boy Kaarle. It means strong and masculine in French as I am given to understand from a French book my sister gave me." "And the girl?"

"I thought to name her Aamu after her mother but the sadness of it overwhelmed me, so I decided she will be called Laila, which as you know means Light. I knew I wouldn't see her until the light of day returned so I call her Light."
"Kaarle and Laila." Mrs. Turhala repeated approvingly. Ahti signaled and his sister Anna entered to help carry the babies to Ahti's waiting coach.

The years passed quickly and the children grew into beautiful platinum haired, rosy cheeked, blue eyed wonders who both looked like their mother. Ahti was a tall muscular man who also had blonde hair and blue eyes. His face was chiseled by the hard winters of his life but he remained handsome. He was a God fearing man and he worked hard in the forests to provide for his sister and his children. His hunting skills matched his farming skills so there was never a day that he didn't provide bountifully for his little family. He owned more than a hundred hectares and had a large herd of reindeer, as well as all manner of animals and poultry. He was considered a catch by many of the unmarried women in the village but Ahti strongly believed he shouldn't even think of a woman to replace Aamu until the children were grown. He taught his children to Telemark ski and traverse with snow shoes and assigned them a full day of work each day on the farm. For their part, the children enjoyed playing winter games and exploring the nearby forests together. They rode the back of Tarja their favorite of all reindeer. Her name meant "Protector" in Finn and she took her job seriously jealously guarding over the children as though they were her own.

The children loved breathing on their bedroom window and watching the ice crystals form. On clear nights they wondered if there were reindeer like Tarja on other planets. "There's only one Tarja in the entire universe!" Kaarle scolded Laila and she cried silently. Seeing her tears Kaarle became confused. "Why do you have tears about Tarja?" "I am not crying for Tarja. I'm crying because I am feeling that like Tarja, our mother was the only one of herself in the entire universe and she never got to hold me. Oh Kaarle you and Papa are also the only ones of yourselves and yesterday I heard Papa and Auntie Anna say that I would be leaving soon for the Norway. I am so sad Kaarle. Please ask Papa not to send me away. Perhaps we could run away in the forest and if Papa loves me he will miss me so much he won't send me away." "Oh Laila. We were born together. No one not even Papa can ever separate us. When he sends you to Norway I will find a way to come and get you. I will grow big and strong so no one will ever hurt you. Ever!" Kaarle promised.

One morning while Kaarle was fast asleep Aunt Anna tip toed into the children's bedroom and carried a sleeping Laila downstairs. When Kaarle awoke to discover Laila's empty bed and closet he shrieked and bounded down the stairs so hard he tripped and nearly rolled into the fireplace. Ahti picked him up and rocked with him in his favorite rocking chair before the crackling fire. Kaarle was sobbing uncontrollably. "There, there my son. Get hold of yourself." "Papa, how could you send her away without letting her say good bye to me? I want to go to Norway too! Please let me join her".

"Nonsense my son. You must learn to think of others before yourself. Without Mama this place was a dead end for her. My sister Anna has stayed with us now several years and longs to return home to Helsinki. Your Auntie Sani in Norway will be like the Mother Laila never had. She will teach her the ways of a woman. Things she could never learn with us." Ahti said.

Sobbing, Kaarle shook his little head yes as though he understood and sat for a long time in his fathers arms staring blankly at the dancing flames in the fireplace. Ahti began to worry on the second day when Kaarle refused yet another meal and his fear turned to anger. He tried once to force feed a spoon of stew down Kaarle's throat but Kaarle spit it out and ran outside falling face first in the snow. That night Kaarle developed a fever that wouldn't break. Ahti sat by his bed all night and in the morning he was awakened when Kaarle asked in a feeble voice; "What's for breakfast Papa?."

Kaarle received letters written by Aunt Sani that described how well Laila was doing in her art class at school and he chuckled when he unfolded a drawing of Tarja with Kaarle and Laila perched on her back. The forest and the lake were in such exact detail that each tree and curve in the shoreline was precise. Kaarle knew then that Laila was suffering perhaps even greater loneliness than he. He vowed that someday when he was rich he would collect his sister and they would travel to all of the large cities and countries he read about in his books. For now, he would work hard and study the ways of a man as his father wished.

On Kaarle's twelfth birthday a strange little man showed up at the door. The man was only a little more than half the height of Ahti, but his frame was very muscular and his face was a map of suffering and the wisdom one receives from living a harsh and dangerous life. His eyes were deep and powerful. Kaarle had never seen such a dark man before and was filled with awe by the contrast of their skin. Ahti rushed past Kaarle and embraced the man. "Kaarle! Come! I want you to meet a man who has been my friend since we were both little boys. Janne this is my son Kaarle, Kaarle, meet Janne." The man grinned and it seemed his face disintegrated into a thousand fragments.

He took Kaarle's hand and Kaarle felt a sureness and a confident strength that only his Papa had ever demonstrated before. " Kaarle, Janne is a Sami. His people are Arctic people. He is a Reindeer Man. I was once hunting in the Arctic and Janne's people rescued me from a fierce Polar bear that wanted to eat me for dinner. I asked Janne to come and stay with us. He will teach you things that only ski soldiers know." The next morning Kaarle awakened with a jolt. Janne had been sitting next to Kaarle's bed for who knew how long just staring. "Ahh you are awake now. Come we have a great many things to learn before sun down my little friend."

They Telemark skied the seventy kilometers to Suomussalmi and back without a pause or a break. When they reached home Kaarle was so stiff he had to take a sauna which Janne prepared with special herbs and camphors. As the three sat in the sauna sweating and feeling the eucalyptus and camphor open their nostrils, Kaarle wondered how many eternities would pass before either his father, or Janne would signal that it was time to leave the heat that had become so hot it had begun to dry even the leaves on the stones.

Finally Janne lifted his palm upward and Kaarle bolted for the door as Janne and Ahti began to laugh. Kaarle slipped on the ice outside and landed upside down in a snow drift. When he recovered he was shocked to see both Janne and his father swimming nude in a large section of the lake that had been cracked open while Kaarle had been on his Telemark.

"Join us!" His father called out. Kaarle ran at full tilt and dove into the moving crushed ice. When he surfaced Janne took him by the hand. "Take a deep breath Kaarle. We will take a small journey beneath the ice to allow you to gradually get accustomed to what it looks like and feels like should you ever fall through the ice. Most important is to shut out the feelings of cold with your mind and orient yourself against, or with the water current to find the air hole again. You will panic, but you must control it. Remember you are holding the levers of control. No one else. There will be air bubbles we can use along the way. Today we won't go far. In time, we will be able to cross the lake under the ice and find weak places in the surface ice where we can make our escape without swimming back to our entry hole. Kaarle looked nervously at his father who sternly nodded his head. Kaarle knew to resist would bring shame to his father. The two began swimming into the dark cold abyss.

Kaarle fought off his feelings about the cold but he became disoriented in the darkness and began to panic. Janne quickly took him by the hand and brought him to a large bubble beneath the ice. They both took air from it until it shrunk and then they swam to another. Kaarle's eyes adjusted to the darkness and when Janne pointed to the entry hole Kaarle easily swam to it with Janne close behind. They emerged with a leap. Ahti was treading water.

Ahti and Janne quickly took Kaarle by his arms and pulled him out of the lake. Kaarle started to laugh from not being able to feel his legs and from the shock of the jolts he felt as his bare feet, which seemed like tree stumps, hit sharp chunks of ice in the snow path. They entered the hot sauna but now instead of feeling the burning Kaarle felt the euphoria of the rush of blood to his brain that had been locked inside his lower body. After a light dinner of roasted pheasant and fish soup Kaarle began nodding to sleep. "You have had a good beginning Janne." Ahti remarked. "He will be a Ski soldier sooner than any of us could have expected.

Have you heard from the others?" Janne asked. "Yes. Colonel Sotavalta has decided that we must soon meet in Helsinki at a secret conference. I will let Kaarle know tonight, in general terms, what we intend to accomplish with this training we are putting him through." Ahti explained. "Do you think it wise? He has friends who are not among the chosen. What if he discusses our secrets with them?" Janne queried. "He won't. I will explain the importance of the program to him and he will be made clear about the fact that if he discusses anything with outsiders he will be breaking a solemn promise to me." Ahti explained. Ahti shook Kaarle's arm gently until he awakened.

"My son are you awake and is your mind clear?" "Yes, father. You want to explain to me why Janne is training me so hard." "Aah! You were only pretending to be asleep." Ahti gasped. "No Father. I was asleep. Since you took away Laila while I was fast asleep, I have trained myself to be able to listen even when I'm sleeping." "Hmmm." Ahti pondered.

"Well, let me explain something to you now that you are awake. Some weeks before your twelfth birthday I was asked to meet with Colonel Sotavalta some kilometers from here at his winter home. Across all of Finland there are three hundred Sami Ski soldiers just like Janne, at this moment, training twelve to fifteen year old boys such as yourself to be Ski soldiers." Ahti said with a serious expression.

"Why are they doing this Papa?" "Well, for as long as anyone can remember our ancestors have fought brutal wars with the Russians. We have always had to fear our great neighbor to the East and it has been our country's winters that have done most of the fighting to defend our Mother Land. Not much has changed. Our choice is to stand and fight, or submit to their will and lose our souls.

"Our wise president Pehr Evind Svinhufvud af Qvalstad has seen the wisdom of preparing for war while we are enjoying the peace won for us by the blood of our ancestors. That is why he has commissioned the Sami to train one on one the young men including yourself who will use their teaching to protect our precious Finland.   Your first year and each year thereafter will emphasize physical conditioning and winter training. Starting this December you will travel with Janne to Mount Halti in the North. You will spend a few months between ski training on that mountain and then in the Lap land, living with the Sami people and learning to live on the land indefinitely without modern support. Next year you will begin weapons training. Your weapons will range from improvised Molotov cocktails for antitank warfare, to pistols machine guns and knives and even some artillery.

The following years until you are twenty will find you spending months at a time in the wilderness practicing ambush tactics and assault formations with other regional teams. You will form friendships as Janne and I did that will last all of your life." "Were you and Janne Ski soldiers Papa?" "Yes my son. As Ski soldiers we are not allowed to train our own sons because we cannot humanly remain objective. Our emotions get in the way every time. We need Ski soldiers who are Vikings without fear who take risks no one else would dream of, who are creative and stubborn to succeed. Fathers would teach their sons a caution that may in a bitter irony be precisely what gets them killed. After your eight years are concluded, if God is merciful and we are still at peace with our neighbors, you will honor Janne by training his grandchildren and so it will go on, back and forth until the end of time. Many of your mates in the village will wonder where you disappear to and will try their best to get you to talk but I have made a promise to your Commander Colonel Sotavalta, also to the President of Finland and of course Janne that you will remain steadfast and true to our precious Mother land and not so much as whisper the smallest detail of your life as a Ski soldier. "Will you before God make this promise to your Finnish brothers and sisters now?" "Yes father. May I go to sleep now? I must be ready for tomorrow." Ahti's eyes brimmed with tears of pride as he embraced his son and nodded over Kaarle's shoulder to Janne. Janne stood and saluted them both then disappeared out into the winter night to check the perimeter.

Janne kept adding a book each day to Kaarle's ruck sack until finally Kaarle carried twenty kilos on their Telemark journeys. Once a week was sauna day. Kaarle soon became able, day, or night, to completely traverse the lake solo beneath the ice.

He found air bubbles in abundance, but carried a sharpened stone Janne gave him to make escape holes in the ice when an air bubble could not be found.

Finally the day came for the secret meeting with Colonel Sotavalta in Helsinki. The meeting was held in the great Presidential hall where rings of desks were in the shape of a semicircle that appeared more like a symphony hall than a conference dome. The sight of three hundred other young men accompanied by their Sami Mentors was breathtaking for Kaarle. It filled him with a strange combination of pride that he had been chosen and a new feeling of belonging to something greater than himself.

Suddenly "ATTENTION" was called and the six hundred sprang to their feet, eyes trained on Colonel Sotavalta. "Please take your seats. As you have traveled from every distant corner of Finland I ask that you please take a look around you and introduce yourselves to new friends and fellow Ski soldiers. Later we will break you up into ten sixty man platoons that will be assigned ten geographic regions. Don't become married to any given region. You will rotate over the years to each region until you have learned them all by heart. Each regional Platoon will wind up back at their home region when your eight years of training concludes. Each sixty man platoon will be divided into ten six man reconnaissance teams. In eight years, your Sami Mentors will return home to Lap Land and their original military units. We believe that three man units able to coalesce on short notice with other three man units will be the optimal defense configuration to protect our country." He explained.

A hand was raised sheepishly in the back row. "Colonel Sir! My name is Rami Into and I have studied military tactics. The average Russian rifle company consists of nearly two hundred soldiers, not to mention the vast numbers in their tank divisions. How can we, broken down into small patrols, have any effect on the notorious Russian forces? It seems suicidal to me if you will forgive me for saying so."

"That is an excellent question. As I am sure Rami already knows, both the Soviet and Finnish armies are organized on a "Triangular" concept. This means that a typical division consists of three regiments and each regiment consists of three battalions. Our Battalions have slightly more soldiers some eight hundred forty five compared with the Soviets who have seven hundred eighty, but of course the Russians have an endless supply of divisions compared to our relatively few. At any given moment, the Russians could overwhelm us with a lightning strike which follows closely with their established order of battle in any case. In addition to our Triangular army, we Finns, however, have our Sissi, or Special operations, Guerilla battalions. It is the Sissi battalions who will benefit most from the special training you will receive. We will break with our traditional Ski soldier training with your generation. You will receive far more than an education in the use of weapons and ski training. We have established an academy here in Helsinki where you will be secretly trained. Your training will include a relentless study of the English Russian and German languages taught to you by native English, Russian and German speakers. . You will each memorize every passage in a book by the great Chinese Military strategist Sun Tzu called "The Art Of War." In it is contained the very heart of your methods of operating as a small fighting force that is able to conquer much larger forces you may be pitted against.

You will study the Napoleonic war, in particular the battle of Austerlitz where the Russians made classical errors in tactical judgement. You will even study naval battles that led to Japan's victory over the great Russian navy." He said. "You will study the political organization of Russian command. You will know and be able to use their weapons as efficiently as you use our own and learn to replenish your weapons and ammunition from dead Russian soldiers and their supply stores. You will be able to get inside the mind of Russian military leaders in order to out think and out decide them on the field of battle. You will gain a respect for the Russian mind when you study General Khutuzov's organized retreat from Moscow and his harassment of the retreating Napoleonic army. You will learn his example of using the weather as a friend not a foe, as Khutuzov taught us all. As your enemy curses the cold you will embrace it as one embraces a lover. You will feel the power when you gain the superior advantage from your most powerful weapon of all, the Finnish Winter."

The vast chamber became as quiet as a tomb. Kaarle was digesting everything the Colonel had just said when a rumble traveled like a wave through the gathering. "Gentlemen I would like for you all to stand as I introduce you to the Father of our Country, our dear President." Colonel Sotavalta then turned and saluted the President. "Gentlemen, please take your seats." The President began. "May God bless Finland's sons and daughters. The program Colonel Sotavalta has just described is in my opinion our nation's only hope of survival. We cherish the peace while we prepare for the inevitability of war. War is in our blood. Our brave ancestors didn't seek war but they most certainly delivered it to those who made a life of bringing it to our door step.

We don't speak of our Viking blood in public so as not to anger the Russian bear, but we all know that the blood of Vikings still pumps proudly through our veins. Shortly before many of you here were born, the Russians experienced their Bolshevik Revolution. Their ideology found its way to our nations workers and by November, 14ᵗʰ of 1917 the Finnish workers declared a General Strike which brought Finland to its knees. I helped organize our middle class Socialist Democratic Party to resist Finland being swallowed by the Soviet Union. Their Red and White Guards civil war had already spilled over into our lands. "I convinced our forces to join with the White Guards because I believed armed resistance to the Bolsheviks to be our only hope of remaining a sovereign nation. With this considerable force I felt confident enough to declare Finland a State independent of Russia on the sixth of December, 1917. It has since become known as our "Independence Day." To my own elation, relief and surprise, Comrade Lenin agreed with me and recognized us as an independent country. That gave me the courage to clamp down on the Finnish socialists who tried to meld our nation with the Soviet Union."

"We crossed into uncharted territory after I announced on the ninth of January, 1918 that I officially commissioned the White Guard to serve as Finland's protector of law and order. This turned out to be an unbearable outcome for the Workers Movement and they attacked our Socialist Party Leadership without warning on the following day. They took over the Socialist Party and called for a revolt on the twenty seventh of January, 1918. I assigned a former Czarist General who is a Finn named Carl Gustaf Emil Mannerheim to be the Commander of the White Guard.

He announced his readiness to face the revolutionaries tit for tat on the twenty seventh of January 1918 while I sent feelers out to invite negotiations, but the Finnish Workers Party proved intractable adversaries and a civil war was begun.

The White Guard consisted mainly of farmers and Landsmen, or Hunters. We numbered Seventy Thousand and occupied the agrarian lands of North Finland. The Reds were urban dwellers and factory workers and had us outnumbered by a ratio of two to one. The Reds as much as the Whites were brave Finns who fought with noble courage for their beliefs. How then, you may wonder, were we able to win against a numerically superior force? Tactics and leadership and I confess, gratefully, with the help of our friends the German Jaeger, or Forest Hunters. They also sent their Baltic Division which many credit for helping us turn the tide against the Reds. The Swedes for their part sent highly professional military officers who helped us organize for major engagements that we won based on superior tactics.

The Russians had forty thousand soldiers still remaining in Finland who helped the Reds with artillery support, but when my staff helped me bring about the treaty of Brest-Litovsk on March third, 1918 these troops were required to leave before the real battles had begun. For each advantage of the Whites, there seemed to be a disadvantage for the Reds. They were nearly leaderless. They refused to leave their cities to meet us for strategic engagements and before long we were fighting a mopping up operation which led to the Reds escaping across the border into the Soviet Union. By May sixteenth, 1918 General Mannerheim entered Helsinki and declared the war to be at an end.

Some of us also observe this day as a second Independence day. As for me, I knew we had tweaked the nose of the Russian bear once too often. I still feel strongly that we may have defeated the Reds within a few years without the help of the Germans and the Swedes but the entire time the foreigners were in Finland I could feel the hot breath of the Russians on my neck, because Russians never forget a slight. True to my anxieties and suspicions the Russians probed our Northern border at Karelia in June of 1919. That border war lasted until October fourteen, 1920 and cost both sides dearly.

I successfully sued for peace which resulted in the treaty of Tartu. We were awarded the port of Pechanga for our troubles and until now we have enjoyed our peaceful independence. In my heart my fellow Finns I do not believe the bear's hunger was satisfied. He is waiting for the right moment to teach us a lesson we shan't forget. The question is not whether we will again fight the Russians, but when we will fight them and absent foreign assistance, will we be ready for it?" Without prompting the entire chamber stood at attention and yelled "God Bless Finland! God Bless our President! We Will Be Ready Sir!"

Chapter Two: Talvisota, The Winter War

Oslo was a nice city. Abundant fresh fish, vegetables and fruit, imported from distant places and no shortage of kind hearted people in every direction, but it wasn't home. Laila proved a fast learner and could soon speak fluent Norwegian. Aunt Sani already had the saddest eyes Laila had ever seen but Laila marveled that when Aunt Sani looked at Aamu's picture, her eyes became even sadder. Sometimes Aunt Sani just started crying without even looking at the picture. Laila was eternally polite, but managed somehow to find a way to escape into solitude even when her Aunt Sani and Uncle Ole were present in the room.

Her Uncle Ole had been a successful fish monger with a few canneries on Oslo's waterfront. After selling his business he drifted into alcoholism and was drunk most of the time. At first he was a happy drunk who laughed frequently. Over the years he became a philosophical drunk and then an existential drunk and finally a sobbing drunk. Aunt Sani's sadness was always the excuse he gave, but in reality everyone knew that it was his own pathetic nature that had caused Sani's sadness in the first place. His redemption was that by anyone's standards he was comfortably rich and had grown to love Laila as his own daughter. His protectiveness of her made some worry that he harbored sinister feelings toward her, the kind no one dare even dream about, but that could not have been further from the true Ole.

Laila called Ole Papa because Sani advised it, but she never really had a daughter's feelings for him. At best she pitied him. Had she told him that, it would have broken his heart. Sani tried too hard to replace Aamu and it only managed to ensure that she never would.

Laila was sad, missed her brother and father and suffered for them with a strange martyrdom that even she didn't fully understand. Laila grew into a beautiful young woman. Her creamy white skin was as smooth as milk and her dreamy blue eyes were as clear as water from the melting snow. This purity created an aura about Laila that seemed to glow and pulsate like the Northern Lights she was born under.

A few weeks after Laila turned seventeen she was walking home from the market with fresh fruit just as a young man, also seventeen, named Arin Olsen was balancing a heavy sack of potatoes on the back of his bicycle. When he saw Laila, his neck craned so far that he ran into a lamp post and potatoes went rolling everywhere. People laughed but not Laila, who gently stooped down to the street and began helping him recover his potatoes. Arin was a dark headed Norwegian and dramatically handsome. His family always joked that he had been a product of the era when Vikings brought home Italian and Spanish women from their southern raids.

Their romance grew from that chance encounter until their love for each other was deep, rich and un-questionable. Laila talked constantly of Kaarle and her father. Arin promised her that as soon as school was out he would travel with her to Finland to surprise her family. Ole even agreed to fund the trip if they would let him come along. When they reacted with silence he finally agreed to let them go on alone.

Then came the letter from Anna of Helsinki. Ahti had gone north to Lapland and Kaarle had joined the Army. The house had been sealed and the livestock sold. Laila went into a deep depression and stopped seeing Arin. He brought flowers each day but was told Laila was too ill to see visitors.

Then one night Arin climbed a wall to the roof of Ole's house and forced his way into Laila's bed room window. He was shocked to see how thin and pale she had become. "Oh Arin I don't want you to see me like this!" Laila screamed. "Then I will live under your bed until I look just like you!" He shouted back. Laila began to giggle and the giggle became a laugh and Arin joined her with deep laughter that released the pain in his heart. For both, the laughter was a desperately needed catharsis. They embraced and stopped laughing. They had never had sex before and only Laila's physical weakness prevented it now. They lay down on the bed together in each others arms and fell asleep until morning.

Some months later, after Laila walked in from her daily visit at the market, Ole was sitting by himself facing the large living room window. Laila spoke to him for a while apologizing that she was unable to find any American whiskey and then she felt the strange chill that gives you goose bumps when you are in the presence of the dead. Sani was collecting the laundry from lines in the backyard. She went speechless when she saw the tears welling up in Laila's eyes. She knew without a word being spoken that it must be poor Ole. She fell to the ground, pulling the fresh laundry with her. She struggled to get up but her knees were too weak. Laila helped her to her feet and steadied her as they walked back inside the house."When?" Sani asked with a trembling voice. "I don't know. I found him sitting in his favorite chair by the window. Ole's face was turning blue around the lips but he wore a peaceful expression. Sani fell to her knees beside him and began to wail. Laila was perplexed. She didn't know whether to leave Sani alone with him, or to linger nearby in case she was needed, so she stayed. After a while Sani dried her tears and sent Laila to the Mortician and the church to begin arrangements for Ole's funeral.

Ole was generous to those he loved. He left the lion's share of his estate to Sani, but wrote a comfortable amount in his will for his "little girl" Laila. He even left enough money to Arin to pay his way into his career. After the funeral Sani gave Arin and Laila her blessing to be married. The two had become nearly inseparable since the night Arin climbed through her bed room window and Sani said she wanted to have a man in the house.

Laila and Arin grew ever more deeply in love but according to Laila's wishes they remained celibate. "I am saving myself for our wedding night." She would say to Arin who found himself taking cold baths even during the winter. Laila and Arin were married on her nineteenth birthday, the twelfth of September, 1939. It was a small wedding with only a few friends in attendance as well as Arin's mother and father and a trio with a Violinist, a Cellist and a Base player, that played Vivaldi all afternoon.

In a little more than two months, on the thirtieth of November, 1939 the Soviet Army came pouring across the border of Finland at Karelia with an invasion force of 400,000 men against 80,000 Finns. The Winter War had begun and poor Laila went wild with worry for her brother and father. She pleaded with Arin to take her home but he responded with silence. She realized that she would only get in Kaarle's way even if she knew where to find him. She prayed constantly under her breath for a letter to assure her of their safety. When no letters came she prayed at least for a sign. It came one clear evening beneath the bright North Star. The star hovered above Finland. Its glow told her Kaarle was alive.

President Pehr Svinhufvud lost the presidential election in 1937 to Kyosti Kallio. In spite of the fact that Kallio was an ardent anticommunist, he was none the less a parliamentarian who shunned using his executive powers to force his will. Consequently a majority arose that believed a repeat of conflict with the Soviet Union to be unlikely. Funds were diverted away from Colonel Sotavalta's war preparation. At times wooden rifles were used for training purposes but eventually he succeeded in finding the funds needed to complete the training and fully equip his ski soldiers. When the Russian 7th Army poured into the Karelian Isthmus with nine divisions Kaarle's six man team had just completed their final training in sniper missions, demolitions and mobile minefield and booby trap placement. They had spent many months training in each region of Finland. They knew every trail mountain stream, fiord and lake and were experts in ski borne hit and run warfare.

The scene along the Northern border was utter chaos. Russia's tanks and infantry became hopelessly clogged in a stream of refugees with cows, goats and chickens and at times sat idle for hours waiting for the narrow roads to become clear enough to traverse. The initial artillery attacks had shocked the farm families and city dwellers. Then came the air invasion. Russian military aircraft dropped leaflets demanding that the Finns turn over General Mannerheim and cease all activities of resistance.

Then closely following the psychological warfare leaflets came the bombing. The Russians were locked into their classical warfare strategy of lightning invasion followed by a Pincer tactic to cut off the enemy from his own logistics and overwhelm him with a Hammer and Anvil finishing action.

The Russians were not ready for what happened next. As the Russians moved in columns on the incomplete roads that meandered through swamps, bogs and across lakes with thinly covered ice, the Finnish Ski soldiers dressed in snow white camouflage lay silently beneath a thin layer of snow on each side of the road. Starting in the rear, they killed first the Russian infantrymen whose responsibility was defense of the tanks blind sides and then they skied ahead to ambush the tanks. Kaarle was laying with his team beneath the snow on a small hill, waiting for the center of the tank column to pass through a small gulch. When the tank column center approached, Kaarle's team skied rapidly down the hill.

As they flew through the air above the open port holes of the tanks they dropped satchel charges and Molotov cocktails that blew up the tanks that were trapped and prevented from spreading out by the gauntlet of the natural terrain. Once the tanks entered a road they could only go forward, or backward, they couldn't turn around. The Finns built tank traps and road blocks which enabled them to divide and conquer. In just a matter of a few hours Kaarle's team destroyed an infantry company and twenty seven Soviet tanks. Kaarle led his team ahead of the Russians who raced forward to catch the Finns. Kaarle led the Russian columns to minefields and across lakes where mines had been strung beneath the surface ice in air tight containers long before the war and the permafrost had arrived. The Russians had believed the war would be a cake walk and over in a matter of days. Their thin uniforms did little to protect them from temperatures that hovered at forty degrees below zero.

The Finns had been trained and specialized in night fighting, which the Russians loathed. The Finn's hit and run tactics, the burning of their own villages and the scattering of their own livestock, neutralized the Russians plan to live on local resources for their invasion. The Finns in particular made targets of the Russian's mess equipment and supply trains which caused the Russians to often fight on empty stomachs with a never ending shortage of food and water. The Finns filled their own wells with dirt, or poisoned them and virtually every object of curiosity was booby trapped, or mined as they burnt their own abandoned villages. Often booby traps would be set in logical sequence, whereby those responding to someone wounded by a mine, or a booby trap would themselves become targets for secondary detonations.

Snipers were an integral part of the plan. Their uncanny ability to pick off drivers, or gunners with their hatches open forced the Russians to "button up" which resulted in diminished visibility, allowing sappers with satchel charges covered with thick pitch to slap charges near the track rollers of tanks. Others crashed Molotov cocktails into the air vents to barbecue tank crews inside their tanks exploding their ammunition stores. Kaarle became a night assassin. He was able to ski and crawl, deep inside Russian defenses and take out battalion and regimental commanders by slitting their throats as they slept. One night a trap was set for him. His target, a Russian General and Division Commander had been moved to separate quarters incognito. Kaarle's forward observer missed the move and assured Kaarle before the mission that the target was in his tent. When Kaarle pulled back the General's tent flap at 0300 he was met by a squad of Russian infantrymen with weapons aimed at his chest. He quickly dropped a grenade and began to run at full speed to his skis.

The Russians were skiers too and the chase was on through the forest during the darkest time of night. Kaarle led them to a lake that had a hidden entry hole. He stashed his clothing and swam beneath the ice from air bubble to air bubble until he reached a hidden exit on the other side of the lake. The Russians were certain they had him and were now puzzled by his sudden disappearance. Kaarle briefly turned on his flash light, as though it had been an accident. The Russians saw it and set out across the lake in the direction of the glint they had seen. Kaarle waited until they were in the middle of the lake, then detonated sub-surface mines that blew the Russians to pieces. Kaarle then rushed to a cave where he quickly built a fire and put on a complete set of dry winter clothing stashed there earlier. He armed himself with a sniper weapon and ammunition and returned to the General's location where a new search team was being organized. He lay still in the snow until he saw the General appear in the lights of a jeep. Kaarle squeezed the trigger and the top of the General's head disappeared. He then killed each of the nearby search team members who weren't even aware someone was shooting at them until it was too late.

Kaarle knew the killing was necessary in defense of his dear Finland. His mind had known nothing else but the preparation for war since he was twelve and his inner soul had become so hardened that he knew he could never go back no matter how hard he tried. He was the perfect assassin. He hadn't yet developed a conscience sufficient to question or regret his sworn duty. He wondered how Laila was and whether she still missed him. He hadn't been in touch with his father who left for Lapland to help support Janne's family since he saw him briefly in Suomussalmi.

Kaarle planned to visit Aunt Anna in Helsinki after his training concluded to see if she had any mail from Laila, but the Russians ended those plans. He knew he would need to shut out all thoughts of Laila in Norway and even his father in Lapland if he were to survive a war where his side was becoming outnumbered by more than ten to one.

He would meet with Janne today. A messenger from General Mannerheim would be arriving with new orders. Kaarle hated the Russians for bringing this insanity to Finland. As did many other Finns, when Kaarle saw the Russians stumbling through the deep snow, without true winter fighting equipment, holding hands and singing Russian battle songs as they were cut down enmasse by Finnish machine guns, he had no small amount of respect for their raw courage, that is until he saw the political Commisars running along behind them ready to shoot them in the back of the head if they stopped, or tried to flee. This was their Communist madness and they wanted to bring it to his homeland.

Kaarle made sure his team of six men, including Janne wasn't followed, or spotted as they made their way to an old abandoned school house in the forest. Waiting there was a tall Swedish officer who was the adjutant for Colonel Hjalmar Siilasvuo. The adjutant brought a platoon of sentries who fanned out to establish a perimeter around the school while the Ski soldiers met inside. Kaarle saw that inside kneeling, or sitting on the floor were teams from a third of all ten regions, or two hundred men. The adjutant didn't waste time beginning his briefing immediately.

"Gentlemen, my name is Major Roland Jergeus I am from Trollhattan, Sweden and am proud to serve in the Finnish army as Adjutant to Colonel Siilasvuo. First I would like to briefly discuss the current command structure." The adjutant pointed to a large map of Finland hanging on the wall. "Our Northern Finland Group is commanded by Major General E. Viljo Tuompo. It's sector of defense responsibility stretches 400 miles from Petsamo to Khumo. They are currently engaging two Russian armies that have established headquarters in Kollaa and Vienan Karelia. You trained in these regions and can imagine what is going on there right now. General Mannerheim sent Major General K. M. Wallenius to command the Lapland Group on the 13th of December. Kaarle your father has been promoted to Colonel and is leading the Ski soldiers there. He sends his love and trust that you will help us all to protect Finland." Jergeus said.

Kaarle choked up and for a moment the boy inside caused his eyes to well up with tears, but the man quickly returned and managed to thank the adjutant for this information. "General Wallenius Lapland Group are facing the Russian's 104th and 52d Tank and Infantry divisions. Commanding the 4 Corps from Lieksa to Sortavala a distance of some 275 miles, is General J. Waldemar Haeggland. The 4th Corps will be defending the critical areas of Kollaa, Tolvajarvi and Aglajarvi against ten invading Russian Divisions. Your region, the Suomussalmi Region is vital at this stage of the war." "The Russians are committing another 500,000 men to the invasion soon which will eventually give them a total of one million men engaged in combat. As you know, the roads that are traversable and the train tracks that bring us supplies from Sweden stretch from here to Oulu. General Mannerheim believes the Russians will expend whatever force is needed to reach Oulu and effectively cut our country in two.

It would cut off our supplies from Sweden and cause us to fight on two war fronts. Currently with only 10 Russians per Finn we have an advantage, (smiling) but to lose Suomussalmi all the way to Oulu would cement our fate. General Mannerheim knows that the fate of the war is in your hands. That you now stand between victory and certain defeat. He sends you his prayers and wishes for a solid victory. On the 30th of November the Soviet 163d tank and Infantry division attacked Finland from the northeast and headed straight for Suomussalmi. It is obvious that Oulu is their ultimate objective. We burnt Suomussalmi to the ground to deny the Russians provisions and we retreated to the other side of Lakes Niskanselka and Haukipera. We had no choice as we could only place a single Finn Battalion from nearby Raate to oppose a fully equipped division. The Russians entered Suomussalmi on the 7th of December and began taking casualties from our mines and booby traps. The Soviets tried the next day to cross the lakes to engage us, but having previously mined the lakes beneath the surface of the ice, we stopped them and forced their retreat back into Suomussalmi." Jergeus said.

"On the 9th of December, Colonel Siilasvuo assembled a regiment of fresh recruits and counter-attacked Suomussalmi but the troops, who were not experienced took heavy casualties and we were forced once more to retreat. Two days ago on the 24th of December, the Soviets attacked once more but we held them in place. Colonel Siilasvuo has managed to acquire two fully equipped regiments from General Mannerheim's reserve forces the JR-64 and JR-65. We will launch our attack on Suomussalmi at 03:00 hours tomorrow on the 27th of December. Your units will be of critical importance.

We need the Soviet forces harassed into directions where we will have massive ambushes waiting for them." "Our ultimate strategy for tomorrow is to execute a Motti. We will use one Finn Battalion to attack the Soviets from the rear. Soon the Finn Battalion will break off and appear to retreat. Once the Soviets are in hot pursuit of the retreating battalion, the retreating Battalion will suddenly be reinforced by the remainder of its regiment and execute a blocking action. Precisely then, our other regiment will attack them from their opposite end. They will be dispersed in order to fight both fronts. Your Ski soldiers will then divide their columns into sections with road blocks and antitank assaults and Sniper operations. Our regiments will then move through them section by section until they are defeated. Have you any questions brothers?" He asked.

Kaarle stood. "I am in charge of Sniper operations Sir. I suggest we be permitted to disperse along the battle area and seek strategic firing positions before the battle even begins. If we wait to select our positions after the battle begins we may not be optimally effective." Kaarle concluded and sat back down. "Yes, I see your reasoning. You could however ruin the entire operation if you are detected before the operation commences. But if you are dispersed you can adjust your positions according to how the battle evolves much better if you are already lying in wait. If the column is one hundred tanks long, first take out the drivers of each fifth tank. That would mean twenty snipers dispersed along the kill zone. I like the idea. I will inform Colonel Siilasvuo." Jergeus promised. "If you do not hear back from me consider yourself to have his permission." The adjutant affirmed. "Gentlemen, may you be victorious for dear Finland's sake!" The adjutant exclaimed. The men stood at attention and shouted "Victory!" Janne embraced Kaarle. "Your father sends his love and prayers.

Word has already reached him of your courage as a Ski soldier. He is more proud than I have ever seen him." Janne said with respect. "Thank you Janne! I'm also proud of him too. A Colonel. That's really something!" Kaarle said with awe. "I think the Adjutant wants to speak with you Kaarle." Janne nodded in the direction of the Adjutant. "Kaarle." "Yes Sir?" Kaarle responded. "By the power vested in me by General Mannerheim and President Kallio I hereby award you a Battle Field Commission. You are now a full Lieutenant. You must repeat that you swear to uphold the honors and traditions of the government, Army and people of Finland. Raise your right hand. Do you so swear?" "Yes I do." Kaarle swore. "Congratulations Lieutenant!" The Adjutant said. Kaarle was dumbfounded, but he knew his new rank would mean nothing to his colleagues. Finns were not impressed by rank.

The only thing they cared about was whether you had courage and intelligence and Kaarle had more than an ample supply of both. Besides, his mind was already on the battle tomorrow and he prayed that he would not let down his father, Janne, his comrades and last but not least, Finland. Just after midnight Kaarle awakened his twenty man Sniper team. To avoid an ambush, he divided them into four five man teams. Each team was assigned a quadrant along the narrow road the Russians would use if they pursued the retreating Finn Battalion. He released each team at ten minute intervals and led the last team himself. They skied as smooth as a twisting silk worm and made certain, as they had been trained, not to silhouette their white camouflage snow suits against dark forest backgrounds. They reached their sniper positions as planned. Each man peeled off from the others to set up his position atop the small knolls and hills that would give them a one hundred eighty degree field of fire.

Kaarle slipped the cover off of his sniper rifle and wrapped white gauze in spiraling bands around the barrel and forward grip to break up its outline and like the nineteen other Snipers curled up in a ball to conserve body heat and energy. At 03:00 hours the Snipers watched as the decoy Battalion moved along the narrow road in the direction Suomussalmi. Within thirty minutes the Battalion reached the Russian sentries and a fire fight broke out. Kaarle waited tensely for the Battalion's retreat that never came. At 04:30 it became apparent that the Battalion had become locked in a death tangle. Unable to disengage they would either have to fight to the death or receive re-enforcements. Kaarle skied quickly along the trail and gathered his Snipers. He then skied a kilometer further and made contact with the Commander of the reserve Battalion. After explaining what had happened the Battalion raced to join the other Battalion and soon an entire Finn Regiment had engaged the Russians in Suomussalmi. Kaarle led his Sniper team to some high trees with a clear view of the Russian flank.

They climbed the trees and began to take out the Russians command structure. Kaarle skied alone across the lake and informed the other regiment that the plan had run afoul of the initial design. Kaarle suggested to Major Aikomus the J-65 Regiment commander that if he used his regiment to attack both flanks of the Russians, they might retreat across the lakes. Major Aikomus agreed and soon with two fresh Battalions on their flanks the Russians felt themselves being squeezed in a vice. At dawn the Russians were in a rout, retreating in the sections the Finns had hoped for. The Finns had their Motti even though it was headed in the opposite direction of the initial plan. Kaarle's Snipers managed to take out most of the tank drivers with head shots as other Ski soldiers set the tanks afire with Molotov cocktails.

When the shooting stopped the Finn regiment had defeated a Russian Division. Kaarle thought his heart would burst with pride as column after column of Russian prisoners were marched back to Colonel Siilasvuo's headquarters. Word spread quickly across Finland that her Ski soldiers had decimated the Russian 163d tank Division and that the Russian attempt to cut Finland in half had been stopped dead in its tracks.

The fighting raged on across Finland with the heavily outnumbered Finns holding the mighty Soviet Tank and Infantry units at a dead stand still. Then one unusually warm morning in February, 1940, General Mannerheim emerged from his winter lodge and saw the ice sickles along the logged roof melting. He knew the tide of battle had crossed over. That same day, the Russians moved their heavy artillery up to the southern defensive line of the Finns and commenced a day and night artillery bombardment of the Finn defensive positions which spanned the full width of the Karelian Isthmus. The Finns held out hope of being reinforced by their French and British allies who never came. The Russians had a remarkable reprieve from the Finnish winter and easily pushed their armored columns all the way to the Northern city of Vyborg. By March 12th, 1940 the Soviets offered a peace favorable to themselves and the Winter War was over. The Finns traded all of Western Karelia and ceded the construction of a Soviet naval base along the Hanko peninsula in order to effect the removal of the Soviet divisions from its heart land. Fearing reprisals should the Soviets invade once more many Ski soldiers were secretly moved to Lapland and provided shelter. Their training continued as though the war hadn't ended and soon enough it would become apparent that the war of all wars had only just begun.

When the Nazis invaded Norway on April 9th 1940 Kaarle made immediate plans to leave Lapland to bring Laila back home but before he could leave he received orders to be assigned along Finland's border with Russia where he remained until June of 1941, when Finland joined with Nazi Germany in Operation Barbarossa. He fought the Russians and by 1942 he received, along with his decorations for heroism, a compassionate leave to travel to Norway to find Laila. Ahti gave him counsel. "Do not trust the Nazis Kaarle." "But we're allies." Kaarle protested. "That's because our president sold his soul to take back from our common enemy the land the Russians stole from us. Trust your instincts in Norway. You may have to kill some Nazis to get back your sister. If so, so be it." Ahti said firmly. "If so, so be it." Kaarle replied. One crisp morning Kaarle set off for Norway with Janne and four of Janne's men as Ahti stood watching, long after they had disappeared into the foggy horizon.

Chapter Three: The Birth Of A Tragedy

As the team skied west, Kaarle let his mind drift to what he had read and heard about Finland's war against the Bolsheviks. He was bewildered that the Germans who had done so much to help Finland rid itself of the Marxists were now, themselves invading a Scandinavian neighbor. Was it the Soviets they were after and just needed to get at them by traveling through Norway and eventually Finland? Kaarle was eager to speak with the Germans and exchange experiences of fighting the Russians. He remained hopeful that Germans were still trusted friends of Finland. Either way, he had to find Laila and bring her home. He would find her and protect her with, or without violence as only fate would determine.

Had someone tried to explain to Kaarle that his future and indeed the future of the world, balanced precariously in the hands of a second hand interpreter of Friedrich Nietzsche and Richardt Wagner, he would have thought the messenger as mad as the man he described. Friedrich Nietzsche, in fact, was stricken with ill health that manifested imaginings about the euphoria of endless power, a Superman to allow him to escape his own wretched reality. In fact not just one Superman, but a breed of Supermen who would lead all of Mankind. A concept the Nazis would grow to call Uebermenchen, or beyond human. Elite in every way to the common man, in particular, intellectually and physically. In his book, "Thus Sprach Zarathustra," Nietzsche described the essence of correcting weak societies by first killing off other worldly Gods such as Christ, when he wrote "Man should be prepared to fly into the abyss like an eagle with talons drawn knowing full well there will be nothing there to meet him when he arrives." No Heaven above, no fairytale ending.

Adolph Hitler didn't infuse the German folk with something that wasn't there before, indeed he awakened it. Wagner's opera "The Ride Of The Valkyries" captures this emotion in music. The very sound of which causes adrenalin to flow rapidly and illusions of endless power to pulse through the veins. In his book "The Birth Of A Tragedy" Nietzsche explains the driving force of his philosophy as the perpetual contest between early Greek concepts of Apollonian and Dionysian central principles of Greek culture. Apollonian is the logical side of man. A unique personage of the analytical thinking man. Schopenhauer described this with his Principium Individuationis, or Principle of Individuation, which is the core of reason for both inductive and deductive logic. Apollonian is described within this framework as form, or individual structure. Form, sculpture and structural shapes are unique and thus are Apollonian because they embody individuality. Rational thinking is structured and therefore Apollonian. Schopenhauer saw this Apollonian principle as greater than the individual because it cannot be neutralized. It is what it is. The best man can hope for is to recognize and understand it for what it is.

The Dionysian principle on the other hand is anything that breaks down the individuality of character. Euphoria, excessive happiness, enthusiasm, anything connected with man's conscious will for the abandonment of logic and reason is Dionysian. Woodland spirits such as Satyrs getting drunk from wine sacs would be completely Dionysian. Music would be Dionysian since it is very much a part of man's emotional chaos and instinctual landscape, versus his more structured reasoning mind. Sigmund Freud would have assigned the Apollonian principle to man's Ego and the Dionysian to the Id.

The music of Wagner is so structured that it allows both the continuation of the Apollonian principle while devilishly permitting the scarce and forbidden elation of darkness found in the Dionysian principle. Listening to it can make those whose souls are already a moth near the flame drunk from its empowerment, an embodiment of power where-in the strong destroy the weak without hesitation, or remorse. The Nazi movement advocated the Apollonian principle and disdained the Dionysian principle, other than its tendency of inebriation of power for its own sake, mixed with an unshakable conviction that their Aryan race was power's only possible heart and by default, its perfect destiny.

Freud described the constant struggle between the Ego and the Id and added a third characterization, the Super Ego, or the Conscience. The Nazi Ego used logic in almost every aspect of life, squeezing the Id and The Super Ego into a corner from which they exploded in the form of racism and the murderous campaigns to eliminate what were considered sub-humans, or, according to Hitler's personal dementia, the Jews. As sociopaths the Nazis had no real conscience. What emerged was a perverted hatred of what they considered to be the mongrelized hybrid races and a burning need to punish and torture them before eliminating them altogether. Nietzsche assigned the name Apollo because as the God of the sun he exemplified brightness and crystal clear form and reason. Dionysus was oppositely the God of wine and drunken euphoria. Their constant diametric opposition was the wellspring of Greek tragedy, which Nietzsche saw as a parallel to life in general. Between his physical illness and his mindset of tragedy, his pen seemed to flow with nihilism. Many have attempted to understand the German mind and nearly all have discovered that obedience to a higher power is intrinsic to the Germanic psyche.

Schuldigkeit, or guilt is easier to deal with if it is transferred to those with higher responsibility. The façade of individualism is at last revealed in its raw truth to be a need to follow and dilute themselves in a greater cause as a place to hide should their mask be removed and their true character be exposed.

As Kaarle's team moved through the frozen tundra they glided with such silence that they nearly skied into a rabid Moose. The Moose was foaming at the mouth and had to be shot as it began a relentless attack. By the scars and fresh wounds on its legs Janne surmised that it had been bitten by rabid wolves. They skied all day and all night again and according to Janne they had already crossed the border into Norway. They made camp in a copse on a hill overlooking a small farming village.

Janne spoke acceptable Norwegian and a plan was immediately struck that he and Kaarle would ski to the nearest farm house to see what could be learned about the Germans in Norway. The remainder of the team would position themselves as snipers until they received an all clear signal from Janne that no hostiles were in the area. Kaarle and Janne skied to a small hill overlooking a farm house and crawled on their bellies, dragging their skis alongside with leather straps. Two large Lap land dogs ran growling toward them barking gruff messages to the strangers. Janne pulled some dried venison from a pouch and in a few moments both dogs were literally eating from the palm of his hand. A man emerged carrying a shot gun and began to walk toward his dogs. Kaarle and Janne's white camouflage kept him from seeing them until he was nearly stepping on them. Janne grabbed the farmers shot gun ripping it from his hands while Kaarle aimed his sub-machine gun at the man's chest.

Janne quickly said in Norwegian; "We come in peace friend!" Erik Carlsson stared at the machine gun and said; "What sort of peaceful bullets does this one fire?" "Sorry." Janne said as he asked Kaarle in Finn to lower his weapon. "Ahh, you're a Finn and you're a Sami." Erik exclaimed. "You are welcome here as long as you aren't working for the Goddamned Germans."Erik said. "We are technically Allies with them against the Russians but we don't trust them should we meet them outside of Finland, Kaarle explained. "We have four more friends waiting on the hill top." Janne explained. "Bring them down. We have good beer good food and a warm fire brothers". Erik said. With this, Janne gave the signal and his four Sami soldiers skied down to the farm house.

The men stood still in the large alcove. Realizing their clothes had become stiff with ice and snow none wished to risk the ire of Mrs. Carlsson, by tracking the melting slush deeper into her house, but she shooed them on into the large chamber with a stone slate floor and an awaiting huge fireplace. Soon their outer shell garments had been removed and the steam from their clothing was rising to the ceiling as the flames licked the higher large black stones of an archive of fires past. A young pregnant woman named Ilsa brought the men a large tray of hot tea. It was explained that Ilsa's husband Magnus, who was Erik Carlsson's only son had gone off to fight the invading German army. The family hadn't heard from him since he left and they were all beside themselves with worry and grief.   The Carlssons prattled away in Norwegian as Janne did his best to translate for all. Erik eyed the weapons the men had laid before them on cleaning mats they unfurled as they felt more welcome and at home. "What sort of pistols are those?" he asked. "9 millimeter L-35 Lahtis," Janne replied. "Do they freeze up on you?" Erik asked.

"When we used to use goose grease they did, but we discovered oil from the liver of a Walrus holds even the extreme temperatures splendidly." Janne explained. "Ask him about the Germans." Kaarle said to Janne. "Yes, can you tell us why the Germans attacked Norway?" Janne asked.

"Well, I suppose the historians shall have a great deal of excitement piecing it all together someday, but it is quite simply that the German arms industry needs Swedish iron ore to build tanks and artillery and Norway falls in the middle of their supply chain. The fools in Oslo believed Norway could remain neutral and we began to believe it ourselves until the Altmark incident." Janne translated then asked "What is the Altmark incident? The men had been silently cleaning their L-35 pistols and their 7.62 mm Lahti Saloranta light machine guns when suddenly their interest peaked and they leaned forward to hear more about the Nazis in Norway.

Janne was about to send a man outside to act as a sentry, but Erik assured him that the dogs would bark well before anyone would come upon them. "Let's see where was I? Yes the Altmark incident. Well, on the 16th of February 1940, the British Navy had quite a tangle with the Altmark, a German supply ship they followed into Norwegian territory quite specifically in the Norwegian fiord Jassingfjord. The Altmark had been scooping up about 300 British sailors who had survived being sunk by the heavy cruiser Graf Spee. " Erik recalled. "The British ship HMS Cossack tailed the Altmark in a hot pursuit and attacked her in Norwegian waters to rescue the already rescued British sailors. From what I picked up on the short wave it was bloody and hand to hand just like the old Viking attacks on the high seas. So much for our Norwegian neutrality after that." Erik said.

The Germans quickly accused us of leading the Altmark to the British and severed diplomatic ties shortly thereafter." Erik searched the ceiling as though he had imagined the entire battle and the subsequent Nazi invasion. "Don't misunderstand me." Erik said. I am not suggesting that the bloody Nazis wouldn't have attacked anyway, in fact, let there be no doubt that to have attacked us as they did with a full invasion by April the 9th could have only been done so quickly with ready made plans. They only needed Hitler's orders and he must have been chomping at the bit to get started." Erik affirmed. Kaarle studied Erik closely, then he said in Finn; "Tell him he's no farmer. He is far too educated to be a simple farmer."

When Janne interpreted, Erik smiled and extended his hand. "Professor Carlsson of Oslo University at your service my friends." "Professor of what?" Kaarle asked. "I am a full professor of biophysics and genetic research. I study what components we are made of." Kaarle, still slightly suspicious then asked; "Why do you live in the countryside?" "Because this is our summer home. We are somewhat early staying here this year because we have been dispossessed of our larger home in Oslo that has been turned into a hospital by the Germans. Don't ask me about any specifics because after I was not successful in talking some sense into my son Magnus, who will soon become a father himself next June, I did the only thing I could and left with my wife and my son's wife while the leaving was still possible." Erik said sadly. "I see. I'm sorry about your circumstances. Can you tell us more about the Germans then? Kaarle asked. "Well, of course the first part of the Nazi invasion occurred on April 9th 1940 with naval battles. The German war ship Bluecher was sunk at the Oscarborg Fortress which gave our King Haakon and his government the possibility of escaping to England.

Then came British attacks at Narvik followed by German counter attacks that couldn't be resisted. By the 25th of April, the British reinforcements were badly damaged at Lillehammer and forced to retreat to Andalsnes. Without the aid of the British, our forces had no choice but to surrender enmasse on the 30th of April 1940. It's been almost three years ago. Those who could manage it rallied in the wilderness and are now fighting a war of resistance that we are calling the Home Front. Would you care to join us? We are scheduled to meet here tonight." Before Janne could translate Kaarle's reply the dogs began to bark. The team began to immediately re-assemble their weapons. In seconds the team was reloaded and ready to react quickly. "Please hide yourselves within the house until I am certain who it is." Erik opened the door and stepped outside.

Soon he was back inside followed by a group of a dozen partisans. The men were heavily armed and were led by a man named Markus Hanssen. Markus was a tall and muscular man who appeared to be a hunter. His followers were a mix of tradesmen and gentile professionals who could have been bookkeepers, or office managers. Erik introduced everyone with Janne's help and the men who were fresh from the cold sat close to the fire. "Markus, our friends from Finland want to know about the Germans in Norway. What can you tell them?" Erik asked. "Well from head to toe they are fanatic and ruthless sons of bitches. They have been rounding up every Jew they can find from Norwegians, to Finns and Swedes, it makes no difference as long as they are Jews. We have heard they are shipping them off to southern Germany and Poland. We hear bits and pieces that they are shipped to death camps never to be heard from again. Perhaps these are just absurd rumors. We cannot verify this. We can however, verify what we have seen with our own eyes.

The darker races have it the worse of them all. They don't even take them prisoner. They execute them on sight. They are hateful and fanatic racists, this we can verify. I see you are mostly Sami here. My advice is to turn around now and return to Lap Land. If you are surrounded by these bastards they will kill you to the last man." Markus said with sincerity.

"Also, we have no hope to use you in our resistance because you would stand out. We need men who can blend in with the local people. It's a matter of life and death to be able to swim in our sea of people without calling undo attention to ourselves. Tactically the Germans are some of the best soldiers in the world. They seldom retreat and they are strangely committed to their Fuhrer. We catch them sometimes in small elements, or in supply operations and columns. This is when we have had the most success in striking hard and fast then disappearing into the forest." He said.

" I can add that prior to the German invasion, our own Nazi party which accounts for about 10% of all Norwegians have been actively conducting espionage against their own people. These vermin are members of the Nasjonal Samling, or "Nazi party" which is led by a traitor named Vidkun Quisling." Erik explained. "As a scientist, the part that disturbs me most is the fact that Norwegian women have been collected, some by force, others by the persuasion of security and food and shelter to take part in German breeding experiments within a program called Lebensborn. It is a genetic experiment for the creation of a Master race." Erik said.

"They believe blonde haired healthy people with blue eyes to be Aryans who they wish to populate the world with." Erik explained. "These are the strange bedfellows your government has decided to call allies. They pretend to be your allies while you fight your common enemy the Russians, but they will turn on you if they conquer the USSR, you'll see. We resist them strongly here. Three men have emerged as our national heroes who have been making the Germans pay for invading us. Max Manus, Gunnar Sonsteby and Max Helberg. When we learned our King Hakkon had escaped the Germans, we formed Milorg as our main resistance, but we now have Distrikt 13 that conducts our espionage and clandestine military operations. I use my University connections as a geneticist to keep in contact with other resistance fighters in Europe." Erik explained.

"My cover is my research which is centered on engineering certain gene splicing that may unlock secrets of nature that will allow us to prevent colds and perhaps someday even cure Cancer but the Germans are writing about completely re-creating the human body using harvested genetic material and cloning the cells to duplicate persons. Unless the German scientists have discovered the secret of human creation, these concepts remain highly speculative. It has, however, been sending shock waves throughout the world scientific community." Erik observed. " Do you support such research?" Kaarle asked as he glared at the professor. "Of course not. I always knew Davenport's work would unleash Satan on earth and now I believe we are witnessing just the beginning." Erik lamented. "Who is Davenport?" Kaarle asked. " I will explain everything I know to you this evening, but for now, my wife and daughter in law have prepared a modest soup with glasses of beer in our dining room. Shall we all be seated at the table?" Erik asked.

The men gathered around a very long table and were served hot soup and steins of beer. "How far away are the Germans now?" Kaarle asked Markus through Janne. "About fifty kilometers. They have taken over every major Norwegian city and will no doubt push east and south until they establish contact with your joint front against Russia to the east. Since Germany is effectively stalled in Russia, Sweden has declared itself neutral and may possibly succeed in staying that way as long as they keep their iron ore flowing in the direction of Germany." Markus replied.

"Does anyone speak German here?" Kaarle asked in Hoch Deutsch, or High German. His question was followed by a palpable silence until Erik replied in the same High German. "We all do." "Good. I have been worried about not being able to speak Norwegian so could we proceed in German and I will translate as needed to my Sami friends." Again silence ensued. "Well, I suppose it makes the most sense, but mind you after what the Germans are doing to Norway and eventually the world, none of us are thrilled with speaking German in this house. Do you speak English?" Erik asked. "I can speak English, yes, let's speak English." Kaarle said. From then on, English was spoken and Kaarle translated to the Sami. "Do you know what type of unit's the Germans have fifty kilometers away?" Kaarle asked. "Yes, an infantry battalion with a few light armored vehicles." Markus replied. "Do they have Ski Soldiers?" Kaarle asked. "No, and most of the bastards don't even have snow shoes." Markus answered. "Well, we may have a slight advantage then because that's what we are." Kaarle enjoined. "Are you the bloody bastards who fought the Winter War against the Russians?" Markus asked excitedly. Kaarle became suddenly embarrassed and looked at the floor. "Yes, we fought the Winter War." Kaarle replied in a soft voice.

"I had completely forgotten to ask why you were here in the first place." Erik exclaimed. "My sister was brought up in Oslo by an aunt. When I learned of the German invasion my friends volunteered to help me find her." Kaarle explained. "Why are you allies with the Germans?" Markus asked with suspicion. "We joined their war against Russia to get back our land but we are Scandinavians, not Nazis." Kaarle replied. "Then will you join us for a raid on the Germans?" "Yes. We will join you but I want to be sure my Sami's return immediately thereafter to Lapland. If they are seen fighting in Norway there would be repercussions in Helsinki." Kaarle advised.

"Fine. Let us make an operations plan against this German Infantry battalion that is currently fifty kilometers from here. After that, I will take you to Oslo as your Samis return to Lap land." "Excellent!" Kaarle replied. "I have some places for your people to sleep." Erik said to both party's. "It was used by previous farm workers and even has a tower with a 360 degree view with glass windows should you decide to post sentries there." "Superb!" Kaarle and Markus agreed. After the teams were settled in for the night, as promised, Erik invited Kaarle to sip some vodka before the fire as Erik described what he now knew about the state of eugenics in Nazi occupied Norway and Europe.

" Kaarle I don't know where to start. I suppose a good place would be what happened in 1929. Those of us who study and practice genetic research were contacted by letter in 1929 by an American eugenics scholar named Charles Davenport, a Phd. out of Harvard who became internationally known after publishing a book titled 'Heredity In Relation To Eugenics.'

It seems he advocated refinement of studies involving local and regional miscegenation between the primary races. He considered cross racial mixing to be negative declaring that it results in a degradation of the pure races resulting in what he calls "Hybridized" or "Mongrelized" people." "His interest with myself and my Norwegian colleague Dr. Halfdan Bryn, who I no longer speak to, was focused on the cross race mixing that had been occurring between the Norwegian Hybrids that resulted in procreation between the darker skinned Laplanders, such as the Sami you have with you and the Alpine, Nordic race. I flatly rejected his thesis about the negativity of cross race mixing, as I saw it for what it was, quite simply a technical justification for the worst form of racism. Genetic flaws can be traced to aberrations in human biochemistry and incorrect alignment of chromasomes that have nothing to do with skin pigmentation and bone structure that evolve from centuries of various physical environments. As far as the inherited diseases and deformities, or even inherited madness, I believe there to be some fundamental code that controls this, a code we have yet to discover." Erik said.

"I'm afraid I still do not understand where this Davenport fellow fits in with the Nazi invasion of Norway." Kaarle said, matter of factly. "Well, he began as a strict adherent to biometric principles, including psychometric studies. He didn't go cuckoo until he had something of an epiphany about Gregor Mendel's Laws Of Heredity and the entire eugenics concepts espoused by the Mendelian School Of Genetics. That's when his extremism emerged. He believed that if you could identify racially inferior persons in society and force them to become sterile you could nip genetic inferiority in the bud and be rewarded with healthier smarter and stronger people who are more productive in society."

"The result of his genetic pruning in America led to the forced sterilization of about 60,000 people. For whatever reason, one which I personally consider to be madness, Adolf Hitler has found in Davenport's writings his perfect connection between Scientific law and insane racial hatred. How euphoric Hitler must have felt when he learned that his hatred for the Jews was being welcomed with open arms as a scientific principle by American science. It now forms the central platform of his Nazi Third Reich. Davenport still maintains editorial positions at two powerful German journals." "This in spite of irrefutable evidence that Hitler is conducting mass genocide against the Jews. In 1939 Davenport wrote an article for the *Festschrift* per the request of Otto Reche who was involved with a program to eliminate inferior segments of Eastern Germany. Davenport writes and the Nazis implement. It's all quite horrible within the context of Hitler's rounding up of Jews wherever he finds them to be shipped off to secret death camps in Bavaria and Eastern Poland. They have long since implemented plans in Germany to sterilize everyone who isn't what they consider an Aryan. Now they simply kill anyone who doesn't fit their standard of what a human should look like, or perform like. It's all quite mad you see." Erik said as he watched the flames flicker in the fire place. "Perhaps Hitler's strongest supporter has been an atheist eugenicist named Margaret Sanger. She has provided both financial and advisory support to Hitler since 1939. Her own writings called "The Negro Project" initiated Planned Parenthood as a legal cover to sterilize and eventually eliminate the Negro race from America." Erik continued.

"Do you think if we help Markus against the Germans tomorrow, he really will help me find my sister in Oslo?" Kaarle asked.

His question startled Erik. It was so distant from where his mind was that it literally yanked him back to the present. "Oh, Markus? Yes, of course, well perhaps not him personally, his face is too well known there, but to be certain, he will send someone with you. To be sure, I will ask him to as a favor. What do you think about the Germans now that you know what is guiding them?" Erik asked. "I think they are pathetic. I've never liked them, it's just that they have always been there to help us with our struggle against Russia, yet I cannot help but question how anyone could just turn their entire country over to an insane man who lives only to hate." Kaarle said.

"I believe it's timing. How could Napoleon have had his way with an entire continent if the timing wasn't right? In the case of Germany it has been the unfair treaty at Versailles and the enforced reparations by the French, from the Alsace to the heart of the Ruhr, that has injected Germania with a desperate need for revenge. Along comes Hitler and pours gasoline on the frenzy until the world explodes with hatred. The German psyche, one half full of logic, the other mixed with narcissism and superiority seems the perfect combination against the possibility of even the slightest desire for peace." Eric considered. "Victory in every aspect of life becomes more than a desire, it becomes a self fulfilling prophecy of success based on the darkest of reasons. The Apollonian who is also the Dionysus." Erik said. " I'm afraid you have lost me with that Professor. I will check on my soldiers and get some rest. Tomorrow appears to be a very important phase of my journey." Kaarle said. "Yes my Finnish friend. Rest for your tasks of the morrow. Sleep well." Erik said. Erik remained before the fire sipping vodka into the wee hours of the night.

His thoughts returned to his native Norwegian language as he considered what he had told Kaarle about the American Davenport, but there had been so many others after him. The Rockefeller Institute of Anthropological Research had been a virtual source of funds to both the American and German eugenic societies. Even J.A.M.A. the Journal Of The American Medical Association extolled the scientific value of German eugenics. Such fools! The eugenic movement though it received its early impetus in the United States had, since Hitler became interim Chancellor in 1933, become an overwhelmingly German enterprise. By June of the same year just six months after Hitler's rise to power, the law governing eugenics in Germany was created. Reich Statute Part One Number 86, or the Law For The Prevention Of Defective Progeny, established Germany's compulsory sterilization program. By January of 1934 compulsory sterilization had begun for nine separate categories deemed to fit the profile of genetic inferiority.

The retarded and those afflicted with mental feebleness such as Alzheimers, Schizophrenia, Manic Depression, Epilepsy, genetic physical deformities and Alcoholism, Huntington's Chorea and inherited blindness, all afflicted were compelled to undergo sterilization procedures. Some 400,000 Germans were sterilized by legal decree. Doctors were compelled to release confidential information and patients who resisted were rounded up and brought to one of the 200 clinics established for the program. The sterilization was comprehensive, including children ten years of age, to men beyond fifty. In spite of continuous international media reports about how inhumane the Germans were in their treatment of the Jews, the American eugenicists continued to heap praise on the technical accomplishments of the Reich.

By 1935 Hitler had demanded and received a standard classification for the percentage of Jewish blood of any given person, which was based on his eugenics math formula. Full, Half, Fourth, Eighth and even Sixteenth. Once the method of determining the degree of Jewishness a person may have was established, a dual law called the "Nuremburg Law" was decreed which removed German citizenship from German Jews and prohibited marriage between a Jew and a non-Jew down to a determination of a quarter level of Jewish blood. Hitler's entire movement was based on the virtue, or lack of virtue of blood. His fellow Nazis who had been martyred at the Bier Putsch in Muenchen before Hitler had been arrested, were carrying his Blut Fahne, or Blood Flag. Their blood from the struggle was soaked into the Blut Fahne and was considered by Hitler to be a sacred part of the Reich. When christening a new unit into his Wehrmacht, Hitler always rubbed the new unit's flag against his Blut Fahne to make the ceremony official and the transfer of reinheit, or purity, complete. Blood and its purity was a central element of his ontological purpose, or what he believed to be his fate that was inextricably intertwined with world domination. Hitler concealed his true aspirations of perpetrating genocide on the Jews in the early phase of military conquest, but by the time he attacked Russia his hatred was "completely unmasked." Erik thought.

Erik had read secret details of Dachau, Auschwitz Birkenau, Buchenwald, Sobibor and Treblinka. Hitler was clever to use the racist eugenic science begun in America and the United Kingdom to hide his real intentions. He knew back then that it was premature to perform mass genocide on the hated Jews, so he pretended to borrow Davenport's ideas about sterilization to at least stop the further expansion of the Jewish population in Germany. Genocide would wait.

He began by adopting Davenport's program of cleansing the human race of the genetically inferior, such as the feeble minded, the insane and those with inherited deformities. He had always considered the Jews a solid fit in each category. Forced sterilization had been child's play. Hitler was now openly eliminating the scourge of mankind with massive genocide. At the same time no eugenic plan would be worth its salt without a plan for re-population with a superior species. A Master Race in "einer Welt frei und rein von Juden." A clean world where even the memory that Jews had ever existed at all would be completely forgotten in a century.

A world where Hitler of course controls the history books. Lebensborn began as a gesture of German responsibility where-in Germans offered shelter to women who had been impregnated by German soldiers. It evolved into a program where the birth became engineered with the express goal of populating the earth strictly with Aryans. One day the plan would be complete and the surviving members of inferior races would be replaced as slaves by machines. The final genocide would then take place. The only humans to be found on earth after that would be Aryans.

Lebensborn under Himmler and Goebbels would apply meticulous management of German geneticists to ensure that a strictly Aryan population evolved. Hitler had been assured by Heinrich Himmler and Josef Goebbels that an Aryan world would be possible in Hitler's own life time. Other German scientists are working frantically on discovering ways to prolong the life of the Fuhrer by another century or longer. "That will continue as well." Erik thought.

Failure is not an option. Now that Nordic populations have fallen before the SS, Lebensborn can emerge as an involuntary assembly line until the Aryan empire is complete. Hitler still won't rest until his scientists discover a way to make it physically impossible for an Aryan woman to be impregnated by anyone other than an Aryan man. Hitler's new rising star Dr. Mengele is personally conducting research and experiments in Auschwitz for Lebensborn, which is the Alpha and the Omega of the Reich, with Hitler its divine leader and protector. Only fools consider the Reich a political movement. "Only the enlightened understand that the Reich is Nirvana, that Lebensborn is its Garden Of Eden and that Hitler is its God on earth." Erik concluded. Erik wondered what would become of himself and his family. He regretted that he hadn't at least pretended to support the racists. He vehemently spoke out against them and he knew the German eugenicists in particular would remember him as a traitor to their cause. Now the Nazis were only 50 kilometers away and unless the partisans were successful, they would soon be on his door step. His only saving grace would come from the fact that he was Nordic, but in his case they would probably use his body for some debilitating torture and experiments and then kill him anyway. With that thought, Erik finished the last swallow of vodka and collapsed before the fire into a deep and troubled sleep.

Erik was awakened by the freezing cold from a dead fire place. His wife was fanning the embers and adding new wood to the fire. The men were given a light breakfast with hot tea and were ready for their planned attack against the German battalion. Kaarle made critical changes to Markus' plan once he learned of Markus' possession of dozens of anti-personnel mines he had stashed away. Erik called Markus to the side and asked him to help Kaarle find his sister in Oslo.

"After we attack the German battalion we will travel with Kaarle to the outskirts of Oslo. My sister will travel inside the city with him to find his sister." Markus said. "Good. If you see my son Magnus please tell him to come home. His wife will soon bear his child." "I will Erik. Good luck!" Markus said. A swirling snow laden blast of wind trespassed through Erik's summer home as the door was swung open. Erik felt so vulnerable. Erik thought how like ghosts the ski soldiers looked as they disappeared in the blizzard ahead. His burden was his knowledge of just how extensive the evil was that awaited these brave young men. Planet earth's last thread of hope. He sensed that his son Magnus was either being held prisoner, or was already dead. As suddenly as they had arrived the ski soldiers were gone. He didn't know how long his wife stood in the pre-dawn darkness watching him weep for Magnus. He wept in silence after the ghosts from Finland left a great emptiness of hope in their wake. How many of them would really become ghosts in this mad, mad war? Dare he hope Magnus would come home? Erik gathered himself up and forced a smile to reassure his wife Ingrid that all would eventually return to normal.

Chapter Four: Ski Soldiers

Erik and his wife watched the disappearing images in their minds for a long time. Finally she broke the silence. "They will be coming here someday soon won't they?" "Yes my love. They will come and we will pretend to be happy they are here. They will pretend to like us and pet our dogs. Then as good Germans they will take our possessions and kill us to take us out of our misery." Erik said with a far away expression.

Kaarle had given a great deal of thought to what the professor had said about the Germans. He personally felt no loyalty to the Germans. They had become invaders like the Russians and after all, the Norwegians were his Nordic cousins. They were willing to help him find Laila which made them allies by default. There was, in addition, an eerie element in all of this race business and hating an entire class of people, not for what they had done as individuals but for who they were by birth. Kaarle wouldn't let it bother him for now. He was sure that the German soldiers were not much different than Russian ones. "They bled and shit like any other man," he thought. If they didn't, he would soon be in a deep amount of trouble because he had been trained only to fight mortals not Supermen. Kaarle spent the night studying the map Erik gave him. It was a military map that showed contour lines of elevation and had symbols for small creeks and bridges. A decent infantryman could use such a map to determine his actual location within a margin of error of ten meters. He imagined the layout of the German camp by visualizing the terrain where Erik had described them to be. Within three hours they were all strapping boxes of anti-personnel mines, bundles of dynamite, and containers packed with grease and nails to their webbing.

The men skied at a constant pace and by late morning they reached the large meadow Kaarle had selected on his map. They set up a defensive perimeter in a thick woods about one kilometer from the German position. Kaarle called a meeting and all except one Sentry huddled together to hear Kaarle's operations order.

" Tonight after dark, we will post sentries along this high ridge, just here. They will alert us before anyone can come to interrupt us. The rest of us will be busy setting up this large meadow with anti-personnel mines. We will use a space between these two saplings. It is very important during our retreat phase not to stray to the left, or right of these saplings. Our corridor will take a 45 degree angle to the right at this large boulder. It will lead us out of the minefield. The Germans will be pursuing us in column. When they detonate the mine clusters near the saplings, their leaders will command them to form a line across the meadow. Ten meters beyond the saplings, our mines will be interspersed all the way across the meadow. If we are lucky, most of the Germans will freeze in place when their lead elements begin triggering the mines in their line formation. I'll need six snipers from you who will be positioned in these trees and will have a clear field of fire on the Germans in the meadow."

"What about the rest of us after we leave the minefield?" Markus asked. "We will circle around and throw Molotov cocktails into the crew compartments of the half tracks, as well as conduct a rear offensive. We do not have the manpower to fight a prolonged battle so when you see a red flare that I will fire, ski to this location where we will be joined by our snipers."Kaarle said. "We will hastily set up a linear ambush on both sides of this lane which the Germans should use on their return to camp.

Don't shoot straight across. Walk your fire from the head of the column backward to the end, or you will be shooting each other." Kaarle said. "How will we get the Germans to follow us to the meadow?" Thomas, one of Markus' men asked. "That's the easy part. We line up and flash them with our rosy red arses." Kaarle said as everyone, including Thomas held their mouths to keep from breaking silence with uproarious laughter. "Seriously, for the initial attack I need the fastest skiers you have. Skiers who can burn leather and turn and shoot without falling down." Kaarle said solemnly."You'll have them." Markus said.

The men checked their weapons and equipment including the bottles of petrol they would rig later with the cotton braiding Erik's wife had given them to use as wicks. They chewed the venison strips she gave them and followed the meal with taffy candy she placed in each mans ruck sack.

Kaarle gazed at the darkening sky and watched a snow falcon hurtle toward earth at maximum speed, ripping the wing loose from a much larger bird. He circled then landed to claim his kill but was chased away by a wolf. "A lesson in warfare." Kaarle thought. "Element of surprise, lightning attack with overwhelming violence and the wisdom not to stand and fight a physically superior foe even when a meal is at stake." Kaarle and his Sami each pulled their extra white shell camouflage garments out of their small packs and handed them to the Skiers who would join them for the initial attack. The men beamed with pride to know they would be wearing the white uniforms of the men who had destroyed an entire Russian Division in the battle for Suomussalmi. Just the thought rallied their courage enough to prepare them to draw their first German blood. They burned with anger that the Nazis had dared to occupy their homeland.

The suddenness was as startling as a snake bite on the face. Two ski jumping formations of six snow-white, death delivering objects flew high over the heads of startled German soldiers who were eating their evening goulasche suppe from metal mess kits.Their rifles were stacked near their tents. They stood paralyzed for a few very long moments before they were able to utter a sound, or run for their rifles. The attackers fired in all directions with their sub-machine guns spraying hot lead across the camp. They threw grenades in the nearby ammo truck and the petrol truck sending shards of steel and plumes of burning missiles and flames shooting hundreds of feet in the air. Even the soldiers who had fought the false war in Poland, to a man were stunned and frozen in awe at the spectacle of military precision and sheer explosive power of the attack.

All twelve of the attackers could have skied to safety while the officers and sergeants were yelling orders to pursue, but they stopped to fire before hop scotching to new firing positions. When the German Colonel who was the battalion Commander learned that his battalion was being ripped apart by only twelve men on skis he flew into a rage. He immediately ordered two rifle companies and six half tracks to engage the sappers in hot pursuit. The skiers were difficult to see at dusk as they crisscrossed and fired without stopping. The pursuing Germans became excited when they saw the assassins head for a meadow they knew to be a box canyon. They would soon be pulling these arrogant and brazen bastards apart by their limbs. Kaarle led the way between the sapplings and the Germans lunged onward through knee deep snow to reach them. Kaarle stopped at the boulder and waved his assault team onward in a 45 degree angle.

Kaarle fired over the heads of the Germans to slow them down just a little, then he also withdrew through the safety passage. The Germans got to their feet and lunged forward until Whooomp! Whoomp! Whoomp! mines began to explode, ripping the German soldiers who stepped on them to pieces. As if on cue the two rifle companies that had been pursuing in a column formation fanned out to the left and right in order to bring maximum fire power to bear to the front. They fired so heavily to the front that their tracer cross pattern looked like a spider web across the meadow. When they reached the mines to their front three German platoons on line were blown to shreds simultaneously.

The trailing company stopped in the open field and Markus' snipers began picking them off in clusters. The Germans lay screaming Hilfe! Hilfe! in the field unable to walk or even crawl away. Suddenly the half tracks began to explode in flames, their crews running and screaming ablaze from the Molotovs. They dropped and rolled to put out the flames just as Kaarle's ambush was sprung. A dozen sub-machine guns opened up on the chaos from the rear. Kaarle fired his rocket flare and the teams rallied to the lane, quickly dividing themselves on both sides of the kill zone to establish the next ambush.

To Kaarle's surprise it wasn't the element he just attacked which came pouring into the kill zone, but instead the Colonel's reserve company rushing forward to the rescue from the rear. Eighteen machine guns opened up on the reserve company mowing the Germans down like blades of grass. The reserve platoon of the reserve company tried to flank the right side of the ambush only to be met by withering fire from the left. Kaarle fired his last flare to signal the break from contact.

Markus performed a head count as each of his men skied past on their way to their pre-determined rally point. Not one of his men had even received a scratch. "My Samis are all accounted for!" Kaarle said as they skied past. "I...." Markus was almost in tears. " See you at the rally point!" Kaarle said as he led his Samis to the forest where excess gear had been stashed. "Don't let your white suited skiers silhouette themselves against the woodlines." Kaarle said. "We should put some distance between ourselves and the Germans. They may have a reserve battalion as a reaction force." Kaarle called out.

Markus led his men to the rally point and held them each in his arms as they all wept with the overwhelming glory they had just experienced. Relieved that none had been wounded, or killed, Markus buried his face in his hands ashamed to let his men see the tears in his eyes. Kaarle and the Samis skied in. Janne immediately shooed Markus men into a hasty perimeter. "I knew you guys were good, but I didn't expect what just took place." Markus said. "It was a team effort and you performed as though you have been Ski soldiers all of your lives." Kaarle replied. "How many?" "How many did we kill? We decimated two rifle companies, about 100 men each and we trashed a third rifle company, say 50 more, so that's about 250 killed and many more wounded. We destroyed six half tracks. That battalion will have to be completely refitted, or replaced."

"Absolutely amazing. Unbelievable!" Markus said. We are twenty kilometers from my sister's house. We'll take you there then we'll disperse until the heat blows off. What about your Sami?" Markus asked. "They must leave now. They won't be safe anywhere in Norway." "I agree." Markus said.

Kaarle embraced each of the Sami and held Janne a few moments longer. "Find your sister Kaarle." Janne said. "I will Janne. Travel safe home. Tell my father that as soon as I find Laila I will bring her to your house in Lapland." "Walk in God's foot steps my brother's son." Janne said and he skied away. Kaarle watched them ski east until they completely disappeared beneath the Milky way. Markus disbanded his partisans in the forest overlooking his sister Elina's house. He arranged to meet them at a new location in two days, then he skied down to the edge of her village and walked with Kaarle to her rear door. It was still dark and at 5 am in the morning Kaarle hadn't given any thought to what she would look like. Markus tapped lightly on her door and in seconds it opened.

Elina had been awake, worried that something may have happened to Markus. She knew that he was hunting Germans and braced herself for the worst. Kaarle didn't expect Markus' sister to be so stunning. Her chestnut colored hair was long and she wore it in a Chinese pig tail. Her almond eyes sparkled and her neck and body lines were perfect and elegant. He thought perhaps when the war is over he would like to look her up again. For now, he couldn't allow even a stray thought to distract him from Laila's safety. Markus embraced his sister. "Elina, this is my new brother Kaarle from Finland. I can't begin to describe what a hero and a Ski soldier he is. He just helped us destroy a German battalion of about 500 men. We killed at least 250 of them. I am still shaking inside. He is looking for his sister who lives with an aunt in Oslo. Please help him without placing yourself in danger. He speaks excellent German but no Norwegian." Markus started speaking German. "Kaarle, this is my sister Elina. She too speaks German. Our parents are both dead. She lives here alone. She will help you find your sister.

Please protect her. We know of at least one of Vidkun Quisling's Nasjonal Samling spies in this village, there could be more. You must travel several meters apart and deny knowing each other if they stop you. Do you have papers?" Markus asked. "Finnish ones." Kaarle replied. "If they catch you together it will result in espionage charges and my sister's death." "We won't be caught Markus, I promise this." Kaarle replied. "I believe you. I'll take your sub-machine gun. Keep the pistol. God protect you both." Tears welled up in Elina's eyes as she watched her brother ski toward the forest as the sun came up along the crystal horizon.

Elina made hot tea and served dark bread with home made honey. Both cast furtive glances at each other without speaking. Finally Elina spoke. "Markus and I both belong to Distrikt 13. We bring in British spies and we help pilots escape. I will consult with our leader Kjakan, it means "the Chin" and he will tell me how to proceed to get you and your sister back to Finland. But as Finns you can probably walk freely amongst the Germans here, no?" she asked.

"No. I would have to be here on official business. Otherwise they would arrest me as a spy like anyone else. You don't need to extract us, just help me find where she is." Kaarle said with a sudden coldness. "I didn't mean to be insulting. I just needed to determine how self reliant you both would be. My brother was right. You are different. Anyway, thank you for keeping him safe from the Germans. He is a brave man but the battle you just fought was his very first. He just recently transferred from espionage to military operations. We never discussed it but he was afraid he would let down his men. It must have been quite a battle." Elina said, probingly.

Kaarle looked around and parted the curtain only slightly to size up the neighboring buildings. "All good soldiers fear they will fail each other. It doesn't end after the first battle. It stays with you each time, but when the dying begins you don't allow it to consume you." Kaarle snapped. "Do you have an address where she stays? " Elina asked. "I have a map where the house is marked with an "X". "May I see it?" Kaarle retrieved the map from his pack and gave it to Elina. Suddenly Elina turned ashen. "My God! This is in the center of the Bygdoy Frogner district. Is your family rich?" "My Uncle Ole was quite wealthy. Why?" "This complicates matters quite a bit. " She said.

"The traitor Quisling occupies the Grand Villa of Bygdoy not far from your sister's house. We will be literally under the noses of the Nasjonal Samling. Oh well. This could get interesting." Elina quipped. Elina busied herself with the dishes as Kaarle soaked in her feminine beauty. Her slim figure but supple and round curves made him inhale deeply. Without turning around she asked in a low voice;"Enjoying the view?" Embarrassed, Kaarle choked, unable to reply. Finally he said; "What man wouldn't?"

"You can look, but don't touch. As my brother always tells me, love is dead until the Germans leave and we are free once more. Until we find your sister and you both depart, forget I am a woman. Emotions could get us all killed." "Agreed." Kaarle said. He couldn't explain it but her clear set of rules only made him want her more. "I must be going crazy." he thought. "Your room is on the right at the top of the stairs. When your sister joins us she can take the room on the left across from yours. My bed room is downstairs. It should only be a couple of days before we have organized your extraction." she said.

"Feel free to go to your room and rest. I will draw a hot bath for you upstairs. The room where you will stay is Markus' room. He has a large wardrobe. Take what you need you are both nearly the same size." Elina said. "I will send you money for anything I take." Kaarle said. "Nonsense. The way my brother spoke of you I am certain you have already done more to aid our resistance than we could ever repay you. We shall stay here until late afternoon. I will wake you when it's time to go to your sisters house." "Thank you." Kaarle said and disappeared up the stair. As the day passed Kaarle had a restless sleep, sometimes yelling out to "shoot the bastards" at other times punching and wrestling the pillows only to awaken and wonder for a few confusing seconds where he was. Finally came the light tap on the door that it was time. Kaarle had been lying across the bed, fully dressed. He had cleaned and oiled his pistol and had cleaned, oiled and loaded five full clips of ammunition. He walked down the steps and asked; "Do you have a knife I can borrow?"

Elina thought for a moment and then unlocked a china cabinet, opening a drawer she pulled out an object wrapped in an oil cloth. Kaarle examined this exquisite object of art and whistled lightly. "Original Fiskar Fisherman's gutting and filet knife. Best ever produced in Finland." He said. "I somehow knew you would appreciate it." Elina said with a smile. "It belonged to my grandfather, then my father and now Markus, but he says he prefers to do his killing beyond reach." It came with a worn, but sturdy leather sheath. "I'll take good care of it." Kaarle promised. "If it takes good care of you then consider it a gift." Elina said. Kaarle slid the razor sharp knife into his boot with the handle beneath his pant leg. "We will walk to the village center. You should follow about twenty meters behind me." Elina said.

"Here are tickets. We will first take trolley bus 17. It will take us to the Tram at Rodelokka. From there we will ride to Frogner, where we will be near enough to walk to your sisters house." Elina said. Kaarle felt awkward at first wearing Markus clothes especially the sweater that hung loosely around his waist. He listened to the crunching noises made by his boots on the freezing, crystallized snow and once nearly lost his footing on a patch of ice that had formed from melted snow during the afternoon, that was once more lying in a shadow as the sun went down. He boarded the Trolley bus a few meters behind Elina and took a seat three rows behind her.

As they traveled through the suburbs of Oslo, Kaarle was amazed at the number of German soldiers and military vehicles. "There must be a half million Germans in Bergen and Oslo." He thought. Kaarle wasn't sure about how large the Home Front resistance really was, but he knew one thing for certain, the Germans would be staying in Norway for as long as they wished. He was saddened to see long lines of Norwegians waiting in ration lines for small parcels of food. He guessed that even at this late hour the people had been waiting all day. He began to hate the Nazis. He found what the Professor had told him at first too incredulous to wrap his mind around but now he was beginning to realize that not only what he had heard was true, but that it had much more horror than a black iceberg waiting beneath the surface.

When Elina reached the house of Ole' she stopped and turned to look at Kaarle. The large gate was locked. Kaarle could wait no longer and closed the distance with Elina. "Return home Elina. This may turn out to be too dangerous for you." Kaarle warned.

Too late. A German sentry had already seen them. "Halt! Wass suchen Sie denn hier?" the sentry barked. "We are relatives of the owner." Kaarle answered in German. "This is now property of the Deutsche SS." The sentry answered. Elina spoke up. "Look it's not the same address. We've made a mistake. Excuse us Sir!" As the sentry eyed them suspiciously Elina pulled Kaarle down the street. Kaarle protested. "I can't just leave! I must find her!" He growled. "We will find her but please do it my way!" Kaarle stood for a moment and then said; "You're right. Lead on. We'll return to your place and make better plans."

Elina walked ahead and they boarded the Tram separately. As Kaarle took his seat a few rows behind Elina an SS Colonel boarded the Tram. He sat beside Elina and devoured her with his eyes. Elina's heart beat doubled. She tried desperately not to scream. Finally a sweat broke out across her forehead and she began to turn pale. When the Tram reached the stop at the Trolley Bus 17 line, Elina stepped away from the Tram afraid to turn around. She walked brusquely to the Trolley Bus and boarded. She gasped to see the Colonel follow her to the Trolley Bus and again take a seat next to her.

"Can you speak German?" the Colonel finally asked. "A little." Elina replied. "I have been admiring your Nordic features. I am Colonel Hartmut von Braunschweig, SS Gruppen Fuhrer for the Lebensborn Project. We have more than a dozen spa retreats in the Oslo region. We are looking for Nordic women who have Aryan genetic history which I can tell from your facial features you possess. If you are willing, I could offer you a very pleasant living environment in one of our hospices. You would never have to stand in line for food, or anything.

You would be pampered by our staff and your children protected and also pampered would become German citizens automatically." "But I have no children." Elina replied. "Oh but you will if you join us at Lebensborn." He replied. "Can I have some time to think about it?" Elina asked. "But of course. I shall escort you home and tomorrow afternoon I shall return to receive your answer." he replied. "Could you just give me your number and I will ring you up?" she asked. The Colonel wasn't to be denied. "I don't release my number to anyone." he said gruffly. The Trolley Bus finally stopped at Elina's village. The Colonel walked along with Elina. In every direction curtains were opened and then suddenly closed. Lights were switched off. To Norwegian patriots a scandal was in progress between that single slut who lived alone without a chaperone and now has a German officer. To the German sympathizers, an SS Colonel was in their village and possible new opportunities might accrue to the village. To all, a piercing fear caused them to hide in their rooms until the Colonel could be expected to have his way and depart.

As they approached Elina's door she thanked the Colonel and repeated that she would make her decision by the next day. "Are you that stupid you little Norwegian whore?" The Colonel growled. Elina tried to shut the door but the Colonel shoved his jack boot between the door and its frame and pushed his way inside. "You are fortunate that I have chosen you to bear children for the Reich. You will begin your apprenticeship tonight!" He yelled. He tore open Elina's dress and exposed her perfect breasts. She screamed and fell to the floor to cover her naked body. When she looked up she saw the Fiskar knife streaking through the air directly into the temporal lobe of the Colonel. He was killed instantly and fell to the floor. He bled slightly from both eye sockets but over all there was a surprisingly trace amount of blood.

"Help me take his uniform Elina." Kaarle said gently. Elina laid on the floor shaking in anger. "Get hold of yourself Elina. We must move quickly. I must wear his uniform and escort you out of this village tonight, or by tomorrow every Quisling in this village will be reporting that they saw the Colonel enter your place and never leave." Not a single drop of blood had splattered on the SS uniform, which was nearly a perfect fit for Kaarle all the way down to the boots.

The Colonel wore, strapped oppositely of his 9 mm Luger a black leather pouch. Kaarle found the Colonel's complete identification papers and several thousand German Reich Marks. Kaarle carried Elina's leather suit case that had his civilian clothes inside. Dressed in the SS uniform, Kaarle led Elina arm in arm to the Trolley Bus. When they reached the Tram station Kaarle waited until no one could see him enter the mens toilette where he changed back into civilian clothes and neatly folded the SS uniform placing it in the suit case. He reached Elina the black pouch the Colonel wore with the German Ausweiss and military identification papers inside. He also reached her his own Finnish passport. "Can your people do something with these? I need my photo transferred to the Colonel's papers. As of tonight I have become a German SS Colonel." "We have a papers man who can do wonders. Why do you want to impersonate him?" "It may be the only way to rescue my sister." Kaarle replied.

Chapter Five: Children Of The Enemy

Just before day break, Kaarle carried the nude German's body to the forest in a white bed sheet. It would vanish within a day as the ravenous wolves would tear it to pieces and drag the pieces away. He noticed a tatoo in Gothic under his left arm with a letter "O". He told Elina who said she would tell Kai about it. In the middle of the afternoon Elina tapped on Kaarle's door. "Come in Elina. What is it?" "I just wanted to thank you for saving me last night. I think he would have raped me then killed me." "Raped you to be sure, but he wanted you for his own reasons. I doubt he would have killed you so soon." Kaarle reflected. "Anyway, thank you." She turned to leave. She looked down at Kaarle's handsome face with blue eyes and marveled that someone who was so handsome could be so lethal.

"Can I stay for a moment?" Elina asked. "Sure." Kaarle said with a puzzled look on his face. Elina sat on the edge of the bed. She had just finished a bath and her lovely hair was still wet and curly. She wore a full length Turkish robe. "Can I just hold you for a moment Kaarle? I'm so lonely just now." Kaarle didn't answer. He pulled her to him and she lay in his arms for what seemed an eternity to Kaarle, who felt his arm go numb. He lay still, feeling the warmth of her beautiful sleek body through the robe. "He called me a whore Kaarle." Elina began to weep. Kaarle ran his fingers through her hair and soothed her. Kaarle watched as Elina's pulse along her neckline pulsated rapidly. He could feel his own pulse thump loudly in his ears and he felt it moving warmly throughout his whole body. "He didn't know you. The whore he was describing lived in his own mind. He had obviously never loved anything, or anyone in his life. He was unable to separate love from violence.

A pathetic man who doesn't deserve to have been able to cause you to shed a single tear from your lovely eyes." Kaarle was still speaking softly when Elina filled his mouth with her own. They kissed and searched each other with their finger tips until they joined in ecstatic bliss.

When they were in rapture in each others arms they fell on their side and didn't separate for the rest of the afternoon. Suddenly Elina arose with a shock. "Kai is coming!" she shouted. "Kai? Who is Kai?" Kaarle asked with a dazed voice. "He's my Resistance leader. He reports to Kjakan. We don't use real names. My name is Fox. We refer to you as Package One and your sister as Package Two." She glanced at the clock. "He will be here in thirty minutes. We must hurry. Kaarle there are three men in Norway who hold our dear Kingdom in their brave hands. Kjakan which means "the Chin" is our top spy. He is a man named Gunnar Tolesby. Gunnar, with Max Manus and Claus Helberg are saboteurs, who, like Tolesby, do not understand the word fear."

"Max fought with your Army in the Winter War. The three founded the "Oslo Group." We have seven thousand members who are ready to die if any one of these men ask them to." Elina said proudly. "Kai reports directly to the Oslo Group." Kaarle's first impression of Kai was that he was a serious man. Kai was obviously very resourceful with keen insight. He noticed everything." Kaarle guessed to himself that Kai was a deliberate, instinctual man who trusted few men if any, a man ever on the alert for sudden surprises. "Kaarle, Fox tells me you tried to visit your sister last night." Kai said. "Yes, we discovered that she no longer lives there. That Nazi SS have taken over the place." "Fox I asked you to wait until my contacts returned with more information before you breached." Kai growled.

"It wasn't her fault. I would have left to find my sister on my own if Fox didn't come with me." Kaarle defended. "Yes, but somehow you managed to bring a Nazi Colonel back into our secret lair. We never bring anyone but packages inside our system. Where is the body? " Kai asked. "I dumped his nude body in the forest. I expect the wolves have made a meal of him by now." Kaarle answered. Kai seemed furious and was about to express his outrage when Elina interrupted him. "Kai, Kaarle didn't bring the Colonel here. He followed me and tried to rape me. He would have no doubt killed me if Kaarle hadn't intervened" "Well are you certain no one heard the gun shot?" Kai asked.

"Kaarle killed him with a knife through his temple. He didn't even bleed on his white shirt." Elina explained. Kai looked astonished. "You killed him with a knife through the brain?" Kai repeated. "and you have his uniform?" "Yes." Kaarle replied. "Kaarle is a Ski soldier from Finland. He fought the Russians in the Winter War." Elina explained. "I see." Kai replied with obviously new respect for Kaarle. "Can you tell me more about the Colonel?" Kai asked. "Well he told me he was a Gruppen Fuhrer with the SS and oh yes as Kaarle dropped his body in the forest he noticed under his left arm a tatoo in Gothic letters with a large "O". Elina described. "My God. You killed a Waffen SS Colonel. The "O" was his Blood Type. What did the rest of the tatoo look like?" Kai asked. "It was a double lightning bolt with a small skull." Kaarle said. "Listen, you said something about hearing back from your intelligence sources. Did you learn what happened to my sister and my aunt?" Kaarle asked. Kai suddenly looked at the floor. "I'm afraid there is bad news. Kaarle inhaled and braced for the pain. "Is she dead, is my sister dead?" Kaarle asked with a quaver in his voice. " No, She is alive. Your aunt was not as fortunate.

When your aunt refused to sign over her property they confiscated it anyway and then created false papers showing that she is a Jew. Your sister was married to a man named Arin Olssen. He had dark features so it was easier to re-create him as a Jew. In his case he actually was a Jew. Fifty percent any way. Twenty five percent is all they need to ship you out to the Death Camps. They shipped both Arin and your aunt to Auschwitz a year ago."

Kaarle's eyes welled up with tears. "My sister! Did they ship her to Auschwitz too?" Kaarle almost yelled. "No. She is in a Lebensborn hospice not far from here. She is with a 1 year old child from a German SS officer. My sources think he's the same officer you killed." Kai looked at Kaarle now with pity. "AAAHHHG" Kaarle moaned in pain. Elina came to Kaarle and embraced him as he moaned. Kai noticed that something more than a natural reaction was involved in the embrace and he buried his large face in both hands as he shook his head no. "Did they make false papers for my sister too?" Kaarle asked.

"No. They would have never accepted her into Lebensborn if they suspected she had even eaten Jewish food. These are insane people who have invaded us. We Norwegians are fighting for our sanity and our souls while we even have Norwegian traitors trying to kill us for the Nazis as well." Kai lamented. Kaarle reeled in pain and slid down the wall to the floor. "I want to hunt down the wolves and cut him from their bellies so I can burn his flesh!" Kaarle screamed. Kai held Elina back until Kaarle settled down. "Can you at least show me where the hospice is where they are holding my sister? I don't need your help I will get her myself." Kaarle growled. "Please listen to me. My contact risked his life getting this information for you.

He is already working under cover at the hospice getting more information about your sister. If you will wait I will return tomorrow and give you an update. But we hope that you understand that you will still not be free to do as you wish. Acting alone, you could get your sister killed and disrupt operations that we are already involved in." Kai said.

"Alright. You are correct. I will await your new information and then I will await your signal as to the best time to rescue my sister." Kaarle agreed. "Thank you. I don't believe the Colonel came here on other business, so it will probably take the Gestapo a few more days to collect enough information from informers to trace him back to this house." Kai said. "What does that mean?" Elina asked. "It means that your brother must be warned and that you need to leave this place or they will hunt you both down and shoot you." Kaarle said. "Precisely." Kai agreed. "I don't know where I'd go. I've lived here all my life until Mama and Papa were killed by the naval bombing." She said sadly. "If you decide, I will have you transported via Sweden to England. If you choose to stay here with the Finn I will take you both to my best safe house where you can hide out until we need you to help us with missions." Kai said. Elina looked at Kaarle. "What shall I do Kaarle?" "Well, it would be much safer in England, but no matter what you decide, once I have my sister I will go to any corner of the globe to find you." he said. "We're staying Kai." She said. "Well, find out first how Markus feels about that. Use your go between to get in touch with him. I'll return tomorrow for your answer." Kai said as he walked out the door. "Can I come to Finland with you Kaarle? I won't eat much and I'll fit nicely in your pocket." Elina pursed her lips like a beautiful child. "Kaarle hugged her tight.

"Of course you can come with me. Your brother as well, but don't you think when you tell him that you and I have fallen in love in only three days that he may not have such a measured response?"

"Oh Kaarle, did you just say you love me?" "Madly. Yes and I want it to go on forever." "Oh Kaarle I love you too, forever." she said. "Just the same, I still must collect my sister and you must convince Markus that we will no doubt eventually have plenty of Germans to fight in Finland as well as Norway." Kaarle said with a sober expression. "Once he hears all of the details how can he refuse? Elina said with conviction. Kaarle held Elina in his arms until dawn. She whimpered a few times but when she awakened in his arms she drifted back to sleep. Kaarle dropped into a purgatory of sleep just before sunrise. His keen senses awakened to a light tapping on the door. Kaarle filled his hand with his 9 mm and bolted from the bed. Elina followed him closely down the stair to the back door. When Elina looked past the curtain she quickly opened the door. Thomas, the joker was leaning against the wall holding a wounded comrade.

"Quickly, bring him inside!" Elina whispered. "Where's Markus?" She asked. Thomas began to cry. "They ambushed us. We didn't see them and suddenly they were shooting at us from everywhere. Hakon and I were the only ones who escaped by playing dead. They were shooting the fallen and just before they got to Hakon and myself they were called elsewhere by their Commander. I didn't know where else to go." Thomas mumbled. "Where is my f--cking brother Thomas?" Elina shrieked.

"He was dragging his men to safety and they shot him to death." Thomas blurted out. Elina painfully dropped to the floor and began pulling at her hair. Kaarle steadied her and she sobbed violently in his arms. "Elina, help me tend to Hakon!" Kaarle shouted. Elina tried but couldn't concentrate. Kaarle felt Hakon's cold body and put his fingers along Hakon's carotid artery. "He's dead." Kaarle said. "Let me look at you Thomas. Where were you shot?" Kaarle asked. "Here I think." he said as he pointed to his chest. "I think that's Hakon's blood Thomas, you lucky devil. "Not a scratch." Kaarle observed.

Suddenly Elina flew at Thomas pounding his chest. "Eleven men shot to death and not a scratch on Thomas? You tell me what really happened you son of a bitch or I'll scratch your eyes out!" Thomas turned pale, dropping into a chair at the kitchen table. "Rinnan's soldiers told me they only wanted to question us. They caught me with my pistol two days ago. They threatened to hang me if I didn't help them." I didn't want to die. Please forgive me. After the shooting died down I tried to go back and help but only Hakon was alive. I'm so sorry!" Suddenly there was a deafening loud pop as the acrid smell of cordite filled the room. Thomas lay across the table with his brains splattered against the wall. Elina stood holding the Colonel's 9mm Luger. "Help me scrape this shit traitor off my kitchen table." she said to Kaarle. "Gladly." Kaarle replied. Kai came early. He rushed in and saw Hakon and Thomas lying in a heap. The place smelled like a butcher shop. "What happened? Where is Markus? The Gestapo is closing in. They traced the Colonel to the Tram station. It's just a matter of hours or less before they trace the Trolley Bus line to this village and start getting reports from your neighbors." Kai exclaimed. "Did you get the update on my sister?" Kaarle asked.

"Yes. The Colonel you killed was indeed the father of her baby. He must have captured her about a year ago." Kai said. "That's the bad news? What's the rest?" Kaarle asked anxiously. "Dr. Mengele from Auschwitz, a mad murderer of children found out that your sister is Finnish and that she is a twin." Kai said sternly. "Apparently you Finns have some of the most isolated genes in the world living where it's too cold for a regular human to live. Anyway Mengele went crazy with joy that he could study your sister's genes, her hereditary history and that of the baby. Mengele will be flying here within days. Initial chatter from our French Resistance cousins inform us that Heinrich Himmler and Josef Goebbels who each, in their own way head up the Lebensborn Experimental program plan to meet him here. This is creating an opportunity we were never sure we would ever have to get the bastards on our turf in order to take them out. All thanks to your sister and the baby. We are hastily making plans to assassinate them. Because it is your sister, we may invite you in on the operation if you behave and follow orders." Kai said.

Chapter Six: Der Weisse Engel

"Kai, Elina just learned that her brother was killed ." "Have something to do with this lot?" Kai asked, looking at the bodies on the floor. "Just the dead traitor on the bottom." Elina said. "He betrayed Markus and his entire unit to Rinnan's assassins who ambushed and destroyed them." Kai winced. "I'm so sorry Fox. Markus will be missed." Kai said sadly. "Let's be off then. I will take you and the Finn to my most secure safe house. I only ask my dear friend from the East that you don't act alone. We have ongoing operations that you could jeopardize." Kai said. Kai had a Volvo parked outside. Exactly fifteen minutes after they left, the Gestapo raided the house in search of a Colonel von Braunschweig but found only two dead bodies lying on the floor.

Arin was knocked unconscious when he tried to stop the SS Colonel from forcing Laila into his staff car. Two strong SS troopers kicked and stomped him as Laila screamed for her husband. Colonel von Braunschweig stepped out of the vehicle slapping both soldiers across their faces with his leather gloves to put on a show for Laila. "You see my dear they will not hurt him as long as you do as you are told. Will you follow my instructions then?" He asked. "Yes, I'll do anything you say. Just don't hurt him any more." she cried. The Colonel told his soldiers to take Arin to the transfer point along with his bitch of a Jewish Aunt. The Colonel had just presided over a hearing regarding evidence his military adjutant produced, that included birth certificates that proved beyond a doubt, both Arin and Sani were Juden. Arin did his best to protect Aunt Sani, but they quickly separated males from females for the trip.

After three days without food, or water he managed to scramble faster for the hard crusts of bread and at each stop he shoved the hardened bread crusts into Sani's grateful hands. During the slow arduous train trip the prisoners were only allowed outside of the cattle cars when the urine and feces saturated straw was removed by workers with star of David insignias sewn on the backs of their ragged shirts. The workers never complained. It was much better to be cleaning the trains than riding in them. Often, the German guards would berate a worker for the most frivolous, capricious of reasons and the worker would find himself shoved into a nearby cattle car to become a "passenger" instead of a Schutt Abladen Arbeiter.

Arin had constant images of the SS Colonel with his arm around Laila as they drove away. He could still vividly see her as she leaped against the rear window screen screaming for Arin as the vehicle grew smaller and finally disappeared. The emptiness he felt at that moment must be what death is like, he thought. One moment you are near everything that life means to you and in an instant it is ripped away as if by a tornado, or a hurricane. Arin wondered what the Colonel would do to Laila. Rape and defile her, beat her, discard her to his underlings until battered and destroyed? Would she in desperation take her own life? The anger and hatred for the Colonel and all Nazis kept Arin alive. He couldn't possibly die until he had ripped out their throats for what they had done to his precious Laila. He trembled with hatred when he thought about the hundreds of thousands, perhaps millions of lives they would destroy before a miracle from God would shut them down. Arin swore that even if he had to drink his own urine, he would stay alive just to watch them all die.

Then suddenly the most powerful weapon in the entire arsenal of the Third Reich hit him squarely in the center of his forehead. Self guilt. He had heard as a child that his father was Jewish, but he didn't really understand, or care what that meant, since religion was never really a part of his life. Was Laila and Sani being punished because of the very blood in his own veins? Had the discovery that his father was a Jew angered the Nazis so much? That couldn't be it. They had claimed Sani was Jewish too. How absurd. She was a Finn. Were there Jews in Finland? Where did they find proof that Sani was a Jew? Wouldn't that mean that Laila was also a Jew?

But the Colonel acted as though he was rescuing Laila from the dirty Jews, so she couldn't be. The anxiety exhausted Arin. He wondered why the Jews accepted their fate as though they deserved it. Why didn't they mob the sentries? It would be worth the risk of being shot, at least they could die fighting. He began to hate the Jews himself for being such sheep. What had Kafka called them? "The Mouse Folk." Then he started hating himself for being a Jew just like all the rest. It hit him like cold water in the face. The Jews were culturally Germans. Their only difference was religion. Both their culture and religion was heavily influenced by authoritarianism that caused them to be good citizens who accepted authority stoically. They cooperated in their own death because rules were never to be broken. Good Germans, good Jews. Acceptance of fate by passive commission. It sickened him to think of how the Nazis had manipulated this quirk of Judaism. "Madness, utter perverted madness!" he said out loud. Then he felt shame. He had witnessed on this very train hundreds of random acts of kindness and selflessness amongst the Jews who had every reason to be filled with anger and self pity.

He had only seen kindness in those around him and at times a tear came to his eye as he felt proud to know that their blood was his blood. He began to understand that if the Jews hadn't been so afflicted with intelligence, kindness and civility they would have already kicked Hitler's ass.

He had fleeting thoughts of befriending a guard or two. Once they really knew Arin as anyone else who had ever met Arin could tell you, they wouldn't be able to resist admitting that Arin is a great guy. He tried smiling at a guard when the train stopped again and received a nearly fatal butt stroke from the guards rifle stock. "Die Homo!" the guard yelled down at him. Arin vomited his own blood and was kicked by guards on each side of him. They were packed in like sardines and the human stench would have defeated him if it had come on suddenly instead of gradually. As the trip wore on, the nostrils became a part of the slow death of the senses. The closer they felt to death the more difficult it was to discern it from life.

Early one morning, as the train rocked and swayed with the many curves it negotiated in the German mountains in Northern Bavaria, Arin pretended to be walking in the meadows between the snow white peaks. Arin loved mountains but as beautiful as the German Alpine horizon was he couldn't feel the elation he once felt when looking at such natural splendor. He glanced over his shoulder and he thought at first he was witnessing an apparition. The man swayed with the movement of the train, his limbs flailing as though he was a music conductor, but how was he able to levitate so well? As splashes of early morning light were cast across the strange scene Arin saw the belts the man had tied together to hang himself with.

Sadness and shock was sent through the poor miserable souls in Arin's car until a man stood and said a few words. He was a Rabbi. "Do not be sad my dear brothers and sisters. Rejoice that he has been set free." He then slid back down again. Arin clung to the words as though they were brick and mortar. Life was a series of freedoms. One progressed from one level to the next until perfect freedom and bliss was finally achieved. What freedom could be greater than death? Without a body one felt no pain, or sickness, or sadness. No beginning and no end, just, just, just what? Of course you wouldn't feel anything without a body, you also wouldn't think anything without a mind. Forget about the freedom of suicide he thought. Instead, he succumbed to thoughts about the freedom of murder. That would be the only freedom he would ever need. The freedom to dream of strangling the Colonel with his bare hands and it gave him such pleasure and comfort, he rarely thought of anything else. His only enjoyment in life had become his vivid and clear step by step dreams of the torture and murder he would inflict on Colonel von Braunschweig.

Arin regretted not trying to escape with Laila back in 1940. It was now late 1941. Aunt Sani refused to leave her home back then and Laila refused to leave Aunt Sani. The Rabbi, whose name was Jakob Stein reached out his hand to Arin. "My name is Jakob and what are you called?" he asked. "I'm Arin." Jakob pulled Arin closer to have a look at his lacerated face and swollen jaw. He delicately traced the jaw bone to the skull and patted the temporal region with his finger tips. "Are you a doctor?" Arin asked. "Yes, University Of Stockholm. You're very hard headed my friend. I saw the blow you took. Many with softer heads would have sustained more extensive injury. As far as I can tell there are no fractures no pesky little bone chips and fragments moving around.

The swelling should subside in a week but I can see pustule formations already forming along both upper and lower gums. If you get a deep infection it could reach your brain and become fatal." Jakob reached Arin a small pill box. "Penicillin 500 milligrams. Take these twice a day until they are gone. It should prevent worse infection." Jakob said. "I will find a way to repay you." Arin said.

"Don't worry. The Nazis would have confiscated them anyway. Worse, they would have discovered perhaps that I am a doctor. I have false papers. I was caught trying to escape to Sweden, but it wasn't my lucky day it seems." Jakob said. "Why wouldn't you want them to know you're a doctor. I'm sure they would have made things easier for you as they allowed you to continue your practice in the camp." Arin said. "My dear young man. Are you from Oslo? I thought I knew all of the Jews in Oslo but I have never seen you at my synagogue before." Jakob said.

"My father is Jewish. He never took me to a synagogue before. I guess he didn't want anyone to know he was Jewish for fear it would be negative for his career as a dentist." Arin reflected. "Hmmm. Well I don't know whether we shall be assigned to the same work, or the same place to sleep, or even if we will remain alive more than a few days, but if you allow me I will do my best to teach you about your ancestry and its religious principles. I would be happy to teach you to be a Rabbi, but I'm afraid that would take a geat deal of time reading the Torah to you and as you can see, the inconsiderate Germans relieved me of my last copy." Jakob smiled."As to your other questions, Arin they are not shipping us to Poland to give us a Kur."

"A nice medical spa retreat in Karlovy Vary would be my choice, but I'm afraid they have something far more sinister in mind. If they knew that I am a doctor I would be assigned as a surgeon's assistant. I would be responsible for painting a line on a perfectly healthy leg, or an arm, to be amputated while the patient screamed because no anesthesia could be wasted on a Jew."

"What?" Arin gasped. "Where have you heard this?" Arin asked. "Oh we sneaky Jews have our little nefarious undergrounds which smuggle letters out of the Death Camps. Arin, my friend you are about to walk around inside the intestines of the Devil. The more prepared you are psychologically, the better will be your chances of surviving. First trust no one. Not even people you knew in your other life. Even Jews I'm afraid will sell each other out for an extra slice of bread, or a small box of medicine."

"How is it that you trust me then?" Arin asked coyly. "Well, perhaps after our friend took his own life I am receding into a state of depression and melancholy, or perhaps it's because I saw a German guard nearly bash your brains in with his rifle. Not many spies would consent to being so realistic in their subterfuge." Jakob Laughed. "Is that it? You have laid in stench and your own filth in a freezing box car for a week just so you can tell Hitler that Jakob is a doctor of medicine?" Jakob laughed. Arin smiled for the first time since he and Laila had been dragged along with a screaming aunt Sani from their house in Oslo. It hurt to smile. "I may have to avoid you for a while Jakob. You're hurting my face." Arin said. Both men chuckled. "Back to my advice Arin. Right now I'm sure we would both trust each other with our lives, but they will break us many times, before we die, that is if they don't march us to the ovens straight away.

In a mere month you will see brothers and sisters agreeing to become spies against each other for an extra ladel of soup each day, or to be diverted from the showers. It must be an unusual experience to have your entire mental and physical existence constantly monitored and controlled by a force that can and will administer pain and torture just because it can. Your soul will leave you many times, angry at you that you have allowed your body to be trapped by such evil." Jakob said with firmness. "Your soul will talk to you like a nagging Mother, or wife agreeing with your Masters that you are indeed worthless and undeserving. They will make your soul hate your mother for birthing you. If you live, it will only be a half life. You will never stop hating yourself for letting evil over power and damage your body, mind and soul, even though nothing in the universe could have protected you from it." Jakob said unable to conceal his anger that burned like a flame in his eyes. Arin suddenly realized Jakob's eyes were passionate and deep and were central to his being.

"When civilizations go mad enmasse it's like an evil storm that tears apart everything it touches. One morning the skies open and the rivers run heavy with innocent blood and you pick up the pieces, if any remain and re-build with the hope that you didn't miss something that could have protected you from the next evil storm. If we live beyond this we will carry a memory that will be like a heavy rock on our backs. It is important to not let the murderers drag you down into their depths. That will consume you and you will be forever lost. You must always let them keep evil on their side while you keep goodness on yours. When they take everything from you, you will still have something they could never possess in a trillion years." "What is that?" Kaarle asked. "Innocence." Jakob said with a whisper so light it made the box car seem a holy place.

If you are lucky enough to survive you can only repay those who died in your place by never forgetting what happened here. That is the singular and only way to prevent it from ever happening again to anyone. Never, ever forget. If you do it will happen again and again. I'm afraid you and I are the little pieces awaiting the worst part of this beast that is just on the cusp of what it can really inflict. It will get much worse before it gets better and we can do nothing but try to hide from the prying witches and war Locks who wait, ever anxious to feed the beast with our very souls." Jakob said as he stared in the distance. "When we arrive they will screen us. Women and children here, men over there. They will ask you if you have a trade. Useful is Tailor, Barber, leather Smith, Jeweler, Shoe maker and so on. Be certain to claim a trade even if you haven't done it before. You can learn it on the job. The worse they can do is kill you if you aren't good at it and they'll kill you anyway so what's the difference?" "I'm grateful for your advice Jakob." "Glad to help Arin." Jakob said cheerfully.

"Say, Arin, didn't you tell me your Dad's a Dentist?" "Yes, was. Both of my parents were killed during the invasion of 1940." Arin replied. "For God's sake don't tell the Nazis about your father." "Why?" Arin wondered. "Because you'll get stuck removing skeletons from the ovens and pulling their gold teeth from their mouths with pliers." Jakob explained.

"They collect our hair when they shave us and melt our teeth into gold bars. Anything useful from our bodies is processed and sold at fair market value. The Nazis have a crude sense of humor and they would no doubt relish the idea that a Jew Dentist's son was pulling teeth in Auschwitz." Jakob said solemnly.

"My God! I want to believe that you are at any minute going to begin laughing and tell me you've been pulling my elbow." Arin moaned. He had actually taken a deep breath waiting and hoping Jakob would confess to having spun a dark tale from a sick sense of humor but no such confession was uttered. Instead Jakob looked apologetically at Arin and reached out to embrace him in a gentle reassuring hug that a father would give a son on his death bed. Arin fell silent and pulled his hat down over his eyes as if he were trying to escape to another place, in another time.

The train arrived at 4 am at Auschwitz. Arin rubbed his eyes and looked out at the train platform which was flooded with search lights and moving sentry patrols. It appeared to be a scene from a Kafkaesque novel. Tall German soldiers with sub-machine guns strapped across their shoulders were being dragged by powerful German Shepherd dogs up and down the train platform. Two half track vehicles had been positioned at opposite ends of the train yard to achieve an inter-locking field of fire if given the order.

Arin felt a lump of fear in his throat. His mouth was dry from the fear and his hands trembled. He thought of Descartes and Spinoza and how we could all be caught in one of their illusionary nightmares. One in which one dreamed they were dying, only to awaken. He prayed that if there is a God he would end this frightening and horrible nightmare and let everything return to sanity. Arin remembered passages from the bible Aunt Sani read to Laila and himself on Sunday afternoons. " Job held his interest the most. But How could there be a God? God watched as they ripped his mate for life from his arms and now the demons wanted his last breath and God was OK with that? If this is a test God, please flunk me and send me home, but where is that now that Laila is gone?

Arin inhaled the crisp morning air and instantly remembered a literature assignment at the University of Oslo. In it Franz Kafka, the famous Czech Jewish author had written:

"To die would mean nothing else than to surrender a nothing to the nothing but that would be impossible to conceive, for how could a person, even only as a nothing consciously surrender himself to the nothing and not merely to a nothing, but rather to a roaring nothing whose nothingness consists only of its incomprehensibility?"

Arin watched the SS Soldaten march their Jewish Security Lackies to the platform and as the gruesome sound of the box car doors grated in the dead silence of morning the dogs became agitated and begged with low howls and squeals to be allowed to attack. "All resistance is futile." Arin remembered from Kafka's "The Trial." He stood and steadied the Rabbi whose knees had gone weak. Their turn came and they were pulled out onto the platform and lined up for their first inspection. A Nazi Sergeant came by with a clip board and asked if anyone had special trade skills. Arin yelled out shoe cobbler and the Rabbi answered the same. The women and young children were already lining up for the march to the camp. Arin saw aunt Sani limping as she walked. Arin quickly surmised that she had been beaten or worse, along the way. He instinctively knew better than to yell encouragement to her. He couldn't take another rifle stroke and he was sure she couldn't either. Then he was dazed by alternating lights and pitch blackness. That's when he saw the White Angel. Jakob whispered "Der weisse Engel. Dr. Josef Mengele, Satan incarnate."

The figure dressed in a flowing clinicians full length white smock was waving his arms first to the left and then to the right to direct those who fit his experimentation profile to a separate holding area. Then the White Angel drew a line across the wall of a nearby building. The line was approximately five feet high. The SS guards had the women with children bring them to the line. Children taller than the line were guided to the holding area, those shorter were given back to their relieved mothers who were not yet aware that to have been rejected was an immediate death sentence for their children as well as themselves.

Women who professed a trade were sent to the holding area, the rest were led to the line of women with small children. "I don't understand what's happening now Jakob." Arin whispered as they stood in the holding area. "Sei Ruhig! Shut up!" an SS sergeant yelled to the formation. In a few moments, Jakob whispered back; "The women with small children will be led to the showers with the women who claimed no trade skills. Instead of the promised shower they will be gassed. Jewish laborers will then drag them to the ovens. See the black smoke yonder in the distance? When it turns greyish white they will be burning flesh."

The SS sergeant leaped into the formation and grabbed a poor man who had a nervous tick that made it appear his lips were moving. He dragged the man out of the formation and shoved him into a group of other men who were waiting in the shower line. "Ich hab's gesagt! Ruhig!" the Sergeant commanded the rest. As the ill fated who were being marched to the showers passed by aunt Sani saw Arin. "Arin! Yoo hoo Arin! They are taking us to get cleaned up from the journey. Don't worry, I told them your father was a Dentist.

They promised to let you work in the hospital!" Aunt Sani cried out. A guard swung his weapon into her ribs, knocking her to the ground. As a Guard with a dog rushed toward her, two women picked her up and half carried her back to her line. She hobbled along and the Guards just watched her, laughing. Arin choked and let out a silent scream. He felt so helpless. He watched his last connection with his previous life melt away, limping in the shadows and he couldn't do a single thing to help her, or warn her. "How unlucky you are aunt Sani. Your sin was owning a house the Nazis wanted. You were not born a Jew but you will now die one. "May God watch over your passing." Arin said softly to himself.   "You! The German Sergeant growled. Why did you lie to me about being a shoe cobbler? So you are a Dentist?" "No, my father was a Dentist, I am a shoe cobbler." "Stand with this group. You will be more useful as a Dentist!" Arin felt as if he may vomit.

Everything Jakob had warned him about was unfolding as if it were some sort of diabolical script. Within a matter of two minutes, he had watched Laila's flesh and blood aunt get swallowed up in a march to the ovens, beaten along the way, while he learned at the same time that he would probably soon be pulling her teeth in search of gold. He had an almost irresistible urge to laugh maniacally and to never stop laughing until he was either completely mad, or they shot him dead. Now he understood why Kafka's drawings looked like the face of death, distorted and painful. Death was as abundant as the sea in this God forsaken place and it came so quickly. Life was the rare and precious side of existence and once lost it was irretrievable. Why couldn't these creatures who must have had Mothers and Sisters, Fathers and Brothers, see what they were doing in the service of evil?

If they could only see themselves as he saw them, they would fall on their face and writhe in guilt. As Jakob described, they were marshaled through a warehouse and all of their jewelry, clothing and suitcases, were collected and stored. An espionage system was in place, so not a single collector dared swallow a jewel, or diamond ring to horde for later. Personal pictures were destroyed. Jewish Barbers with electric razors gave every man, woman and child the same haircut; bald with nothing left anywhere. They were dusted for lice and issued prison clothing with a Star of David sewn on the front. They slept on cold slabs and blankets were all but nonexistent.

Those who succumbed to the harshness in the night were carried out to mass graves and throw into them like sacks of garbage. Arin soon discovered that he was actually assigned to what they called the hospital which was in reality a filthy butcher shop for humans. He was at first horrified to learn that it was his job to collect the amputated limbs removed mostly from children without anesthesia. He took them, along with their corpse in an open wheel barrow to the mass graves and tossed them onto the piles of dead already there. Lye and chlorine powder was sprinkled across the graves to lower the incidence of disease. When he returned he rinsed away the blood with a water hose after Dr. Mengele finished with his surgeries. There was a tremendous amount of blood because unless Mengele wished to keep the patient alive for further studies, no effort was made to tie off arteries. In fact before each procedure, it was assumed the patient would die, if not from the shock, then from the blood loss. Arin saw a small cage with a set of twins inside, boy and girl, 9, perhaps 10 years old.

They were half starved with death masks for faces and had been intentionally kept in the cramped cage to test what their heart muscle fiber would be like compared to another set of twins that had not been deprived of food, water and sleep, but who would also provide heart specimens the next day. Arin fully expected that at any moment he would discover that a secret gate would be opened and he would be forced directly into Dante's Ninth Circle. Then he chided himself. He was already in a river of shit that must be very near Circle Nine on Dante's scale of human misery. How much worse could it be to be buried upside down in ice with white hot fire above in Dante's Hell? At least he wouldn't be able to see the suffering of others and hear their startled screams as they were being butchered alive by the most evil demon in human history.

He ceased thinking of Laila. He never wanted her to see him in this place so he reasoned that if he stopped imagining her while inside the wire it would keep her safe. Now, when he wanted a mental escape he concentrated on more tangible thoughts such as his memory of being a child in a loving family. Then sudden stark images of the suicide on the train jumped into his thoughts. Arin now had a different opinion of that fellow. He pitied him before, now he envied him. He hadn't seen the Rabbi in weeks. Then fear became a loathing. He made a vow that as long as he didn't see the Rabbi's corpse in the mass grave he could hang on. One morning he had a greater than usual load of limbs and Mengele needed the blood cleaned before the afternoon's experiments. As he dumped the arms and legs of the children he slipped and went tumbling into the grave with them. The Lye began to burn his hands as he scrambled to be free.

He fell flat and then, suddenly staring directly into Arins's face were the now lifeless eyes of the Rabbi. His head had been severed, no doubt as a result of some test about blood flow to the brain. Arin screamed but no sound came out of his paralyzed throat. He was pulled from the pit by other laborers and rushed back to the hospital with Mengele screaming for the blood to be washed away from the walls. Arin didn't even have time to mourn his friend Jakob. He rinsed the Lye from his hands with the water hose and began scrubbing the floor and the white ceramic tiled walls hoping to clean the evil place before Mengele decided to use Arin as another specimen.

His work perhaps saved him from going completely insane. Arin now kept to himself. Jakob, even from death had one last lesson to teach him. If he didn't let anyone inside his heart as he had the Rabbi, then he could endure watching death take them. Yet to know them, not simply as fellow human beings who didn't deserve what was happening to them, but as friends, stretched Arin's mind beyond its endurance limit. He learned from a woman laborer who worked in the office that Mengele would be traveling to Norway for a fort night and that he was leaving in the morning. Had he known that Mengele's purpose for the trip was to examine his wife Laila at Lebensborn in the nude, with her fat baby boy, whose father had been the SS Colonel who sent himself and Sani to Auschwitz, he would have gone completely mad. The woman also informed him that Mengele had personally ordered that Arin be assigned Dentist duties until he came back. He would be handling skeletons, pulling their gold teeth, then dragging them from the ovens and stacking them for burial until Mengele returned.

She warned him that Mengele nearly ordered his death for letting blood accumulate on the operating room walls and would surely do so next time.

Chapter Seven: Norges Hjemmefront

(Norwegian Resistance)

Kai's safe house was perfect. It was a converted barn that still appeared to be a barn from the outside. Animals occupied the first floor. Access to the very comfortable suite beneath the barn floor was a trap door under a small pile of straw and animal manure, that was refreshed often. Its downside was the fact that it had no windows. It had instead a periscope salvaged from a German U- Boat and hidden within a hollow beam that gave Kai a 360 degree view of anyone approaching from a kilometer away. One wall of the living room held a small armory of rifles, submachine guns, pistols and knives. The armament was loaded and the safety's were off. A bin held hand grenades and a rack held a bazooka with a canvas vest that carried four anti-tank rockets.

Elina offered Kaarle some Swedish coffee. "Kaarle, I told Kai what you and your Samis did to the German battalion when you first arrived, but he already knew. He just didn't know what your contribution was until his sources informed him. It's a pity the training you gave Markus and his team went to the grave with them. Norway has a detachment that fought in the Winter War. They returned with shocking stories of the incredible courage of your Ski Soldiers and the rest of the Finnish Army." Elina said respectfully. " As I told you, Norway has placed its future in the hands of three men; Gunnar Tolesby, Max Manus and Claus Helberg. Kai, which means 'Earth' reports directly to Gunnar Tolesby. Gunnar is perhaps the greatest spy who ever lived.

He is gifted at many different impersonations and has walked and talked in the midst of high level SS and Gestapo without them having even the slightest suspicion he is in Norwegian Resistance. As a co-founder of the Oslo Group with Max and Claus, he helps decide every mission and every sacrifice that our Resistance Movement makes. Without him there would be only chaos for Norway. I share this information with you because you have already proven beyond a doubt to be a brother, if not a son of Norway." Elina said. "Thank you." Kaarle said as he kissed Elina's hand.

"Once the Gestapo learn who we are they hunt down and torture our loved ones and threaten to kill them until we can't stand it any longer and give ourselves up. That has already happened sadly enough. We lost a key person to the Gestapo not long ago and we worried that he may give his torturers enough information about us to write a biography about all of us, but he found a way to bite the veins in his wrist and he bled to death rather than risk betraying the Resistance. Sadly we only knew his operations name. Many Norwegians are dying for Norway and we may never know their sacrifice or true identity." She said. "Max is an amazing saboteur. He came back from Latin America to help you with your Winter War and when the Nazis invaded Norway he could have easily escaped to Sweden, but he remained here to join the "Oslo Group." she said.

"He has been trained in Scotland, England and America and has cost the Germans dearly by blowing up key Nazi military ships like the Donau, in Norwegian waters, with home made Limpet mines. The man is fearless. I can't even imagine swimming in freezing ice water with explosives that could suddenly vaporize you along with an enemy ship, can you?"

"No. That is indeed brave." Kaarle agreed, as he silently remembered stringing the explosives in the frozen lakes in Finland. "He has destroyed countless enemy aircraft on the ground. He has built homemade torpedos and launched them from a canoe. Can you imagine blowing up a huge ship from a goddamned canoe?" she asked. "No. It's incredible. I hope I meet him to thank him for fighting in our Winter War." Kaarle said. "Kaarle some have wondered how much we can trust the Finns now that you are fighting alongside the Third Reich against Russia." Elina said. "I assure you that the alliance is temporary, a measure to gain back lost land after the Winter War. Once we have our land back the Finns will quit Germany. We share battlefield information with them about the Russians, nothing more. Our leaders knew we would be drawn into the fight between Russia and Germany. Given Russia's historical belligerence with us it was a natural choice to go against the Russians." Kaarle said.

"As I'm sure you already know, not a single Finn would support the insanity that we ourselves have been shocked to hear about regarding the Nazi Genocide. We would never betray a sister Nordic nation I swear this to you." Kaarle said emotionally.

"I believe you. For God's sake look what the Nazis are doing with you. They raped your sister, sent her husband to Auschwitz along with your aunt. They are all bloody mad! What they are doing with our women in their Lebensborn program sickens every decent Norwegian. There have been nearly twelve thousand fatherless children born to Norwegian women and anonymous German soldiers in the Lebensborn project in Norway alone. Even more if you tally all of the Lebensborn clinics across Europe.

I expect the number will go even higher before the war is over. These orphans will face an incredibly unforgiving society when the Germans lose their war. Some of the names already being assigned to these children by society are quite pejorative." Elina said. "I can imagine. What are they saying?" Kaarle asked. " Even though most of the women are kidnapped, coerced, or simply promised food in their bellies Norwegians call them Tysketoser, or German whores. They are calling the children Naziyngel, or Nazi Spawn." She said in disgust.

"That's horrible. All I care about is my sisters safety. Any child she gives birth to will be welcomed into my family as if it is 100% our own. I worry about the fate of her husband though. Should he survive the death camp how will he react to the fact that the Nazis have been growing his family without him? I have never met him but it burdens me so to think of how the Nazis have ruined his life and the life of my sister. My aunt who is 100% Finn did not deserve being sent to a Death Camp over a piece of land." "Neither did any of the millions of Jews who have been slaughtered like sheep in Germany and Poland deserve it either." Elina said. "I quite agree." Kaarle concluded. "So this Quisling government is searching for us even more than the Gestapo?" Kaarle asked. "No. There is a particularly hateful Norwegian who works directly for the Gestapo who is even more active than Quisling's thugs. His name is Henry Oliver Rinnan and he's from Trondheim. They say he's almost a midget standing only at 1.61 meters." "His method of operation is to engage fellow Norwegians in public, on the bus, or tram for instance. He and his followers involve people in conversations intending to entrap them about their feelings about the occupation. Then he arrests and tortures them. He has killed hundreds of unsuspecting Norwegians like that.

His organization specializes in infiltrating Resistance groups and then calling in the Gestapo. Willing, or unwilling Thomas collaborated to set up his own team. I am sure that's how they were able to trap Markus and his men." Elina said. "Does his organization have a name? How many of them are there?" Kaarle asked. "In German they call them Sonderabteilung "Lola." In Norwegian we call them Rinnanbanden." "There's probably between fifty and one hundred members. Their greatest accomplishment is making us unable to trust fellow Norwegians." she said. "Unbelievable heroism and unforgivable treason from the same nation of people." Kaarle said. "They speak Norwegian but once they cross over to the Nazis we don't consider them Norwegians anymore." She said. "If you and I will be working together it will be a good idea to give you an idea of who the good people are as well as the bad." Elina said.

"On the good side, as I already mentioned is Gunnar Sonsteby who was first a Ski soldier when the Germans invaded Norway. He tasted his first action as a member of Philip Hansteen's Skiloperkompanie. Later he was recruited and trained in Britain by the "Special Operations Executive" and became known as Agent 24. He had been especially well trained in sabotage and has destroyed countless petrol installations, aircraft, military munitions and weapons factories and other military installations. He is at the top of the Gestapo's list of most wanted resistance saboteurs. After his training with S.O.E. in Britain, he helped found Milorg our national resistance organization. He became the 'go to' contact for all S.O.E agents in eastern Norway and currently heads up our Norwegian Independent Company 1 Group here in Oslo. If you repeat anything I am about to tell you I will be shot." "No one will shoot you unless they shoot me first." Kaarle said grimly.

"Gunnar controls an espionage ring that provides daily information to Special Operations Executive branch in London about every troop movement, every arrival of naval ships and even changes of command and troop strength. The allies know the Nazi's weakest and strongest points in Norway thanks to Gunnar's tightly controlled organization. He is beyond a doubt one of the most important resistance fighters in Norway and he operates right under the noses of the Reich and they haven't a bloody clue who he really is. I swear Kaarle, I would die for that man and so would everyone else in his S.O.E. network." Elina's eyes teared as she said those words. Kaarle hugged her. "Then I would die for him too." he said. "It is important to understand the distinction between Milorg and the S.O.E. she said. Milorg is not involved in sabotage to the extent that Gunnar's group is. He operates in coordination with an ultra-secret organization known as "XU." X stands for unknown and U stands for Undercover agent. Some suspect it's Gunnar but I believe it is probably a British agent he works closely with to organize Commando missions both to collect intelligence, or to act on it." she ventured.

"Because of the high profile of our proposed kills of Himmler and Goebbels, XU will jointly run the sniper teams . Max Manus will probably choose to be one of the snipers and I would expect Gunnar to be the other. XU will provide a back up sniper in order to guarantee a simultaneous kill. Each sniper will have a spotter, trained in target analysis so don't feel left out because you will not be a part of the actual assassinations." Elina said. "My specialty in the Winter War was solo sniper. I didn't need a f--cking spotter! I took out top Russian Generals with a sniper rifle and sometimes with a knife, or pistol with silencer at close range." He snapped.

"I'm glad we're having this conversation away from Kai." Elina said. "Why do men have such egos? You should be glad that in spite of the merits of what you did against the Germans last week he is bringing you along at all. This is Norway, not Finland." Elina said painfully. She immediately regretted her words. She fully expected Kaarle to storm away angry, or even slap her. Instead he softly touched her face and said; "Elina what you say is quite true but if you would have had an opportunity to be in the fire fight that killed Markus you know you would have been there even if it meant your own death. I don't give a damn about the monsters who will be killed, or who gets to claim credit for the kills, I simply want what's left of my sister returned to her family." "Nothing more and nothing less." he said. "I don't care what it takes we will get your sister back for you." Elina promised.

The Volvo ran without lights for three kilometers to ensure it wasn't being followed before Kai finally turned onto the country road that led to the old farmhouse. He parked on a small lane inside the nearby forest. He had his sub-machine gun under his coat at the ready just in case. He stomped on the barn floor three times followed by silence and then two stomps. Elina unlatched the trap door and Kai climbed down the ladder to a waiting cup of coffee. He smiled at Elina. "What is it Kai?" she asked. "I don't know. I've only known you as a Partisan. But you look cheerful and well…… domesticated. It suits you. But don't relax too much." He cautioned. "Well it's on for tomorrow night at twenty thirty hours. They will be flying to the Oslo airport in a Dornier aircraft. They will be met by a heavily armed company of Waffen SS . It would be suicide to try to take them at the airport.

The Waffen SS has an entire battalion within ten minutes of the airport on 24 hour reaction reserve." Kai laid out a map. "The three will be moved by staff car to the Lebensborn hospice where your sister is being held. You see this 'S' curve just before the street that leads to the hospice? There will be two recon motor cycles leading the way. We will let them pass beyond two trucks we will have parked across the road from each other filled with petrol and explosives. Once the staff car with targets one, two and three, or Goebbels, Himmler and Mengele, respectively, pass beyond the trucks they will be command detonated simultaneously which should effectively separate our targets from their support, who will no doubt fan out and proceed forward on foot." Kai said.

"We will take out the motorcycle escort first and then shoot the staff car with an anti-tank rocket. Our snipers will engage targets One, Two and Three and the ground team that will take out the motorcycle escort will put a bullet in the head of each target to confirm the kills." Kai said. "What of us?" Elina asked. "You have the most important mission of all. You will arrive at the hospice at twenty fifteen hours riding in a stolen German ambulance. Kaarle will be dressed in the Colonels uniform. He will be presenting you as a new member of Lebensborn. Your sister, Kaarle, is in unit E723 on the ground floor. Take this hand drawing with you study it ahead of time then burn it. As soon as you hear the explosion down the street get your sister and baby, they will be in the same room. Return to the ambulance and pick up our ground team at the bottom of the hill. They will take over the ambulance and drop you off here. Here is a second set of keys for the Volvo which will be waiting parked just here on the map.

Take your sister and yourselves back to the safe house and we shall begin the exfiltration of you and your sister back to Finland." Kai said. "Impressive plan. Thank you Kai." Kaarle said. "Kai I want to be extracted with him."Elina said. "Very well Elina, you have earned the right to leave." "Be warned there are always two armed guards at the hospice." Kai said. "I'll take you to the ambulance at nineteen thirty hours." Kai said as he left. Elina looked at Kaarle for a long time. "You are frowning Kaarle. What is troubling you?" "Oh nothing. Just reflections." Kaarle answered. "Kaarle please, don't shut me out." "Alright. I was just thinking how much simpler this could have been if Kai had just given me the location of my sister and let me handle the rest. Now it has turned into perhaps one of the greatest assassination missions in history. Can you imagine what Hitler will want to do to Norway when he learns that his top henchmen have been killed by Norwegian snipers? He has about a half million combat soldiers in Norway right now. He won't even need to send more. I've heard that in all of Norway you only have about 40,000 men in Milorg." Kaarle said.

"There will be a blood bath. Hitler will bomb you into oblivion and raze your cities and countryside." "Are you saying we should let the monsters come and go freely?" "No. I'm only asking if it's worth losing at least a million Norwegian men women and children in order to kill three pigs?" "I can answer for my Resistance without even asking them. The answer is yes." Elina said unflinchingly. "Good, that's all I needed to know." Kaarle said firmly with even deeper love and respect for Elina than he felt just a moment before. Elina and Kaarle held each other all night and slept until late afternoon. Neither said another word. Elina chose a 9mm from the rack and put its safety on. She loaded five clips and put them in her purse.

Kaarle kept the German Luger he had taken from Colonel von Braunschweig and added a Thompson .45 caliber sub-machine gun that fit nicely beneath his folded overcoat. He packed four extra magazines in his overcoat pockets. Elina gasped and began to tremble. "What's wrong my love? Kaarle asked. "I don't know. You standing there in that uniform just now brought it all back." She said. "He's dead Elina. You saw me kill him." "I know Kaarle. Sorry. "She said embracing him.

When they heard Kai tapping on the barn floor above they were already standing on the ladder. Soon they were riding in the stolen ambulance with Elina at the wheel. Kai jumped out near a Tram station and Elina continued on to the Lebensborn hospice. They arrived at exactly twenty fifteen and parked according to plan. A Sentry was posted both at the main and the rear entrance to the four level building. Kaarle walked boldly up to the Sentry and flashed his identity card. "Good Evening Herr Colonel!" the guard snapped. "Heil Hitler!" "Heil Hitler!" Kaarle replied. Suddenly the hair stood up on the back of Kaarle's neck. "This was too easy!" He thought. He was met by a cruel eyed woman who was a member of the Gestapo. Kaarle expected her to protest about registering a member female late in the evening, or that he didn't call first but nothing, not even a mean glance. Kaarle looked toward the door and down the long hallway extending from the reception area where he now stood, all the way back to the rear exit. Suddenly Kaarle reached out and grabbed the woman by her mouth. He ripped the telephone cord out of the wall and used it to bind her hands to her ankles behind her. "What in the Hell are you doing?" Elina screamed. "Reach me that bandage beneath the counter!" Kaarle ordered. Elina reached it to him and he used it to cover the woman's mouth.

"It's a trap Elina. Look at your watch. No explosion down the street." Kaarle shoved the woman behind the counter and ran down the hallway to unit E-723. The door was locked. Kaarle backed up and gave the door a powerful kick. Sitting inside was the second guard aiming his rifle directly at Kaarle's chest. Kaarle dropped to the floor and fired two shots into the man's chest. Kaarle quickly recovered and ran back to the receptionist counter. Elina had drawn her weapon with both hands and was turning in circles to cover all directions. Kaarle ripped the bandage from the woman's mouth. "Where is she?" The woman remained silent. Kaarle then shot off her right knee cap. "They took her last night!" she moaned. "Where to?" Kaarle screamed. The woman remained silent until Kaarle aimed at her left knee. "Wait! I heard them say they were putting her on a plane to Muenchen last evening at twenty three hours."

Still no explosion. It was ten minutes before twenty One hours. Suddenly there was small arms fire near the ambulance. The ground team could be seen taking up firing positions as they dragged a wounded comrade toward the ambulance. The Sentry ran toward the reception area firing wildly. Kaarle took aim with the 9 mm and placed a shot in his forehead. He grabbed Elina and ran for the rear entrance. As they jumped down the landing Kaarle could see a half track speeding to a rear approach to take up a firing position. The half track had a search light that flashed on Kaarle and Elina's image and then froze. Kaarle fired his Thompson and put out the light. He dragged Elina to the side of the hill and they slid down the snow capped icy surface to the street below. Kaarle watched the ambulance try to make a run for it, but when it reached the main road, it was hit by a German antitank rocket and exploded in a ball of fire.

Elina sprained her ankle during the slide down the hill and was limping badly. Any minute Kaarle expected the German half track to come crashing around the curve. Instead, from the opposite direction Kai's Volvo was speeding in reverse with the rear doors open. Kaarle threw Elina in the back seat and dove in behind her. Kai sped forward as Kaarle leaned out of the rear side window and opened up on a squad of SS running on foot trying to catch them.

"What happened Kai?" Elina screamed. "Breach!" He yelled back. "We obviously have a mole who infiltrated us. Tolesby is sure he knows who it was. Targets got diverted to Bergen." "Damage?" Kaarle asked. "Severe." Kai replied. "We managed to pull the sniper teams but they got our ground team. I thought you two were finished. How did you manage to escape?" Kai asked. "Kaarle knew something wasn't right so he tied up the Gestapo receptionist and destroyed the telephone line. He went to the room but one of the Sentry's was waiting in ambush. Kaarle took him out and the forward Sentry as well. Then we rushed out the rear entrance before the German's had us sealed in. Kaarle shot the woman in the knee to make her talk." "What did she say?" Kai asked anxiously. "She said that my sister had been removed at twenty three hours last night and flown straight off to Muenchen." Kaarle said. "Sorry Kaarle. But that gives us a time line to work with regarding when they received and acted on the traitor's information. You two have been together the entire time, so unless you have known each other longer than your attack on the German battalion, which borders on the absurd, you may consider yourselves cleared. We shall see how all of the other alibis hold up under serious interrogation." Kai said. "You were limping. Will you be ready for extraction tomorrow?" Kai asked.

"I don't think I'll be able to walk on it for about a week." Elina said. "Fine. There are plenty of provisions for you in the safe house. Make yourselves cozy for a week and we will check with you again to see how you are." Kai replied. "Kai I want to go to Muenchen to find my sister." Kaarle said. "I know. You will. But first please allow our intelligence collection resources to exhaust what may be known. " Kai pleaded. "If you can wait a week we will have travel documents and false identity papers for you and Elina. You can then travel as husband and wife. We will work on the cover story and when you go, you will have safe houses and underground contacts before you even arrive." Kai explained.

When they descended the ladder Kaarle had to climb down first to accept Elina who was lowered carefully by Kai. Kai had a nervous cup of coffee then excused himself and soon they were alone again. Kaarle put ice on Elina's ankle and made her warm tea. He found a half loaf of bread and some jam and made toast on top of the stove. Before long the wood stove warmed up the place and Elina began feeling sleepy. "I love you Kaarle." "I love you too Elina." He replied. "You saved us tonight. I would have waited for the SS to arrive if you hadn't been there." She said. "Nonsense! You performed brilliantly by holding them off until I nearly got myself killed in a room ambush." he said. "You took out both Sentrys and dragged me to safety. You're my Ski soldier and I love you dearly Kaarle." She said as she drifted off to sleep. Kaarle took a cross bow and a quiver of arrows and went out in the forest. He soon had three rabbits he tied with a string after he gutted and skinned them, carefully scattering the blood and entrails and leaving the fur strewn in tufts. To anyone but an expert tracker it would appear that a wolf pack had made a meal. He counted on wolves scavenging the place, leaving behind their tracks.

He carefully used a pine branch to sweep his own tracks clear all the way back to the main trail. He found a few vegetables in the pantry and when Elina awoke the place was filled with the delicious aroma of rabbit stew. "Oh Kaarle. I wish there wasn't a war outside. I could live with you in this little place forever." She said. "I feel the same Elina." He said with a sadness in his eyes. "You're wondering where they took her and if she's safe." Elina said. "Yes, of course. Actually it eats away at my insides each passing day." He replied. "Trust my people Kaarle. Their connections even in Germany are as good as they get." Elina reassured him.

Elina walked on the ankle which Kaarle had her soak in ice water for ten minutes each day. By the end of the week she was completely healed. Both were getting cabin fever and only their love seemed to mollify the confinement. Kaarle at least left the confines to hunt at night but Elina began feeling quite trapped. Then one evening they heard several footsteps on the barn floor. Kaarle gave Elina a 9mm and he armed himself with his Thompson. The foot taps were correct so Kaarle slid the latch open on the trap door. To his relief Kai was smiling down at them. "It's only me, why the artillery?" He joked. "Because you sprouted extra feet." Kaarle replied. Two men accompanied Kai down the ladder. Both were wearing ski masks. "We apologize that we cannot show ourselves to you Kaarle, but the less you know about us the better off you will be in case you are ever captured." The tallest man said. "I understand." Kaarle replied. He guessed but was never certain that he was in the presence of Gunnar Tolesby and Max Manus. Elina fixed hot tea and they all sat around the dining table in the center of what appeared to be the living room. "We have heard the story about how you decimated a German Infantry battalion east of here with just eighteen men." The tall man said.

"The story has increased the size of the German unit, it is now a regiment." The shorter man said. Kaarle chuckled. "Well, I suppose I should reserve comment until it becomes a Division." Kaarle said with self deprecation and modesty. Even Kai laughed at Kaarle's remark. "We regret deeply that our operation last week was compromised. We found the source and have eliminated him along with his Gestapo contact." The tall man said. "We like to always kill both the traitor and his contact whenever possible." The second man said. "We came here to make you a proposal." The taller man said with directness. "We lost a total of six good men last week. I mean our very best ground team. We are currently involved in a Top Secret mission that we will divulge to you only if you agree ahead of time to our proposal." The Tall man continued. "Let me hear what you are proposing." Kaarle said. "Yes, well we need those six men replaced." The tall man said.

"Can't you simply draft them from Milorg?" Kaarle asked. "We don't have time to send them to Scotland and America to get trained in sabotage and demolitions work. We could train them ourselves but our current intelligence and operational demands are too vital to dedicate the time and effort, by shutting down everything and running a school in Special Operations. You on the other hand have the expertise and the experience to train as many men as we send to you." The tall man said. "You can train them while we go on business as usual." The second man said. "Gentlemen, you are fighting the most noble kind of war, a war to take your country back from some of the most evil villains who have ever lived and I respect you for it, but I came here to simply rescue my sister from these same villains. I can't waste a single day in my pursuit. I hope you understand." Kaarle said.

"Well, that's why we said we have a proposal for you. We are in close contact with the French and German underground. Your sister we have learned, is being held against her will in a small village near Augsburg. Both she and her son are in fine health. It seems Dr. Mengele travels there twice weekly to visit a group of "special" patients for his experiments regarding the genetic structure of Aryan twins. They consider your sister Aryan and thus a precious commodity and as far as we can determine, Mengele would have to answer to both Goebbels and Himmler if he dared harm a hair on her head." The tall man explained. "Not like the poor Jews who he dismembers without anesthesia." The second man added. "So if you will help us train a dozen men for just one operation that is vital for not just Norway, or Finland, but for the entire world, we will rescue your sister and get both herself and her baby to Sweden to sit out the rest of the war without further threat. We need your word that once she is in Sweden you will visit her for just one day to confirm her good health and spirits and return immediately here to train our people and participate in our vital mission." the tall man said. "How can I be sure the underground won't get her killed?" "The only people dying in the underground are the very brave members of the underground itself." The second man said.

"You won't find anyone more selfless and prepared to sacrifice themselves for God and country than these courageous people. Besides we already have the people and where with all already in place to get your sister out of Germany. You are an Operator. We don't need to calculate the odds for you of successfully getting a woman and a baby out by yourself, I'm sure." The tall man said.

"I don't need time to think about it. My answer is an enthusiastic yes." Kaarle said as he extended his hand to both men. "Elina, get the sword." Kai said. "We have a small ritual for every person who agrees to join us." The second man said. The tall man took the sword from Elina. "This sword belongs to the King of Norway who is currently running the country's resistance and official government from England. Please kneel and repeat after me. I Kaarle from Finland, who will henceforth be known by the code name Wolf, do hereby swear upon pain of immediate death that I will protect the secrets and the efforts and affairs of my Norwegian benefactors with my very life if need be. That no amount of torture, or pain will cause me to jeopardize my comrades in arms, so help me God." Kaarle repeated each word.

As soon as he declared "So help me God" the tall man laid the sword lightly on Kaarles shoulders and lightly on top of his head. "Congratulations you're now a member of the Oslo Group 1." The tall man said. Kaarle stood and shook hands with everyone, including Elina. She wanted to embrace him, but instead squeezed his hand so hard he felt a sharp pain in his fingers. "Now then, let's get started." The tall man said. "You will see our faces someday but for now, not even Kai knows what we look like." The tall man scanned the ceiling with his eyes, obviously searching for a place to begin. "Kaarle, there is a race going on between the allies, in particular the United States and Germany to develop the most horrible weapon in human history. I don't completely understand how it works, but a British Physicist once told us that the first one who completes this weapon will win the war immediately." The Tall man said.

" It is based on the atom studies of the Curies in France and Albert Einstein of Switzerland. The best we have been able to determine is that the Nazis made wasteful strategic decisions regarding what to spend their resources on when they began the war against the world. They took rocket science to new levels in Peenemunde and could certainly deliver an atomic weapon, possibly even to the United States if they had one, but they simply do not yet have it. If they did they would have already used it." The Tall man said. "There is a material known as Plutonium, or pu-239 which is needed to create what they are calling an atomic bomb. Pu-239 needs what is called heavy water or a 2% element of purified water. This Heavy Water is separated by electrolysis. The Heavy Water somehow moderates the refinement of pu-239 into fissionable material. By coincidence, the Heavy Water production facility that supplies the world with Heavy water is in Norway . They produce it as a part of their ammonia and fertilizer processes. This company, the Vemork Hydroelectric plant operated by Norsko near Rjukan and near Telemark was taken over by the Nazis shortly after the invasion.

If we can shut it down the Germans will be denied access to a critical material they need to build an atom bomb. In October, 1942 myself and four other Norwegian Commandos who had also been trained by the British Special Operations Executive were parachuted into the wilderness. We skied for days to reach the plant. We called this Operation Grouse. A month later, a team of British engineers arrived by Glider. When we made contact they gave us our challenge which was; What did you see in the early morning of Wednesday? Our reply was 'Three Pink Elephants.' We were all ready to start shooting until we were verified. The next phase of what we then called Operation 'Freshman' however was an unmitigated disaster.

Two gliders were to be towed by air to a landing site on the frozen lake Mosvatn, not far from the Plant. Bad weather caused the British assault team's gliders to crash separately into the mountains and the Gestapo reached them ahead of us. They were tortured to death and of course it became a wake up call to the Nazis that we too were interested in Heavy Water." he continued.

"We had hoped they may have thought that we wanted it to make vodka with it, instead of denying it to them." He grinned. "Their efforts to create an "A" bomb have since doubled. Their spies, I'm sure must be telling them that America is getting closer. They put a price on our heads and combed the region for us but we survived in a cave, living on Lichens and tree moss until we killed a reindeer to add some meat to our green salad." The tall man said. "We have now reached a point of cooperation and joint planning with British Special Operations Executive Branch whereby we are prepared to redouble our efforts to destroy the Hydroelectric Plant before it can complete the production and delivery of the Heavy Water to the German Atomic Weapons Laboratory. If we destroy the plant, as well as the shipment of Heavy Water it will kill the German Atomic Weapons program. There are other methods of creating the fuel needed to build an Atomic bomb than the Heavy Water method, but the Germans would be forced to essentially go back to square one and lose at least three years of development. They know this and are therefore protecting the Hydroelectric Plant with some of their best soldiers. We have begun the planning for what we believe will be the last and hopefully final successful destruction of the plant. " he reflected. "We call it Operation Gunnerside, the meaning of which is to be found in the hallowed offices of S.O.E.

We had planned to launch the Operation jointly with the British, in January of 1943 next month, but our set back with losing our ground assault team has caused us to consider a delayed launch by the end of February instead. This will give you slightly more than two months to build us an assault team. We will provide you with twelve students. We want you to train them all, but only you will decide which six will join the men of Grouse, who we are now calling "Swallow". Your students will also be inserted by parachute. We will provide you with operational details soon to help guide your training curriculum." The tall man concluded. "Excellent! I will do my best." Kaarle replied.

Training for Gunnerside was a complicated affair. Kaarle first had to study the drop zone and the layout of the factory and the central operations order for the Swallow team. Then he had to conform the training for his students, who would, in spite of having specific tasks during the infiltration still need to merge with Swallow as though they had never been a separate force. All of this literally under the noses of the German Luftwaffe who flew frequent air patrols over the sector of wilderness Oslo Group had chosen. It helped that the men wore white camouflage suits and were quick to hear the drone of oncoming aircraft. After eight weeks had passed Kaarle finally contacted Kai to tell him that of the twelve he had given his nod to five. Kaarle told Kai that he personally wanted to volunteer as the sixth man. Two days went by and the answer came back "Permission Granted." Kaarle and his team went into isolation. Elina moved to another Safe House and a planning briefing was called on the 15th of February. The team met with the two masked leaders in a secret bunker and were given initial individual assignments.

"Team Swallow has been mainly staying out of sight but they have sent back considerable intelligence information through an S.O.E. agent. I just learned myself that S.O.E. Branch has had an asset under cover as a worker in the actual Plant for some weeks. After the disaster of "Freshman" the Nazis moved in a three thousand man defensive force to protect the Plant and the Heavy Water supply. Main access to the Hydroelectric Plant is restricted to a 75 meter bridge that spans at a height of 200 meters above the river Man. Our reconnaissance confirms the bridge to be well defended by machine gun placements at regular intervals. I'm afraid you may find yourselves getting wet before this mission is finished." The Tall man remarked. "At least now we understand why Wolf had us swimming beneath ice at a frozen lake!" One of Kaarle's trainees spoke up. The rafters in the bunker shook from the laughter. Once the laughter subsided, the briefing continued.

"At twenty One hours tomorrow night you will board an RAF Halifax bomber from the 138th squadron. It shall land on a makeshift airstrip in the wilderness, just here on the map. Your parachute drop zone is just here. There will hopefully be no one there to meet you, as we have no communication with Swallow at the moment so the only possibility would be to land on some German's head. Don't go near the plant until contact with Swallow has been made. Leave signs in the forest and Swallow will track them back to you. Once you connect with Swallow, their leader becomes your leader. He will issue detailed assignments in accordance with fresh intelligence." The Tall man said."Check and re-check your weapons and ammunition. Any questions?" "Sir, what about ammunition re-supply?" One of Kaarle's trainees asked.

"Along with your jump the Load Master will drop three C.L.E. containers. One is loaded with demolitions equipment and supplies. Please lose anything else but that. The containers are designed to pull easily across snow and ice. Be certain to cover any trace of your parachute landing. Any further questions? Alright then. Good Luck to each of you." The Tall man said. Kaarle thought of Elina. He wished he could spend the last evening before the mission with her but it was standard procedure to quarantine the entire team twenty four hours before the mission commenced. Kaarle went to bed early and soon drifted in his troubled dreams back to the forests near Suomussalmi and fighting the Russians in the Winter War. At precisely Twenty One hours on the 16th of February, the Halifax bomber landed and the six men boarded the plane. They flew at a very high altitude which required donning oxygen masks until just before they reached the drop zone. The jump was executed with precision and soon the team was gathering their white silk chutes rolling them tightly as they would be used later to keep warm inside small holes burrowed in the snow.

They recovered two of the C.L.E. Containers. The third had a parachute malfunction and wound up buried somewhere in a snow bank. The men breathed a sigh of relief to learn that it wasn't the container with the demolitions. The team spent the next three days leaving small signs to reveal they were in the area and finally contact was made on the third day. The men were jubilant that they had the honor of having been selected for such a vital mission for Norway and mankind. In spite of the harsh weather and sleeping in the snow, morale was very high. Swallow's leader was code named Badger. Kaarle thought how unusual it was that some man resemble the code name of the animal, or object, he was named after. Badger looked tenacious.

Badger took the newly expanded Swallow team to a cave that was large enough to accommodate a small camp fire in the center of its great chamber. The men went over the details again and again until they could see it in their sleep. "The S.O.E. agent has supplied us with shift schedules and a detailed layout of the Plant. We will ski at night fall at Twenty Hours on the 27th of February. On that day, the moon will not be bright. The bridge is too well defended. Our only hope is to swim across the icy river. We will cross just here as it is blinded from the bridge. We will use logs to keep our clothes, weapons and gear dry. We will scale the face until we come to the railway. We will follow the railway and take out any guards silently along the way until we are inside the Plant. You have each practiced applying demolitions to objects that are similar in size and shape to the Electrolysis Chambers you will blow at the plant. Once the demolitions are placed and the fuses lit we will leave as a team. Any questions? Good get some rest gentlemen you will need it." Badger said.

Kaarle helped the team members secure two logs per raft with the straps of their weapons. Their skis had been organized separately beneath some dead tree branches to allow a quick get away. The water was shockingly cold no matter how many times you felt it. Halfway across the river Kaarle looked up to see a search light scanning the river bank but they had chosen their insertion point well and were not seen. It was difficult with frozen fingers to button and zip their clothing once on the other shore but soon Badger gave the signal to begin the climb. Narrow slippery ledges caused the ascent to go slowly, but finally all had reached the railway level. Badger whispered to Kaarle to take one of his men forward to scout for guards. "If there are too many, don't engage. We will all make a silencer assault together if there are more than five." Badger said.

Kaarle and Rolf moved with caution but deliberate speed until they discovered that the Germans had placed all of their security on the bridge and on each floor of the laboratories. There was virtually no one to stop them all the way to the loading dock. Once there Badger consulted his layout and led the team into the main basement through a cable tunnel and by breaking a window.

Soon they were inside and on their way to the Electrolysis Chambers. On the way they met a Norwegian Caretaker who was thrilled when they told him what they were there for. He guided them to the Chamber array and to the storage room where 500 kilograms of Heavy Water was stored. He chatted jovially as the demolitions were placed. Just as Badger was ready to ignite the time fuses, the Caretaker noticed that he had misplaced his glasses. The entire team started searching until the glasses were found on a ledge. Badger smiled as he lit the fuses. A British sub-machine gun was left on the tracks to make the Germans believe it was a strictly British operation in the hope that revenge wouldn't be taken out against Norwegians.

The men crossed the river again and were sliding their pointed toe shoes into their ski bindings when the enormous fire balls shot straight out from the rail dock. The raid had finally succeeded. 500 kilos of Heavy Water, the entire amount produced since the Germans had taken over the plant had been destroyed. In addition vital equipment needed to run Electrolysis Chambers had also been destroyed. When Team Swallow reached a summit they had chosen for their release point Badger stopped and shook everyone's hand. "Gentlemen, ski like the wind. God Bless Norway, God bless our King!" The skiers headed in three different directions.

Six who were to be given new missions by S.O.E. skied 400 kilometers to Sweden, four who had trained under Kaarle skied to a cave complex more than fifty kilometers away. They would join local Resistance forces and remain near Telemark. Kaarle and Rolf, skied back to Oslo. Not a single man was captured by the three thousand Germans who searched every square inch within miles of the plant and found nothing, or no one. After Kaarle returned to the Safe House near Oslo, Elina joined him again. She was beaming and proud of Kaarle. He was met by an ecstatic Kai and the Secret leaders who were effusive with gratitude. As they all sat by the wood stove drinking coffee and tea Kaarle asked the "Tall" one if the German Atomic bomb were nothing more than a dream in some scientists mind. "If you can wait just a moment a friend of yours is on his way down the ladder to greet you. He would be more technically able to answer your question than I." The Tall man said.

Professor Erik Carlsson shook the snow from his coat as he greeted the group. "I understand things have gone both good and bad for you Kaarle." He said as they embraced. "Yes, we came very close to rescuing my sister from Lebensborn, but a traitor betrayed us before we could get to her. They have since moved her to Augsburg." He replied. Professor Carlsson looked grim and remained silent. The room became quite still until the Tall man broke the silence. "Erik, Kaarle wonders whether our destruction of the Electrolysis Chambers really stopped the German Atomic weapons program, no wait I think his question was whether such a weapon could be developed at all." He said. "I'm afraid the answer is both yes and yes." Erik responded. "In 1939 the possibility of splitting the atom was first discovered by the German chemists, Otto Hahn and Fritz Strassman.

They conducted a test that included bombarding atoms with neutrons. The result was the production of Barium which is approximately one half the size of Uranium. They didn't quite grasp the significance of their discovery until Lise Meitner, their learned Jewish colleague who later escaped the Nazis to Sweden, immediately realized that they had split the uranium nucleus in two. The news traveled like wildfire around the world and soon every major country initiated Atomic scientific programs." he said.

"The Germans assigned an ordnance scientist named Kurt Diebner to study the feasibility of using nuclear fission in a weapons program they quite simply called "The Uranium Project". Along with his fellow physicist Werner Heisenberg it was determined that when the method included the use of a contained device, or nuclear reactor, the result would be the creation of a chain of nuclear fission reactions that would produce controlled power. Without the reactor, the chain reactions could theoretically continue on throughout the atmosphere and destroy the world, at the very least, create an explosion many times more powerful than TNT." Erik explained. "If such an energy were to be considered feasible for a weapons application it would be imperative to select a method of moderating, or slowing down the neutrons liberated by the chain reaction fission. The Germans quite in the beginning chose our Heavy Water Hydroelectric source and have since taken their research to a level where they now realize that by using Heavy Water as a moderating substance for Uranium-235 they will be able to mass produce detonatable devices, or bombs. As far as we know, our continued existence is our proof positive that they did not choose an alternative moderating system or else they may have already started to use such weapons particularly in Russia.

Your team's success in Telemark hasn't completely stopped them but it has most definitely added a couple of years delay to their possibility of success." Professor Carlsson stated. "Given what we know about the Nazis other super weapons programs, it is difficult to imagine why they did not choose early on, at least since the discovery of fission reaction in 1939, to place this weapon at the top of their development list regardless of cost." Kaarle wondered out loud. "Well, let us not forget that since their early successes in toppling other countries throughout the rest of Europe, not the least of which has been Norway, they must have felt they wouldn't need any super weapons until, like Napoleon they repeated the mistake of getting bogged down by the fierce Russian winter in Stalingrad. Quite obviously history does indeed repeat itself. There is no doubt if they had such a weapon all of their enemies would have been targeted." The Tall man said. "Whether the Americans who are using centrifuges to separate the isotopes, or the Germans, who are using Heavy Water to moderate the rate of neutron chain reactions succeeds first, may God help us all if we should ever have such an evil force in our midst." Professor Carlsson concluded.

Kaarle studied the lined face of Professor Carlsson. "Is your family well Erik?" He asked. "As good as can be expected without Magnus. At least we are togeth".... He stopped in mid sentence, suddenly feeling the mistake he was about to make. "Kaarle, I was asked to come here because we've met before and because as a friend it was felt I should bring you the news. Your Sami friend skied alone to my house from Lap Land to tell you that your father was captured by the Russians near Petrograd and executed as a spy though he wore the uniform of a Finnish Colonel.

You were away on this secret mission so I promised I would inform you when you returned. Before I could get Janne to come inside he disappeared in a cloud of snow." Erik said sadly. "I'm afraid we have even more bad news Kaarle." The Tall man said.

"The operation to rescue your sister in Augsburg went poorly. A much larger German force of Gestapo and Waffen SS were assigned to the small hospital where she was residing. They tortured the underground members until the entire network was compromised. Only a few escaped into Switzerland with their lives. We are quite certain that based on a clandestine observer's report they took her by guarded train to Muenchen and she is now within the confines of the Cell Research Department at the Max Planck Institute. As a geneticist Erik can give you what we think they are doing with her there." He said. Kaarle turned away from the men and slapped his hand against the wall. He was crying in his heart but was too proud to let anyone see his tears. The Tall man gently ushered everyone except Elina toward the ladder. Each man patted Kaarle's shoulder on the way out giving condolences for his father's death and reassuring him that a way would soon be found to rescue Laila.

"Wait Erik! There's an extra bedroom. Will you stay the night and return to your home in the morning after a good nights rest?" Kaarle asked. "Why of course Kaarle. Is there anything else I can do for you dear friend?" Erik asked. "Yes. I want you to explain this genetic and eugenic stuff to me once more, only this time I will pay closer attention." The men had each brought down an arm load of fresh firewood and placed it in the wood bin. Kaarle held Elina tight and after she prepared some soup and brought out a full bottle of vodka, she excused herself for the evening and went to bed.

"I suppose you'd like to know all of the technical details surrounding what is happening with your sister?" Erik asked. "Yes. Absolutely." Kaarle confirmed. "Kaarle I think I mentioned to you when we had our last discussion that there exists an underground in Academia. Even as the war rages around us, we scientists seem to have a way of sharing otherwise secret information." Erik said. "Yes, I recall your having mentioned that." Kaarle replied. "Let me first give you some history of genetics and then we will culminate with some philosophical origins of the false science of eugenics summarizing finally with the current state of the genetic break through in German microbiology." Erik said. "Fine." Kaarle replied. "Are you sure after learning about your father..." Erik asked. "I will suffer his loss for the rest of my life. Learning more about what has caused the Germans to treat my sister like a lab specimen and a prisoner can only give me the power I need to take her back." Kaarle said sternly.

" Very well. Scientific discovery is seldom understood while it is being discovered. Instead, more dramatically, a curiosity begets a suspicion which is followed on by others who prove the original hypothesis. Such was the case when a Swiss micro-biologist named Friedrich Miescher in 1896 was tinkering with pus cells he extracted from discarded bandages. He isolated the cell nuclei and discovered a substance with a dense concentration of phosphorous. He named this substance "Nuclein". He further determined that the cell nuclei contained both an acid property, what we now refer to as nucleic acid and a protein portion that we now refer to as Histones. Although Miescher suspected that nucleins had something to do with cell inheritance, little was done with this information until this year 1943."

"Some American geneticists of the Rockefeller Institute named Oswald Avery, Colin Macleod and Maclyn Mcarty discovered that Nuclein, which we now have more elaborately named deoxyribonucleic acid, or DNA contains a basic deterministic code of genetic information that is replicated by cells. The Americans harvested DNA from a highly virulent strain of bacterium streptococcus pneumonae and implanted it into a nonvirulent strain. Cells of the non-virulent strain quickly became recoded, or transformed into the highly virulent strain."

"Sorry Professor, I'm still having difficulty in understanding what this all has to do with my sister." Kaarle said. "I suppose I should be more blunt."Erik responded."This will sound insane to you, but we believe the Nazis are far more advanced than the rest of the world in this field and have already secretly cloned animals in their research institutes. That your sister is one of several Aryan specimens they are trying to replicate into clones of themselves. Such a program would allow the Nazis to quickly populate the globe with a Master race. Lebensborn is a front. It provides a collecting point for healthy Aryan type women to serve as multipliers in the old fashioned birthing method of procreation, while at the same time the women are virtual living laboratories for Nazi genetic experiments. The Nazi scientists are harvesting DNA from blood and tissue samples. They must have mapped the human genome and are able to select superior genetic structures and eliminate inferior ones." The Professor said. "I still do not understand." Kaarle said with frustration. "Kaarle, they have quite obviously discovered a way to take what are called "stem cells, or cells without DNA and inject the DNA they wish the cells to grow into. With cloning, they would not need a man to impregnate a woman in the natural way.

They would create a completely manipulated embryo and implant it in a host body to grow into a fully grown deliverable baby. In effect they can mass produce people they have genetically engineered who have a list of unique traits such as immunities to diseases, body types, hair color, eye color, physique, everything Aryan." The Professor explained.

"My God these Nazis are monsters. What do you think they will do to my sister?" Kaarle asked. " I would say they are probably treating her like some queen Bee that holds the key to their biological future. Aside from harvesting eggs from her ovaries, or taking DNA samples from her blood or tissue, they are probably pampering her. They must have found in her Finnish genetic structure a nearly perfect template for their replication program. The Nazis are on the one hand Genocidal when it comes to what they call the Hybrid races and Jews who they believe to be one colossal mistake of nature, yet protective of the gene pool of their Aryan model. Rudolf Hess said it very clearly; "National Socialism is just applied Biology." An entire movement that is built on first cleansing the global demography of the undesired, through forced sterilization until a genocidal system is in place, while all the while using eugenic breeding techniques to control the outcome of the species. There have been many genocides in human history but as far as I know none that have been so technologically fashioned." Erik said. "Did Adolf Hitler start this nightmare all by himself?" Kaarle asked. "Alone? That would give him far more credit than I think he deserves. Many others were worshiping the promise of a perfect human species well before Hitler came on the scene. His genius, if you wish to call it that was recognizing and exploiting the warrior pride that still beats in the German breast. German history is replete with success through power since the ancient tree worshiping Germanic tribes.

They were brow beaten by economic misery during the Weimar Republic. The war reparations they had to pay to their detested enemy France after they were outright lied to by Woodrow Wilson began a burning need to exact revenge through conquest. If you tell a soldier he is special, over and over, you both awaken in him such a self belief as well as program him to use it. Apparently Hitler has succeeded in convincing all Germans that they are special and they believe him. Your question I believe was did he get any help? Yes, absolutely yes. Davenport did not influence Hitler. Hitler was way ahead of Davenport's eugenics racism of forced Sterilization. Hitler manipulated Davenport and exploited his research to justify his own forced sterilization." "Using Darwinian biology and evolutionary theory as a base or a core postulate, they developed Social Darwinism as a vehicle to implement Hitler's primary concepts. Eugenics is in fact applied Darwinism. The actual subtitle for the book was called; "The Preservation Of The Favored Races In The Struggle For Life." The book became a manual for all Nazi scientific belief. He later published a book called "The Descent Of Man" which introduced the high probability that Man had evolved from Apes.

Only as a result of genetic challenges in his environment, followed by corrections and improvements involved with natural selection, or, survival of the fittest, had mankind evolved to a level several layers higher than the lower animal kingdom. Some races within this development were believed to have not developed as highly as others. His writings were concurrent with the existential movement of the likes of Kierkegaard, Nietzsche and others that helped many in the atheist movement reinforce their reasons for rejecting God and the Bible as a believable answer to the origin of the species.

124

You see Kaarle, genetics is the bioengineering of cells to improve the physical condition of future humans. Aside from the medical ethics and altruism involved, it is sterile of philosophy. Eugenics, on the other hand introduces a value judgment that one combination of cell structure is superior in either an ethnocentric, cultural, religious, or ideological way to another and the science becomes dedicated to isolating superior genes to promote their survival while intentionally ending, or killing alternative genetic combinations." Erik said.

"Darwin, however, wasn't the original thinker I'm afraid. That distinction goes to a fellow named Jean-baptiste Lamarck who published " Philosophie Zoologique" in 1803. His theories of descent became the universal reference on evolution for a century. Darwin first learned about Lamarck when he read geologist Charles Lyell's book ; "Principles Of Geology," wherein he provides a long explanation of Lamarck's theories on Descent. In these books the concept of "Transformism" is introduced and discussed. The belief that a species can evolve into an entirely new species. In one felled swoop it describes why species disappear and new species appear in their place. It explains that the evolution involved is a dynamic process, not a static one.

Where-as the Bible offered an explanation that the world was suddenly created and completed in six days with God resting on Sunday, Lamarck introduces the evolution of one species into another over millions of years." Erik explained. "I see." Kaarle replied. "Wait! There's more. Where-by the Bible describes an ever improving world beneath the guiding hand of god, the evolutionist's concept places nature itself in that role.

Rousseau's "Discourse On The Origins And Foundations Of Inequality Among Men" published in 1755 describes Natural Selection using Ancient Sparta as an example. Nature, like Sparta, supported the strong and let the weak die. This system removed all moral consideration of compassion for the weak and less fortunate to obtain the highest condition for the well fated. This sort of thought absolves the National Socialists. They see themselves as the neo-Spartans. Their role is to promote the strong and remove the weak from human history." Erik reflected. "Social Darwinism promotes this concept entirely." Erik continued. "I'm beginning to understand it better now. The National Socialists have assumed the role of God and Nature by demanding a monopoly to decide who lives and who dies." Kaarle said. "You have it in a nut shell young man." Erik cried out. "They began as a watered down version called "Fabian Socialists." The main difference between progressive socialism and National Socialism is that the National Socialists seem to be in a far greater hurry to transform humanity, but the end is unfortunately the same, a perfect species." Erik observed. "The last intellectual impetus for National Socialism comes from their interpretation of Malthus. Malthus believed that man would eventually over populate himself beyond earths resources.

That natural occurrences, such as fire, flood earthquakes and so on would not be sufficient to return the balance to the population. He encouraged man's interference such as with wars and disease as a final remedy. This has been used by the Nazis to justify their Lebensraum style of Genocide. Prune back the population with war and executions to make it a better place for the 'survival' of the fittest." Erik concluded. "I've heard that description often. Is that from Darwin?" Kaarle asked.

"Well he claimed it, but it was actually first used by an evolutionist philosopher named Herbert Spencer a good eight years before Darwin published his Origin Of The Species." Erik said.

"So I can take from this that the Nazis are not just greedy murdering bastards but Atheistic sons of bitches who believe their plans for a master race will be what is best for the planet and their right to proceed is based on a one sentence slogan; that they are allowed to survive while the weak perish because nature has determined them to be the fittest?" Kaarle summarized. "I believe you now know as much as anyone knows about Nazis." Erik exclaimed. "I can now give you the news you have been waiting for." Erik said mysteriously.

Kaarle wore a surprised expression as Erik poured two more glasses of vodka. "What news?" He asked. "One of the underground members who escaped to Switzerland managed to steal a folder from your sister's room. It contained the usual reports about her daily tests, but it also contained some logistical information you may be able to use." Erik said. "Such as?" Kaarle asked. "Well such as the name of a certain SS Hauptman Bernt Weisner who is a Lebensborn courier. The best part is that he fits your physical appearance to a letter T.

The plan has already been approved. Our people will intercept him in Oslo, torture him for a few days until we know what his first birthday present was and then kill him. You will assume his identity and travel to the Lebensborn facility in Muenchen with orders in hand to transfer your sister to Frankfurt by staff car. The staff car will be driven by our underground friends who will take you instead to Switzerland and then you will travel together to London, where King Hakkon wants to meet you personally." Erik said.

Elina had been listening the entire time. She emerged with tears streaming down her face. "Take me with you Kaarle." She pleaded. "I can't." Kaarle said softly. "It's far too dangerous. Will you please wait for me in London?" Kaarle asked tenderly. Elina ran to Kaarle. They embraced. "Oh Kaarle I would wait for you in Hell, you know that don't you?" "I know it now." He said.

Chapter Eight: Bavarian Nightmare

Hauptman Bernt Weisner enjoyed his job. He loved traveling but his destinations made the job all the more pleasant as he had been verified by Heinrich Himmler's SS-Ahnenerbe as having Aryan features and a traceable lineage of Aryan ancestry in excess of 90%. This mandated the responsibility of doing his patriotic duty by having sex with at least one, sometimes two Lebensborn women, one after the other per visit who were in the peak moment of their fertility cycle. Weisner estimated that he averaged sex at least five times a week, or two hundred sixty different women a year. Only occasionally the same one twice.

If he enjoyed a particular woman more than usual, he would write down her location, name and fertility cycle to be certain he was in her city when duty called. He gave himself a 33.3% probability of impregnating the women he had intercourse with, for a final estimate that he fathered approximately eighty six children each year. He started his assignments shortly after the invasion of Norway in 1940, or three years ago which meant that give, or take a few here, or there, he had fathered two hundred and sixty children since his work as a Lebensborn courier began.

He carefully tallied the files he signed for and locked the metal attache case he carried them in. Mostly technical junk and medical reports Bernt had little interest in. He was just happy that he hadn't been assigned to the Russian front. He looked up his Lebensborn assignment for tomorrow evening. Just one woman. He enjoyed the assignments much more since Josef Goebbels correctly observed that production of pregnancies would be greater if the donor were allowed to behave more naturally, even pretend it to be an experience with a girlfriend, or wife.

Nothing kinky allowed such as sado-masochism. What a nightmare that had been for a Leutnant who actually took a strap to one of the women one evening. To the Leutnant's sad misfortune, Himmler was visiting the same clinic that evening to impregnate a woman down the hallway. When Himmler entered the room and saw the bleeding welts on the woman's backside, he pulled out his revolver and shot the Leutnant in the temple. Since then the donor males were all exceptionally polite. The women seemed to appreciate the foreplay much more than the previously clinical, mechanical sex that characterized the launching of the program.

Bernt always enjoyed fondling and kissing first and then mutual love making. When he had only one assignment he took his time with a great deal of foreplay, but if he had a follow on assignment he was far less sensual. Bernt looked at his watch. He enjoyed the last sip of coffee and headed out of the café to his waiting staff car. When his driver missed the right turn that led to the Oslo Lebensborn clinic, he yelled at him. "Achtung Dumbkopf! You missed the bloody turn!" Bernt shouted. With sudden shock Bernt realized the driver wore a German uniform but was a stranger. The driver pulled over to the curb and a heavy set muscular man jumped in beside Hauptman Weisner. Bernt tried to pull out his side arm but the huge man hit him solidly in his diaphram bending him over while he pulled the 9mm Luger from Bernt's holster. A judo chop expertly delivered to the back of his head put Bernt to sleep.

When Bernt began to awaken he realized he was lying flat on his face on a cold stone floor. He heard various voices and saw a half dozen pairs of boots. He thought of pretending to still be unconscious but a voice cried out; "Herzlich Wilkommen an Norwegen Berntie mein schatz!"

Bernt looked up. It took a moment for his eyes to adjust to the bright light being beamed on his face. He was yanked to his feet and securely tied to a hard wooden chair. The first blow came so fast Bernt felt as though he were an unattached and distant observer of someone else's pain. The second blow flattened his nose and caused him to realize in panic that he wasn't a detached observer, but instead the recipient of raw and brutal violence. Bernt screamed a high pitched primordial scream. Then came the third and fourth blow to his ribs. He fought desperately just to get his lungs to inflate with air again. He released his bowels and the heat traveled down both thighs. A voice in the background shouted; "Don't kill him, leave someone in the chair I can talk to." Then came the foul odor. "Damn Bernt! What are they feeding you Nazis? That has to be the most miserable stench I have ever smelled. Is that what Nazi shit smells like? Take him outside and dip him and then bring him back smelling nicer." Someone ordered.

Bernt was dragged through the freezing snow outside to a small lake. The ice had been broken in an area large enough for a man's body. Bernt was stripped and forced beneath the freezing water. When he began to inhale the frozen water he was pulled back out wheezing, coughing and struggling for air. "He's clean!" Came the same voice. He was dragged back inside the cold warehouse that seemed hot to Bernt now. He was tied up again but this time in the nude as he shivered and shook in the same hard wooden chair. "Bernt let me explain something to you. You are now a prisoner of the Norwegian Home Resistance Front. Do you understand?" Bernt sat quiet and still. With cruel malice a man grabbed the small finger of his right hand and chopped it off with a Blacksmith tool.

Bernt tried to scream but he had lost his voice from the earlier scream. He grimaced, forcing air through his nose as tears streamed down his face. "Bernt, I need your full attention here. You have been treating Norway like your own private whorehouse. Did you just think you could come here and knock up thousands of our women and not have to pay for the pussy? Eh Bernt?" A red hot poker was brought near his penis. Bernt fainted. He was splashed with a bucket of ice water and the misery of waking up from one nightmare to a worse one was overpowering. "As I was saying Bernt you need to pay full attention. I am going to have my people take you to a warm comfortable back room. You can take a bath and someone will bandage your little finger. We have some hot coffee waiting for you and you have my personal assurances that no one else will harm you. Do you understand me Bernt? Do you understand me Herr Hauptman Weisner?" Bernt vigorously shook his head yes.

"Good. Because I will be asking you some very personal questions and the game we will be playing is simple. You don't know how much I know about your personal life. If I discover, or even suspect you are not providing honest answers we will come back out here. We will cut off a digit for every lie you tell. The final lie will mean we use the cutting tool on your little Bernt. Ist ja Alles klar Commissar?" Bernt slowly dipped his right hand into the warm soapy water and his eyes filled with tears. How could his stupid driver have allowed this to happen? If he survived this, the driver had better hope he was already dead. He began to feel the warmth return to the rest of his body. His uniform was hanging on a chair minus his soiled trousers and under wear. Instead they had given him a pair of red wool trousers. How could he escape wearing those? he thought. Time to be serious. What did he have to lose?

He would tell them any f--cking thing they wanted to hear if it meant leaving with the rest of his fingers and Schlange still attached. The Tall One appeared suddenly from the shadows outside. "Hello Sir!" The muscular man said. "Hello." The Tall One replied. "How much time do I have Sir?" "No later than tomorrow morning early. Try to get names of people he works with. Their functions. How our man agent Wolf might expect to encounter them, when, where, why. His favorite Gasthofs in different cities. Names of Bartenders. Waitresses, lovers. Is he also queer? Get the names of his parents, brothers, sisters, wife." The tall one said. "We found a personal diary. I don't know how he could stay so sexually active and take care of a wife too." The muscular man said. "I don't want you to assume anything. Maybe he has an estranged wife, or a homosexual lover. I want to know every goddamn thing!" "Yes Sir.' "We learned from his papers that he has an 'assignment' tomorrow night at twenty hours." The muscular man said. "An assignment?" The Tall One asked. "Let me see the documents." The Tall One said. He studied them carefully. "He has an assignment with Birgit in unit A-6743 at twenty hours. It's a sex encounter at the Lebensborn clinic. Find out what he normally does at those. Leave nothing out!" "Yes Sir!"

"How long he stays, whether he must sign any paper work. Must he pick up more documents tomorrow to take back with him to Muenchen? Must they sign for all of his delivered documents? Every detail. I want this information delivered to me at first light." the Tall One said. "What do we do with the prisoner later Sir?" The Tall One looked incredulous at the muscular man for a few seconds before answering. "Kill him and bury him far from here in a snow bank." "The car sir?" "Our Man will need it and a driver for tomorrow that will take him to Lebensborn and await him.

Get the dead drivers name. The new driver must take our man to the Luftwaffe Air strip. He has a flight to Muenchen at 11:00 in the morning, day after tomorrow." "Very well sir, just one last thing." The Tall man looked at the muscular man with an angry expression. "Yes, what?" "Well sir, the German shit himself and the trousers are so foul we aren't sure we can get them clean." "Goddamnit! Don't bother me with things of this sort. Wash the f--cking things seven times I don't care as long as our man who wears them smells tomorrow like the Rosen Kavalier." "Yes Sir!"

Kaarle studied the data the Tall Man had just given him. "Assignment?" "Yes. Sorry Kaarle I know you have feelings for Elina but I swear she will never be told." "I can't do it. I won't do it. It would make me just like them." Kaarle growled. "Do you want to see Laila again Kaarle?" "Yes." "Well, start reflexively believing that you are Bernt. He likes to always poke twice so we learned. So you poke twice make it last an hour with foreplay. If you deviate one iota from the character and habits of that Nazi Captain it could cost you your life." The Tall One said. "Here is his uniform. I can already see that it should fit you like a glove Herr Hauptman Weisner. Here. You may want to wear this eye patch. You look incredibly like the SS Captain, but someone may notice a slight difference in your facial structure, so the eye patch should throw them off. If they ask what happened to your eye just tell them you picked up an eye infection. We have learned that Weisner and his driver were staying at the hotel near the Lebensborn Clinic." the Tall one said. "Be sure to check out for both of you. Here's several thousand Reich Marks. Sometime after your plane leaves, the body of the real driver will be placed in the staff car which will be rolled over on a desolate road.

The dead driver will have the contents of an entire bottle of vodka in his stomach to lead any suspicions as to his cause of death away from you." The Tall One said. "You have thought of everything." Kaarle said. "Let us hope so." The Tall One said.

Kaarle came back out in the Captain's uniform. It looked tailor made for him. Elina came out to embrace Kaarle before he departed. "I'll wait for you in London Kaarle. Please be careful." She said as she kissed him good bye. She became teary eyed and went back into the Safe House. "Do you think she suspects?" The Tall One asked. "No, because I already told her." Kaarle replied. "You insufferable fool! Oh well, she's a good soldier, perhaps she forgives you but I promise she will never forget." The Tall One said. "I couldn't cheat behind her back. I respect her too much for that." Kaarle said. As Kaarle was climbing in the back of the staff car a vehicle turned onto the farm house road with the lights out. Kaarle unholstered his pistol. "You won't need that. It's Erik. He is delivering the latest intelligence report from Muenchen. Once you board that plane tomorrow, we will have no further way of reaching you until you make contact with the underground. Our messages can sometimes be delayed for weeks if our short wave transmitters get compromised." The Tall One said.

Erik walked brusquely to Kaarle and reached him a leather folder. "Kaarle, we have learned that they moved your sister from Muenchen to Berlin. She is apparently the central element of some Top Secret project started by Mengele. We only know that she has been taken to the Kaiser-Wilhelm Institute of Anthropology, Eugenics and Genetics in Berlin-Dahlem. It's a suburb of Berlin. Once you read the material I prepared for you please burn it.

Some of the information could only be traced to me if the document is siezed in Norway." Erik said. "Don't worry, I will read it and burn it before tomorrow." Kaarle assured him. Kaarle jumped in the staff car and was taken straight to the Lebensborn Clinic for his assignment.

The staff was new since the failed mission. The security was doubled and appeared to be on a high state of alert. It wasn't known whether Hauptman Weisner's driver knew the guards, or not, so in order to be assured not to be compromised, Kaarle's driver let him off and left to re-fuel. He would return at twenty two hours and wait near the front entrance to the clinic. Kaarle flashed his ID and stiff arm saluted the guards. "Heil Hitler!" They all repeated to each other. He walked up to the clinic counter and opened his metal attache case. "Shall you receive the documents here?" He asked. "Hauptman Weisner. Good evening. What happened to your eye?" The Head Nurse asked. "It's nothing. An eye infection that I'm sure will be healed soon." Kaarle held his breath wondering if the ruse was working. The Head nurse counted the documents and signed a receipt which Kaarle placed in the attache case. Have you documents for me? He asked. "Yes, not very many, but these are marked AM STRENGSTEN GEHEIMNIS. TOP SECRET. I'm glad you are taking them away. The responsibility for them is frightening." She smiled. "Well, imagine how frightening it is to be responsible for them all the way to Muenchen." He said.

"Oh they are not bound for Muenchen. They are to be delivered to Berlin." She said. "But Berlin is not in my circuit.' Kaarle protested. "Here! These are special orders signed by Dr. Mengele and countersigned by Heinrich Himmler.

These are the patient history documents for the Finnish girl who was here." "How do you know this?" Kaarle asked. "I prepared them for shipment." She defended. Kaarle held his finger to his lips. Am Strengstens Geheimnis. He said in a low voice and grinned. "Is my assignment ready?" Kaarle asked. "But of course Herr Hauptman. Do you know which unit?" She asked. "Certainly." He replied.

Birgit was a tall woman, twenty four years old and extremely attractive. She was born and raised on a small farm outside Bergen, Norway. Kaarle had expected a frumpy woman smelling of rubbing alcohol and wearing a hospital gown that ties up in the back. To his utter surprise, Birgit was wearing make up with a sheer negligee that showed her supple breasts and every line and curve of her solid, smooth body. She had honey blonde hair and deep blue eyes that were as clear as water from a mountain stream. After some small talk she joined him on a small sofa and began to caress his inner thighs with her long finger nails. "It looks to be your lucky night, I'm not in the mood tonight. Travel sickness." He said. Birgit began to sob. "You don't find me attractive!" She moaned. "That isn't true, I find you most attractive." He shot back. "Then why do you want them to make me leave the clinic?" She asked. "Do you want to stay?" "Yes. I am treated well here. Good food and shelter and protection from the madness. I saw my entire family burn to death when a bomb hit our house. I wouldn't know what to do out there." She lamented. "Well, I promise you, I will give glowing reports about you when I leave." Kaarle said. "Who are you? Don't you know they perform extensive post assignment examinations here? After you leave, they will make a swab to measure and test your sperm count.

There have been many women dismissed for being empty. It is considered the worst form of failure and insult to the Reich. "Yes. I'm sorry I momentarily forgot. Please come back and sit down." Kaarle apologized. They began to kiss and before long Kaarle was making passionate love with Birgit. They finally finished and lay sweating and gasping for air, which only moments before had seemed completely unimportant. Birgit begged Kaarle to have a second session and when he declined she asked him to take her with him.

Kaarle felt ashamed and unclean. Making love with Elina was different. It was all based on his love for her. Birgit drained him of his self respect. "War brings out the best and the worst in people," he thought as he leaned into the arctic wind while walking to the waiting staff car.

When Kaarle finally made it to Hauptman Weisner's hotel room he was surprisingly clear minded and not at all sleepy. He gathered Hauptman Weisner's personal belongings and packed them in the canvas suitcase he found in the closet. He found some Cuban cigarillos which he was about to throw away, but quickly decided to keep when he remembered the Tall One's admonition about details.

Kaarle reluctantly pulled the leather folder out that Erik had given him and began to read.

"Kaarle I know some of what I have written here will seem redundant. We thoroughly covered the origin of eugenics in the Third Reich from a historical standpoint, but given that your sister has fallen under a specific part of the Reich's progenetive endeavor in Berlin, I think perhaps some duplication risk may be well worth taking. The Kaiser Wilhelm Institute of Anthropology and eugenics in Berlin-Dahlem was founded in 1929. It established the first international scientific conference held in post WWI Germany on eugenics.

I mention this because it was anything but a coincidence. It was attended by a long list of like minded eugenics scientists the world over. The Institute was begun by a chap named Professor Eugen Fischer whose primary academic attention had been for some time focused on the anthropological and anatomical research he had done in the African territories colonized by Germany. He developed a eugenics approach steeped in prejudicial theory and blatant racism. There was no question in his mind that certain races were inferior to others. His was a quest to discover the best way to achieve racial hygiene, or a cleansing of the inferior races from the human family. Along comes our fellow Adolf and a match was made not in heaven but in Hell. Fischer immediately declared his institute completely capable and willing to support Hitler's new government sterilization programs and to provide eugenic studies to the sky if need be to justify racial hygienic programs. A particularly enthusiastic research scientist in Fischer's Institute, who advocated and who was a proponent of Hitler's racist policies and programs was a man named Dr. Otmar vonVerschuer. He now runs Eugenics research for the Reich."

"Dr. von Verschuer is a world renowned authority on the genetics of twins. His incipient research at Dahlem was in fact funded by the American Rockefeller Foundation before they discovered the news later about Hitler's Death Camps. By 1936 von Verschuer was brought to Frankfurt to head up the Genetics and Racial Hygeine Department of the University Of Frankfurt. This soon became The Frankfurt Institute Of Eugenics and Racial Hygeine, the largest and most authoritative Institute of its kind in the world. The Frankfurt University's medical studies became a part of the Institute as a compulsory curriculum." "No one became a Medical Doctor without being thoroughly versed in racism. In fact Frankfurt's Institute scientists helped write the laws of 1933 mandating forced sterilization. Dr. von Verschuer's first assistant at Frankfurt was none other than our favorite Wunderkind Josef Mengele. Dr. von Verschuer's mantra became an "Endloesung" or Final Solution for the Jewish problem. He modified it slightly when he later called for a "Gesamtloesung" or Total solution for the Jewish problem. By last year, 1942, von Verschuer was made Fischer's replacement at Dahlem."

"Surprise, surprise, his right hand man Dr. Mengele was assigned to Auschwitz also last year at the same time and has been dissecting Jews and Gypsies ever since, sending their body parts to Dahlem for von Verschuer to experiment with and test. These hapless victims are being murdered to keep von Verschuer's laboratories filled with specimens! I do not wish to frighten you my good friend I only want you to be prepared for anything and everything you might find there. In fact, it is quite positive thus far that your sister has been carefully preserved as a live specimen.

They will no doubt wish to keep her that way since most of their other research subjects were murdered by Mengele before being sent to von Verschuer, so her life is as precious to them as it is to her, scientifically speaking. One last very important item. S.O.E. has an asset in Berlin. A German woman who despises what Hitler has done to Germany. Her code name is Medussa. We have no way of contacting her. If she decides it's safe she will contact you. She knows you only as Wolf. God Speed my brave friend."

NOW BURN THIS !

ERIK

Kaarle sat watching the document Erik had given him fold and curl in the flames of the fireplace. He found a silver flask of Scotch in the breast pocket of Weisner's over coat and took a large swill before tumbling into a frightful and tormented dream state. Kaarle had crystal clear nightmares until early dawn. He dreamed of the Winter War but his dream scenes abruptly changed to dreams of Mengele dissecting Jews in Auschwitz. Then he saw Laila being cut straight up the middle as Mengele ripped organs and tissue without anesthesia while she screamed . By the time his driver knocked on his door Kaarle was ready to fight anyone to the death.

The Norwegian Resistance Driver packed the dead driver's suitcase and loaded both suitcases in the staff car. There was an awkward moment when the front desk ran out of change for Reich Marks but Kaarle told them to give him a credit balance to apply for his next visit.

Soon the Dornier twin engine passenger plane taxied for take off and Kaarle watched the splendor of Norway's fiords slip slowly by far below. He had only ridden in an airplane once when they executed a night jump at Telemark. This ride would at least bring him back down again he thought as he drifted into a sound sleep with his metal attache case hand cuffed to his wrist. Kaarle fell asleep listening to the engine's drone and was dreaming about the night jump at Telemark when it happened.

In his dream he could feel the arctic wind on his face as he leaped into the darkness. He could see the feet and backs of the other jumpers descending like a swirling centipede in physical disconnect, but firmly connected in the order of the falling pattern. Then came the gut wrenching air brake as the parachute opened with a shock slowing his falling rate from 200 feet per second down to 32 feet per second. The dream of the opening shock awakened him abruptly. When he opened his eyes he saw the other passengers screaming and bracing against the heavy G force. The Dornier had gone into a steep dive to avoid the attack by the British Spitfires that were met suddenly by a heavily armed escort of German Messershmitts. Kaarle strained to remain near a window to watch the spectacular display of aerial combat taking place across the sky.

He knew the reason his plane had the escort. It was the documents the Germans wanted so badly. The documents from what ever they had done to his sister. Men were fighting and dying just outside his window for what he had secured to his wrist. He had to watch, that was the least he could do. He fought off an urge to unlock the handcuff and open the door to throw away the contents of the attache case.

He would have done so but he didn't know whether the documents would save her, or seal her fate. Until he had the answer he had no choice but to take them to her captors. He looked down at the earth far below. Land! They were somewhere over the North European continent. France Holland, Germany, he had no way of knowing which.

The Dornier strained for altitude and finally leveled off. Then came the loud cracking noises like flat bladed steel against steel from a strafing Spit Fire. Large holes appeared along the ceiling of the aircraft. Smoke invaded the cabin and Kaarle could see inside the cock pit that both pilot and co-pilot were dead. A man was passing out parachutes and Kaarle quickly strapped himself into a chute as the plane began a roll to the right falling into a death dive. Kaarle struggled to get to the door. As the dive began he felt himself floating weightlessly about the cabin. Soon he was sucked upward against the holes in the fuselage made by the Spitfire .50 calibers.

Someone managed to open the door which blew away immediately. Along with a tornado of debris the wind sucked Kaarle out into the open sky. He saw two German officers hurtle out of the plane behind himself. One pulled his rip cord too soon. The silk caught on the rudder. Kaarle saw the man whip saw as the plane fell to the earth. He fell free hugging the metal attache case which caused him to roll and tumble. He strained against the pull of the attache case which was now spiraling behind him. When he felt the case near his waist he reached across his chest and pulled the rip cord. His chute opened and he was sent sailing diagonally on a wind current high above a large open patchy snow covered meadow below. As Kaarle looked down he saw two Germans running for their lives.

Across the wide meadow he heard shouting in Dutch. Then he heard responses in German. The night silence was shattered by the sound of submachine gun fire, then abruptly dead silence again. Kaarle landed hard. He rolled to distribute the shock, but he felt a sharp pain in his left knee. He lay still for a moment massaging his knee. Then suddenly three sub machine gun muzzles were aimed directly at his face. "Haende Hoch !" They shouted.

"Ahh Dutch Underground!" Kaarle thought to himself with relief. The relief disappeared when one of the men gave Kaarle a sharp kick to the abdomen. Kaarle could only speak German, Russian, English and Finn. He said in German; "Ich bin kein Deutscher" I'm not a German, but this elicited only laughter. The meanest of the three obviously concerned that someone may have heard the other shots aimed his pistol at Kaarle's head. Just before the trigger was pulled Kaarle spun around disarming the man then holding the man's pistol against the man's head. "Waffen auflegen!" Lay down your arms! Kaarle commanded. The Dutchmen obeyed. One of the men spoke German. "Why did you say you aren't German? You wear a German Captain's uniform!" He said. "I'm on a mission. I am under cover." As he said this, he returned the man's weapon pistol grip first. The Dutchmen looked dazed. "What of the ones we killed? Were they your allies?" "No. Good job. I'm operating alone." "I see. Good. What's in the brief case?" "It's complicated. I'm from Finland and the Germans are holding my sister in a Lebensborn research facility in Berlin. They need these papers I intercepted but I don't know whether delivering the papers will help, or hurt my sister." Kaarle said honestly. "You're right, that is complicated. Came the reply. Can you verify your identity? If not we can't release you without approval from our leadership." The mean one said.

"Would I have given you back your loaded pistol if I were not telling the truth?" "Perhaps, perhaps not." The mean one replied. "Listen do you have access to a short wave that can put you in touch with S.O.E. Branch in London? Tell them you have captured Wolf. Tell them Wolf claims he is from Finland but is now working with the Norges Hjemmefront, or Norwegian Resistance." Kaarle said. Kaarle was taken to a Safe House five kilometers away. He was held under guard until the short wave connection was made. A tension filled the room as a reply was awaited in code. The coded response came back and as it was being decoded, Kaarle could feel the tension tightening on a dozen trigger fingers. The decoded message said "Wolf is an authentic agent. [Stop] Ask him the name of Wolf's Sweet heart [Stop]. "What is the name of your sweetheart Wolf?" The mean one asked. "Elina." Kaarle replied. The coded response came back; Wolf challenge verified. [Stop] Please help him get to Berlin. End of message. The relief was palpable. Even though he wore a mean expression, the Mean One was horrified that he had nearly killed an innocent man.

The mean one held out his hand. "Sorry brother, but we have learned as a matter of survival to be extremely cautious. My name is Hatchet." Kaarle took his hand. "I fully understand. I would have behaved the same if the circumstances had been reversed." Kaarle said. "Wolf, we will do everything we can to get you to Berlin, but I'm afraid it could take as long as a month." Hatchet said. "I don't have a month. What I do have is my cover and orders directly from Mengele and Himmler to deliver these documents to Berlin." Kaarle replied. "They must be very important for Himmler to get personally involved. Shall we open them?" Hatchet asked. "No. My sisters life may depend on the seal remaining unbroken.

They are sealed by wax at every possible entry point. I checked." Kaarle said. "I see." Hatchet replied. "What you can do for me is get me to the nearest German military post. I will report my aircraft being shot down and show them my orders signed by Himmler. I'm sure it will be the quickest, if not the safest way to get to Berlin." Kaarle said. "Yes, you are right. Very well, my friends will take you to the German airfield at Eindhoven. It's not far from here. Then we shall all move our operations from this area for a few weeks. Once they find the Germans we shot, this piece of real estate will be very hot indeed." Hatchet observed. Kaarle wandered into the Guard post at the Eindhoven Luftwaffe air strip. Soon he was joined by Major Kraemer and Horst Feldner, the local Gestapo representative who decided to grill Kaarle on the details.

"Well, Hauptman Weisner, we must check out these details just to be careful. We should be concluded with our investigation in a day, or so." Horst said. "I am on a high level mission as a courier for Heinrich Himmler. Are you quite certain that you wish to delay my travel to Berlin? Where is your telephone. We can ask Herr Himmler himself what he wishes for us to do." Kaarle said. "But it is 3 am Major Kraemer protested. I know how I felt when my guard awakened me." The Major objected. Not to be outdone Horst reached for the phone and placed the call. After a few minutes of ringing a voice came on the line.

"Himmler. Wer ist das?? "Herr Himmler, Horst Feldner Gestapo in Eindhoven, Holland. We have a Hauptman Weisner who is claiming to have survived being shot down on a flight from Oslo to Berlin. He claims to be a courier for Herr Dr. Mengele. He is asking to be flown immediately to Berlin and I…" Before he could finish Himmler cut in. "Did you see the goddamned orders I signed?"

"Ja wohl Herr Himmler but documents of course can be forged." Horst tried to reason. "Are you now calling me a forgerer?" Himmler said excitedly. "Of course not Herr Himmler but I was trained to…" "You were trained to follow f--cking orders, now get Hauptman Weisner to Berlin if you have to get on your knees and become his horse. Einverstanden?" "Of course Herr Himmler! Heil Hitler!" Horst said in shock. "Put the ranking SS officer there on the line." Horst reached the phone to Major Kraemer who shot a dirty look his way.

"This is Waffen SS Major Kraemer Sir!" "Kraemer arrest the dumbkopf I was just speaking with and send me his personal file." In the meantime get Hauptman Weisner in the air on the way to Berlin immediately. Wait. Let me speak to Weisner." "Jawohl Herr Himmler here is Weisner." "Weisner, do you still have the documents? Are they safe?" Himmler asked. "Yes Herr Himmler. In accordance with regulations they have remained locked to my wrist even during my parachute escape from the burning aircraft." There was a pause of silence. "Good work Hauptman Weisner. You shall be decorated for your loyalty and bravery." Himmler said gratefully.

"If the dumbkopf I spoke with first, Horst whomever tries to impede your travel to Berlin you are hereby ordered to shoot him in the forehead. Ist ja alles klar?" "Yes Herr Himmler. Heil Hitler!" Kaarle shouted. There came a sudden click as Himmler hung up the phone. His rant was loud and Horst Feldner heard every word. He blanched white and sat down in an office chair, perspiring. "Please come with me Hauptman Weisner. I will have an aircraft and pilot ready to fly you to Berlin in a matter of minutes." "Thank you Major." Kaarle said.

"Horst remain here and consider yourself under arrest. If you try to leave orders will be issued to shoot you on sight." The Major said with anger in his voice. Kaarle was met at the airport in Berlin by a staff car sent by Professor von Verschuer. "The Professor wishes that you take the documents to him at the Institute immediately." the young adjutant said. Kaarle wondered what this old city looked like before the bombing destruction it was marred with now. He adjusted his tunic and changed wrists with the handcuff in order to be able to salute and shake hands with his right hand. The driver stopped at the front of the Institute to let the adjutant and Kaarle climb out.

Soon Kaarle was led to a large office that had several microscopes and lab testing equipment in an adjacent room. Kaarle saluted von Verschuer as they both exclaimed "Heil Hitler." The adjutant excused himself and Kaarle was left alone with the Professor. "Please sit down."von Verschuer said as he anxiously awaited the documents. Kaarle reached the Top Secret documents to von Verschuer who used a letter opener to break the wax seals. He perused the documents for a few moments and squealed like a little boy. "Yes! This proves the analyses I have myself made. She is a 100% direct descendant of the Aryan race. These DNA samples taken before during and after her pregnancy at the Norwegian Lebensborn Center are an exact match with skeletal remains we uncovered in the area of the ancient Harappan Civilization northwest of India. The Fuhrer will be so pleased to get this news!" von Verschuer said.   "Look at me. After risking your life to save these documents that are vital to national security I haven't even offered you a refreshment." von Verschuer waved to his adjutant who commanded a secretary to bring a tray of cookies and a pot of Brazilian coffee.

"I hope you enjoy this coffee, I designed the mixture myself." von Verschuer said. "I'm sure it will be delicious." Kaarle replied. Von Verschuer seemed like an entirely different person than the man Erik described in his dossier. Kaarle became almost ill when he knew he had to pretend not to know that this man was personally responsible for hundreds of thousands perhaps millions of deaths of men, women and children. Kaarle smiled as though he were genuinely entertained, even as thoughts of von Verschuer examining body parts of twin children passed through his mind.

Dr. von Verschuer remained jubilant. Quite on impulse he took a set of caliphers from a desk drawer and began measuring Kaarle's forehead, cheek bones and lower jaw. "Your file seemed to be an exaggeration when I read that Himmler's people rated you at 90% Aryan. I would say you are most probably 98%. I would like to schedule you next week for a complete examination." von Verschuer mumbled.

"The Fuhrer will grace our ball this evening when we make our announcement that Project Lebensborn is on schedule. This is a code word which means our Top Secret project is a smashing success. Would you care to take a stroll? I can show you much quicker than I can explain it." "But it's Top Secret Herr Dr. von Verschuer." Kaarle protested. "You risked your life to get this Top Secret information to me. You have earned a right to know the value of your service to the Fatherland nicht wahr?" Kaarle was now nearly as jubilant as von Verschuer that he would get a VIP tour of the project where others had given their lives but had never come so close. They walked through the main corridors of the Institute until they came to an elevator accessible only by key. The elevator plunged with speed, ten levels below ground.

When the doors opened Kaarle saw an enormous room with rows that totaled 100 tanks filled with liquid oxygen. Connected to hoses that monitored vital signs were human fetuses in varying levels of development within each glass tank. "Ahh you are attracted by the children. This is everyone's reaction." von Verschuer exclaimed. "Can you see what they have in common?" von Verschuer asked. Kaarle was speechless. "Everything!" von Verschuer beamed. "They are all exact clones of our Finnish Princess as we like to call her." von Verschuer exclaimed. In a glass encased room Kaarle saw his sister Laila asleep on a hospital bed with tubes connected to her abdomen. We bring her down here when she is ovulating to harvest the eggs." von Verschuer explained.

"Then we replicate the eggs with her own DNA inside a stem cell which becomes an embryo that is deposited in a maturation environment. At first we used host females to carry the cloned infants to term but we had a high failure rate of the embryos. We believe the host DNA was influencing the embryo DNA somehow by genetic readjustments. When our scientists invented the exact environment found in a female womb, without host DNA interference, we were able to grow the fetuses, using liquid oxygen and it was suddenly like magic, zero failure so far. The results of this project were made possible by some very bright scientists of ours who took what was known about genetics and DNA since the last century and added our goal of genetically engineering 100% racially hygienic Aryans to populate the Reich. As we proceed further, we will take a mature clone and attempt to use its DNA to replicate itself until we have perfect control of world population. Once we populate the entire globe with a hygienic race we can sterilize those who were loyal to the Reich. When they live out their lives that will be the end of their genetic contribution to mankind.

All others beyond the loyalist group will simply receive the total final solution." von Verschuer said matter of factly. Kaarle struggled deeply to constrain himself from strangling this man with his bare hands. What a nightmare. These monsters had created a hundred clones of his sister and were excited about creating clones of her clones!

Kaarle knew that if he made any attempt to kill von Verschuer and rescue his sister, she would probably bleed to death before he could leave the building with her. He ached to speak with her and to protect her, but she was in an induced coma and he had zero chance of success. Kaarle pretended to be in awe of von Verschuer's accomplishments while in his heart he suffered anger, shock and disgust beyond anything he had ever felt before in his life.

"Hauptman Weisner you have demonstrated such true dedication to our cause I would like very much that you will meet with our Fuhrer at the ball tonight. With the good news you brought the mood is certain to be quite festive. If the Fuhrer doesn't decide to make you his own personal Adjutant then I will gladly do so." von Verschuer said. "But you already have an Adjutant Professor von Verschuer." Kaarle replied. "Him? Well he never risked his life for anything. I will send him to help with the experiments in Auschwitz with Dr. Mengele. Mengele will be at the ball tonight also and wishes to meet you in person. A driver will pick you up at your hotel tonight at twenty hours and bring you to the ball. Go now back to your room and get some rest my son." von Verschuer said affectionately. You will need it for the ladies tonight."von Verschuer said laughingly. "Vielen danke Herr Professor von Verschuer." "Nichts zu danken Hauptman Weisner."

They returned to ground level in the elevator and in moments Kaarle was hopping into a waiting staff car, his head spinning with the dark images of the Nazi world of horror and moral mayhem of unspeakable secrets. When Kaarle entered his room he found a dozen roses, a basket of fresh fruit and a bottle of French champagne waiting on a table with a personal note of gratitude signed by Heinrich Himmler and Josef Goebbels. Hanging in the closet was a black SS uniform with skull bone insignia and red trimmed sleeves with a white shirt and black tie. The measurements were exact. He would be a special guest of the Fuhrer tonight and he'd only just arrived. Kaarle tried to sleep but he couldn't get the images of the clones out of his mind. The worst image was Laila lying there in the nude with tubes poked into her abdomen as though she were just a massive lump of tissue to be done with as they pleased. First they ripped her away from the man she loved. No doubt a good man. Then the Colonel that he himself killed recently had forced a child on her. For the first time Kaarle wondered where that child might be. For Laila and the child's sake he hoped it was nearby to comfort her when she wasn't sedated. It would add complications to the rescue but he would somehow pull it off. He had to.

Kaarle began to imagine a plan in his mind. A subterfuge that would allow him access to Laila when she wasn't being held ten levels beneath the ground. He didn't know where they kept her between ovulation harvesting and other experiments. Perhaps he should accept the Adjutant's position von Verschuer was offering. It would give him access to the entire building. The possibility someone would expose his impersonation would increase daily. Things were in the air. Details missing. He would learn them tonight and make his decision according to the highest probability of success.

He never thought he'd miss the battle field, but things were wonderfully simple there. You fought and you either killed or you died. Here you had to calculate vastly complex characters and make multi-layered plans with even greater contingencies that relied on the capriciousness of maniacs. Whatever it took Kaarle was anxious to get started. His greatest challenge would be to hide his emotions from others about his love for his flesh and blood sister when he was near her, his sister who was so pitiful to see in her current state.

Kaarle wore his eye patch to the ball. He couldn't be certain whether someone there may have met Hauptman Weisner before. If so it would end his cover before he had a chance to use it. He looked menacing in his black SS uniform with his black eye patch. He would no doubt cause many curious whispers at the ball. The driver made several turns and stops on the way to the ball in accordance with Hitler's latest counter assassination policy.

March of 1943 had been a busy month for the German Resistance Movement which by now had begun to attract high level conspirators, such as General von Treackow and his Aide who tried to plant a bomb on Hitler's private aircraft. It was discovered just before the plane taxied for take off. In the same month, in fact a week later, Colonel Rudolf von Gertsdorff planned to explode a bomb near Hitler as he stood in the Zeughaus in Berlin but just minutes before the bomb was to detonate Hitler made an abrupt change in schedule and departed early. Frantically von Gertsdorff flushed the live fuse down a toilet just before the bomb was detonated. Hitler had doubles who he sent to parades, but the ball would not be a place for a double as people would be close enough to spot a fake Hitler.

It was only because of the significance and importance of the Lebensborn Project for the Reich that Hitler agreed to attend at all. Kaarle was ushered into the ballroom by the Adjutant of Professor von Verschuer who commented on how elegant the SS Captain appeared in his uniform. Kaarle gave a smug and curt nod to the compliment which only added authenticity to the role he was playing. There was some milling around near the stage and suddenly all of the military officers and ladies stood at attention and in one voice shouted "Heil Hitler! Adolf Hitler entered the ball room surrounded by SS storm troopers and Gestapo agents who faded back as Hitler walked up to a microphone.

"Guten Abend Meine Damen und Herren. I have some excellent news to report tonight. Our soldiers in Russia appear to have had significant victories and I am assured we will have beaten the primitive Russians down into defeat within weeks. An even more exciting bit of news is that our scientists have made a major break through in our Lebensborn Project. They inform me that within my own lifetime I will see the creation of an Aryan race. I am able to make this announcement tonight because one of our heroic SS officers Hauptman Weisner escaped by parachute from a burning aircraft to bring proof to me that our Aryan race is indeed 100% Aryan. "He could have merely protected himself by separating his wrist from the heavy suitcase he had handcuffed to his arm. A suitcase that nearly caused his death by making his parachute unstable, but he disregarded himself and remained secured to our precious inheritance, which is the proof of purity of the Aryan blood of our sacred Reich!

Hitler said almost tearfully, his voice breaking.

"Himmler was shocked. Hitler was insane to release such information prematurely. "Was he that desperate for good news to counter the fact we are in fact being driven from Russia?" Himmler wondered silently. Hitler motioned for Hauptman Weisner to be brought up on the stage. Kaarle stood stiff and erect. Hitler's Aide whispered "Bow down." Kaarle bowed slightly forward as Hitler placed a ribbon around Kaarle's neck. The German Cross. Kaarle stood erect again and saluted as he shouted "Heil Hitler!" Kaarle nearly extended his hand to Hitler, but he instinctively waited for Hitler to make the first move, which never came. Hitler had a germ phobia and disdained hand shaking. Applause erupted and when Hitler held up his hand palm down, there was immediate silence. Hitler motioned with his right hand as though he were directing a band and suddenly music began to fill the ball room. Kaarle bowed again slightly, saluted and left the stage.

A line formed to congratulate Kaarle for his award. Waiting at the end of the line was a very attractive blonde lady bedecked in jewels and wearing a sparkling gown. She leaned forward to expose her left cheek for Kaarle to kiss. As he was kissing her cheek she whispered; "Dance with me Wolf." "Medussa!" Kaarle thought to himself. Kaarle retrieved two glasses of champagne and gave one to Medussa. While at the bar he asked the bartender who the lady was. "Oh her. That's Graefin von Neustadt. A real German Countess. Congratulations Herr Hauptman Weisner!" "Thank you." Kaarle said as he nodded to the bartender then returned to the Countess. "Oh such a gentleman!" She said loudly. They sipped from their glasses and joined the other couples on the dance floor. When the music slowed Medussa leaned slightly forward to conduct a conversation more privately. "Quite impressive Hauptman Weisner.

You really know how to make a grand entrance. You do realize that the German press will soon visit your family I believe in the small village of Bad Bruckenau to get their reaction to your heroism and award of the German Cross?" Kaarle looked stunned. "They will run photos of you in the papers from infancy to the present." She said. "How much time do I have?" "Four , maybe five days on an outside bet." She said. "What made you take a visible profile like this?" She asked. "It wasn't my plan to get shot down and without delivering the documents it would have taken me a month to get here. Also are you aware of why Hitler is so excited about the documents I delivered?" he asked.

"Yes. They verify some archeological and anthropological studies Professor von Verschuer has been conducting with Himmler's Aryan authenticity board." She said. "It's far more than that. Ten stories beneath the Eugenics Institute in Dhalem is a laboratory that contains 100 clones made of my sister. They are breathing liquid oxygen and are growing rapidly. My sister is in an induced coma so they can perpetually harvest her eggs to be used to create additional clones. They are apparently on the verge of being able to exponentially make clones from existing clones. The documents somehow show that my sisters DNA is closely matched to artifacts from the ancient Harappan civilization of north west India where the Aryans are to have originated. Without this verification von Verschuer and Mengele may have been creating a false Aryan race. They are quite happy to think they are not. My only interest is getting my sister out alive and her Lebensborn baby if she has it here." He said.

The Countess von Neustadt stiffened at the information she just received. "My God the insane sons of bitches actually did it. What do you mean by DNA?" She asked. "It's apparently some genetic technology that's been around since the last century but it has obviously been taken to advanced levels by von Verschuer's scientists. It's a genetic map of every human being. It provides a blue print for creating humans by exact specification. Clones are babies that receive this code from an injection of their mothers code into their embryo cells. I don't completely understand it myself, in fact. When it was explained I really didn't believe it, but now I've seen it with my own eyes. Von Verschuer took me on a VIP tour." Kaarle said.

"This changes everything. We must stop this. We must destroy the Institute." She said. "Not with my sister in it you won't." He exclaimed. "Of course not. Look, not far from the Berliner Hof Hotel where you are staying is a small Pensione Ilsa. When you leave here go to your room and dismiss your driver. Get changed into civilian clothes and sneak out of the hotel from the rear entrance. You must absolutely make certain that you are not followed. If we are seen together we will both lose our lives at the hands of the Gestapo." She said.

"Pensione Ilsa?" "Yes, Pensione Ilsa. I own it. It is a safe house. Everyone there is a member of the German Resistance. This matter is urgent or I would have never made contact with you." she whispered as the music ended. "Vielen danke! Thank you for the dance Countess." Kaarle said. She smiled and walked away. Kaarle stayed to dance with other ladies who asked him to dance and within an hour he excused himself with professor von Verschuer and left for his hotel. He excused his driver for the night.

"Damn! German press. I hadn't thought of that. The Countess is really a Pro." Kaarle thought. Kaarle changed into some clothes the Adjutant left with the dress uniform and within minutes he was slinking into an alley behind the Hotel. After a brusque fifteen minute walk he saw the small sign "Pensione Ilsa." He made certain that no one followed him. He ducked inside. Kaarle was led by the receptionist down a dark hallway and taken in a lift to the penthouse level. He was ushered into a large suite with an expansive living room and a sitting area enclosed in glass that afforded a view of the major streets below. Whether by car, or on foot, no one could reach the place without someone knowing they were coming. The windows were full of tropical plants which only accentuated the wintry weather. The Countess changed into a comfortable gown and was flanked by four men and two women. "Wolf, this is my entire team except for the receptionist who brought you here and her two sons who are aware of our work but who do not get involved with us on a day to day basis." she explained.

"I am placing an immense trust in you by informing you that I have a junior scientist under cover at the Institute but he has only been there four months and has not been granted access to the secret project you discovered on your first day. I assure you that caused no small amount of jealousy and envy here." She smiled. "I would introduce you to everyone, but I'm sure you understand that we do not hope that you will be here for more than a few days. If you get yourself captured it is best that we keep names to a minimum." Medussa said. "I understand and agree." Kaarle replied.

"I have already briefed my team on the information you gave me. Would you mind answering any further questions they may have?" she asked. "Certainly. Ask away." Kaarle said. The tall intellectual man began. "Are you really suggesting that we kill 100 babies by exploding von Verschuer's laboratory?" The Countess broke in; "Mister Wolf I am proposing to S.O.E. Branch in London that a joint mission be conducted to end Hitler's Secret Master Race Lebensborn Project. This unfortunately must by necessity include the destruction of everything in that evil place. I realize these fetuses were spawned from your sister diabolically without her knowledge, or permission and I regret they must be destroyed but this monstrous project is a crime against God, nature and humanity." She said. "I concur, but I do not want the baby she gave birth to before coming here killed. Although the fetuses were mass produced they contain life from my sister. I consider even pre-born life sacred. I hope with no small amount of anguish that what we propose to do is the right thing in God's eyes. How do you propose conducting the mission without unduly risking my sister's life?" Kaarle asked.

"Well there are two missions and an exfiltration. Mission one will be the rescue of your sister shortly before Mission two which is the demolition of that underground laboratory. It has to be so completely destroyed they must not be able to start all over again, however, if they do, next time we must make certain the world will know exactly what they are up to. In order to accomplish that at least one of our number must survive and reach London." Medussa said. "What sort of explosive will you use and how do you propose to get it down there? Kaarle asked. "Well, we have our hands on a few hundred pounds of TNT and some plastique as well.

We need to determine the re-supply schedule of the Liquid Oxygen and kidnap the regular delivery fellows for a brief while. My men will deliver instead blue cylinders packed with demolition material." She said. "My inside man cannot use the telephone, it's too dangerous, but when he sees them taking your sister to a room upstairs he will move a cactus plant from his desk to his window. That will be our sign that she is out of the laboratory. We will then send in two women dressed like nurses with lab slips which will give them an excuse to wheel her out in a wheel chair. We will have an ambulance waiting outside prepared to take her and the rest of us to an abandoned air strip. A captured S.O.E. plane we stole from the Luftwaffe will fly us all to London under R.A.F. escort once we cross over the Dutch border." she said.

"This will be my crowning mission. None of us will be safe when Hitler learns what was done to his precious eugenics program. Let us synchronize our watches. We believe your sister is only taken downstairs during her ovulation cycle so she could conceivably be brought back up at any time over the next few days. We must remain prepared to execute our plan at a moments notice." Medussa said.

The same man who asked a question earlier, now asked another question. "What if she gets moved sometime tonight. Will our demolitions be ready? Will the plane be waiting at the abandoned airstrip?" "Good questions." Medussa replied. "No. Consider the mission to commence a 24 hour stand by status as of twelve hundred hours tomorrow. That will give me time to coordinate our escape route with S.O.E., target our airplane and get my people started on preparing our demolitions in a warehouse I own not far from here. Any questions? Fine. We shall meet here one last time to launch the mission.

I will send a driver to pick you up Mister Wolf, so don't wander away from your hotel very far. Then we shall all only see Berlin again after the Nazis are defeated." Medussa said." Kaarle walked several blocks in the wrong direction just to be certain he had not been followed before returning to his hotel room. He wondered whether he made a major mistake in trusting Medussa with the fate of his sister and himself. He had never worked with her, or her team before. Things could go horribly wrong. On the other hand, they were locals. Medussa apparently was financially independent and other than intelligence support from S.O.E. Branch she could not have survived this long without some capabilities. She seemed to be cautious enough to reflect both professional experience and logical thinking. He didn't know how she might behave under combat circumstances but S.O.E. trusted her. As he saw it, he had no choice but to trust her too. Kaarle was relieved to discover after a few days that medals for heroism, even with the pomp and circumstance of being awarded by Hitler, himself, quickly faded from public attention. He received an invitation from von Verschuer's office to attend another ball next month, but for the most part Kaarle was left hanging without contact from anyone. His only worry would be sudden contact with someone from the Lebensborn Project but perhaps because of his award of the medal by Hitler, he had gained a few days before all Hell would break loose from several possible directions. In the meantime, he would only venture from his room to collect a newspaper and check his messages.

He knew when the moment came for the mission launch he would be collected in person but he always checked his message box anyway. He took all of his meals in his room and listened to Deutsche Wella the official war time radio network in Berlin.

He was always alert for the wrong knock on the door which he figured wouldn't be a knock at all, but instead the sound of someone crashing through with weapons at the ready.

Horst Feldner spent an anxious week under house arrest. Major Kraemer told him the arrest was merely protection if Himmler decided he wanted to follow up on his threats against Horst. Horst had access to a telephone and he called his protectors to let them know what had happened to him. His protectors had the ear of Hermann Goering.

When they explained what had happened to Goering he informed them that the Courier Captain had been awarded the German Cross personally by the Fuhrer and that if any decisions were made about the Captain that made Hitler seem foolish, they would all be hunted down and shot. Horst was beside himself with worry. Life just wasn't fair. He had only been trying to do his duty of verifying the young Captain's identity. Why should I be punished for being loyal? He wondered. Then it came to him. He would still do his duty even if he died in the service of the Fuhrer. He called his brother Aloise, who worked at the ball bearing factory Kugel Fischer in Schweinfurt. Aloise was a high level manager thanks to Horst. It would be nothing for him to visit the Weisner family. "Halo Aloise! Ja hier ist Horst. Aloise, listen carefully, I need for you to drive to Bad Brueckenau to visit a family Weisner." Horst said. "Horst you know I cannot do these things you do. You promised me." Aloise said.

"Just be quiet and listen. This is not an official business of the Gestapo, not yet at least. I want you to go there to congratulate the family Weisner that their brave son Hauptman Bernt Weisner was decorated in Berlin by the Fuhrer with the German Cross.

Ask them for their most recent photograph of him. If there is a choice, select one that is a full frontal view. Then drive the photo to Fulda. I will have a man waiting to fly it to me in Eindhoven. Aloise, this is a matter of life and death to me." Horst said sincerely. "Consider it done." Aloise said. He hung up the phone and told his secretary he was leaving early today.

When the parcel arrived in Eindhoven Horst was called by Major Kraemer. "Horst what are you up to? A parcel has arrived from Fulda. House arrest does not mean that you are conducting official business." The Major said. "Yes, I know Major Kraemer, but if you would be so kind as to open the parcel and tell me what you see, I would be most grateful. If it is nothing, I promise you I will conduct myself as a friar from now forward." Horst replied. Major Kraemer took out his dagger and slit the parcel open on one side. He shook the parcel until an 8 inch by 10 inch photo slid out. "I am looking at a photo of a German Captain taken last year. Why did this photo come to you Horst?" The Major asked with curiosity. "You mean you don't recognize Hauptman Weisner?" Horst said with excitement. "You mean the Courier? This photo is definitely not of the Courier!" "Bring it to me and we must decide together how best to proceed. I would be within my rights to have you arrested Major for interfering in an official Gestapo investigation but that would no doubt be embarrassing to Herr Himmler for which we would then both be punished." Horst considered. " I think the best direction in which to proceed is to have you call Herr Himmler and tell him we have irrefutable proof that the man who we both let go a few days ago is an imposter." Horst said. "Mein Lieber Gott!" The major groaned.

The young scientist working at the Institute under cover for Medussa, swallowed hard when he saw a nurse and two orderlies wheel Laila out of the special elevator. He quickly moved his cactus from his desk to the window and grabbed a folder to make it appear that he was on official business near the hallway. After he left another scientist who was allergic to plants in general moved the cactus back to the young scientist's desk.

The young scientist saw Professor von Verschuer walking in his direction so he turned and walked back to his cubicle. He nearly fainted when he saw the cactus sitting back on his desk. "Who moved this?" He asked. "I did. I have allergies." The other scientist complained. "Could I please leave it by the window just for a few minutes? It will die without at least a few sun rays." He said. The other scientist just scowled and busied himself with paper work. The young scientist returned to the hallway in the nick of time to see Laila being wheeled into the regular elevator. He ran up the stairs until he saw her being wheeled onto the fifth floor. He got the room number and returned immediately to his cubicle. He moved his cactus back to his desk and opened some files to appear engaged in work.

A tap came at Kaarle's door. It was the Intellectual who asked questions. He entered the room quickly. "Come with me now. There has been a slight change of plans. We will execute our assignments straight forth without a launch meeting." He said. "What happened?" Kaarle asked. "Something about some confusion with the cactus but it's on as soon as we can get there. Everyone is proceeding normally. I have the ambulance in the alley. We must go to it now and put on white medical uniforms." He said.

The young scientist watched as his two colleagues for whom he had made a wax impression of the special elevator key entered the clinic with four large blue cylinders marked "Liquid Oxygen." They wheeled their cart to the special elevator and soon disappeared. When they wheeled the cart into the lab one of the scientists called out. "What in the Hell are you doing here? Only special personnel have the authority to enter here. " he grumbled. "Sir, we were told you needed an emergency supply of Liquid oxygen. The other scientist hurried over to aid the first scientist in scolding the two workers. Suddenly the workers pulled knives and hastily slit the scientists throats.

They shoved their bodies into a corner, then placed their home made bombs at opposite ends of the laboratory and lit their five minute fuses. It seemed like an eternity until the elevator arrived. They wheeled their empty cart inside. When they exited the elevator they saw their two nurse colleagues wheel a mobile litter out through the front entrance. They helped the nurses load the litter and then they pulled their blue truck ahead of the ambulance that was being driven by the tall Intellectual. The women one of whom happened to be a genuine nurse attended Laila. Kaarle sat on the passenger side and loaded his sub-machine gun. The young scientist told his secretary that he had to visit the men's room. He walked straight out the front entry way and hopped in the back of the blue truck which held Medussa and her entire Resistance operations group. The ambulance and the blue truck sped away. The secretary became suspicious and called security. "What is the problem fraulein." They asked. She explained the strange behavior of the young scientist who said he was going to the men's room, but left in a blue oxygen delivery truck. "As a matter of fact, I saw earlier two oxygen delivery men take the special elevator without an escort."

She reflected. "Why didn't you call us then?" They asked. "Because since they had a key I thought they had authorization." She said defensively. "Do you have a key?" They asked. "No but my superior has one." She retrieved the key for the two Security agents who took the elevator down. They reached the 10th lower level just as the bombs went off with precision. The blast belched up through the elevator shaft with such force that it lifted the institution off its foundation and set it down sideways against a row of trees. Institute workers were walking in circles bleeding and dazed as emergency vehicles and people who happened to be nearby rushed to their aid.

"Halo, Herr Himmler. Guten Tag. Hier ist SS Major Kraemer, in Eindhoven, Holland." "Ja what is it Major? I am very busy." Himmler said gruffly. "Well it seems that with further investigation Herr Horst Feldner of the Gestapo and I discovered that the Courier Hauptman Bernt Weisner is an imposter. We suspect he is a spy who took away Hauptman Weisner's identity to use it to get to Berlin for a secret mission." Major Kraemer said. "What? Are you mad?" "No Sir!" "Can you prove this?" He asked. "Yes Sir! We have a photo provided by his mother in Bad Brueckenau that proves the man who flew to Berlin is not Hauptman Weisner." Before he could say another word an enormous explosion in the distance shook his office, breaking several windows. "Wait! My emergency line is ringing!" Himmler said. "Ja! Himmler hier wass ist passiert? What? Are you sure? Mein Gott! Ach du Lieberzeit!" "Let Me speak to the Gestapo agent." Himmler snapped. "Hier ist Feldner." "Listen to me carefully Feldner. Are you alone?" Himmler asked. Feldner shooed the Major into the next room. "I am alone now sir." Feldner reported. "Gut! I want you to lure the Major into a dark hangar and shoot him in the head." Himmler demanded. "But Sir he…"

"If you say another word I will fly in a team of Kommandos and have you both killed." "Yes Sir, I will take care of it right away." Feldner assured him. "Not a word of this to anyone. If you even tell your mother I will erase your entire family. Bring me the photo." Himmler said. "Sir, I am Gestapo. We do exactly as we are told." Feldner exclaimed. "Yes, I know this to be true. The Fuhrer decorated your imposter with the German Cross. Did you know that?" "Verdammt noch mal! Wirklich? Really Sir?" Feldner exclaimed. "It is even worse. The eugenics Clinic has just been destroyed by saboteurs who must have been working with the spy. Did you know that the fuhrer already decorated the schweinhundt with the Iron Cross?" Himmler said. "Mein Gott! Do we have any leads as to where to find him?" Feldner asked. "No. Get your ass to Berlin after you take care of the Major. Report only to me. We may need you to identify the spy." Himmler growled.

With the numerous bombing raids over Berlin it wasn't unusual to see the creamy white ambulances with red crosses driving chaotically, however, there were so many ambulances heading for the eugenics clinic this day that an ambulance heading the other way did indeed stand out. Soon they were surprised by an impromptu road block formed by a half track and two motorcycles with side cars. An SS Leutnant motioned for the ambulance to pull over. "Our patient is near death!" "So are you if you don't pull over!" The officer yelled. Kaarle slammed open the passenger door and rolled out of the ambulance cutting down the Officer and the driver of the half track with two short bursts of his sub-machine gun. The two motorcycle drivers dove behind the half track. Kaarle also dove down and sprayed both of them full of bullets.

Kaarle jumped on a motorcycle and pulled on the Leutnant's overcoat, grabbing a helmet he sped down the road, looking back only at intersections for directions from the ambulance driver whether to turn right, or left. When it became apparent no other road blocks stood between them and the airstrip, Kaarle ditched the motor cycle and jumped back in the ambulance. The Resistance nurse attending Laila looked distressed. "Is everything alright?" Kaarle asked. "I don't like her vital signs. Her pulse is thready and her blood pressure is low. I'm not sure she is fit enough to take an airplane ride to London." She said.

"Pull over along that row of warehouses." Kaarle ordered. Kaarle moved to the back of the ambulance. He lifted the sheet and saw that his sisters body was pasty white and her fingertips were slightly blue. His eyes teared at the thought that he had come so far only to lose her. Laila opened her eyes. From her point of view everything was a blur but then an indescribable sixth sense known only to twins kicked in. "Kaarle. Oh my God Kaarle it's you. You've come to rescue me like you promised me you would when we were children." She sobbed. "Rest my love. I'll get you out of Germany forever." He answered as he massaged her hand. "Are we still in Berlin?" She asked. "Yes but not for long." He replied.

Medussa entered the ambulance from the rear. "What's wrong? We don't have much time before they close the city!" She groaned. "She isn't stable. She shouldn't be flying until she is." The nurse volunteered. Medussa looked sympathetically down on Kaarle and Laila. "What do we do now?" she asked no one in particular. "You all leave. I will take my sister away from Berlin. If any of you are caught you will receive incredible torture for helping destroy their secret Lebensborn project." Kaarle said.

"You are right. Alright, listen. I will draw a quick map to an estate I own near Prague. I will also write a draft for several thousand Reich Marks you may cash at any Deutsche bank. There is a new Mercedes car there that is always full of petrol. There is food in the pantry to last a month. An old caretaker named Fritz will do anything you need him to do when you give him my signed note. Stay there with your sister until she is ready for travel. Then in Prague, make contact at this address. This resistance leader may be reached at a book store with a book shaped lantern in old Prague near the university. Ask for a biography of Beethoven that is a first edition. That is our code to reach the Czech Resistance leader. His code name is White Knight." "He will help get you further south to Tirol and Switzerland. Everyone move back with me to the blue truck. You stay here with your sister and drive the ambulance to a place where you can abandon it far from my safe house after you secure your sister there." She said. "Can I remain with them?" The nurse asked.

"Heavens no my child. They would butcher you slowly if they caught you." Medussa said. Take the extra fuel from our blue truck right now. You will need it to reach Prague." She told Kaarle. Medussa wrote the notes, drew the map to her safe house and signed a bank draft and shooed her people into the blue truck like a flock of chickens before a storm. "Go with God Medussa." Kaarle said as he re-loaded his sub-machine gun. "I would gladly do this but he hasn't been around here for quite some time." She replied.

Hermann Goering immediately grounded all air traffic within 500 miles of Berlin except for a squadron of Messerschmitts as soon as he received word that saboteurs had destroyed von Verschuer's Lebensborn laboratory and eugenics clinic.

The Messerschmitts patrolled at low level searching for any sign of unauthorized aircraft. Suddenly the sky was black with British and American bombers. S.O.E. had coordinated the timing of a bombing mission to aid Medussa's escape. When her blue truck pulled inside the large hangar her awaiting twin engine Halifax bomber was already revving its engines. The Resistance group quickly boarded the aircraft. As they taxied, a Messerschmitt appeared from nowhere to begin a strafing run on the departing plane. Before it could train its guns, two American Bomber escort P-51 Mustangs swooped in behind the Messerschmitt and drilled it until it exploded in an enormous fire ball. Medussa and her entire Resistance group would fly to London safely to sit out the war.

Kaarle used secondary highways and somehow managed to slip south before road blocks were established. He drove all night using the extra cans of fuel from Medussa's blue truck. He finally arrived at Medussa's estate. He was met by Fritz, Medussa's caretaker who helped Kaarle get Laila inside and tucked warmly in Medussa's favorite bed with down comforters. After some hot tea she began to get color back in her face. Fritz explained that this region was considered secure by the Nazis, who seldom patrolled it any longer. Prague was a different story. "Many Partisans there. The Nazis are there in heavy numbers too. They only come here to Karlovy Vary for the mineral baths." Fritz said. Fritz led Kaarle in Medussa's Mercedes, as Kaarle drove the ambulance several miles away to an abandoned slate mine. Kaarle drove the ambulance inside the mine and set it ablaze. When they returned Kaarle chopped wood for the fireplace. When the great room was heated he carried Laila to a large sofa and spoon fed her soup that Fritz prepared. "It's like a dream to me that you're here Kaarle." Laila said softly. "Please never let them take me away again Kaarle." She sobbed.

Kaarle's eyes filled with tears. "No one could ever do that again Laila. I promise you." Kaarle choked on the words. "Tell me of papa." She said. "He was made a Colonel in the Finnish Ski Troops Laila. I wasn't there but he received many medals for his courage against the Russians. The Russians executed him in Stalingrad." Kaarle's voice trailed off. "Kaarle when things were horrible, as it was when they took away my husband Arin, or when I was raped, Tarja came to me and carried me on her back to look for you. Every time I saw the Milky Way, or saw a picture of a Reindeer I was with you Kaarle." Kaarle's tears fell as he held his beloved sister Laila in his arms. He was grateful that she didn't mention his childhood promise never to let anyone harm her. He felt personally responsible for everything they did to her and it ripped his heart in two.

He felt like telling her that he had killed the rapist quite by coincidence but he sensed that it may only burden her more so he kept silent about Colonel von Braunschweig her baby's natural father. Laila brought up the baby, however when she described how she suffered when they took it from her. Kaarle burned with anger. "Do you have any clue about what they did with your baby?" He asked. "Oh Roland is probably still at the Lebensborn clinic in Oslo. Because he has my genes they wanted to keep him for further documented studies." "Laila I promise you, I will do everything possible to get your baby back and now that we are here, why leave without being sure that Arin is alive, or dead.?" "Oh Kaarle. You have grown up to be a man like Papa." Laila said as she drifted off to sleep in her brother's arms. Kaarle watched the snow flakes fall outside the large bay window. For a brief moment as he felt his sister's heart beat near his own he felt they were home safe and sound before his father's fireplace.

Horst couldn't believe his luck. One minute he expected to be assassinated by Major Kraemer on the orders of "Herr Gott In Himmel" Himmler and now it was he who would be the assassin and Kraemer the victim. He knew better than to argue with fate and switched the safety lever to the firing position as he held his 9 millimeter in his coat pocket. "What did Himmler want? Major Kraemer asked. "He wants us to confirm that our hangar has not been broken into. Do you have the keys to the side door? We can enter from there and then check the perimeter from the inside." Horst said. "Hangar broken into? Is he insane?" The Major exclaimed.

"Just following orders. Who knows what Himmler is thinking at any moment in time." Horst shrugged. As the Major bent over to get a closer look at the key slot, Horst pulled and fired. He aimed at the back of the Major's head but the slug entered the Major's right shoulder blade, tearing out a part of his lung and fracturing his ribs. It crippled the Major's right arm. He instinctively reached across his waist with his left hand to retrieve his own 9 millimeter but by then Horst moved closer and put a round behind the Major's left ear.

When Horst Feldner was escorted into Heinrich Himmler's office by a comely young secretary, a meeting and briefing by Ernst Kaltenbrunner, head of the Geheime Staatspolizei, or Gestapo, was just concluding. The room was cleared of everyone except Himmler, Kaltenbrunner and Feldner. Kaltenbrunner remained silent but his piercing eyes scanned Feldner from his tired face to the dirty slush on his shoes. "So! Herr Himmler informs me that you first questioned an imposter who was somehow able to be decorated by the Fuhrer with our nation's highest honor, the German Cross nicht wahr?" "Yes, Herr Director Kaltenbrunner.

I was immediately suspicious, but Major Kraemer influenced Herr Himmler to believe that the man was not an imposter and should be allowed to fly on to Berlin. As soon as I learned of this unforgivable act I killed Major Kraemer as an enemy of the Fatherland." "Is this right? You killed the only other witness?" Kaltenbrunner asked with suspicion.

"I ordered Kraemer's death for his traitorous act Kaltenbrunner now let us proceed with everything we know since Kraemer's unforgivable mistake." Himmler said. "Of course Herr Himmler. "Kaltenbrunner said, changing the subject. "We have learned that the imposter of Hauptman Weisner stayed in his room eating like a rat, not coming out to do much more than check his messages. His only other human contact that we are able to verify was the Fuhrer, Dr. von Verschuer, who he delivered important documents to and five women he danced with at the Berliner ball." Kaltenbrunner recounted. "There it is Kaltenbrunner! Bring me these five women. One was his contact in Berlin!" Himmler shrieked. "Most likely either the leader of a pack of assassins or at least high in their chain of command." Himmler said.

"We located four so far. Their cover stories all seem quite proper at this point." Kaltenbrunner remarked. "And the fifth?" "Almost too incredible to consider. The trusted advisor to the Fuhrer, Graefin von Neustadt." Kaltenbrunner reflected. "What? Graefin von Neustadt? Are you certain?" Himmler coughed incredulously. "She was the first to dance with him at the ball. We have checked everywhere. She is nowhere to be found. " Kaltenbrunner said. "One of our road blocks was breached shortly after the explosion at the clinic. It was on a road that leads to an abandoned airstrip. We found a blue oxygen delivery truck in the hangar and evidence that an aircraft recently received maintenance was also found there.

A survivor of the explosion reports seeing two men arrive in a blue truck to deliver oxygen cylinders shortly before the explosion. The blue truck obviously was also used as a get away vehicle after the crime." Kaltenbrunner said. "We must make a joint report to the Fuhrer this evening at his bunker. Do you have the photo Feldner?" "Yes sir! Here it is." Feldner said. Himmler took the photo and studied it for a while. "So this is the real Hauptman Weisner." Himmler mumbled. "Yes Sir! He is probably buried somewhere in Norway. That's where the imposter began his journey." Feldner replied.

"I want an urgent report sent to all offices of the Reich, to be on the look out for a man impersonating a German Captain with a young woman in poor health as an accomplice." Himmler commanded. "Right away Sir!" Feldner barked."I will make my recommendation to the Fuhrer that the scoundrels responsible for this be hanged on sight. Keep looking although it is sadly apparent they escaped from under our noses immediately after their heinous crime against the Fatherland." Himmler growled. "Do you know whether von Verschuer escaped the explosion?" Himmler asked Kaltenbrunner. "Yes, but he is despondent. He can only whimper about how his life's work was lost and that it is impossible to start over. That the two scientists who unlocked the DNA code died in the blast along with all of their notes." Kaltenbrunner lamented. "GODDAMN HIM!" Himmler shouted. "How many times did I tell the old fool to have everything photographed and duplicates recorded in case of a disaster such as this one? He believed ten levels beneath the ground was all of the protection he needed. The old foolish bastard! I want all of the family members of Graefin von Neustadt arrested.

Arrest all of her acquaintances as well. One of them knows of her involvement with the Resistance Movement and possibly where the airplane took the traitorous bitch. " Himmler concluded. Horst Feldner led the raids against Graefin von Neustadt's family and friends and had them tortured, but none would, or could, devulge any information at all. It was only when Horst began going over her bank accounts nearly two weeks after the Institute had been destroyed that he hit pay dirt. A bank draft had been made to an account of a Fritz Becker in a large sum over six months ago. The bank was in Prague. Horst anxiously called Himmler with the good news. "Horst if you catch these traitors you will be made an assistant to Kaltenbrunner himself!" Himmler promised. "I will leave now for Prague and investigate this Fritz Becker." He said. "Yes. I want to have a daily report on your progress in this matter!" Himmler demanded.

Exactly ten days after arriving at Karlovy Vary Laila was on her feet making breakfast for Kaarle and Fritz who hunted daily for their food. Snow hares, squirrels and partridge made up the daily menu. One day, Kaarle brought down a large buck and they fashioned a sled from branches to drag him home. They quartered the carcass of the deer and hung the sections of venison in the cellar to cure. On the twelfth day Kaarle decided it was time to visit the book store in Altstadt Prague. Kaarle marveled at the beauty of the Karl's Kirchen twin spires and the ancient bridge that led to the Altstadt. He parked the Mercedes in an alley and walked across the Karl's Bruecke. The Saints that lined the sides of the bridge seemed to stare at him with warnings on their faces.

When he saw the book store he pretended to be looking for his way. When he didn't see anything unusual, he wandered in and asked a bookish looking woman if she had any first edition biographies of Ludwig von Beethoven. The woman looked down at first to gather herself and then answered; "No. They were sold out months ago." She said. "When would you recommend that I check again? He said. "Well, after the war?" She replied sadly. No one else was in the store.

"Look it is a matter of life and death. I must meet with the White Knight." Kaarle said with desperation. The woman looked shocked. "He is dead." She replied. "When?" Kaarle asked. "This morning. They…. She began to cry. "They shot him. He was informed on by a bank manager. The bank manager was tortured. He gave them the name of the White Knight and also the name of a man named Fritz Becker. The bank manager didn't know where Becker lives so they are going door to door to find him. "Will the White Knight's trail lead them here to you.?" "No. The White Knight had a business in the center of Prague. He never came here, we always went to him when someone such as yourself gave us the password phrase. Are you Fritz Becker?" She asked. "No. The less you know the better off you will be." He said. "Yes, I know. I just wanted to warn him that the ones who are hunting him are Gestapo." She said. "Yes, I know." He turned to leave. "Wait." she cried out. Here is the address of Vaclev. His code name is Spider. He owns a trucking business that transports chickens to distant places. The White Knight used him to transport Jewish refugees escaping to Switzerland. Be careful, perhaps the banker may give him up too if he knows about him." she warned.

"Thank you!" Kaarle said as he walked carefully outside. He crossed the bridge and headed back to the car. He had to move fast to get Laila and Fritz as far away from this place as possible. Kaarle found Spider's business and walked in as Vaclev was loading chicken crates. He looked frightened. "Vaclev, I am a friend of the White Knight." Kaarle said. "That sounds like crazy talk to me. Who are you?" Vaclev asked nervously. "I know you are called Spider. I also know the Gestapo is looking for myself, my sister and Fritz Becker. You are code named Spider and you are our only hope of getting to the Tirol. We need to get to Switzerland before we are found and tortured." Kaarle said. "Who gave you my name? Whomever they are they are lying. Go away or I shall report you to the Germans myself." He growled.

"I can understand your fear Spider, but it is keeping you from thinking properly. It doesn't matter who gave you to me because you already have a serious interest in my safety. Do you think if you send me away and they capture me that you will be safe? When they apply the fire, or electricity, or nearly drown me in my own urine that I will not use you to gain a few more moments of life without pain?" Kaarle said. "What do you want from me?" Spider asked. "Just hide us the way you have hidden the Jewish refugees. I will pay you for your benzin and for your troubles." Kaarle said. "F--ck you and your money too. You think I risk my life for your money? I piss on your money. I do this because my wife is a Jew and so far no one but you, her and I know this because they already killed her entire family. She was away at University in Bologna, or they would have killed her too!" He said angrily. Vaclev eyed Kaarle carefully and weighed the wisdom of his words. This man was experienced he thought. A soldier, or a spy. "What choice do I have?" he thought. "When do you wish to leave?" Vaclev asked.

"I must return by car to Karlovy Vary to pick up my two others." Kaarle replied. "Good. On the way here from Karlovy Vary you passed the Black Boar Inn. It is at the intersection of the main road that leads to Muenchen and Vienna. Be there at twenty thirty hours. If you are even one minute late the deal is off." "I will park in the back with my chicken truck. There is a crawl space and a small compartment concealed in the flooring of my truck. Dress warmly. Bring no suitcases. There is no room. If we are caught we will all be shot. If there are Nazi vehicles parked at the Black Boar proceed instead in the direction of Muenchen. Five kilometers along the main road you will see a truck turnout. I will be waiting there instead, but try the Black Boar first. "Thank you Spider." Kaarle said. "Thank me if we make it." Vaclev answered. Kaarle glanced back at Vaclev who had buried his face in his trembling hands.

Had the Gestapo managed to break someone who knew where Fritz lived? He tried to suppress images of Fritz and Laila being tortured in the cellar but he couldn't shut them out. He recalled quartering the deer and hanging the sections on the meat hooks. The images now created a feeling of panic because of Laila's vulnerability. He made it back to the estate in record time and ran inside to see Laila sipping tea. Fritz was outside chopping firewood. He called Fritz into the house and explained to both Fritz and Laila that they needed to dress warmly. "Borrow some things from the Graefin von Neustadt. Pack no bags and hurry. We don't have much time." Kaarle poured a bucket of water on the fire in the stove and the fireplace. "I don't want them to guess how close they are behind us." He said. He poured out the pot of tea in the sink.

"Herr Kaarle, I appreciate your concern but I am a simple farmer. Surely they will understand this. I cannot leave the Graefin's house unprotected. She would never forgive me." Fritz said. "Fritz, I will not force you to come with us, you are still a man of free will, but how many estates do you think the Graefin owns?" Kaarle asked. "Oh many to be certain." He answered. "Well two weeks ago she left them all including this one and she won't be back to visit them until the war is over. The people who are coming will cut off your fingers until they think you are no longer holding information and then they put a ball in your brain. What use will it be to the Graefin if you remain here and get tortured to death." Kaarle asked. "Not much I suppose." Fritz answered. "The Gestapo is only coming here because they think you know where the Graefin is." Kaarle said patiently. "They tracked you with the money she transferred to Prague for your maintenance, the way we tracked the rabbits and the deer from where they feed." Kaarle said with finality. He took Laila by the hand and walked toward the barn where the Mercedes was parked. "Kaarle we can't leave him here." She shouted. Suddenly there was a loud explosion with towering flames that burst through the windows and licked to the roof. Fritz emerged from the black smoke and turned to take one last look at his home for the last half century. "Graefin von Neustadt is a lady. She would never have forgiven me if I left her private things for them to put their nasty fingers on." He said.

Kaarle hid away on a small trail in a heavy pine forest until thirty minutes before rendezvous time. He pulled slowly toward the main road and quickly used his hand brake to stop so as not to trigger his brake lights as he saw two staff cars whizzing by followed by two Nazi jeeps. The staff cars were using police flashing lights to clear possible traffic. There was no room for doubt. The Gestapo had broken someone.

They were Hell bent for leather to rush to
Medussa's estate.   Within twenty minutes Kaarle was pulling
into the Black Boar Inn parking lot. He had his lights off as he
circled around to the back. Sitting in the shadows, as
promised was Vaclev's chicken truck. Vaclev leaned inside the
driver window of the Mercedes. "If you need to use the bath
room I'm afraid you must go quickly there in the bushes. You
will find a large bottle of water inside the compartment but sip
it slowly, or you will have to piss it away on yourselves. If this
becomes necessary there is a hole in the floor of the
compartment and use it only when the truck is traveling down
the highway. Once the door to the crawl space is latched it
won't be opened again until we are in the Tirol." Vaclev said.
"How long will that be? Kaarle asked. "Two days and nights
maybe less depending on how many road blocks we
encounter. Don't be afraid of the strange odor you smell. It is a
mixture of vinegar and bleach to put off the scenting dogs.
There is an adequate air supply from a radiator hose I have
piped into the compartment. Of course you will smell chicken
manure but that cannot be helped." Vaclev shrugged.

"Don't light matches, or candles. The fumes
might explode. Vaclev said. Kaarle gave Vaclev the keys to
the Mercedes. "You can re-paint it and perhaps sell it if you'd
like." Kaarle said. "We will burn it and bury it so they cannot
trace it to us." Vaclev said. They climbed out of the Mercedes
and under instructions from Vaclev they crawled across the
card board on their backs until they reached the small portal.
The compartment was a square metal box that was sound
proof. They had to clear their nose and ears to equalize the
pressure. The floor was carpeted and as Vaclev had
promised, a stream of fresh air came in through the vent
formed by the radiator hose, however, the odor Vaclev
described was thick and nauseating.

Even Kaarle felt squemish when they heard the metalic finality of the steel latch slam together. The combination of vinegar and bleach was overwhelming. Laila suddenly began to scream. "I must get back out of here Kaarle. I feel as if I am in a coffin." She gasped. "Here my love. Feel this along the wall? It is the air vent Vaclev described. Put your face just here and I will hold you. Lay back against me and close your eyes. I want you to pretend you are flying on the back of Tarja to the Milky way. Kaarle sang sweet Finnish childrens songs to her until she fell asleep in his arms." The compartment was as quiet as a tomb and pitch black.

"Are you alright Fritz?" "I am fine Sir." Fritz replied. They felt the bumps and the G force when the truck took heavy curves but after a while they lost all concept of direction. The mind played tricks on their ability to discern up from down, but after Kaarle advised raising ones arm and then letting it drop it was possible from the direction it fell to temporarily discern up from down once more. Finally after losing concept of time but what seemed an eternity they heard the latch being opened. Their legs were numb and they moved slowly toward the portal through the crawl space. Laila was first, followed by Kaarle. When they were out and crawling on the card board toward the side of the truck, Kaarle noticed that Fritz was not with them. He crawled back and again entered the compartment. He found Fritz' neck in the dark but couldn't detect a pulse.Kaarle dragged Fritz backward through the crawl space and then pulled him down through the portal and from beneath the truck. His eyes were wide open and blood shot but his face was jet black. The corner Fritz lied in was the furthest away from the air vent.

He suffocated sometime during the first twenty four hours of the trip without as much as a whimper, or a complaint. Kaarle buried Fritz in the snow and embraced Laila. "Thank you Vaclev." Kaarle said. "I'm sorry about your friend. I have had entire Jewish families in there and this is the first time anyone died." He said apologetically. "He was getting old Vaclev. Never forget, thanks to you at least he died a free man." Kaarle said. Kaarle looked at the magnificent mountain ranges in the distance. "You see that Cornice just there?" Vaclev asked. "Yes." Kaarle said. "Well try to stay to the right of it and you will find a valley that extends all the way to the Swiss border. It looks close from here, but it's about a three day hike with snow shoes. Follow this trail until it comes to a dead end. Keep going straight on and you will come to a small log cabin. You will find fire wood and matches in the kitchen. Stay as long as you wish, but please replace the water from the mountain stream in the jug you will find in the kitchen and use the axe to gather more firewood before you leave. There are four sets of telemark skis and snow shoes. I hope you find some that fit. There are several sets of snow shoes. I will replace them on my way back through. Use them to trek through the mountains and stay safe. Watch out for German ski patrols when you pass beyond the Cornice." Vaclev said. "Shalom Vaclev." Kaarle said. Vaclev looked surprised at first.

"Are you Jewish?" He asked. "Since right now? Absolutely yes!" Kaarle replied. Laila gave Vaclav a hug and in a few minutes they could hear his engine roaring as he down shifted to negotiate a steep decline down the narrow mountain road. Kaarle and Laila stumbled and rolled through the snow until they soon reached the log cabin. It was sparse. Probably built for Forest Meisters who were responsible for paring back the forests and regulating the trout and wild game. It had a pot bellied stove which Kaarle immediately kindled.

The wood in the bin was filled with too much pitch filled young Pine. Kaarle didn't want clouds of smoke hovering in the sky above the cabin so he went out and gathered drier older wood which would burn cleaner. There was one large bed with old and rotting blankets. The food was mainly dried foods and spices. After a grueling two days in a cold metal coffin Kaarle worried about Laila's health. Their imperative not to remain too long in one spot was weighed against Laila's need to rest and build up her strength for the Telemark trek they were about to embark upon. Kaarle decided that if Laila's health improved, they would continue their journey to Switzerland within three days. Four pairs of Telemark skis with wooden poles were in a hand made rack by the door. Kaarle selected the best ones for Laila and himself but after considering Laila's weakness he strapped her skis to a sapling frame he made into a sled.

He hunted rabbits with a bow and arrows he made from leather boot laces he found in the cabin and a strong, flexible, sapplings he found in the forest. He whittled arrows and grooved them with his knife to tightly accept the chopped chicken feathers he scooped up from Vaclev's truck. He found some empty shell casings on the floor of the cabin. Holes in the wall suggested there had been a shoot out not long ago. He forced the casings onto the arrow tips and used an edge of the iron stove top and the flat side of an axe to beat the casings into a point. He could have used his 9 millimeter to shoot game but he was concerned about who the sound may attract as well as a high probability of starting an avalanche. He made Laila some herbal tea from bark and winter berries he knew not to be poisonous. Then he left with the bow to shoot a rabbit for a nice stew.

He was able to find a pair of curved toe ski shoes for the Telemark journey. He skied to a small copse that gave him a commanding view of the expansive meadow below. He built a snow igloo with a dead pine roof. The pine made his little wall of packed snow look like a natural part of the landscape. He saw a pair of snow hares romping in the center of the meadow. He knew them to be beyond the range of his bow so he patiently waited for them to draw nearer. Suddenly they scattered and ran toward the forest. "Damn! He thought. "What spooked them?

"Then he saw them. A four man German Ski recon patrol. They were headed toward the cabin. No doubt with intentions to rest there until the next day. They carried carbines strapped diagonally across their backs as typically ski soldiers do. He estimated they would pass within fifty meters of his blind within two minutes. He crawled out of the blind and readied his bow and arrows then placed them near the snow blind. He covered them with some branches from the pine. As he had been taught in Finland he burrowed into the snow bank from the opposite side of his kill zone and punched a small hole to observe. The German ski patrol was perspiring from having traveled all night and were just thinking about drying out and getting some much needed sleep. Kaarle watched as they skied past. As soon as they were a few meters beyond, he slipped into his skis and came within ten meters of the last man in the column. He drew as far back as possible and let his arrow fly. It entered at the base of the soldiers skull severing his spinal cord. He repeated another arrow shot with the third man who also immediately lost control of his legs and fell silently to the wayside. The second man however, happened to look over his shoulder to see the man fall with Kaarle close behind still aiming his bow.

The man yelled out to the patrol leader as he tried to twist his carbine to the front. He fell on his back trapping the carbine in the snow beneath him. Kaarle didn't even stop to fire. He shot the man in the center of his forehead as he skied past.   The lead man skied frantically off trail and put his Telemark skis into a straight down the mountain direction. Kaarle was close behind. The man tried to twist his carbine around but lost his balance tumbling head over heels down the mountain side. Kaarle didn't want to risk an avalanche by using his pistol. He removed his Fiskar knife and drew it so deep across the man's throat it nearly beheaded him. Kaarle took two knapsacks from the Patrol. Inside each was an insulated sleeping bag, some energy snacks and ammunition. He took a carbine and all of the extra clips from all four knapsacks. Then to his delight he found two fresh white camouflage outer shells. The ones the ski patrol was wearing were soaked in blood.

Kaarle and Laila would wear them and remain nearly invisible especially as the snow was falling. Kaarle carefully buried each man in snow banks and used the dead pine to sweep away his own tracks. As he skied back to the cabin he collected his bow and shot a pheasant to prepare for their dinner meal. Kaarle knew that when the Ski Patrol failed to make their next rendezvous point within a day, or two, other patrols would appear to back track and discover what had taken place here. He shortened his departure to two days. He used the boot laces he removed from the Germans to further stabilize weak joints on the sled he built to drag Laila . "Why were you gone so long Kaarle?" Laila asked. "Oh I saw a German patrol but they went the other way." He said. "Will they come here Kaarle? She asked. "No. They seemed quite in a hurry to head in another direction." He said.

"I'm afraid I will hold you back Kaarle." Laila said. "Shhhhhh. Let's not hear that sort of talk anymore. You are the only reason I am here. We will take as long as we wish to make it to the Switzerland." Kaarle assured her. On the next night the snow began to fall in large feather like flakes. Kaarle knew this would be a perfect time to leave. Their tracks would be covered by the fresh snow making them very difficult to track. Laila slept all day while Kaarle kept alert for new German patrols. "Laila, I'm afraid we must leave soon." Kaarle said. "That's good Kaarle I have been feeling bad premonitions today. I think to stay here longer would be a drastic mistake." She said. "You have been feeling this too?" Kaarle asked.

He marveled that twins really were connected in a psychic sort of way. They dressed in their warm clothing with their snow white shells. Kaarle put their knapsacks on the pine sled. Before he began to ski toward the Cornice Kaarle tied a long rope around Laila's waist and then tied it to himself in the case of a white out, or in case the trail gave way near the cliff edges beside the trail. The pine sled was very light and served the purpose of sweeping away their ski tracks which were being covered as well by the thick falling snow flakes, but if it veered over the cliff Kaarle knew he couldn't hold the sled as well as Laila.

Kaarle skied all night and watched the glory of an Alpine sunrise as a gentle breeze of progress caressed their faces. At times the trail many others had taken before them came to unnatural and tragic ends. The depth of the valleys below reached distances of a mile or more, but Laila and Kaarle were Snow people and Snow people instinctively knew when to ski and when to stop. After two nights and a day the Cornice was behind them and the trail disappeared.

It was then that Laila, weak from the physical stress and the effects of the sub-zero temperatures agreed to continue laying down on the pine branch sled. Kaarle covered her with both sleeping bags one under and one over. He pulled her along narrow ledges that defied gravity. Finally when only a true mountain man could know it he reached the peak. There remained only the treacherous descent and sudden dangers of negotiating the down hill trek with hidden ice chasms that offered depths of a thousand feet.

His exertion increased on the downward slope to keep the pine sled from flying over a ledge to the distant valley below. Just when Kaarle began to question his own senses he saw them. A German Ski Patrol of twelve Skiers headed in his direction at maximum speed across a slanted slope with layers of fresh powder. They skied frantically to reach him and he wondered why they felt a need to hurry, they already had him served on a platter. They would soon reach Kaarle and Laila and the extra burden of bringing them under arrest would be so dangerous on this mountain that it was clear they would merely overwhelm Kaarle and cut his and his sister's throats to avoid the noise that may start an avalanche. "An avalanche." Kaarle thought. He unstrapped the carbine he took from the previous Germans and aimed at the crown of the snow peak above him. He let forth a series of short bursts and one minute before the German Ski patrol would have arrived the entire side of the mountain came down. Kaarle lost the pine sled immediately as the tonnage of snow released itself from its attachments along the slope. Kaarle could see the shock on the German Ski soldiers faces as they were devoured by the roar of the swiftly moving snow. Kaarle was tied to Laila and the rope held.

He was buried in darkness and didn't know which way was up until he forced his right hand to his face and spit to see which way the saliva rolled from his lips. It rolled into his nose so he knew that he was upside down. He wriggled until he could push with his knees and kick with his feet.

Fortunately, he was between large clusters of snow and was able to fight his way to the air above. When he reached fresh air he pulled and pulled on the rope until he could grasp Laila's hair which he used to pull her head to open air. She gasped and sobbed at the same time. They were alive and they had both been reborn from one of the most horrible experiences Mother Nature had in her arsenal of death.

Kaarle half carried and half dragged his sister until they reached a trail that led to the valley below. He knew that if they were still in Austria they would be turned over to the Gestapo immediately. Either way, Kaarle realized that any further endeavor would automatically kill Laila. He was ready to throw himself at the mercy of the Nazis when he staggered to a farm house door and begged for help. He soon discovered they were not just in Switzerland but had been even when the last German Patrol had attempted to capture them. Laila was safe. Kaarle broke down when it became apparent to him that without any uncertainty no one would ever harm her again. Laila spent a few days in a Canton hospital and Kaarle rented a small flat with two bedrooms which he got ready for Laila's release. The Swiss diplomat who began their application for political asylum assured them that it would just be a matter of days before they would be granted asylum.

Kaarle managed to get word back to Erik through an S.O.E. contact in Bern that he and Laila had escaped into Switzerland within weeks after the secret clinic in Berlin had been destroyed. He sent a request to S.O.E. in London for an extraction of only his sister from Switzerland to London. "Please tell Elina I will be coming home soon but not without Arin. Elina sent back a letter describing how good the life was in a free London in spite of the bombing. She promised Kaarle that she would take care of Laila until he returned. Laila didn't mention it a single time but Kaarle never forgot his promise to find Arin for a second. He took time to heal his wounds from the frost bite of his ear lobes but kept busy studying maps of Auschwitz and the escape routes from Poland. He would find him. He broke one promise to Laila and he would never break another.

He trained every day as though he were still with the Ski Soldiers in Finland. He thought every minute about Elina. When he read of Hitler's V-2 rockets he cringed. If anything happened to Elina he would be forever devastated this he knew without discussing it. "How did you meet Arin?" He asked Laila. I want to know everything about him." He said. "Please Kaarle, Arin is dead. It hurts me too much to even think of him." She said. She reflected a moment and gasped. "My God you intend to go back into the nightmare." she exclaimed. "He'd do the same for me I'm sure." Kaarle said. "That's crazy Kaarle. No one ever escapes the Death Camps." She said with a pained expression. "Then it's time someone tried!" Kaarle exclaimed. Kaarle arranged to meet secretly with the S.O.E. agent on a bus, per Erik's instructions. Erik informed Kaarle that the agent's code name would be Falcon. They got off the bus separately and both walked to a small café. Falcon put his hand inside his jacket pocket and aimed the muzzle of his weapon at Kaarle's chest.

"Where did you receive your commission?" He asked. Kaarle responded that it was in a small church in the wilderness on the way to Suomoussalmi, Finland. "You can put your safety on." Kaarle grinned. "Yes, quite. It's indeed a pleasure to finally meet you Wolf. You have become something of a legend with the boys back in London." Falcon said. "Glad to meet you too." Kaarle said. "We have a Swiss aircraft that will leave Bern at fourteen hours tomorrow for London. We'd like for both you and your sister to be on that plane. You will be issued British passports on the plane. You have both been granted British citizenship based on your bravery against the Nazis. The King of Norway wants to meet you at the airport in London." Falcon said.

Falcon reached a .45 caliber pistol to Kaarle beneath the table. "It's an extra." "But the Swiss are so peaceful." Kaarle replied with a smile. "Kaarle the Nazis are conducting an international manhunt for your sister. Somehow a Dr. von Verschuer believes she is the purest Aryan alive and they want her badly. Switzerland is crawling with Gestapo who would not hesitate to kill anyone in Switzerland who tries to stop them from getting her back." Falcon said. "Have you had any discussions with anyone since you arrived?" Falcon asked. "Just the diplomat who made us fill out an application for asylum." Kaarle said. "What? Asylum?" "Yes." Kaarle said. "Without it he said they would simply have their border patrol take us to their nearest border." Kaarle said. "Goddamnit! Let's go. We may not have much time." Falcon said.

As they left the café a dark sedan with it's head lights off crawled slowly to Falcon's location. They jumped inside. "Number 6 Heilbrunnerstrasse!" Kaarle shouted. "Hurry!" Falcon added. In minutes they were at the Land Haus where Kaarle and Laila were staying.

The door was wide open. Two Gestapo agents were running with Laila thrown over the lead mans shoulder as they hurried to reach their car. Kaarle and Falcon leaped out and drew their weapons. "Don't fire! You may hit Laila. "Kaarle shouted. The lead Gestapo agent was nearly at his sedan when Falcon's driver raced forward smashing into the Gestapo man's sedan. The Lead Gestapo man dropped Laila on the ground and took aim at Falcon. Kaarle shot first and dropped the man where he stood. The other tried to run but Falcon took an arm supported bead and shot the man dead.

"Put her in the car." Falcon ordered. "We can't wait until tomorrow. That plane leaves tonight!" He said. "How did they know where to find us?" Kaarle shouted. "The Gestapo has the Swiss government more infiltrated than the cheese they put holes in." he replied. On the way to the airport Falcon wrote down an address near Zurich. "Are you sure you won't leave with your sister? How will you get to Auschwitz?" Falcon asked. "I can't live without at least giving it a shot. How will I get there? By becoming conspicuously Jewish if needed." Kaarle said. Falcon wanted to discuss Kaarle's plans in more detail but he knew he had to concentrate on getting Laila safely out of Switzerland so he simply filed it away. "Alright then. Once you find Arin you'll need to get him and yourself out. This is the address of a safe house in the Zurich suburbs. The man you will meet is known as Sorcerer. He will provide you with his underground connections. There is a resistance movement in Poland but it is on its last legs from massive starvation. I would guess that you will be on your own and walking straight into Hell but I won't digress any further." Falcon said. Laila was sobbing. "There, there, Laila." Kaarle comforted her. Soon you'll be safe in London." He said. "I'm not crying for me, I'm just afraid Arin is dead and that they will take you too. Then I will be completely alone." She cried.

"I won't go down easily Laila you know that." Kaarle said. After Kaarle saw Laila safely to the plane and watched her plane disappear, Falcon drove him to the train station. He gave him some extra clips for the .45 caliber and watched his train leave bound for Zurich. "Stay safe Wolf. I'd like to have a pint with you when you make it back." Falcon said. "Just one? I'm buying for what you did to save my sister tonight." Kaarle smiled back. "That's what they pay me for." Falcon smiled back.

Chapter Nine: Descendance Into Hell

Kaarle made his way from the Hauptbahnhof Central train Station of Zurich to the cobble stone streets of its old city. He found the small Gasthof that Falcon had given him the address of and went inside. He sat near the fire. No food was available other than a potato soup with more soup than potatoes inside. The soup was included once daily as a part of the price of a room. "Is the owner here?" Kaarle asked. "And who might you be?" She asked. "I'm an old friend of his." Kaarle lied. "I know most of my father's friends and I've never seen you before." She snapped.

"Yes. You're very sharp. I'm a friend of a friend who is in need of a Sorcerer to get out of his troubles." The girl looked around. No other customers were within ear shot. "I see. When you finish your meal walk back to the end of the hallway. Before you reach the door turn left and go down the stairs. He will be waiting for you in his private chambers. "Thank you." Kaarle said.

Sorcerer was a slight man. Almost frail. Balding with a moustache he could have passed for a Librarian, or a school teacher. The lines on his face and the suspicious expression resident in his eyes, however, told a much different story. As an Hassidic Jew, he had lost countless relatives and friends to the Nazi genocide machine at Auschwitz. His birth as a Swiss citizen had been the only thing that kept him from the ovens. He kept an incredibly expansive and detailed record of Nazi crimes against humanity which he intended to provide to the emerging international authority after the war was concluded. "Please sit down Mister Wolf." Sorcerer said.

"How may I be of service to you?" He asked. "That depends on the strength of your contacts. Since you already know my code name I assume S.O.E. Branch in London told you to expect me. How much has S.O.E Branch told you about me and what I intend to do?" He asked. "Both a little and I suppose a lot." Sorcerer replied. " I admit I was skeptical and still am about your stated mission. You do know that our underground systems were designed to infiltrate, not exfiltrate the concentration camps? The other part, which I must confess has been giving me the most trouble is the fact you are from Finland. Your country has been fighting side by side with the Nazis against the Soviets in what is called the "Russian Front' since 1941. It has only been your own active combat against the Germans in a region of Norway as well as the mission against the Hydrolelectric Plant near Telemark that got you this far within my coils." Sorcerer said matter of factly. "Did you know in fact that Auschwitz was patterned somewhat after your Finnish prison in Petrozavodsk? This prison that serves the needs of your Finnish Army which occupies East Karelia in conjunction with the Nazi invasion against Russia known as Operation Barbarossa?" Sorcerer said matter of factly. "Your people had about 6,000 Russian Army prisoners and 3,000 ethnic Russian refugees from the Svir River region incarcerated there. 4,000 of your Russian Army prisoners starved to death within a year. Your own country does not have clean hands in this sordid affair I am afraid." Sorcerer said bluntly. Kaarle buried his face in his hands and then looked the Sorcerer straight in his eyes."This is the first I have heard of this information. I confess it shames me deeply. I fought in the Winter War against the overwhelming Soviet invasion and I fought in the initial stages against the Russians in East Karelia, but I wasn't there to starve Russian soldiers.

I was there to shoot them to take back the land they stole from Finland." Kaarle answered. Sorcerer knew instinctively that he had pushed the envelope with Kaarle but he knew that unless Kaarle had the exact reaction he just displayed that S.O.E. could go to hell before he lifted a finger to help the Finn no matter how noble his mission. Sorcerer looked straight into Kaarle's eyes and sensed the contradiction belonged not to the man but to the personal nature of what drove this man to walk straight into the mouth of death. Sorcerer sensed that Kaarle wore an aura of danger like a long coat. That he was highly trained to kill without hesitation was obvious. After a lengthy stare Sorcerer decided to help Kaarle but not without first ensuring that Kaarle knew the full story. "I believe you. Well, if this information brought you personal shame, I wonder how you will feel when I tell you that no less than three Finnish Divisions agreed to join the Waffen SS? "I can't believe this!" Kaarle said. "Oh you can believe it but don't think I am singling out poor little Finland. At least Finland's cooperation with the Nazis is a part of its grander strategy of fighting what it is calling the "Continuation" War against the U.S.S.R. The others have no excuse for their collaboration with the Nazis." Sorcerer said.

"If we are serious about performing this mission together I must be sure that you know exactly what you are getting yourself into. Do you want me to bring your knowledge of the enemy up to a good operational level?" Sorcerer asked."Yes. Please." Kaarle answered. "Good Mister Wolf. Then we shall begin with the formation of the "Brown Shirts" or Sturmabteilung, or Storm Troopers. The SA grew from an initial gathering of Ordnertruppen.

These were the fellows assigned the job of protecting Hitler from his Communist detractors during his speeches before he attempted to overthrow the Weimar Republik with his now infamous "Bier Putsch" at the Hofbrau Haus in Muenchen." "The disastrous outcome of the Bier Putsch landed Hitler in jail so when he got out he instructed his personal body guard Julius Shreck to gather eight men in uniform who would receive special training and recognition as his Schutzstaffel, or SS. The SS was assigned as a part of the SA, but an immediate eliteness ensued, whereby the SS was considered to have been formed from Germany's higher classes and the more rough edged SA was more of a Peoples Army. When Heinrich Himmler took over the authority as SS ober fuhrer he began to restrict recruits to Aryan type soldiers with blonde hair and blue eyes. By the time Hitler was appointed Chancellor of Germany the SS had grown in ranks to 83,000 men. It's estimated figure today exceeds one million men.

A central theme in all of these organizations seems to be that as soon as they spring up and are successful, a more elite, or specialized organization emerges. For example the SS were considered more elite than the SA Sturmabteilung but begat more specialized elements. The Waffen SS, for example is the Kommando, or special operations element of the SS. When the Waffen SS began combat operations they were subordinate to the Wehrmacht or Regular Army, but they now have 39 Divisions and are parallel to the Wehrmacht. The elite factions had their major victory over their arch SA competitors when in 1934 during an action that is now referred to as "The Night Of The Long Knives" Theodor Eicke SS Gruppenfuhrer and General of the Waffen SS arrested and executed SA General Ernst Roehm."

"This consolidated power for the Waffen SS. General Eicke was already the Commandant of Dachau, but he soon became the Chief Inspector of all Nazi Death Camps and head of the Totenkopfverbaende, or "Death Head Unit" which, with its ominous appearing skull and cross bones insignia is the most elite of the elite in terms of an allegiance of loyalty until death. The skull and cross bones is supposed to infer that they will surrender to death in behalf of the Fuhrer but as they now run all of the death camps the effect is that they are a part of the aura of death they are sworn to protect against. The Totenkopfverbaende run all of the prison guards in every camp, including Auschwitz."

"If we are to get you into Auschwitz and back out again we must create a prison guard persona for you. Choose a Finnish alias for yourself and we will do our best to get you identity papers identical to the ones from Petrozavodsk and orders to Auschwitz that assign you as an observer and an advisor. We will prepare a layout with details of daily operations for the Petrozavodsk Prison which you can study beforehand in case they ask you how you handled this or that prison matter sort of probing question." Sorcerer said.

"You may call me Fredrik Aito." Kaarle said. "Fine, Fredrik Aito it is. You shall have the documents within a week." "Thank you! Sorcerer." Kaarle said sincerely. "You are rescuing one, or more Jews from the Devil's lair Mister Fredrik Aito. It is I who thanks you." Sorcerer said. "Sorcerer, was Finland the only country to provide troops to the SS?" "My goodness no. In addition to the 39 German SS divisions Berlin lists 20,000 French soldiers from the Charlemagne division, as well as a Flemish division for which we do not have an accurate head count. Probably between 8,000 and 10,000 men.

Then there is the ethnic Germans from Romania, Yugoslavia and Hungary who number about 310,000 men and another 200,000 men believe it, or not, who are British and Polish. About 50,000 Dutch, 40,000 Spanish and 40,000 Belgian soldiers too. Quisling's Norwegian volunteers number about 5,000 and some of these fought beside you on the Russian Front. We Jews may be docile but we can still count both our friends and our enemies quite accurately." Sorcerer said.

"Now perhaps you understand why I initially questioned your loyalties but after I learned about what they did to your family I have been eager to meet you and call you a friend of the Jews and friend of free men everywhere." The Sorcerer said as he reached out his hand to Kaarle who gripped it strongly.

Kaarle remained in his room at the Sorcerer's Gasthof. Sorcerer's daughter brought a fresh apple or an orange each day and a large bowl of potato soup. Finally the documents arrived. The forgery was too perfect to be detected by the naked eye. Sorcerer explained that Frederik had been given the rank of Sergeant to minimize his interaction with the Waffen SS Officers of General Eicke's Totenkopfverbaende who may have once visited Petrozavodsk. It would also give him more direct access to the prisoners. Both a field uniform and a dress uniform of the Finnish Security services had been tailor made from photos. Sorcerer gave Kaarle the map coordinates of an old bombed out church five kilometers from Auschwitz. Plan your escape to occur at a time that will allow you to rally at the ruins at exactly Midnight on Wednesdays and Mondays. It is the only rally point outside of Warsaw and Krakow for the Underground to take people out of Poland." he said.

"Memorize the coordinates and then destroy the paper." Sorcerer said. Kaarle thanked Sorcerer and his daughter and was soon aboard the train from Zurich to Muenchen. Each train heading for Auschwitz left Muenchen for Warsaw late in the afternoon. There was a lead engine attached immediately to the security officer's car, then the Unteroffizier's car followed by the cattle cars that contained the Jewish prisoners. The last two cars held security guards who dismounted at all required stops to prevent escape. Supplies requested by prison staff were also located in the last car. Kaarle was stopped at train side by the Gestapo. "Good evening Sergeant you are a long way from the Russian front yes?" "I am no longer assigned to the Russian front." I am a prison guard from Petrozavodsk on temporary orders to Auschwitz." Kaarle said as he turned over his papers.

Suddenly, the Gestapo agent began to speak perfect Finn with a slight Swedish accent. " Where are you from in Finland Sergeant? Were you in the Winter War?" "Everyone in Finland was in the Winter war. I am from Suomoussalmi." Kaarle replied. "Yes that's true, I would have been in the Winter War too had I not returned to Stockholm before the Russians came. I suppose you are wondering what a Swede is doing in the Gestapo?" "The thought crossed my mind." Kaarle said. The Gestapo agent laughed. "My father is German. My mother is also from a German family who emigrated to Sweden and then Finland before the war. What will you do for the Reich in Auschwitz?" The agent asked. Kaarle hadn't expected questions in his mother tongue and he worried that he may misspeak by saying too much. He hadn't rehearsed a cover story about the job.

"As you may have been told, since you are with the Gestapo, there has been considerable thought given to the impracticality of shipping so many inferior races all the way from the many regions of the USSR to Poland. This is taking combat soldiers away from the war effort. Prison guards and officials from the Finnish sector shall be assigned to your various prisons over the next several months so we can return to our sector with enough operational information to construct our own contribution to the final total Jewish solution." Kaarle lied. "Quite impressive Sergeant. Oh just one thing. When the USSR attacked Finland there arose a public slogan. Do remember what this was?" The Gestapo agent asked. "Of course! As any Finn can tell you, our war cry was "There are so many Russians, where shall we find room to bury them all?" Kaarle repeated. "Ha! Excellent! Sergeant here is a copy of your new orders. Signed by the Fuhrer and Heinrich Himmler himself. Perhaps you may have heard, since one week we have an emergency in the Jewish Ghetto in Warsaw. Before any of us may return to Auschwitz and the other prison camps, we must rally in Warsaw to put down the insurrection that is taking place as we speak." "What reasons are they giving for the insurrection? Kaarle asked.

"Oh the typical Jewish nonsense. Let's face it, they must all die sooner, or later anyway. We built a perfect camp in Treblinka. There is no bantering or pretending anyone has a chance to survive by asking them if they have handicrafts or talent at fixing things." The Gestapo agent said. "We march them straight from the trains to the ovens and are done with it. Better for guard and prisoner alike. Somehow the word got back to the Ghetto in Warsaw, now the little monkeys are standing off Waffen SS with wine bottles filled with petrol and homemade pistols. It should all be over soon and then it's off to Treblinka with their nasty little arses in any case."

The Agent said. "Here, come with me and I shall outfit you with a sub-machine gun and some ammunition. Where we will be going things may get testy for a while. Better to be prepared. Not true?" "Yes, better to always be prepared." Kaarle replied. "But what shall I do about my original orders to go to Auschwitz?" Kaarle asked. "Keep them. These General orders are temporary. Just until the emergency is lifted and then we can all be on our way besides you would have had to go first to Warsaw in any case as I'm sure you know there is no direct train to Auschwitz." The Agent said. "Yes. I knew that, but I thought it would be a simple matter of changing trains." Kaarle said. "Well, I shall fill you in on what I know along the way and the trip to Warsaw should proceed faster. Ja?" The agent asked. "Excellent. My own briefing. Thank you." Kaarle said, knowing that this blow hard was the type who liked to impress others with his knowledge.

Arin was nearing death. His weight had dropped sixty percent and his organs had all but ceased to function properly. He had clearly reached a fork in the road. As it was a goal of the Nazi power structure to instill in their prisoners minds a feeling of being sub-human, many merely succumbed and committed suicide through starvation by just giving up. Arin was not the sort of person who would give in to his murderer's desires. He found strength in helping others and by always being available to help if only in a small way. He was rewarded one day when two prisoners approached him with an invitation to join the "Kampfgruppe Auschwitz". The prisoners were Rudolf Vrba and Alfred Wetzler. "Arin, we have smuggled cameras into Auschwitz. We have taken pictures of the Crematoria ovens. Even with pictures the extent of the evil is so great here that no one will be able to fathom it. We are mostly German and Polish Jews here. You have an advantage. You are a Norwegian Jew my friend." Rudolf said.

"Some advantage. I am starving in my own peculiar Norwegian way, I suppose." Arin said dryly. "Don't joke. That is not what I meant. I meant that as a Norwegian you will be believed more than a Pole or a German Jew would be believed." Rudolf replied. "Why?" Arin asked. "Because Norway was picked off not for its Jewish population, in fact oppositely, most of its population fit's the Nazi ideal of Aryan features. Norway was attacked simply to secure iron ore supply lines from Sweden to Germany and to give German U-boats a harbor from which to launch attacks across the North Atlantic." Rudolf explained. "I don't understand what this has to do with me." Arin said.   "We need someone to take these photos to the Allies. We have no illusion that if you make it back we will be magically rescued by a caring world. We are Jews. We shun mixing outside our religion and it has reaped a world without pity for us. Many feel we deserve everything we have received but we are still humans and no human deserves the monstrous treatment we have suffered in the death camps. We want only that no one shall ever forget what happened here." Vrba said sadly.

"When they shoot us in the back of the head and roll our bodies like logs into a fire we return to ashes, but our spirits will walk this place eternally. Our voices will haunt our oppressive murderers and their children eternally for what they have done not just to us but to the dignity of all mankind for all time. Our greatest nightmare is that mankind does not discover this moral outrage. That it will be kept secret." Wetzlar growled angrily. "Of course to have died in silence beyond the eyes of mankind is unbearable of and by itself, for it means our deaths and therefore our lives will have been meaningless and lost in vain.

An even greater imperative than this is the possibility that such a genocide could ever be repeated, which we believe it shall be if no one knows of us." Vrba continued sadly. "We have all voted and our decision has been made. We will entrust you with the sacred mission of delivering this evidence to the outside world." Rudolf said. "I am honored, but just how do you propose getting me out of this place with the evidence?" Arin asked. "Each fortnight on Monday, they take the salvaged materials to the railhead for transport to Warsaw." Rudolf explained. "The salvaged items?" Arin asked. "Yes, hair, skin and gold teeth harvested by the Sonder-kommando supervised Jewish laborers. The material is transported in wooden chests that have large steel locks. We will lock you inside one of these. One that has a false tray above you filled with gold teeth, in case they open it to inspect.

Your chest will be just like all the others except that yours will have small burrowed holes on the bottom to let in the air. Yours will have a screw driving tool inside that you can use to escape when you reach the foundry. Four heavy screws and the bottom falls out." Rudolf explained.

"This sounds good so far, but how shall I know when it is safe to emerge?" Arin asked. "You won't. It will be completely dark inside and once they load you onto the train you could be placed at the very bottom of the entire shipment. You can only judge by motion that you are being carried first to the rail head. Secondly to the box car. Thirdly to the truck that carries you to the foundry in Warsaw that melts the teeth down into gold ingots and fourthly from the truck to the foundry where ingots are made. Don't trust even the Jewish workers there. The fact that they are there instead of here with us suggests a special arrangement.

Once you slip away from the foundry it should still be dark. Take this hand drawn map and memorize it, then destroy it." Vrba concluded. "Your destination will be number 27 Cholodna street near where it intersects with Zelazna street connecting Little Warsaw with Big Warsaw. Ask to be taken to Mordechaj Anielewicz. He is the senior Commander of Jewish Resistance. Ask him to get you out of Poland by exfiltration. Explain your mission to him and mention that this was my idea. He shall not refuse you." Rudolf said. "How do you know this?" Arin asked. "He is a very good friend." Rudolf said proudly. "Best friends!" Wetzler repeated.

"What of those who work in the salvage abteilung? Surely they will be punished when it is discovered that I am no longer here." Arin asked. "That is the other reason you are perfect for this mission. Unlike us, you have no one who can be punished because you escaped. Secondly, no one at the foundry will dare make a report that someone was smuggled out through them. You shall only be missed by der Weisse Engel when he discovers he has not you to torture any more." Rudolf said with a wry smile.

All week long Arin's spirit traveled first like a rocket exploding in the sky and then when he thought of the misery of the others he would be leaving behind, the rocket's nose cone would come smashing downward until it was beneath the surface of the earth. He cried at night at times from the raw euphoria of daring to believe he could leave this place alive and at other times the tears were for his Jewish brothers and sisters who were torn from their tender lives by a collective of maniacal monsters. How stoically the women comforted and assured their beloved children right up to the moment they were gassed, or burned alive.

Never before, or since could the family of mankind be more proud of these courageous and tragic souls than Arin was at this moment. How sad it would have been to have never known they were his blood relatives. How sad now to leave them in the same Hell he had tasted and died in a million times. Arin wondered. Would mankind remember? Would they even believe this diabolical triumph of Satan ever happened at all? Could these photos silence deniers? Arin was utterly ashamed when he realized how selfish he had been at first not to have immediately accepted the sacred mission he had been entrusted with. He would get the photos out, or die trying.

Arin thought of the millions of people butchered because a few mad eugenic scientists believed they could play God by destroying an entire people, while artificially creating an ideal, a myth, that could only be taken to the level of a value preference in the demented mental landscape of Hitler, Himmler, Goebbels, Eichmann, Mengele and many others who followed them without asking a single question.

The tap on Arin's shoulder came and he crept through the shadows to the loading dock. Skilled hands guided him to the large wooden trunk and tucked him inside with the leather pouch full of photos tied securely to his waist. In a moment he was lying down tucked in a fetal position in his own perspiration. He perspired in spite of the tomb-like coldness of the trunk's surfaces. It seemed an eternity passed. Finally, he heard muffled german and then came a rattling and vibration. To his shock and despair, Arin realized his trunk was being opened! He could see the tray being lifted and the rifle blasts as they filled him full of bullets. So close. So close. But the tray never lifted. Instead, he felt the slam of the lid and heard the click of the lock.

Then came the motion of being loaded on the truck that would take him to the train. Arin was giddy. At any moment he could be discovered but for now it was working. Dare he hope at this early stage? When Arin's wooden trunk was finally dropped at the foundry he immediately located the screw driving tool and began removing the large screws in each corner in the dark. Arin fainted while trying to push the trunk off of himself. He realized in shock that his legs were too weak. They cramped horribly from the deprivation. His weakness would cause him to remain trapped in this tight dark space until he starved to death. A man who once prided himself in his ability to lift heavy objects simply lacked the strength to lift an otherwise ordinary wooden chest from himself. To remain where he now lay was a guaranteed miserable death, a death in the darkness, unable to see the world about him as he died. From darkness to darkness, ashes to ashes and dust to dust." his mind was edging toward delerium.

Hours passed and finally Arin heard a metallic click. Someone was placing a hoisting hook to a metal ring on the top of the chest. Suddenly a bright light was shining down from the ceiling directly into Arin's eyes. When his focus returned Arin saw that a man was standing over him with an axe. The man, Boleslaw Sawa was not a Jew. He had been captured by the Nazis and forced into labor outside the concentration camps because he was not Jewish and at the time he was captured Hitler had not yet ordered the total solution that would enforce the genocide of Gentile as well as Jew. He had been captured by the Nazis and forced into labor outside the concentration camps because he was not Jewish. Boleslaw was classified merely as a "Forced LaborerLevel Two Trustee" because he had never tried to escape.

He looked down at the disgusting lump of human flesh and wondered to himself as he had so many times, who were the people who had once owned the gold teeth he melted into liquid? Now, finally, there it was not just a set of teeth, but a live and squirming human body. Boleslaw was a strong man, not always a friendly man especially when drinking, but now he became as liquid as the gold teeth he melted for the Nazis. His legs became weak and he dropped to his knees, tears streaming down his face. "What have they in the name of God done to you ?" He asked out loud in Polish. Arin didn't understand Boleslaw's words. He prepared himself for the inevitable chop from the axe he had glimpsed for a moment in the huge man's hands. He felt a lightness, an ascending and it occurred to him that perhaps from some mercy of God that he was spared from remembering the blows from the axe. He saw the light become brighter and was convinced he was experiencing the death so many had embraced in his presence.

Then he opened his eyes and was thrilled to see the axe lying on the floor. He felt only the arms of this strong but compassionate, gentle, mountain of a man holding him as though he were a small child, or the frail and light skeleton of a bird. Boleslaw secreted Arin away to his small apartment and spoon fed him cabbage and potato soup. Within two weeks Arin felt stronger although his body was still emaciated and his hands shook and trembled. His face was sallow and his teeth had fallen out like over ripe pieces of rotten fruit, but he was alive and the stubbornness of youth beat firmly within his breast. He had long since forgotten the once powerful hatred he felt toward the Nazis even his powerful hatred of Colonel von Braunschweig. His soul had moved well beyond obsessions. He pitied the evil and the ignorant for they had but one path to follow.

He didn't condescend because his inner constitution was above, or holier than anyone else, he merely accepted that evil does exist and that its singular reward is itself. Those who were fortunate, as he considered himself to be, were better off as victims without blood on their hands than their tormentors and torturers who couldn't remove the guilt and shame from their lives in a million life times. The blood on their hands couldn't be removed even if their hands were cut off. Arin knew that the short life of a single innocent person was infinitely preferable to a long evil filled life, or even a multitude of evil lives.

The world seemed so full of evil that Arin was amazed that anyone like Boleslaw was still to be found on earth. The man's human compassion and tenderness caused Arin to feel tears again long after the very memory of them had been all but forgotten. When Arin could walk without assistance he used his hands to describe his need to find an address in Warsaw. Boleslaw gave Arin a pencil and paper and he wrote out the address at 27 Cholodna street. Boleslaw shook his head to show he understood. Boleslaw didn't begin his shift at the foundry until midnight. As soon as darkness fell Boleslaw put Arin inside a burlap potato sack and carried him over his shoulder half-way across Warsaw until they reached the Jewish Ghetto. Several times Boleslaw ducked behind trees, or trucks parked near the street as German jeeps and motorcycles whizzed by. Boleslaw knocked on the door and there was no answer. Just as he was turning around to leave three men surrounded him with pistols. "Who are you? What do you want here?" They asked. "I was asked to bring this man to Mordechaj Anielewicz." he replied. "What man? I only see a sack of potatoes." "This man." Boleslaw said as he lowered and opened the sack. The men instantly recognized that Arin had escaped from the Death Camp.

They were immediately grateful to Boleslaw and escorted both Arin and Boleslaw to a secret hide out deeper in the recesses of the Ghetto. When Mordecaj saw Arin he held him close as though he were a brother. He shook Boleslaw's hands several times. When Arin described the condition of Mordecaj's friend Rudolf in Auschwitz, Mordecaj excused himself, went into another room and although he tried to muffle the sounds his sobs could be heard throughout the building. When he returned he looked as though someone had ripped out his human heart and replaced it with one of steel.

He accepted the photos and thanked Arin for risking his life to deliver them. All in the room wore expressions of anger and hatred as they saw the gruesome photos of the lines of men, women and children awaiting their fate in the Crematorium. They shook their heads in disbelief when they saw the stacks of bodies and the bones of skeletons and the arrogant guards watching over their prey of death. The anger increased when they saw photos of the Jewish Brigade Guards who they had already encountered fighting alongside the Germans in this very Ghetto. "Vermin!" Mordecaj spit out angrily. It occurred to both Arin and Boleslaw while they watched the facial expressions of Mordecaj and his men as they witnessed the photos that not only had the photos provided the sacred mission of getting the message out to the world, but that it steeled the resistance members more than ever before. The fight Mordecaj had been fighting based on highly reliable rumors, had now been transformed into a fight to the death based on evidence. Surrender was not an option because the choice was merely one of dying in battle, or dying like sheep being led to the slaughter.

Boleslaw suddenly stood up and declared to the room. "I have been model prisoner of Nazis. I melted gold teeth for them in foundry and though I often wondered, I never allowed my mind to imagine who had given up all these teeth. I have now met one of you and in these short weeks I have come to feel the protectiveness for Arin one would feel for brother of blood. I am not the Jew. I am not even good Christian, but I cannot go back to the foundry after seeing these photos. I would feel the great honor if you would let me stay with you and fight this evil." Boleslaw said as he bowed his head. Spontaneously, with misty eyes, all of the Jews in the room stood at attention and saluted Boleslaw. "We cannot permit this. Your life would end with 100% certainty within weeks from now. If you are unfortunate enough to be captured they would take you with us to Treblinka. We must face this as Jews, but we are infinitely grateful for your kind heart dear friend of Israel." Mordecaj replied. "I'm sorry honored leader but what I choose to surrender life for is choice of the Boleslaw." he said respectfully. "The Boleslaw can either fight them standing beside you or alone." Boleslaw said. "I suppose if the Germans are using our own Jews to fight us we can hardly refuse the help of this brave Pole." Mordecaj said. The group welcomed Boleslaw and Arin and the word spread quickly of two heroes who had come to help defend the Ghetto of Warsaw from the evil Nazi tide.

Kaarle studied the face of the Gestapo agent. Obviously developed in a sheltered and wealthy atmosphere. His philosophy carefully watered and cultivated within the elite atmosphere of German royalty, even though his youth had been spent in Scandinavia. Kaarle disassembled the sub-machine gun, cleaned it, oiled its moving parts, re-assembled it and loaded a large clip in five minutes. The task would have taken many people at least an hour to accomplish.

"That's quite good Frederik!" The Gestapo agent said. "I'm sorry, I don't know your name." Kaarle said. "I don't usually tell people my name. You may however call me Juergen." "Thank you Juergen." Kaarle said. "We may be killing Jews together Frederik. We should at least be on a first name basis? Ja?" Juergen asked. "Listen, I should brief you about the history and important persons involved on both sides of what some are now calling the Warsaw uprising." Juergen said. "That would help me with my duties Juergen. Thank you!" Kaarle pretended to be intensely interested.

"Well as you must already know, the Fuhrer began to separate the Jews from German society when we dispossessed them of their stolen loot during Krystal Nacht. This was the turning point when the Reich began to reverse centuries of trickery by Jewish loan sharks and cut throat Jew bankers. The Fuhrer's plan was a bit too conservative however." Juergen lamented. "How so?" Kaarle asked. "It's obvious. He worried too much about world opinion. He implemented the Forced Sterilization plan to end the proliferation of the Jewish population. They populate with the frequency of rats, did you know that?" Juergen asked suspiciously. "Of course." Kaarle played along. "He should have said f--ck world opinion and implemented the Final Total Solution from the beginning. Then we wouldn't even have the bastards in Ghettos as they are today they would already be gone." Juergen said. Kaarle wondered how much of Juergen's racism was genuinely his own and how much came from his upbringing. "Well anyway Hitler didn't so now while we are fighting the Red menace we have to keep combat troops tied down in a backwards country we already defeated." Juergen continued.

"Since last year in 1942 the Jews have all been moved from Germany to the concentration camps. We estimate three million just since the deportation code named "Grossaktien Warsaw" was initiated under the command of SS Oberfuhrer Ferdinand von Sammern Frankenegg. He managed to exterminate about 300,000 Jews in an until now secret facility called Treblinka and another called Sobibor. There were a couple of other ones, but these are the main ones. Frankenegg became too relaxed Ja? He didn't closely watch the Jewish administrative labor who somehow discovered that Treblinka wasn't a labor camp, but instead one of the most efficient killing factories we have ever made. Ja? There was no f--cking fake German village there. We marched the f--ckers straight from the trains to the ovens. To keep the system moving, we had them dig enormous trenches and then sit on the edge of them while we marched along behind them to give them a pistol shot to the back of the head. The memory of Juergen's role in the genocide still blazed in his eyes. "Then we rolled them into the flaming pit." Juergen said with hatred dripping from his lips.

"We had to wear two pistol belts with four pistols and we still ran out of ammunition. This was crazy! Ja? When we ran out of ammo we had other Jews loading our clips. If they had any courage they would have resisted at this moment. Ja? Now that they have heard of Treblinka the little bastards are only now resisting." Juergen laughed. Kaarle smiled but inside he had to use every ounce of his self discipline to prevent strangling Juergen to death. "What is the order of battle." Kaarle asked. "What does this mean?" Juergen asked. Which are the German units? How many Resistance Fighters are there estimated to be? What are the weapons and equipment on each side?" Kaarle clarified.

"Aach! You sound more like an Infantry officer than a prison guard sergeant." Juergen said as he cast a suspicious glance at Kaarle. "First of all Frankenegg was relieved by Himmler for allowing such an interruption to occur and replaced him with SS Polizei Fuhrer Juergen Stroop. Things have gotten better since they brought in a policeman for what is essentially a civilian insurrection, but yes, they are still using crack infantry troops to open the street blockades. Our main forces are Waffen SS, OrdPo or Ordnungs Polizei Wehrmacht and of course Gestapo. I don't trust the bastard Jews but we also have help from the Jewish polizei and the Occupied Polish Polizei. It's funny, when the fighting gets heavy, we send the Jew cops in first. If they survive that then we f--cking kill them after the battle subsides. Juergen laughed again and Kaarle nearly sprang for him. "What do we know about the Resistance forces?" Kaarle asked.

"Oh those bastards and miscreants! They are led by a man named Mordechaj Anielewicz. I will personally piss down his throat when we capture him. There are two major Jewish Resistance forces; the ZOB and the ZZW. They are reinforced at times by the Polish Resistance Forces which are the AK, or "Home Front" and GL or "People's Guard." Cowardly bastards all. As far as weapons we have our sub-machine guns and heavy mounted machine guns. We use anti-tank rockets to bring down cement barriers and walls. We ride half tracks and jeeps. The resistance use pistols and shot guns. Theirs are home made pistols that occasionally give us great laughter when they blow up in their faces and cause them to lose a hand, or half their face. Their most fearsome weapon has become their petro bottles which they use to blow up the fuel tanks and engines of our vehicles. As for your question about troop strength we field about two thousand men in the Ghetto each day.

Highly trained SS and Waffen SS make up about half of our troop strength. The resistance field about six hundred fighters each day if you also count the women and young children who we shoot like any other bastard who can throw a petrol bottle at us." Juergen said with a wicked smile. Kaarle didn't know how much more of this he could take. His impulse to kill Juergen was overwhelming. "I'm stepping out of the train cabin for some air Juergen." He said. "I hope I didn't frighten you about the subhumans in Warsaw." Juergen snickered.

"You are so f--cking close Juergen!" Kaarle thought to himself as he smiled and stepped out into the aisle of the train car. As the sun began to send its first beams across the horizon Kaarle secured his weapon and his small bag and returned to his cabin. "Well, all freshened up Frederik?" Juergen asked. "Yes quite. Thank you." Kaarle replied. "While you were gone they brought us some bandoliers and ammunition cannisters and clips for our weapons. I divided them, there's your stack." Juergen said. "Excellent!" Kaarle replied.

As the train pulled into the station, Juergen was met by Waffen SS Hauptman Werner Stroud. "Are you ready for some excitement Juergen?" He asked. "Of course, but look who I brought along. A Finnish prison guard friend from Petrozavodsk." Juergen smiled. "I see. I was once visiting Petrozavodsk. I knew a Finnish Captain named Peter Andersdotter did you know him?" "Oh yes, you mean the queer who wore woolen dresses?" Kaarle responded with a laugh. "Huh? I'm afraid I don't understand." Hauptman Stroud seemed perplexed. "First of all, it's not a Finnish name. Actually, it isn't even a Swedish name.

Andersson would be an appropriate Swedish name for a boy named Peter, but Andersdotter would only be suitable if the first name was Petra." Kaarle said with a grin. Juergen shrieked with laughter. Hauptman Stroud gave Juergen an annoyed glance. "He told me to ask you this question." Hauptman Stroud attempted to explain. "If you answered yes, I was supposed to shoot you." Hauptman Stroud concluded. "As well you should have!" Kaarle said with a smile. "It's alright Hauptman Stroud, I have interrogated his ass off along the way. He is a bonafide Finnish Nazi. Come let us board a half track and kick some affen asses." Juergen declared.

Kaarle saw no one in this desolate city. He had never seen a place so desolate. An occasional shadow of a person scavenging a dead horse for food, but nothing else not even a stray dog, or cat. "Of course not. Those would be food sources." Kaarle thought sadly. He didn't know quite what to do about Juergen. He wasn't sure how much longer he could stand the racism, hatred and anger. As a member of the Gestapo the association might add some legitimacy to Kaarle's orders to report to Auschwitz, but he had seen Juergen's empty soul along the way. Juergen should be given the same trust one gives an African Black Mamba. Kaarle considered. His plan was to spend only the shortest time possible to learn where Arin was being kept in Auschwitz and then devise an impromptu plan to spring him from the place and head for the rally point the Sorcerer had given him. If it were possible to spring some wheels all the better, but if he had to carry Arin the entire distance to the rally point, so be it. He thought.

Suddenly there came a loud crack!, crack!, crack! Pistol fire from a nearby window! Hauptman Stroud was leading in a half track. Juergen and Kaarle were in the trailing half track. Stroud immediately halted his vehicle. "Big Mistake!" Kaarle yelled out. A petrol bottle came flying through the air and hit Stroud's engine compartment squarely. Juergen and Kaarle followed it to its source. The little boy who threw it couldn't have been a day over nine years old. Just before Juergen had a chance to squeeze the trigger Kaarle buried his Fiskar knife into Juergen's brain. Five little boys between the ages of nine and fourteen were completely shocked to see Kaarle save their brother's life.

As the Waffen SS troops began to dismount from their burning vehicle, Kaarle opened up with his sub-machine gun. The troops in his own vehicle began to dismount but the five young boys pumped them full of lead. Kaarle jumped down from the half track and began gathering weapons and ammunition from the dead bodies and from the burning half track before it exploded ten feet in the air, landing on its side. Kaarle motioned and the boys climbed inside his half track. He shoved its dead driver out of his seat and revved the engine. A wounded Waffen SS soldier who pretended to be dead got a good look at Kaarle's face. Soon the half track was near the end of the street and a large truck blocked its forward progress. In seconds a group of eight men pointed their pistols and shotguns at Kaarle's head. Wait! The little boy who owed his life to Kaarle shouted. "He helped us kill the Germans. He blasted five of them!" the boy yelled. "Yes, he helped us steal the half track and a shit load of weapons and ammo." Another boy shouted. "Yes. He's with us!" The other boys joined in. "Out of the vehicle Mr. Kraut. We will see what you're up to and then we'll kill you." One of the men said in German.

"I'm not German, I'm from Finland!" Kaarle protested. "Kill the f--cker! He was riding with the Germans and was armed just like they were." Another man enjoined. "If you shoot him, shoot me too!" The little boy named Marik Nussbaum yelled out as he pointed a nine millimeter at the man's head who called for Kaarle to be killed. "Mordechaj will decide." An older man in the group announced. "Yes, hide the vehicle in the warehouse and take him to Mordechaj." Another shouted. Soon Kaarle found himself tied and bound and then marched to Muranowski Square. He was taken to a heavily fortified underground bunker while a man kept a 9 mm pistol trained at his temple the entire time. He was kept standing in a room so fortified it was virtually sound proof and when the heavy door was closed it left little air to breathe. Kaarle realized when he saw that all of the men had a string with ear plugs dangling around their necks that he was standing in an execution room. "One wrong answer and you get the main course." He thought to himself. Soon Mordecaj opened the door wide and entered with a body guard on each side.

"My men tell me you killed most of the Germans you came in with and helped us capture a half track vehicle and several weapons as well as save the life of one of our young boys. Yet you were armed and not a prisoner of the Germans. Would you please be so kind as to explain this glaring inconsistency?" Mordecaj asked. "I am an agent of S.O.E. Branch in London. I came here quite by accident. My cover was that of a Finnish army sergeant, who as a prison guard from Petrozavodsk was sent to learn Nazi Concentration camp techniques for the elimination of Jews. I was encountered by a Gestapo agent in Muenchen and compelled by him to come here instead of Auschwitz." Kaarle related.

"When I saw the Gestapo agent on the verge of shooting the young boy I reacted as any decent man would have." Kaarle explained. "So far, so good. " Mordecaj said. "But there remains one burning question." Mordecaj continued. "If we cannot get even bombing support from London, why would they dispatch a single agent to rescue us? You obviously are a very well trained fighter but we are being contained in this section of Warsaw and will either be sent to the fire ditches of Treblinka or hunted down like rats in a maze. Also, why were you going to Auschwitz if you were not actually intending to serve as a prison guard? To rescue the Jews who are being killed in the ovens too?" How did you get to Muenchen and from where?" Mordecaj asked.

"The Nazis were holding my sister captive in their Lebensborn program. They believed that she carried perfect Aryan genes and they were trying to use her as something of a queen bee to be cloned for purposes of propagating a Master Race. We blew up the eugenics laboratory in Berlin and escaped with Jewish help into Switzerland. S.O.E. Branch flew my sister to London while I carried on with the help of the Sorcerer in Zurich. My sister's husband Arin is being held as a Jew in Auschwitz and my sole purpose for coming to Poland is to ascertain first if he is alive and if he is, to take him to my sister his wife, in London." Kaarle said firmly."I have heard many amazing stories about the Nazis and as a matter of survival I have learned to believe them all. What a nut factory. They are committing mass genocide against us while they rape innocent victims to create their own bee hive. Three mad scientists drunk from vodka could not have created such a fiction, but I believe you. I will need your code name. My contact in the Armia Krajowa, or Polish Resistance Home Army operates a secret radio transmitter that connects them to S.O.E. Branch in London.

We should have verification either way to tell us whether your truth is stranger than fiction." Mordecaj concluded. "My code name is Wolf." Kaarle said. "Very well Wolf, but I must inform you that an even greater coincidence is that we have an escapee with us who is a Norwegian not a Finn. He is called Arin. He brought us valuable photos that we need to get to S.O.E. Branch for world wide dissemination. These photos prove beyond any doubt that what the Nazis are doing is even more horrendous and miserable as crimes against humanity than even we could have believed possible." Mordecaj said.

"You have my sister's husband here? With you now? Can I please see him?" Kaarle began to choke with emotion. "Yes. We will fetch him now. When he arrived he was in very bad shape. He is much healthier now but you will probably not recognize him." Mordecaj observed. "Oh, I wouldn't have recognized him anyway. My sister and I are twins. Our mother died in labor. My sister was sent by my father to live with an aunt in Oslo. I saw my sister last when we were small children. I first saw her as an adult when I rescued her in Berlin. I have never met her husband." Kaarle said matter of factly. Mordecaj slowly shook his head in disbelief as he sent for Arin. Arin was trembling more than usual as he was led inside by Boleslaw who stayed near Arin as a protector. "Arin? I am Kaarle Laila's brother. She sent me here to take you home my brother." Kaarle said with emotion. Arin began to shake even harder. "What was Laila's favorite pet? What was its name?" Arin asked. "A female reindeer named "Tarja." Kaarle quickly replied. Both men embraced as tears streamed down their cheeks. Even Mordecaj choked with emotion as he spoke. "We will run the verification but I can see already what the answer will be." He said. Over the next few days Kaarle more than pulled his weight.

His ambush experience from the Winter War proved invaluable. He devised a plan that Mordecaj quickly adopted that increased the casualty figures of the Nazis twofold. He established with Zydowski Zwiazek Wojskowi (ZZW) Jewish Military League, a system that he called "pattern reserves." The main ingress avenues to the Ghetto were covered at choke points with standard ambush teams but if a large enough column became stymied by Molotov cocktails, all other pattern reserves were notified and overwhelming force was placed on the active choke point. By the same reasoning if an overwhelming Nazi force were concentrated with continued mobility, the patterns disappeared back into the maze of alley ways where the Nazis dared not go. The location and strength of the enemy determined the pattern applied.

Kaarle became numb and listless when he saw a dozen children and two young women immolated in flames by a tank-borne flame thrower. He sadly realized that these valiant and courageous people were all doomed. Not by the military prowess of the Waffen SS but by the imbalance of weaponry. No matter how formidable the enemy SS troops they threw into the battle were, as long as one could use his mind to outsmart the enemy, or his bravery in charging a mechanized vehicle, or a tank, there remained a hope. But no one on earth could fight raw fire. No one could survive, or escape the fifty feet high wall of flames of the Nazi tank flame throwers. No one could continue the fight when the thick and clinging, black, acrid smoke filled their lungs and burnt their eyes until their vision became hopelessly blurred. When Kaarle saw the Nazis wearing gas masks he knew the battle for the Warsaw Ghetto was finished.

Just the day before two brave lads climbed the flag pole rising high above the Ghetto and affixed the Red and White Polish flag along with the Blue and White Jewish flag. A new hope became palpable and grew for everyone except Kaarle who knew the gas masks portended a new and unwinnable war, a war of poison gas with no masks of their own in defense. When it came the effected fighters gallantly continued to fire their pistols standing in open defiance until the yellow clouds encircled them and they began to vomit blood and die in place. "The time has come for you and Arin to take the photos and leave. I predict we have a week at most before the Nazis poison us all to death. There is no weak point along the perimeter where we can evacuate our people." Mordecaj said with sad acceptance. "I draw daily sustenance from knowing that as long as freedom exists somewhere there will be people who can say the Nazis did not take us without a fight." Mordecaj said.

"I would give anything to free my people but alas it isn't possible. There are still thousands of us here, hundreds of our elderly and feeble. We can't just forsake them here for the hyenas to devour. Where would the dignity be in that? If we attempted an escape the Nazis would hunt us down in the fields and kill us all like frightened wild animals. We are better off remaining here and taking a few more of the bastards with us." Mordechaj said defiantly. "As for a weakness in the Nazi perimeter, we would have to blast one and there wouldn't be much secrecy involved in that. For you and Arin we have an exfiltration we haven't used precisely because we didn't want it discovered before it was really needed. We have informers who are with us even now, as incredible as that may seem. A mass evacuation would fail because the traitors would find a way to signal Stroop.

You and Arin will have the honor of burning the last match. Your escape will take place through a sewer the Nazis have no blue print of. The Muranowski tunnel. Once you exit the tunnel in the small hours of the morning you should proceed to the Michalin Forest. It is thick and ideal for a prolonged escape. Your mission to deliver the photos is sacred for us. You must go and soon." Mordecaj said. "Does the escape route lead to a church not far from Auschwitz where on Mondays and Wednesdays at midnight we may rally with the Polish Underground?" Kaarle asked. "Heavens no. That system was compromised a few months ago. When you reach the outside please inform the Sorcerer that he should keep his information updated. You will be given a map. There are no more resistance patrols. You will be on your own. Stay in the forests and use the map and you should succeed. I will offer the opportunity also to Boleslaw. It isn't fair to drag him down with us into a Jewish grave." Mordechaj said. "What can I do before we leave?" Kaarle asked. "You have done more than I can thank you for by becoming a brother in arms against the disease. There was a time when we felt hated by all non-Jews, but your willingness to risk your life has inspired hope for the future in our breasts where we thought none existed. Just please tell our story lest history forgets us and then becomes repeated." Mordecaj said.

"I have been reluctant to tell you something because I didn't want to soften your desire to get these photos to the Allied Commanders, but we have been sending reports about Auschwitz and other camps back to S.O.E. Branch in London by messenger and radio coded messages since 1940 but they simply have not believed us. As far as we can tell they consider our reports wild Jewish exaggeration. I wish I knew why it is so hard to find a Gentile who believes a Jew.

Perhaps they are in some form of shame or embarrassment that has caused them to plunge themselves into denial for allowing this to happen to us, I don't know." Mordecaj said with resignation. "That in itself is incredibly difficult to fathom, or understand. Who received your reports?" Kaarle asked incredulously. "We are quite certain they have been read by Churchill himself." Mordecaj said. "Was there just one report in 1940?" Kaarle asked. "Hell no. Look there is a hero from the Polish Army, a Captain who allowed himself to be taken prisoner specifically to investigate Auschwitz. He is there now almost three years and every report is smuggled to us at the risk of immediate death to him and others who are collaborating with him. His name is Witold Pilecki. "

"As long as a single Jew remains alive, this man's heroism will always be remembered. He has detailed the selection process in his reports. They send the weak and feeble as well as all women and women with children straight to the ovens. They lie to them. They tell them they will be taking a shower to prepare for the evening meal. They even have fake shower heads to calm them. Then they drop Zyklon-B pellets from the ceilings and apertures in the walls to fill the place with Cyanide gas. In Auschwitz II- Birkenau they kill up to 20,000 people a day! There is a sign above the main entrance to Auschwitz made of wrought iron. It says; "Arbeit Macht Frei", or "Work Sets You Free." That is the only way anyone survives another day in Auschwitz. If their body is still able to squeeze out one more day of hard labor they are free to live another day. Ask Arin. He has seen it. He has lived it and survived it." Mordecaj said. "Please help me understand why the Allies refuse to believe our goddamned reports. Sometimes we feel trapped. As though the Allies also want us to die. They will have to believe these photos Rudolf risked his life to get to us." Mordecaj exclaimed.

"I don't need to imagine why you feel betrayed Mordecaj but the answer may simply be that they are unable to do anything right now and they can't find the courage to admit it to you. For example, if Churchill tried to bomb the Death camps he would kill more Jews than Nazis. If he bombed the rail head it would be Jews who would be worked to death without adequate food to repair them. " Kaarle said. "You may be right Kaarle. Since I first met you, you have spoken only the truth with me and I with you. Why can't the people at S.O.E Branch answer when we send them reports even if it's to correct the goddamned spelling?" Mordechaj said in disgust.

"I can't answer for them, but I give you my solemn promise we won't just deliver these photos, we will hold them in front of the leaders noses until they answer. What you have done here for decent men everywhere will never be forgotten dear brother Mordecaj. I promise you this." Kaarle said. "Go now and make plans for your escape. Take the weapons you need but leave us most of the bullets." Mordechaj said. "I will take my knife. If I need a rifle, or a pistol it will be supplied by a Nazi that I have killed to get it." Kaarle said. "You are truly a snow soldier my dear friend." Mordecaj grinned. "Read the exfiltration instructions carefully, memorize each name, grid coordinate and detail. Then destroy the paper before you leave the Ghetto. If you are caught with this information, dozens in the Polish Underground would perish. Take this one piece of intelligence information with you to S.O.E. Branch that we have uncovered from a Waffen SS officer we tortured for it, that in addition to Operation Reinhard which we have generally reported on, which calls for the genocide of Polish Jews, a secret program having to do with Hitler's Lebensraum is about to be implemented."

"This will not be the Lapanka round ups of Gentiles in Warsaw, this is also not a program for the removal of Poles to Russia, but rather the ambitious genocide of the entire Polish population to make way for a new Reich society." Christian Poles will be completely destroyed along side of the genocide against we Jews. We have since confirmed this intelligence with other reliable sources." Mordecaj warned. "You will meet at the map rally point in the Michalin Forest with a small exfiltration team. They will hide you for a few days until it is safe to travel north to a small abandoned airstrip. In the meantime I will arrange a hasty landing operation for an RAF bomber to pick you up. We will arrange this by short wave radio code." Mordecaj said. Kaarle embraced Mordecaj, took the map instructions and photos and left to alert Arin of their secret departure in the night.

Boleslaw tapped on Mordecaj's door and peeked inside. "You sent for me sir?" He asked. "Yes, brother Boleslaw. I wanted to thank you personally for your gallantry and for your aid to the Jewish people but the time has come for you to go back out into your own lands. Arin and Kaarle are leaving tonight. It is my wish that you travel with them to protect them." Mordecaj said. "Kaarle is a relative of Arin. He has proven more than capable of taking care of Arin. I have but one wish sir." Boleslaw said as he looked at the ceiling. "What is your wish Boleslaw?" "I didn't live my life as a Jew but I wish to die as one. Would you please ask Rabbi Markewicz to perform the ritual for me?" Mordecaj gasped. He was humbled by the innocence and bravery of the request. "Are you certain?" He asked. "Yes sir with all my heart." Boleslaw said softly. "We will be honored to perform the ceremonies if this is your wish." Mordecaj replied.

The tunnel was over run with rats that jumped up on Kaarle and Arin's legs as they splashed their way through the blackness. Anticipating this their Jewish comrades wrapped their legs with thick rags to protect them from the plague producing bites and scratches. They emerged well beyond the wall of the Ghetto. All through the night they hid in the shadows until they reached the Michalin Forest. Neither spoke as they pressed onward but neither could stop thinking of their brothers in Warsaw.

Chapter Ten: Sacred Mission

Horst Feldner was in shock. He was just given the news that his son Juergen had been killed, not by a resistance fighter in Warsaw, but instead by the imposter from Finland. Juergen made extensive notes about Frederik Aito and had even included a sketch. Horst held a copy in his hand and agreed it was the same imposter he'd seen in Holland. His investigation had led him to conclude that the man who he now knew to be Kaarle Tuuri of Suomoussalmi, Finland was an identical twin brother of the female test subject of Eugenics Cloning Project 001. He had standing orders to dedicate a thousand agents to nothing besides the capture of Kaarle Tuuri, then to turn him over to Dr. Professor von Verschuer who was beside himself with elation to learn that his lost female eugenic specimen had a twin brother.

Horst wanted permission to shoot Kaarle on sight for what a witness said he had done to Juergen, but he knew he would have to follow orders. This didn't prevent him from notifying Dr. Mengele that Kaarle was an identical twin to the test subject that had produced such perfect clones. Himmler was sitting on Mengele's request to dissect Kaarle while promising von Verschuer that if his scientists could repeat the cloning process he would have Kaarle delivered alive and breathing to von Verschuer's brand new eugenics Laboratory hidden now in a secret cave in Bavaria. Either way, Horst intended to extract his pound of flesh on Juergen's behalf. Horst had already let Stroop know that a fugitive who was considered a top priority of the Fuhrer himself was wandering around in Stroop's Warsaw Ghetto. Any amount of torture and mayhem had been authorized by Himmler to locate this Finn named Kaarle Tuuri traveling with the Norwegian Arin Olssen an escaped Jew from Auschwitz.

Heinrich Himmler was busy with the coordination of his plans to complete the Total Final Solution in Poland. It had been far too complicated at first because Jews had been separated at least in the major East European cities from the Gentile Polish population. With the latest plans things would be simple; kill every human being in Poland without restrictions. Hitler would finally get his Lebensraum. Quite by coincidence when the Sonderkommando began rounding up both Jew and Gentile from the public streets it turned out that the majority of the initial prisoners sent to the ovens in Auschwitz were actually Polish Gentile all along. With the current plan it was estimated that even the secret Death Camps at Birkenau and Sobibor would not be able to accommodate both populations. Plans had been formulated to use the swamps to both receive and execute Gentile as well as Jewish prisoners in large fire trenches.

As was his practice the Fuhrer suddenly appeared in Himmler's office with his coterie of Gestapo and Waffen SS escort unannounced. Himmler jumped to attention and gave his best "Heil Hitler!"salute. Hitler was annoyed about the incredible reports he was receiving about the losses at Stalingrad. "How is the new Total Final Solution Plan coming along?" Hitler asked. "Perfectly my Fuhrer. We have been wasting too much effort in trying to solve the sub-human problem separately from the Jewish problem, so now we are using the same facilities and consolidating our forces." Himmler explained. Hitler began playing with an ash tray on Himmler's desk. Suddenly he threw it through a glass window. Himmler braced himself for another long ranting speech and Hitler didn't disappoint. "Why in the f--ck do you think I attacked Poland, Austria and the Sudetenland first?" "Lebensraum, mein Fuhrer." Himmler answered on cue.

"Yes. Quite right. Our Fatherland needs to build first its base and a solid perimeter of protection in order to systematically cleanse mankind from its mistakes of nature. The sub-human countries fell before our mighty armies because they are inferior. We should have just waited and Stalin would have eventually crawled from beneath his bed and stopped shitting himself. I would have let him stay on to run his affen reserve for perhaps a few years until we could duplicate the Auschwitz camps in Russia. But no, the same plotting Generals who I should have sent to Stalingrad tried only a few months ago to kill me in the Zeughaus using this assassin Colonel von Gertsdorff. General Kluge actually promoted the motherless affen von Gertsdorff to be his Chief of Intelligence. They are all conspiring against me." Hitler sobbed. Himmler knew the exact opposite to be the case. He and virtually Hitler's entire top staff had argued against Barbarossa but Hitler was euphoric from early victories and launched the invasion against better advice.

"They don't deserve me! Germany doesn't deserve me! I am the only person on earth who is dedicated to the creation of our Master Race and the vile sons of whores are trying to f--cking kill me." Hitler screamed. "Himmler, take dictation!" "Yes mein Fuhrer!" Himmler shouted. "I want the Twelfth Army taken out of Stalingrad tonight. Move their asses down into Poland and kill everyone. Stroop is a policeman. I need a soldier to finish this job. You shall take direct control of the Twelfth and use the Waffen SS and kill everything that moves in Poland. Bring me back this perfect Finn and give him to von Verschuer. He can do again with this perfect specimen what has been done with the twin sister. von Verschuer now has the same laboratory he had in Berlin hidden in an obscure cave in Bavaria." Hitler ranted.

Himmler knew that a Rueckmarsch had begun at Stalingrad and that the Twelfth Army as well as all the others had begun a massive retreat to a line near Kursk, but Hitler talked as though the Twelfth Army were still engaged in Stalingrad. "But my Fuhrer, if I remove the Twelfth from the Eastern Front it could embolden the Russians to advance on Berlin. It could tip the balance in favor of Stalin's forces!" Himmler protested. "F--ck Stalin and his forces. They are affen who pick fleas from each others asses. They are a freak of nature that only since the last century stood up from their knuckles to walk erect. When did we lose our way? If you all would have listened to me we would have stopped the Lebensraum along the Russian border until our entire reason for being alive was completed. Our Master Race. We must find this f--cking Finn and harvest his sack until the world is marching with only Aryans. Then our Aryan armies will destroy all who are not considered pure. How could the Russians stand up against Aryans? How much clearer do I have to make this? Begin Operation Citadel. I have 5,000 tanks and 4,000 aircraft in reserve waiting to push the bastards back into Stalingrad and into Siberia if need be." Hitler screamed as he glared.

Himmler knew any counter argument would be futile. He would organize a five thousand man force from the German Home Guard using every Ordnungs Polizei available and begin a massive manhunt for the Finn. As far as killing all of the Poles in Poland regardless of whether Jew, or Gentile weren't they already trying to do that? He would focus on finding the Finn. It would be far less complicated. When found Himmler would turn him over to von Verschuer as Hitler had ordered unless the Finn had been killed during his capture, in which case, Mengele could dissect the left overs.

Himmler was a true believer in the Reich and had proven his loyalty to the Fuhrer many times since the Bier Hall Putsch in the early days, but he was also quite aware that Hitler had begun to unravel as he sensed that he wasn't the infallible leader he convinced himself he was from the very beginning. Hitler was an "Ideas Man" and as such, he believed all he had to do was provide the road map for the "Details Men" and his followers would, like robots, sacrifice themselves gladly for the future of the Reich. The fallacy of this concept was not the soundness of Hitler's understanding of eugenics, but rather his simple lack of appreciation that Nazi soldiers may be tough and willing to die for Hitler's cause but that their human frailties made them vulnerable to failure and collapse if implemented with complete disregard for their particular human vulnerabilities.

The same sociopathic characteristics of Hitler's persona when applied to the massive suffering his programs caused, made him insensitive to the nuances as well as the needs of his own troops. Himmler had initially scoffed at the intercepted psychoanalyses of Hitler, done by Allied psychiatrists, but resist as he may, at times, the definitions and descriptions of Hitler were profound. Yet, Himmler believed their pronouncements that he was a megalomaniac a sociopathic mass murderer, a manic depressive with catatonic schizophrenic tendencies, were wide paint brushes meant to win the moral high ground for the Allied cause. What was missing in Himmler's opinion was the side of Hitler that few people other than he and Hitler's close staff would ever see. The man was a genius. Of course eugenics was the answer. Himmler had to simply find a way to re-direct Hitler's military strategies to protect the genius from harming the Reich and himself.

If a person was born with a strabismus condition it only made sense that surgery be performed during the brief time window allowed by the natural receptiveness of the muscles that controlled the eye balls, lest the person become an inoperable cross eyed person for all time. But in the case of the sub-human species, genocide, not surgery was the answer and could only be performed at the point of a gun. "The cancer can only be removed from the pan-systemic human organ with genocide, that much is clear." Himmler thought. Nature made the mistake when it permitted the Jews and the darker races to multiply and contaminate the human population. Now it was up to superior men to correct the mistake. Himmler thought.

Then healthy genetic beings would not be competing with unhealthy genetic beings for vanishing resources. Nature's mistakes could be corrected. It followed for Himmler that if an entire race of people were dimwitted, or genetically inclined toward inferior physiology, or pathological behavior, it made perfect sense to first sterilize them to prevent proliferation of their hybrid and inferior subsets and then remove them entirely from the path of progress as the obstacles they were. Only in this way, by enabling the inevitability of a Master race that is genetically engineered to remove nature's mistakes could complete success be achieved.

With a carefully engineered folk, resources such as described by Malthus could be better spent, leading to an efficient and proper Master race throughout the world. So many subhumans had been confused by acquired morality that states that every human being has a right to live. Darwin clearly debunked this myth with his "Survival Of The Fittest" thesis that describes natures own "self corrective power."

Were the Nazis not fulfilling Darwin's thesis by eliminating the weak while propagating the strong? Himmler reasoned. Where was Hitler in this over all schematic? Himmler dared not discuss his private thoughts with anyone but he certainly had them. A case study in Darwin's theory was Lavretiy Beria who had been brought by Stalin to Moscow to serve as Deputy Head of the Secret Police, the NKVD. Within a few months he had the Head of the NKVD Nikolai Yezhov replaced. The Great Purge that established the Gulag soon followed that resulted in the purge of a third of Stalin's military leadership. Himmler knew that Hitler too was afraid of his own vast military machine which he created to project the power of the Reich out into the areas where Germany needed lebensraum, both to operate and to secure vital natural resources, but at least in the case of the Eastern Front, Hitler sent out the people he feared most would kill him. Only those whom he calculated would assassinate him just to gain power over the Reich. He assumed that if they were preoccupied with their own survival in the war against Russia they would not develop intrigues that sooner, or later might succeed. It was a calculated decision that Hitler was already beginning to regret because it was reaping unintended consequences as evidenced by the abysmal losses at Stalingrad. He was learning painfully that military strategy and politics are anathema to each other.

To be sure Hitler could have used a Beria to purge the potential assassins from his midst but his choice had been to let Russia do it for him. The blow back was now obvious. If the 5,000 tanks and 4,000 planes headed for Kursk were unable to push back the Red menace to Stalingrad and beyond, the war and the goals of the Reich would be lost. This was obviously to be the turning point of the entire war. It's equivalent in chess would be the loss of the Queen.

Hitler's inability to learn from Napoleon's Russian Winter mistake was to be etched in the history of warfare as a glaring and terribly unforgiving miscalculation.

A week after Kaarle and Arin escaped through the Muranowski tunnel, Stroop's Waffen SS found an enclave of ZZW fighters. ZZW lost all of its leaders on that day who fought to the last man. Small pockets of ZZW fighters continued to fight to the death but within a few days, they were all either burnt to death by flame throwers, or poisoned with gas. In yet, the final week of the Warsaw uprising the Nazis found Mordechai's last stronghold. A fierce battle ensued and Mordechai's corpse was later found where he had chosen to die, within a pile of bodies of his loyal resistance fighters, one of whom was Boleslaw still clutching his pistol that was aimed at the door. Mordecai knew his Warsaw Uprising was doomed from the beginning. He simply chose to use the lives of his Resistance fighters including his own life to make an indelible statement that Jews were willing to fight to the death to stop the genocide. This was made clear in his last letter to his friend and confidant Yitzhak Zuckerman:

> *My life's dream has now been realized: Jewish self-defense in the ghetto is now an accomplished fact....I have been witness to the magnificent, heroic struggle of the Jewish fighters.*

Mordecai Anielewicz

Kaarle made contact with the Polish Resistance and was hidden well inside an old abandoned mine shaft to await extraction. Arin developed pneumonia and it appeared he may not last until the rendezvous with an R.A.F. Halifax bomber scheduled by S.O.E. to land on an abandoned farm road at first light. Kaarle made a bark tea for Arin. He held the cup as Arin choked while trying to swallow the warm liquid.

The Poles tried to be cheerful, sharing their last scraps of food with Kaarle and Arin as though it was a banquet for royalty. The Poles sang folk songs and shared home made vodka while taking turns at watch all night long. There was nearly an incident when one of the Poles wanted to see what Arin had inside his pouch. When the pole grabbed the pouch, Kaarle reached for his Fiskar, but before he had to use it the photos fell out of the pouch and scattered across the earthen floor. Seeing the Death photos the Poles were very apologetic, or so it seemed, as no one understood each other. The leader of the small Resistance group pulled a piece of paper written in broken English and reached it to Kaarle. It had been transcribed from an underground radio transmission by some one in the Polish Resistance regarding the rendezvous. The transcriber's English was poor.

Dear English: Your fly London tomorrow at 0600 hours. S.O.E say von Verschuer has new lab in Bavaria cave for to make clones. Serious you leave before capture. They know you have same body like sister. If they catch you, they make clone many from you.

Cheerio! Erik

Kaarle re-read the note over and over. "So, von Verschuer was still in business with his scheme to clone a Master Race!" Kaarle thought. At dawn the S.O.E. Halifax bomber landed hard on the dirt road. Kaarle ran with Arin straddling his back to the plane that kept its engines revving. He reached Arin to the assistant bombadier. He had to yell at the top of his lungs. "He has pneumonia. Please keep him warm." "Please give my sister Laila at S.O.E. Branch my assurances I will be home soon. Got that?" Kaarle asked. "Yes Sir!" The bombadier said.

"Good! Please ask my sister Laila to tell Elina I love her and I want with all my heart be with her." "Want me to kiss her for you too mate? The bombadier asked. Kaarle grinned and shook his head no. "Cheeky bastard!" Kaarle said. "Tell Erik that von Vershuer's lab in Bavaria must be destroyed. Got it?" "Got it mate." "Good. Be sure this leather pouch full of photos from a prisoner at Auschwitz named Rudolf Vrba are turned over to the head of S.O.E. it's critically important. Last but very critical, tell S.O.E. that the Nazis have launched a new campaign to kill all Poles regardless of religion." Kaarle said. With that, the pilot began rolling down the road. Kaarle watched as the bombadier wrapped a blanket around Arin. The doors were closed and the plane lifted skyward heading northwest high into the morning sky.

Kaarle used sign language and the note but the Poles didn't seem to understand that they were his only hope of communicating with Erik and S.O.E. He followed them until the leader began barking in Polish for Kaarle to stop following them. Their mission had been completed. Finally the Resistance group leader made the mistake of pointing his 9 mm at Kaarle's head. He was lying on his back seeing stars before he knew what happened. Kaarle had the weapon pointed at the other two who had no intention of tangling with Kaarle. Kaarle then offered his hand to help the man up and returned his pistol to him pistol grip first. Kaarle pointed at the note then pointed to his own eye and then made a shrug that suggested he didn't know who wrote the note. The group leader then understood and shook himself off. His feelings had been hurt but he had a new respect for the Viking as his two men had been calling Kaarle since they met him. The Resistance group used hidden trails and hid away beneath shrubs when planes flew over head. Within two hours they reached an old abandoned warehouse near a small village.

The group leader went in first and soon came out to signal Kaarle and his two group members that the coast was clear. When Kaarle entered the warehouse he was led down a private stair visible only after removing some false planks. Kaarle was astonished at first when he saw that the Resistance Cell Commander was a silver haired older woman. "Why you don't leave with plane? You am crazy man?" "No Maam. Well maybe just a little." Kaarle smiled sheepishly. "My job isn't finished. I must go to Bavaria." Kaarle said. "So what you tink? I run travel office here?" She asked. "No Maam." Kaarle replied. "You just happen to be my only contact with S.O.E. Branch. Can you please contact Erik and tell him I need another Halifax and a parachute with a full load of weapons and mountain gear. If he can pick me up just like the plane picked up my brother today, I will be out of your way." Kaarle explained. "I make contact once each month except emergency." She said.

"I think this qualifies as an emergency." Kaarle said. Suddenly the room erupted in Polish from every direction. Each of the Poles looked at Kaarle as though he were a criminal. Finally the old woman reached Kaarle a note pad. "You write short note big letters, I send tonight after midnight." She said. Kaarle wrote the note in block letters:

ERIK,

NEED HALIFAX RIDE TO BAVARIA. NIGHT PARACHUTE INSERTION. ANY CHATTER OR HUMAN INTEL REGARDING CAVE CONSTRUCTION? NEED MAP OF CAVE AREA, SUB MG, PISTOL, GRENADES, 3 DAYS AMMO, BINOCULARS, RADIO THAT CAN CONTACT RAF TO GUIDE POSSIBLE BOMBING MISSION.

WOLF

The next evening Erik's reply came:

"Insane to do what you did, but I'm growing to expect it. Cave is Maxmillian Grotte north of Nurnberg, south east of Bayreuth near the Krottensee. Not certain which tributary houses the lab. Night recon only! Sending Halifax at 0100 zulu in two days/Saturday. Landing at Coordinates 094875. Proceed with night parachute insertion. Drop zone 3 kilometers east of objective. Choose (OP) observation point at a distance. Sending radio with frequency set. Your call sign Wolfhound 10. Birds are Eagle 10. Sending map, combat weapons and equipment package.

DON'T GET CAPTURED!"

Erik

Kaarle was certain he had the map coordinates interpreted accurately but it was already 01:30 hours and still no aircraft. The tomato cans filled with sand and kerosene to delineate the flare path had nearly burned themselves out when the Halifax bomber came lumbering in for a rough landing. Kaarle shook hands with the Poles and ran to leap into the still moving aircraft that maneuvered, then took off again. Kaarle didn't have to ask why they were late. Two crewmen lay dead on the floor and there were so many bullet holes in the fuselage Kaarle wondered that none of the cables and control systems had been damaged, or destroyed. Kaarle cast a sympathetic look to the crew chief who returned a grateful nod. No explanation was necessary. The Halifax had obviously been involved in a heavy bombing mission and air battle. No one had to mention what Kaarle had already guessed. That the extra thirty minutes of air time would mean they didn't have enough fuel to make it back to base.

Their choice was to try to make it to Dover, or take a chilling midnight swim in the English channel. The slight deviation to make a night drop over northern Bavaria wouldn't make that much difference either way so in spite of their own problems the mission came first. It humbled Kaarle to be among such silent heroes. Before long Kaarle had donned his chute and tied down his weapons and equipment in a P.A.E. bag that he would release on a long line just before landing. He could see the glimmer of the Krottensee as he stepped up to the chilling wind to await the green light that signaled his time to jump. Suddenly the interior of the aircraft glowed green and Kaarle dove straight out of the aircraft and felt the cushion of air take him ever downward. He pulled the cord and felt the reverse pull on his torso and inner thighs as the canopy opened. His head was pushed downward by his riser straps but the pressure disappeared as his body untwirled from the twisted risers. In seconds he saw the dark features below him getting closer so he released his P.A.E. bag. He didn't realize in the darkness how close to the ground he really was. He was suddenly surprised as his feet, then his legs, collapsed into his rump as he hit the ground like a sack of coal.

Kaarle lay silent for a few moments but as he began to get out of his webbing and roll up his parachute he heard the yelping of distant German shepherds. He couldn't tell if the barking was getting closer, or not, so he hustled to stash the chute in a hole he quickly dug with his collapsible entrenching tool. Soon Kaarle was scurrying to reach a large thick forest that surrounded the main area of the cave complex. Kaarle froze when he heard the sentry dogs barking from the direction of the forest. "Concentric inter-locking patrols, this one would not be easy." He thought. Kaarle knew there wouldn't be enough time for an initial recon, so he looked for a hiding place until the next night fall.

He found a stack of logs that had been cut for several months evidenced by the growth of weeds between the outer logs. Kaarle carved lumps of pitch and resin from the logs and smeared himself, his weapons and equipment thoroughly. He avoided the temptation to cut evergreen branches from live trees that would have left a trail, or evidence of his presence. Instead he found a freshly cut tree and took its branches to make a soft, dry bed for himself. Kaarle re-stacked the logs leaving a hollow chamber and used a bundle of bound dried branches that appeared to be collected kindling wood as a movable trap door. Kaarle designated one log on each side of the pile that he could remove quickly to establish a firing position. Just before first light Kaarle crawled inside his hideout, organized his weapons and gear and studied his map and reference points until he fell fast asleep.

When Laila learned that Arin was enroute to London, she was torn between the excitement and anticipation of being reunited with her husband and a feeling of shame that another man had made her a mother. Added to that was the inhuman feeling she experienced in knowing that her eggs were being harvested to clone children without fathers. Worse than what Dr. von Verschuer had called in-vitro fertilization had been the injection of what he called her DNA into stem cells to create clones without fathers. She worried that Arin would turn his anger toward her. Arin was fighting for his life. His lungs were filling with fluid and every breath he took was a major effort of survival. Yet the thought of seeing Laila once more gave him a strange inner strength based on his love for her and the hope that he would recover. Laila had been warned that Arin had suffered unbearable physical torture and denial and that his appearance would be shocking. Laila didn't care.

As long as Arin still loved her and didn't blame her for what had happened to herself she would nurse him back to health. Elina had been working as an intelligence analyst with S.O.E. Branch since she first arrived in London and was keenly aware of Kaarle's dangers and his progress. She was deeply hurt when she learned Kaarle had elected to stay in Poland when the aircraft had landed to exfiltrate Arin and Kaarle, but as an operator herself, she was also immensely proud of his courage. Arin was rushed to hospital upon landing in London where he was met plane side by Laila. She waited impatiently for the report from the doctor.

She could only see his eyes as his face was mostly covered by an oxygen mask. The tears streamed down her cheeks. His eyes were overwhelmingly expressive. Those eyes had once held only innocence. Those eyes had beheld her naked body and tenderly traced its lines with the desire of a lover and a husband. Those eyes had once held nothing but laughter and love for the world. Now they were bottomless with pain and suffering. Things had been bad for Laila, she had been abused, raped and treated like a lump of tissue but Arin's eyes held vast memories of the unimaginable pain of others. Self pity and horrible memories was one thing but constant exposure to the visual violence of watching children ripped apart without anesthesia, mothers charred bodies found still clinging to an infant to protect it even after both mother and child were dead. All of this was written indelibly across his mind. It was simply something the human mind wasn't designed to deal with and continue to be sane. The hatred a man would feel toward the person who took his wife transcended by the exposure to unending death. Laila didn't know it but she didn't have to worry that Arin would blame her about what had happened to both of them. His mind was in a much different place.

What she had to worry about was far more dangerous. She had to worry that Arin's mind had not traveled too deep into the darkness, the abyss from which nothing ever returns. She had to worry whether her love for him would be strong enough to provide a delicate but enduring bridge that wouldn't shatter with the weight of both of their souls. Just the weight of their burdens could, without warning, cause them to lose their way in the fog and darkness where the slightest misstep would send them both hurtling down into a sea of insanity.   After two very long days with Penicillin injections Arin began to improve. Laila had fallen asleep with her head extended across the foot of his bed. His voice was weak, but he spoke with her. "I love you Laila." "Oh Arin, my darling Arin I love you too. But I have to tell you some things that may make you hate me." She said while inhaling deeply. "You mean about our son? Kaarle already told me. We will find him Laila, I promise you this. But do you still love me?" he asked. "I look like an old man."

"Oh Arin, you look beautiful to me. Are you sure you want to be his father?" "I already am Laila. He's a part of you and that makes him a part of me. I just don't want you to tell him I'm not his natural father right away. Let him have a childhood. I had a sweet childhood and that is the single reason I survived." Laila leaned down and kissed Arin's forehead. "I always knew you were a special man Arin, I just didn't know how very special you were until this very moment." She sobbed openly. "Do you really think we can find him?" She asked. "If we can't find him in Norway, we'll search every inch of Germany but yes, we will find him as soon as it's safe to take you back to Oslo. Let's pray the war ends soon." Arin said softly.

Although Richardt Wagner was born in Leipzig and spent his early years in Dresden, his epic writing took place in Bayreuth where he completed his famous "Ring des Nibelungen" which consisted of four famous operas; The Valkyrie, The Rheingold, Siegfried and Goetterdammerung. Although Rheingold was played for the first time in Muenchen in September of 1869, the same year he completed Der Meister Singer von Nurnberg and Tristan und Isolde, as a part of his Norse sagas, the complete Ring wasn't assembled and played until August, 1876 when he performed them in the Bayreuth Festspielhaus, which was constructed especially for Wagner.

His work was based on a belief in the racial superiority of Aryan Norsemen. His racism appeared as early as 1850 when he wrote "Das Judentum In der Musik." a polemicist's argument about the mediocrity of Jewish contribution to music. He was a member of Nietzsche's inner circle in the 1870's and by 1880 his anti-semitism was blatant when his influence from the racist Arthur de Gobineau and his book; "An Essay On The Inequality Of The Races" began to be interpreted in his music. Gobineau's book eventually became mandatory reading for Hitler and his entire National Socialist party.

Kaarle was lying on pine branches, trying to sleep as Nazi patrols crisscrossed in opposing directions all around him. Had he known that Wagner was one of the strongest influences on Hitler's plan to design a Master Race, he may as a Norsman himself have found it ironic, but certainly not amusing. Wagner had written his finest work just a few kilometers away but Kaarle was only waiting for the first opportunity to blow the eugenic freak show to Hell,

Suddenly the logs shook and the ground rumbled beneath Kaarle so viciously that he wondered if it may be an earth quake. He had no way of knowing that the Eighth Air Force and the British Bomber Command had just begun Operation Point Blank which initiated round the clock bombing, the British at night and the Americans by day, to relieve pressure on the Eastern Front. Their current bombing was taking place as an initial probe in the Schweinfurt industrial sector against the precision ball bearing factories the Germans needed for the production of their war machines. The effect was immediate.

The Luftwaffe moved a major element from the Russian front to Central Germany to intercept the bombing campaigns. Its desired effect by the Allies was accomplished as it thus reduced the pressure felt by the Russians. Both America and Britain agreed they were not yet ready to open a second front, so the bombing campaigns served as a temporary replacement. Kaarle realized that the ground was vibrating as a result of the 500 pound bombs being dropped on the factories. He tried to go back to sleep. As he lay there he tried to count the time intervals between the bombing raids in hopes that he may use the noise and distraction to his own advantage when his recon would begin, but there was no specific pattern.

When darkness falls on a thick forest, it renews the very concept of darkness. The slightest glimmer of light is swallowed into the shadows. German Shepherd dogs however, are immune from this concept. Their pupils widen and their sensitive vision receptors pick up even subtle shades of contrast from long distances. Even if German Shepherds had been born as blind as humans their highly sensitive olfactory nerve would pick up scents from great distances.

Kaarle had thoroughly rubbed his body with pine pitch, but once in the open forest all bets were off. A three man patrol of Waffen SS soldiers were about five minutes away from their turn around rendezvous with an opposing patrol. Kaarle was able to see movement near an old abandoned woodsman's hut with his high powered binoculars. The patrol there was stationary and waiting. Kaarle correctly determined they were waiting for contact with their opposing patrol. If either patrol failed to show up an alarm would be sent immediately after an established interval had expired.

Without warning, the large German Shepherd from the nearest patrol began pulling its human master in Kaarle's direction. It whined slightly but didn't yelp, or bark. "Damn but that's a well trained dog! Kaarle thought as he crawled behind a large tree stump. The German Shepherd tore away from its master and leaped through the air above the stump Kaarle was behind. By the time the dog landed it was missing its heart. Kaarle rolled away from the stump and sprang upward slicing his Fiskar through the mans breast plate, up through his pulmonary artery and his Larynx. The other two soldiers were close behind. Kaarle hit each one with a round from the silenced 9 mm pistol Erik had included in his combat pack.

By the time Kaarle reached the Woodsman's hut the other patrol arrived. A German Shepherd began spinning and rolling, but like its colleague it also didn't bark. The Patrol leader was angered slightly at the dogs behavior but took it to mean that the dog from the opposing patrol was getting expectedly closer. Suddenly the dog that had been straining at the leash yelped and then fell flat. The patrol leader groaned as the 9 mm coughed once then two more times killing the entire opposing patrol. Kaarle reached down and lifted the Patrol leader's radio.

He set about collecting all of the Potato Masher Stick grenades from the dead bodies. There were twelve total. He emptied a German's pack and shoved all twelve grenades inside in a bundle. He turned the squelch knob on the German Patrol leaders radio to silence, then he moved quickly through the forest. When he reached the main entrance to the Maxmillian Grotto he cursed silently. He saw that no construction had occurred there. The lab must be in one of the distant tributaries to the main cave Kaarle figured since he had encountered the two patrols along the east sector above the caves. There must be at least two more patrols operating along the west sector. Suddenly a piercing ray of light was emitted from the east sector. He saw the vehicle path but had somehow walked right past the entrance.

He back tracked along the east sector and nearly stumbled over the army motorcycle with side car. He crept over to a large sliding door that was covered with earthen live foliage. No wonder he missed it. He looked for a lever, or a handle and realized there wasn't one. Access could only be gained by radio with a pass word. "Damn it! Sooner, or later the Patrol Commander would be checking in with his patrols. All of them. If he was challenged for a password an alarm would go out immediately. He could pretend to be one patrol leader, but not two." Kaarle thought. Just then the massive door slid open and the Motorcycle messenger emerged. Kaarle shot him in the temple with the silenced 9 mm. He then shoved a large stone in the doorway. A group of scientists and technicians dressed in white smocks and full length coats began screaming A-L-A-R-M! One reached for a telephone and Kaarle shot him right away. As he was replacing his clip an older scientist opened a desk drawer and began to pull out what Kaarle believed to be a weapon. Kaarle shot him center forehead.

When Kaarle walked over to his desk he saw the man had a file, not a pistol in his hand. Kaarle almost opened the file but he already knew what it contained. It contained the evil science that enabled Nazis to re-create humans using only their own cells. He put the file inside the pack full of grenades. He looked down a spiraling stair and saw the same set up of liquid oxygen glass tanks he had seen in Berlin. The scientists and technicians had all begun to run deeper into the recesses of the cave tributary. "No doubt they're running to a bomb shelter. Better be a good one." He thought as he looked at the blue Liquid Oxygen tanks along the walls. Kaarle unscrewed the cap from the bottom of one of the Stick grenades and pulled the short cord which triggered the fuse. He set the activated grenade back inside the pack and dropped it in the center of the lab below. He shoved the rock out of the path of the sliding door just as the belly of the cave complex belched forth a horrible, collapsing, rumbling explosion that blasted the heavy door ajar with flames licking along its edges. Kaarle stripped the uniform from the messenger and shoved his body inside the still flaming cave. He put on the uniform and threw his clothing inside the fire.

He drove the motorcycle in the direction of a landing strip on a large rounded mountain top in the Rhoen mountains called the Wasserkuppe. Erik picked it as a possible extraction point and had it marked on the map as a primary. Alternative two was near a city called Amberg and looked too congested and too far away. The other choices looked worse with a half dozen plots near Schweinfurt. "Too dense with Germans." he thought. Wasserkuppe looked somewhat isolated on the map and had a symbol of a glider near the center, so Kaarle felt reasonably certain he could get the RAF, or S.O.E. to pick him up there.

As the first glimmer of dawn glowed along the horizon Kaarle turned onto a side trail. Using the small tool box he found in the saddle bags he detached the side car and covered it with tree branches. He could now ride faster and go off road if need be.

Chapter Eleven: Basque Country

Kaarle skirted the small villages, choosing instead to ride across open fields to avoid road blocks. He stole a can of fuel from a farmer's barn and walked the cycle almost a half kilometer down a narrow trail to avoid waking the farmer. Soon he was riding near a small village called "Oberweissenbrunn." He saw a sign that pointed toward "Bischofsheim" and another that said "Wasserkuppe." He rode with his lights out in the direction of the Wasserkuppe. He was happy to see that the place was perfect, except for the low lying cloud cover two thirds of the way to the top. The Allied pilot would have plenty of room to land because the strip had been designed to accommodate towing gliders and was nearly twice the length of other small airstrips but if the cloud cover reached the top for any reason, it would be impossible to land.

Kaarle found a thick pine forest near the landing strip and made himself a hide out, covering the cycle with pine tree branches. Just before sunrise the cloud cover brought a dense fog to the top and it remained there until early afternoon when it receded somewhat back down the mountain side. "It would have to be a night extraction." he thought but he would attempt to communicate with the bombers day, or night once he heard them flying over head again. When the two patrols from the west sector heard the explosion they thought at first there had been an accident in the lab. They attempted to contact the East patrol Commanders but their radios had been strangely silent. After some deep anxiety about leaving their patrol sector they finally decided to investigate the secret cave. When they discovered the destruction of the secret cave with several charred bodies inside, they woke up the Battalion Commander who was staying in a hotel he had commandeered for himself in a nearby village.

The Battalion Commander immediately phoned Horst Feldner per his instructions and reported that a platoon of Sappers had somehow managed to wipe out two Waffen SS Patrols, kill their dogs and blow up the underground laboratory. Horst was beside himself. He knew that he had "better have a goddamned good story for Himmler" he thought. He called Himmler in Berlin and gave him the report he had received verbatim from the battalion Commander. Himmler was silent for a moment. "I hope you understand Feldner what this means. It means that Lebensborn has been stopped dead in its tracks. Were any of the research files rescued?" "No Herr Himmler. All of the personnel and all of the equipment was melted when a large explosive device was ignited from within the cave." Feldner responded. "How many of the Sappers were killed, or captured?" "None Sir."

"What? Do you mean to tell me that a platoon of Sappers were, I assume, dropped in by parachute and that with two German Divisions in the area not a single road block or a single citizen has reported seeing them, or witnessing their extraction? I want you to take every Goddamned person soldiers, farmers f--cking goat herds and comb the forest where the two patrols were found dead. Don't move the bodies, I want to know the angle of the bullets. I want a count and type classification of all of the shell casings. I will have one hundred German Shepherds brought in to look for foot prints before the trail gets cold. I want a count of how many Sappers were there. Then you call me back. I won't even go to the W.C. until I hear from you. Do you understand my orders?" "Yes Sir!" "There is no possible way anyone less than a rifle company could have done this much damage. Hitler will want someone's balls for this. Yours are looking rather large right now." Himmler warned.

Within thirty minutes Feldner called Himmler. "Sir you are a genius!" Feldner exclaimed. "Get your nose out of my ass Feldner! What have you found?" Himmler shouted. "Sir, we found a total of six shell casings near both sites where the patrols were murdered. All casings were 9 mm." Feldner observed. "That doesn't add up. Six men were killed and two dogs that's eight casings." Himmler said. " No Sir. Five men were shot and one dog. One man and one dog were stabbed to death." Feldner explained." The location of the wounds suggest highly trained assassins performed all of the murders. One thing seemed strange. Each patrol member was missing his grenades but there were no holes in the ground to suggest explosions had occurred." "Feldner you embecile. It was a single man who did this using your own explosives! Verdammt noch mal! A one man platoon. Why did you tell me this was done by a platoon Feldner?" "This was the information I received from the Battalion Commander Sir." " Is the battalion commander a member of the Gestapo?" Himmler asked. "No Sir!" Feldner replied. "Then why is he doing your f—cking job for you?" "Sorry Sir! I was in a hurry to notify you." Feldner pleaded.

"Listen Feldner. We can discuss this again later. Right now it is clear that a lone assassin is attempting to get his ass out of Bavaria. Verdammt! One man kills two patrols and destroys Lebensborn with your own grenades? Unglaublich Feldner! Draw a circle with the Maxmillian Grotte at its center. Then keep drawing ever larger circles and call them zones one through ten. Make each zone five kilometers wide. Highlight every flat space in each zone that can accommodate a long range aircraft. Make abandoned, or lightly used air strips priority one. I will wait." Himmler said. "Yes Sir!" Feldner replied. Within fifteen minutes he was back on the phone. "There are eight places Sir.

Five near Schweinfurt, one near Bad Kissingen and one that seems quite distant in Amberg." "Where is the eighth one Feldner?" "On an isolated glider path called Wasserkuppe." Feldner reported. Silence ensued. "Wasserkuppe is the most isolated from populated areas?" "Yes Sir! But it's only for gliders Sir." " Feldner you are a dumbkopf. A glider path is twice as long as a power runway. It's perfect for a long range plane. The man who murdered your son can be found there if you hurry. He has anger for what happened to his sister. That is why he destroyed our lab in Berlin and that is why he destroyed our lab in Maxmillian Grotte. Since he destroyed our last hope of exponentially expanding the Master Race until after the war, I no longer care if he is captured dead, or alive. I only care that you cut out his genitalia and preserve them in Formaldehyde in a jar for our geneticists. Alles klar?" "Yes Herr Himmler!" "Good. How many soldiers do you have immediately ready to travel?" "About five thousand Sir!" "Get their asses moving toward the Wasserkuppe. I want the Finn's balls in a jar before sunset! Himmler growled. "Yes Sir!"

Kaarle began transmitting with the radio Erik sent him. He repeated the call sign several times. "Eagle Ten this is Wolfhound ten, come in over." He was about to go silent until night fall when suddenly a voice came in first with static and then as clear as a bell. "This is Eagle Ten, come in Wolfhound Ten over." Kaarle had never heard English spoken with an American accent before and it caused him to hesitate slightly. "Eagle Ten Wolfhound Ten, request extraction, over." Kaarle said. "WolfhoundTen be advised I am the escort leader of a flight of twenty Mustangs but we are all single seaters." EagleTen said.

"In your favor, however, is the fact that we are escorting a bomber squadron of very frustrated B-24 Liberators who can't find a place near Schweinfurt to drop some heavy ordnance because of thick cloud cover. I will have their squadron leader peel off someone for you, over." As Kaarle was speaking on the radio a large separation in the fog opened up, revealing an enormous convoy of truck borne infantry fanning out near the base of the Wasserkuppe in the valley below.

"Eagle Ten, my ground coordinates are 094770. I have an enemy force of approximately five thousand men bottled up in the valley below me. Would your Liberators be interested? Over." Kaarle asked. "I see them. What the..F… Why are that many troops holding down in such a tight spot? Over." Eagle Ten asked. "I believe they are interested in me. Over." "Sweet Jesus! OK Wolfhound we're gonna turn this into a fair fight. I'll be going off station for a few minutes, you just sit back and enjoy the fireworks son. Out." Kaarle switched frequencies until he found the Escort leaders new channel to listen in. "Apache Ten this is Eagle Ten over." "Copy Five by Five Eagle Ten. Preparing to return home heavy. No targets over." "That's a negative. Follow your escorts. We are coming down to your elevation. We found a hole in the clouds and there's nearly an entire division of enemy infantry in the open. Be advised we have a very important friendly on the mountain top. Try not to scatter off target. Over." "Lead on Eagle Ten. Friendly is noted. Out." The Mustang patrol dove down through the opening in the clouds and led the bomber squadron to the scrambling Nazi soldiers below. The rumbling massive bomb detonations in the valley below caused the entire mountain to sway as though it was about to sink into the earth. Kaarle was thrown to the ground.

He managed to return his radio to the original frequency just as Eagle Ten was sending. "Wolfhound Ten Wolfhound Ten, do you copy? Over." "Five by Five. Over." Kaarle said. The Escort leader chuckled. "You learn fast Wolfhound. There's an infantry company still headed toward your location. My team will neutralize them for you and then I'm going to bring one of the Liberators down to pick you up so stay close but not on top of the runway. He will stop and go so fast you won't have a chance to take a piss break. Are we clear on that? Over." "Loud and clear Eagle Ten." Kaarle replied. "Eagle Ten. Out."

Kaarle watched as the Mustangs chewed up the remaining Waffen SS. A single jeep in the lead made it to the top of the Wasserkuppe. Kaarle was confused for a moment. He had seen that face before. EINDHOVEN! It was the Gestapo agent! Feldner stood up above the windshield and began firing at Kaarle. "You killed my son Juergen you dirty bastard!" Feldner was screaming. Kaarle opened up with his submachine gun drilling Feldner across the chest. He shot the driver in the face with his 9 mm. The two SS soldiers in the back seat dove out. Kaarle finished his clip killing them both. Suddenly a huge shadow passed over the ground as the B-24 Liberator came in for a landing. Kaarle ran until it felt as though his heart would burst. The crew pulled him inside and soon the smooth aircraft was lifting up above the pines and back above the clouds where it was soon rejoined by its flight of Mustang escorts. Kaarle was strapped into a parachute and given a flask of whiskey to help hold down his airsickness or so the crewman said. A crewman sat down beside him and shook his hand. "Apache Five, pleased to meet you Wolfhound Ten." The man said. "Who is Eagle Ten, what's his Christian name ?" Kaarle asked.

"Eagle who?" The man responded. "The escort Leader." Kaarle replied. "Oh, we don't use names, we use call signs." he said. " You see, the truth is not many people you meet in either the fighter group, or the bomber command will still be around a day, week, or month from now. If you ask a guy's name then the bastard may show you a picture of his kids and if you have to clean him out of his cockpit, or gun turret it takes away a piece of your soul. If you lose a call sign and you don't even know whether he had a family, you're a lot safer. Then it's just his ugly puss you have to forget which isn't so goddamned easy either know what I mean?" "I see." Kaarle said as he shook his head slowly and felt the collective madness of combat catching up with him at last. He took a deep swallow of the Kentucky whiskey and fell asleep as the aircraft dropped and gained altitude almost continuously. The crewmen sensed his need for solitude and didn't wake him even when the formation of Messerschmitt fighters came down from high altitude to do battle over Lyon, France.

The pilot of the B-24 Liberator, Captain James Ellis watched the skies above as his Mustang escort fought an intensely pitched battle in his defense. Messerschmitts were exploding in flames and streaming black smoke as they hurtled earthward all around him. The Mustangs skillfully owned the sky. One Messerschmitt, however, that had been hiding beneath the cloud cover suddenly broke through just to the right and rear of Ellis' bomber. Kaarle was awakened when the B-24 turned on its side to avoid a line of machine gun fire from the Messerschmitt that came so close Kaarle could see the pilots face. Blood sprayed from the turret gunner who was killed instantly. The crewman Kaarle had spoken with pulled his body out of the Gunners seat and crawled in behind him until he too was shot to death.

Kaarle was about to pull out Apache Five and take his place when an enormous blast ripped a hole across the top of the B24's fuselage and caused the plane to go spinning earthward. Kaarle managed to grab a sub-machine gun and a metal box of ammo as he spun suspended and weightless through the air in a counter direction until he was sucked free of the plane. The B-24 was trailing thick black smoke. Kaarle watched as it broke into two pieces. He saw the crewmen trying to climb free but lost sight of the plane and crew when it penetrated the cloud cover below. Kaarle waited until he punched through the clouds before pulling his rip cord. He nearly lost his weapon and ammo with the opening shock of his canopy. Kaarle was already thinking about his last hard landing and was getting ready to brace when the hot molten lead whizzed in front of him. Then he saw what was happening. Three other canopies were drifting above him as the Messerschmitts were coming in for the kill. He watched in horror as the crewmen he had been flying with just moments before were screaming as they watched their canopies go up in flames.

One of the crewmen hung lifeless from his parachute harness. Kaarle felt a deep burning in his rib cage. He looked down and saw the ammo box glowing red. He saw the large round hole in the side of the metal box and realized the box and the ammo clips had protected him from being killed by the projectile. He quickly dropped the ammo box and snuffed out the burning embers of his jacket. "He was lucky twice," he thought. First the box stopped the bullet and second the ammo inside didn't explode. Kaarle was still staring upward at the falling crewmen whose canopies were burning away when he hit the ground. He tried to roll but it all happened too fast and he was temporarily knocked unconscious.

Still above, hidden by the thick clouds Captain Ellis craned his neck in every direction to watch for marauding Messerschmitts. He knew they were ordered by their Air Marshall Goering to eliminate all flyers while they were vulnerable in parachutes, or else face the prospect they will return to finish you in the next battle, but Captain Ellis knew he personally would never murder a fellow airman even if he did wear the wrong uniform. As he landed, a small group of French Maquis surrounded him and began cutting away his chute. "Don't worry Monsieur, we are French Resistance. Maquis from Brittany in the north of France. We patrol the air corridors to rescue airmen. I am sorry to report that your entire crew was killed by the shit Nazi Messerschmitts. Captain Ellis grimaced as tears filled his eyes.

"Please Sir to come with us. We will take you with us to Brittany and then smuggle you by fishing boat to England." Abruptly the Resistance leader noticed James was bleeding from a left shoulder wound. The Resistance Leader called his medic over who quickly removed a shard of shrapnel and dressed the wound. Captain Ellis insisted on seeing his dead crewmen. The resistance leader became anxious about remaining too long, but Ellis was not taking no for an answer. He limped supported by the Resistance leader to the pile of bodies the Resistance assembled. "OK, They're dead alright but we had a passenger. Did you find his body?" "No Sir. He is most likely dead somewhere across these fields. We really must leave now Sir, or we will all join him." They boarded a stolen German truck and left for Brittany, picking up other downed airmen along the way. Captain Ellis made it back to London, but the surgeon reluctantly informed him that a nerve in his left arm had been permanently damaged. He would never fly again for the military.

He was quietly assigned as an Air Force mission analysis officer at the S.O.E. Branch Tactical Operations Center. As soon as he reported for duty he was met by the prettiest Norwegian woman he had ever seen. It saddened him when he had to tell her that her friend Kaarle, who he picked up from a mountain plateau was aboard his plane when it was shot down. That they searched the surrounding fields and that his body was never found and that he was believed killed. Over time, Elina began to grow accustomed to the idea Karle was gone. She felt a closeness with James because he had been the last person to have had contact with him. She avoided Laila and Arin because she couldn't bear to discuss with them Kaarle's highly probable death.

When he awoke Kaarle heard the smooth, silky soft rounded words of French. He was looking up the barrel of a Thompson sub-machine gun at a very unfriendly man. "Thees one is Le Bosch." Alain said. "Keel him then." came the decision from Jacque the apparent leader of the small resistance group. "Wait. We can interrogate him later and perhaps learn some intelligence about what the Luftwaffe is planning since it has moved away from the East." Came the opinion of Michelle a pretty young French woman. "She's right. See if any of the others survived the jump." Jacque ordered. In a few minutes Alain returned. "All dead. Fokking Bosch shot them as they descended. Fokking Bosch." He repeated. "That's too bad for this one who is wearing a German uniform but it doesn't make sense that it is the uniform of a German Corporal. He should be wearing the uniform of a Luftwaffe pilot. Furthermore he was wearing an English parachute and apparently jumped from the same American bomber these dead Americans were riding." Jacque said. "Perhaps he was their prisoner?" Alain asked. "Ha Ha! Brilliant Alain."

B-24 bombers flying through the sky taking German Corporals prisoner who are getting drunk with Bavarian beer angels on clouds that wear the perfume of German beer? " Michelle laughed. "Well, let's ask him. Monsieur Le Bosch parle vous Francaise? " "I speak English. I am from Finland and I am an agent of Special Operations Executive Branch, in London. I was being taken back to London by the Americans to deliver my after action report when we were suddenly shot down." Kaarle said.

"Hmmm. Good so far, but please to explain how you jumped from the ground into a B-24 Bomber? They are not welcome at most German airports and we didn't see one land." Jacque paried. "I am an S.O.E. Agent. My mission was in Northern Bavaria. When it was completed I stole a German motorcycle and borrowed the drivers uniform in order to get to an abandoned glider path on top of a mountain called Wasserkuppe." "Ha are you proud Alain you embecile? You nearly shot a spy from S.O.E. Branch." Michelle quipped.` "Who could tell. He looks like one of those f--cked up Aryans and he is still wearing the German uniform." "Why are you in Northeast France when you operate in Southwest France?" Kaarle asked. "His mother dies two days ago from German bombs. We came for the funeral. Of course he couldn't attend but we watched from a distance to pay our love and respect. Within our current mood, you are truly lucky we didn't just shoot you." Michelle said. "I see. My condolences Jacque. I won't make trouble for you. Once you find out that I speak the truth, what then?" Kaarle asked. "That is a problem. Our main camp was destroyed by the Fascists. Our radio destroyed we have no further contact with the Allied forces. If you are truly an anti-fascist you will have many opportunities to prove it. We stay busy against the fascists and you can either help us, or die." Jacque said.

"Until we can trust you we must bind you. You can ride in the boot." Jacque said. "One last question, where are we?" Kaarle asked. "Why should I tell you?" Jacque stared hard at Kaarle. "We are near Lyon. Why?" "I'm just amazed we are this far south. We were headed for London. We should have at least been over Normandy." Kaarle replied. "Do you think Monsieur that Allied pilots fly in straight lines? They avoid known alley ways where Messieurs Messerschmitt make their home. Come everyone let's get going before we attract flies." Jacque said. T Michelle wrapped Kaarle in a wool blanket and rolled up some old rags to make Kaarle a pillow. "I am betting that you are telling the truth. If not, I will be the first to shoot you and it won't be pretty." She said as she hurried back to the waiting passenger door. They boarded an old Mercedes Benz and headed for the highway south. Kaarle was grateful for the warm blanket and the rags for a pillow. They took bumpy back roads and Kaarle was tossed around severely. By Midnight they reached an abandoned mill near Toulouse. The car was refueled by local resistance members and Kaarle received his first toilet break. They blindfolded Kaarle in order not to endanger the identities of the local Maquis.

They later untied Kaarle's hands and he devoured some potato and cabbage soup. He enjoyed a glass of local wine and became very sleepy. By two am he was back in the boot of the fuel smelling car trying his best not to return the red wine and potato soup. They drove for an hour and stopped again. This time they were near an old warehouse. A man came out and exchanged keys with Jacque. Soon they boarded an old hearse. It's engine purred as though it had just been wheeled out of the factory. The old man embraced each of the Maquis and gave them light kisses on the cheek and then they were off.

Kaarle had the most comfortable place in the vehicle. He was covered by a white sheet on a collapsible Guerney traveling as a dead body. "Jacques is really a good driver." Kaarle thought to himself, as they flew through curves in the Pyrenees with breathtaking precision. Once when Jacque came too close to a rocky ledge for Michelle's satisfaction they broke out in an argument in a language that Kaarle had never heard before. "What language are you speaking?" He asked. They all looked at each other and roared with laughter. "We are speaking our Mother tongue "Euskera." Michelle answered.

"We are Basque. We have been fighting since 1936. First against the Spanish dictator Franco and now against his brothers Hitler and Mussolini. We despise all fascists equally." She said. "We feel safer now that we are back in the French Basque country, so I will tell you this much. We have a hideout not far from here. If you are who you say you are we have been laughing because we will use it as a cause for killing chickens and filling our wine sacs. Alain made us laugh because he said if you are not who you say you are we can kill you instead of the chickens and still fill our wine sacs. I suppose it's only funny if you hear it in Euskera, no?" She asked, still smiling. Kaarle didn't smile which made them laugh all the harder. He instantly liked these people. He had read of how Franco did his best to erase the Basque for resisting his government during the Civil War. Executing men women and children alike. Franco even tried to outlaw their language and culture. So this is what happened to them. They have thrown in with the Allies and are still resisting to their last breath. What absolutely marvelous people he thought. Kaarle didn't know much about the Americans, but he sincerely hoped they would look out for the Basque according to what ever deal had been struck with them.

If not, there would no doubt be Hell to pay. They were met about thirty kilometers from the Spanish border by a farmer with a truck full of goats and chickens. They followed the truck into the mountains. The truck was also filled with armed men hidden behind the chicken crates. Soon they reached a farming village hidden away in the forest. Every farmer carried a shotgun. Even if Kaarle wanted to escape, he wouldn't have made it 100 meters without being blasted by a shot gun. "That's probably why they untied me as soon as we met the truck." He thought.

"This small house is used for our guests. Since we have none at the moment, it's all yours." Michelle said. "May I ask you something?" "Certainly." Michelle replied. "Why do you all have French names?" He asked. "Well we operate mostly in France and when we're here we speak French. It's just easier. I certainly hope you aren't a disappointment. You are getting to know us far beyond our comfort level." She said. "Their comfort level? Or yours?" Kaarle asked. Michelle blushed. "My Basque name is Yenega. It means Fiery in English." Kaarle's eyes widened. "Yes, I can see that." He said as she blushed even more. "What of Jacque and Alain?" He asked. "Jacque's name is Albar. It means noble guardian and Alain is Benat, it means a brave bear." She explained. We do not believe in eating alone so please wash up. There is a rain barrel with soap and a towel over there behind the house. Your shirt size is equal to Albar's. I laid out a fresh shirt and trousers for you. As I said I'm betting that we won't have to put any holes in Albar's shirt." She smiled. "You'll win your bet." Kaarle grinned back. Kaarle was completely overwhelmed with both the beauty and simplicity of the meal and the ambient candle lit surroundings. The table was surrounded by six people including Yenega, Albar and Benat.

The other two present were an older couple who Kaarle surmised had cooked the meal. A giant flat pan sat between them in the center of a floor level set of cushions. Each person sat straddle legged and used their fingers to retrieve pieces of rabbit, pork, chicken and mussels in a delicious tomato sauce with savory golden rice. Hanging from the high wooden ceiling above were chains with a silver hook at shoulder level. Hanging from each silver hook was a leather sac filled with delicious red wine. One could either drink from the bag, while it remained on the hook, or drape it over a shoulder and guide the hollowed out deer antler that served as a spout. Kaarle couldn't drink fast enough. Splashes of red wine covered his face and painted the front of his shirt. Michelle laughed. "Those of us outside will think we already cut your throat. " Everyone except Kaarle roared with laughter. When it dawned on him that he had been keeping a sadness bottled up inside Kaarle began to chuckle. Then as the wine relaxed him a flood gate of laughter opened. His too serious life pent up since childhood was released. Kaarle wished it would last forever but he already knew it wouldn't. These wonderful people showed him in just a few moments of human warmth that he had never had a real family, but his sadness resided far too deep to go away for more than the breadth of a few single heart beats. His Mother had been taken away from him in the same bed he was born in. His sister had been ripped from him in the middle of the night and her life all but ruined. He had traveled straight through a lost childhood and become an efficient killing machine. An assassin. No where in his entire life had he come even close to having what these people have. His brief stay with the Sami was at least a semblance of a family structure, but even they had not dared completely relax as tragedy and violence became as commonplace to their warring existence as the onset of another arctic winter.

The Basque were somehow different. They stood their ground against the fascists and the dictators, but when they were together the excitement and the warmth was as though they had never witnessed the dark side of mankind. Kaarle's memories of Elina were growing dim. His heart had never been this far south before and the warmth was showing up in the people around him and yes, even in himself. He didn't know how to handle this new part of himself. He was as vulnerable as a child. He didn't love killing, he hated it. He only did what was needed to stay alive himself yet he sensed that taking human life was wrong and that he would some day have to answer for it. His only consolation which wasn't much was that he'd never really asked for it, he was born into it. The old man asked Kaarle why he was fighting Germans when his country, Finland had chosen to fight with them. "There is occasionally a time when we must follow our own heart." Kaarle said. "The Germans forced their armies upon my neighbor Norway. They took my sister and her husband away. "My sister was raped and forced to bear a child by a Nazi officer while her husband was delivered to a Death camp called Auschwitz. I discovered they wanted to use my sister's body to create Aryan babies for their Reich. In a more direct answer to your question, I suppose, at least in my opinion my country chose the wrong side." Kaarle replied. This drew an understanding grunt from everyone around the table. "Why do you fight the Germans?" Kaarle asked innocently.

"We have experienced a similar problem to your own I suppose." The old man answered. "In 1936 when the demon Franco joined with the other dissident Generals, Mola and Sanjurjo against the Republic, we Basque didn't really think much about what being a country really meant. To be sure we have a language that is not the same as Spanish, or any other.

Racially, our ears and other appendages are quite different from those of other people. Maybe we are from another planet." the old man joked. "I suppose we just never applied too much thought to how completely different we are from the country of Spain which claimed us based soley on geography. Our culture is also different from theirs. We were divided amongst ourselves and since we could not agree some of the Basque who are called 'Carlists' sided with the Franco. They called themselves traditionalists. We were only interested in annexing ourselves from Spain, to be left to our own devices, so this was a promise we received from the Republic, that our people and its borders would always be respected. So like the great Finland we chose one side over the other based on our projection of who would win and what that would mean to our own precious independence.

We formed a government that we still call Euskadi and though we had never really formed an army before, we assembled 45,000 soldiers to defend the Republic in a very short time. General Mola, building on early successes in Pamplona and Vitoria led the Carlists while we established ourselves in Vizkaya and Guipuzcoa. What our soldiers lacked in experience they made up for in dedication to our cause, but we placed far too much reliance upon fortifications." the old man lamented. "We built magnificent barriers around Bilboa. For example, during the winter of 1936 and the spring of 1937 the weather was always cloudy along the Bay Of Biscay. Not the best weather for aerial bombing and surveillance.This caused Franco to turn his attention away from us for a while to concentrate on the fierce Republican siege of Madrid." He continued. "As luck would have it however, things went poorly for Franco in Madrid and the weather changed to sunshine where we were in Bilbao.

They must have decided that Bilbao looked too much like a ripe apple to be ignored because they came to us in force. They laid siege to us at Bilbao and we counter attacked but our losses were not sustainable.

We lost 800 men in a pitched battle south of Bilbao in the direction of Vitoria with 4,000 wounded. Our president Aguirre was a gallant man but with certain defects he was unable to address. The first was the fact that Franco had air superiority thanks to 120 German fighters of the Condor Legion. We on the other hand had only six worn out Russian fighters flown by Spanish pilots without much experience. The second was that so called neutral countries had signed a pact that denied them from shipping weapons to us. Our weapons were limited to small arms and a few small mortars. Aguirre's response was called the "Cinturon de Hierro" or the belt Of Iron. The initial plan was to build a barricade that was to stretch from Somorrostro by the western sea shore around Bilboa to Sopelana on the east. In total distance about 200 kilometers of barbed wire, trenches and machina guns not unlike the famous Maginot line of WW I. We had a belt but were without pantalones."

"It was poorly constructed and had enormous gaps where no barbed wire, or fortifications were present. This was not the worst part. A son of a bitch engineering officer, a Captain Goicoechea deserted us, possibly because he had lack of faith in his own work and provided Mola not only with a detailed map of the best attack lanes, but an inventory of all of our weapons and troops. The attack came soon and it exploited the Cinturon as though it wasn't there. The German bombing of Guernica and Durango was merciless and against mainly civilians.

Some say Air Marshal Goering used the cities to practice bombing strategies for his future air campaigns, but of this I cannot say." the old man pondered. "We tried to surrender with dignity to the Italian forces but their Mussolini tried to claim us as a conquest, so Aguirre told them to kiss his brown spot." The old woman slapped her husband on the arm. "Well, it's true." He said. I obscenity in the milk of Franco and Mussolini's mothers.

"Anyway, young man, know that we fought even in retreat into the Basque regions here in Southern France and are still fighting. Our main resistance has been against the Germans and the Vichy French who are afraid to chase us into these hills. When Franco declared victory he did everything including selective genocide to destroy the Basque people. He made our language and culture illegal and the poor souls of Bilbao, were sent to death camps by the thousands." the old man reflected.

"Winston Churchill has said that our Maquis are the same as fifteen complete divisions. We will help the Allies because they fight our enemy the Germans, but there will come a day when they have no use for us and they will cheat and murder us like Franco did." the old man reasoned. Kaarle was silent. "I will pity them if they do. There will be much unnecessary blood spilled if that is true." Kaarle said. The man looked Kaarle in the eye for several seconds."Yenega, I like your boyfriend." He said with a grin. She blushed and looked at the floor. "Grand Papa he is not my boyfriend. He is a Partisan like us, or so he claims." She said. The old man stared into Kaarle's eyes and he became suddenly agitated. "You have many kills, my friend." Kaarle tried to look away, but soon stared back into the old man's eyes. "You have more than I." Kaarle said with a serious expression.

The old man erupted in laughter and slapped Kaarle's shoulder. People outside had all been waiting for the old man's sign of approval. The tension left the men as they re-shouldered their weapons. Other men rolled an enormous wine barrel to the old man's steps. "What is happening?" Kaarle asked Yenega. "I believe you have just become a Maquis." "A Basque Maquis?"Kaarle asked. Yenega flashed a look of anger. You will need another lifetime to earn that!" She said without a smile. Kaarle rested over the next weeks but soon grew uneasy and filled with excess adrenalin.

He watched patrols leave on long range missions and longed to go with them. Some never returned and some came back chewed up and wounded with stories of ambush deception and complaints about German air power. He could take it no longer and finally pressed Yenega to allow him to go on a mission. "We will take you. You have one last person to meet. He is expected to return from a deep sabotage mission he has been involved with in conjunction with the Spanish Maquis near Barcelona. They have successfully blown up a German ship full of munitions in the Barcelona harbor. There will be much celebrating tomorrow. He has been with us since the Civil war. His Basque name is Commandante Bikendi, which means "The Conquerer." She said. "Is he French, or Spanish?" Kaarle asked.

"Neither, he is Russian. His name is Yevgeny." "This may not go well." Kaarle said. "We are all aware of this. We have decided that if the two of you do not get along, he stays and you must go. He has earned the right to have a name in Basque. You have not. He is proven in battle and you are still a question mark. If you must go, we will guarantee safe passage to the Bay of Biscay where meets the ships that smuggle foreigners to England for a price.

It is quite dangerous because often the price the Nazis are willing to pay the smugglers is more than you may have to pay for passage yourself. I wish you great success tomorrow with the Russian. He is a little older than you, but probably stronger. His specialty is fighting with the knife. I have seen him kill Nazi prisoners by hand. He could have just shot them but he enjoys this thing of the knife." She said. "Thanks for the advice." Kaarle said. Yenega stood for a moment staring at Kaarle wondering if tomorrow he would still be alive.

Albar always awakened before dawn. He checked the perimeter several times during the night and slept in episodes. Benat, like a bear, hibernated. This early morning however, it was Benat who was awake and Albar who had slept from midnight until dawn. The smell of the rich Turkish coffee awakened Albar from his dream state. "Why are you awake so early Benat?" "It is the day of the return of Yevgeny have you forgotten." Benat asked. " Since we brought home this question mark, I have thought of nothing else. Where did you find the coffee?" Albar asked. "I have been saving it for a special occasion. It was a part of the treasure I took from our ambush of the German Colonel near Toulouse." Benat said proudly. All day long Kaarle worked in the fields with the Basque who told him incredible stories about the inhumanity of the Franco forces. Kaarle thought he had reached his limit of hating an ideology, or a political system with the German Fascists, but now he found a vast new capacity to hate the Spanish Fascist culture as well. The common thread of all of the Fascist dictatorships was the low value they placed on human life and the bizarre lengths they were willing to go to inflict suffering and pain on the poor and downtrodden to secure selfish objectives.

Independence was all the Basque ever wanted and they were tortured, imprisoned and raped because of it. Man is at his worst when compassion for the defeated and injured is completely absent. The fascists lacked both common decency and feelings of mercy for their adversaries. Kaarle knew his mission would be incomplete unless he helped them to be free in any way possible even if it meant staying beyond the war to take the fight back to Franco in Madrid. When he had such thoughts he became torn by his promise to help Laila find her Lebensborn child and his promise to return to Elina.

He managed to get Arin back to Laila but his commitment to the other promises was growing weaker each day. Elina suffered over her perceived loss of Kaarle, but after a respectable interval she began to reassemble the pieces of her life. The loss of her parents and then her only brother Markus was devastating, but after losing Kaarle she drifted aimlessly in a whirlpool of emotional pain and depression. Once, she stayed in bed for three days even during a bombing raid. S.O.E. sent an agent to look in on her. The next day she forced herself to go through the motions of her daily routine and before long she was coping again. Captain Ellis brought her flowers and during the remainder of the week he spent an unusual amount of time coordinating flight missions with her. His patience and understanding was exactly what she needed and before long the two fell madly in love. She was sure that Kaarle would have wanted her to be happy and the initial guilt she felt about letting another man come into her life subsided as time went by. That she gave herself to a man who had risked his life to save Kaarle made it only more fitting.

Chapter Twelve: Survival Of The Fittest.

Roland was in many ways a prodigal child, but he wasn't a super child. He was merely a blonde haired, blue eyed natural baby with an average intelligence potential and genetic traits of his Finnish Mother and German father. Just another child who would have to develop through his nurturing years alone when what he needed most was the love of just one woman. His Mother whose voice he could recognize and single out from a crowd of a thousand other voices. When they took him from Laila's arms he wouldn't stop crying for several days. He somehow knew in desperation that his loving protector could no longer even protect herself.

All of the children in his group had long since been marshaled out to adoptive parents in Germany, or to orphanages scattered throughout Nazi occupied Europe. They kept Roland in the clinic near Oslo because his mother had somehow escaped from Dr. von Verschuer's clinic in Berlin and he was their last genetic repository. He was nearly acquired by Dr. Mengele in Auschwitz who wanted to dissect him as a sibling of a twin parent but Himmler vetoed the request. This was after all an Aryan child with nearly perfect genes. He would grow to adulthood as a stud, or if the cloning technology was recovered perhaps the cloning source of many spawn. His daily routine was the same. Tests, feeding times and children's books about the Reich. He looked at the pictures and wondered about what lay beyond the windows of the children's ward. He dreamed of his Mother and fell into dark dreams that took his little mind to a place that imploded into inner space only to then explode into outer space, in the breadth of a heart beat. He awakened in sweat that soon turned to chills and he felt a loneliness his little mind was not equipped to deal with.

He stayed the night with various women. Some coddled and held him. Others shook and even beat him when he cried, or soiled himself. Men would come and the women would scream and moan as he lay in frightened silence in the dark. He thought the men were demons who came to punish the women for the times they had beaten him, but he couldn't understand why the demons also punished the women who had been good to him. He grew to understand that other children, many hundreds, would always leave while he remained right here, in this place that had become his entire world and the last place he had seen his Mother. He wondered where the other children traveled to as he imagined floating on a leaf beyond the windows that grew dark and cold to his nose, as he peered out in search of his Mother. He kept a drawing of a reindeer she sketched for him one night before a demon came and punished her. He never showed it to anyone. Instead, he kept it folded and tucked in a spring beneath his bed. As it was later explained to him by a ward nurse, who found it when she was changing sheets it was a reindeer named Tarja from the Lapland. From then on his dreams changed from riding on a leaf, to someday riding on this reindeer to find his La La, the only name he was able to pronounce when he thought of his Mother.

When Yevgeny rode into the village, rifles were fired to celebrate a victory whose news had traveled home like a prairie fire ahead of him. He lifted his own rifle high in salute of the Basque whom he had come to claim as his own people. Benat was the first to tell him of Kaarle. He digested the information and his rough face turned beet red. "Bring him out in the open! Why does he hide?" Yevgeny yelled. Kaarle walked out into the village center and extended his hand. He spoke in perfect Russian. "I would like to join you as a brother in the fight against the Fascists." Kaarle said.

Yevgeny stared at Kaarle's hand and then he spat into Kaarle's palm. The old man came out on his porch just in time to see Kaarle's gesture of friendship followed by Yevgeny's brutal response. "You are a Nazi as are all Finns. My brothers fought you all in the Winter War where your kind fought like yelping dogs. You poisoned the water. They had to eat snow to live. They f--cked your women and killed your men who fought like cowards. No one was brave enough to stand and fight." Yevgeny taunted."Out of curiosity before I kill you, what did you do in the Winter War Finn?" Yevgeny spit out the words as though they were poison on his lips. Kaarle switched to English. "He just asked me what I did in the Winter War." Kaarle translated. "I killed ugly Russians who came to my home as conquerers and left as broken men." Kaarle replied. Yevgeny dove forward with his knife that reflected the sun light across the entire clearing. Kaarle stepped sideways and planted his Fiskar into the base of Yevgeny's skull just at the Occipital bone down into the Foramen Magnum which houses the spinal cord. He died instantly. The entire fight lasted less than thirty seconds.

The men who returned with Yevgeny from Spain aimed their weapons at Kaarle who stood alone in the clearing. The old man shouted across the village from his porch. "Shoulder your Goddamned weapons! Did you not see that the one who calls himself Wolf offered his hand in friendship only to receive the vile sputum of hatred that could not be taken back? It was Yevgeny who chose the path of a fight to the death and it consumed him. Can we not mourn Commandante Bikendi while at the same time welcoming a brother who like ourselves is an enemy of the Nazi's?" The old man asked.

"Commandante Bikendi made our enemies his enemies. Should we not make his enemies ours?" Albar asked. "No. The bad blood between these fine men ended here in an honorable way. We shall not bring dishonor to an honorable fight regardless of who was the fittest to survive. We have struggled to control our own fate, let us not enter into the business of trying to control the fate of others." With this, the old man stepped back into his house and all further discussion was closed. Yevgeny's commrades carried him to a small Basque cemetery nearby and put him in the hole that had been dug earlier for Kaarle. This night no one would celebrate the death of a Maquis hero who had been replaced by a man who killed with the beauty of a Matador. Not even Barcelona would be celebrated. The mystery of Kaarle only grew as some considered him a bad omen, a man who would lead them all down the path of death and ruin. Others, not yet willing to voice their opinions, saw an awesome new leader who could bring high honor to their nation. Kaarle didn't sleep easily that night. He saw the flash of hatred in the eyes of Yevgeny's close followers. Especially Gorka, who had an evil scar across his face. Any one, or all four could perhaps drink too much and decide to test their luck with the man who killed their Commandante.

After midnight Kaarle heard a twig crack outside the window. He quickly drew his knife and stood behind the open door. He nearly planted his knife in the throat of a shadowy figure that floated inside closing the door softly, until he realized it was Yenegy. She undressed in the candle light and Kaarle thought his heart would stop. She was, even in the candle light the most beautiful woman he had ever seen. Both were silent. They sensed that what was happening between them was too rich and too pure to be spoiled by words.

Yenegy brought Kaarle to the edge of the universe and back again. Her sweetness was nectar from divine and secret places, where the air itself was an elixir that took away Kaarle's breath and returned it to him more pure than it was when her power first sucked it from his lungs. He penetrated her very soul with his own until they collapsed beads of sweat spread across their backs like the early morning droplets of dew on an autumn vineyard.

Neither said a word even after they collapsed in each others arms, satiated and floating in a blissful state. Yenegy got dressed and slipped away into the night as if in a dream that Kaarle wished would be stilled by the hands of time. He lay there in silence until just before dawn, unable to believe that it really happened. Kaarle never thought much about fate before, but clearly his life's path had been altered this night by a woman who he would now be perfectly willing to give his life to protect. Kaarle was surprised to learn that the old man, whose name was Endika, which meant "Home Ruler" was a great deal more than just a figurehead. He was the operations planner for both strategic deployment of Maquis forces in Southern France, as well as providing day to day tactical leadership of his immediate force of three hundred resistance Fighters. If he issued an order, as many as 3,000 resistance fighters could be set in motion simultaneously throughout France. He didn't participate in field operations, or patrols any longer but he had been a fierce Commander of guerilla operations against Franco's forces during the Civil war. Kaarle had the rare privilege of having been invited to listen in on an important mission to destroy a Wehrmacht supply train between the cities of Montauban and Toulouse.

Endika poured over the detailed assignments of where the defensive snipers would be positioned to protect the placement of demolitions and where the team would rally after escaping from the area separately. Kaarle remained silent throughout the meeting. As the meeting was drawing to a conclusion, Endika introduced Kaarle as a new force against the Fascists. "Wolf, have you any questions, or things you would like to add?" Endika asked. "On the operational details? No. It is a perfect plan. You have partitioned the assignments and phased each important element of the strike and have avoided rejoining the mission's members until they have left the kill zone." Kaarle said.

"The only question I have has to do with enemy forces. Who are they?" Kaarle asked. "That is an excellent question. Other than their unit designation, our intelligence is quite thin. They are the lead element of the 2d Waffen SS Division. Have you heard of them?" Endika asked. "Yes. That Division, known as "Das Reich" is considered one of the Waffen SS' most elite divisions of all thirty nine. It first saw action in the invasion of France and was then moved to Romania. It accepted the surrender of Yugoslavia, then moved into Poland and was an important element in the invasion of Russia. They reached the outskirts of Moscow before they were pushed back to the line along Kursk. It has been said that Das Reich lost as much as sixty percent of their fighting force in Russia. That they are now moving into southern France would suggest that they are being refitted most likely in order to conduct operations against us. This means that they are most vulnerable currently because their heavy losses will mean a new commander with new troops who may not have served together before." "This may offer opportunities for us as they struggle to inter-lace their units.

I haven't heard very much about whether the Allied invasion of North Africa and Italy will somehow become a coordinated invasion in Northern Europe, but you can rest assured the Russians will not stop with a victory over Germany's forces in Kursk. As they drive the Nazis in our direction we must be careful not to become hopelessly encircled by the Nazi's retreating forces. The Russians will come as far west as they can. When they fought my country, ejecting them afterwards was like removing armed fleas." Kaarle concluded.

"This is excellent input, so how do you think we should tailor our missions, including the current one?" Endika asked. "Well, to be honest, I would cancel the current mission. Conducting it now plays our hand and neutralizes our greatest advantage which is the element of surprise. You will be killing logistics personnel and destroying supplies that can easily be replaced. We can reach these supplies by burning down warehouses when the time is right. Supplies are usually sent forward from two to four weeks before the troops who will be using them are sent. If we have connections with intelligence gatherers who are monitoring troop trains along the Russian front we should wait for hard information about trains carrying soldiers and focus our efforts there. When we were invaded by the Russians, we waited for their convoys to become caught up in bottlenecks. If there were none, we created them. A stationary force in column is like shooting ducks in a small pond." Kaarle reflected. "He speaks from experience!" one of the Maquis leaders shouted out. "It's settled then. I will contact our spies in the east and ask them to alert us when a troop train with many troops is headed for southern France. We will pick the place of battle and hit them with all we've got. By the time they recover we will hit them somewhere else." Endika said.

Kaarle noticed that a few women were in attendance. He was impressed that many women were Maquis fighters and then he remembered what Yenega had mentioned, that so many men were imprisoned by the Carlists when they vanquished Bilboa that women filled the empty spaces. Women who crossed over into combat were every bit as good a soldier as any man. Courage and skill with weapons was the great equalizer. Over the next few weeks Yenega all but moved in with Kaarle. She stopped trying to hide the fact that they were madly in love, but she was none the less a Basque woman and risked violating the Basque ethic. This was a time of war and her status as a Maquis fighter allowed her to love her man as long as the light of dawn never crossed their brow together. Endika knew of everything that happened within his command. He was uneasy that two of his best soldiers were involved emotionally, but as long as it didn't effect a mission, he was, for now, willing to turn a blind eye.

Albar and Benat, as well as the other Maquis were getting edgy as they did nothing. The close followers of Yevgeny were already complaining that if Yevgeny had lived they would have already conducted several missions by now. Had the new foreigner taken over command from Endika? If so, they had a right to decide whether they wanted to be commanded by him, or allowed to move to another Maquis resistance Group. Endika received his answer at midnight. The train would be arriving in Montauban at 10:00 Hours. It would be carrying the lead Regiment of the 2d Waffen SS, some 2,000 Nazi soldiers from the Russian front. Endika called a meeting for the next morning early at 07:00 Hours. "Who can say what may have transpired exactly, had we not heeded the advice of the Wolf? All we can say for certain, is that his advice is unfolding like the petals of a rose.

We would have killed at best, 150 Nazi supply soldiers and destroyed some weapons and munitions with a train derailment. To be certain, security will have tripled. Now we have 2,000 Nazi soldiers and their security level is normal. Perfect! For this reason, I am assigning the Wolf as the leader of the mission. Wolf are you prepared to offer an Operations order or do you need more time?" Endika asked. Kaarle wasn't caught by surprise and he reacted quickly. "Thanks Endika for your trust, thank all of you for accepting me into your midst. I will try to equal the honor of being one of you. Endika I have studied the train map you gave me at our last meeting and in anticipation that you may invite my advice, I wrote an entire operations order. The only information that is critical, but still lacking, is the length of the train. Can we get this information?" Kaarle asked. "That depends, Wolf. The train may indeed add or subtract cars right up to time of departure. Someone must risk their life to be caught within a kilometer of a departing troop train. They are constantly monitoring their trains and tracks for sabotage especially as they depart. Why do you need this information?" Endika asked.

"Please take my word that it is critical to know as much as possible about the train. Which cars hold the troops, which hold supplies and which hold weapons. Where their train sentries stay do they patrol outside the train on the roof? Any bit of information. The length will help me determine where to place the explosives. By the way, what type of explosives do we have? What type of detonators? My objective is to destroy all 2,000 in their sleep. Kaarle explained. "My God. Are we now as monstrous as the Nazis?" Danel, one of the Maquis leaders shouted. "YES! I certainly hope so!" Endika shouted back. "Have you forgotten the fire bombing of our cities? Have you forgotten the death camps they sent our people where they rot away in the darkness?

Have you forgotten their policy of executing us as soon as we are captured? Did they hesitate to burn our babies to death? Anything we do to these vermin is too good a death for them. Do you want to give up your command and join the priesthood?" Endika yelled an inch from the man's face. "No Sir. I'm sorry. I forgot only for a second, the history of what they have done to us. But just for a moment, the thought of two thousand people dying like fish in a frying pan overwhelmed me." He said apologetically.

"You are a good man Danel. I have fought beside you and know you to be brave but I need to know you will not hesitate for a second to execute your part of the mission. Do I have your word?" "Yes Sir! You have my word." "Good. I believe you. Wolf as for the explosives, we have all of the TNT and Plastique you would need to destroy the entire mountain the tunnel runs through. We have Primers and detonators that can be ignited with an electrical crank handle. I have four of the best demolitions experts you could possibly hope for. They were personally trained by an American OSS officer named Rene Guiraud. He was much man Wolf. He was captured a few months ago by the Gestapo and subjected to the most severe forms of torture by Klaus Barbie's thugs, but he never cracked." "How do you know he never cracked?" Danel asked. "Because you would either be sitting in the dungeons, or you would have been executed by now at Natzweiler-Struthof if he had talked. I have reliable information that Guiraud was transferred by the Gestapo to the Dachau Death Camp where he is still even now organizing resistance inside the prison. Please continue Wolf." Endika said. Kaarle laid out a precise and well detailed operations order assigning each partition of responsibility along a very tight time line with exhaustive contingencies.

Kaarle insisted on at least three complete dry run rehearsals. After the third rehearsal Kaarle felt assured that in spite of never having worked together with them, each man would do his part. The word came back that the train was six hundred meters long. Kaarle closed his eyes and whispered to himself. "Perfect! the tunnel is twice that." "Do they know the order of the cars?" Kaarle asked. "Yes, immediately trailing the engine is a flat bed which carries nothing. It is no doubt there to trigger mines. It is followed by supplies in a closed car. After that are some forty cars that are packed with armed troops. The only Guards are riding two in the engine and four in the caboose." Endika said.

Kaarle calculated the average speed of the train by cross referencing two observations from spies in sequential cities. The train should reach the tunnel by 04:00 Hours, give or take 30 minutes. He had four hours to rig his explosives and position his men. At that hour there were no other trains scheduled, but to be certain they didn't attack a civilian train observers were posted with phones spliced into the lines that ran along the railway. The first detonation would be triggered at the entrance to the tunnel after the last car of the train had passed inside. This detonation would seal off the northern end and prevent an escape on foot by the troops from the train once the train stopped inside the tunnel. The sound from the first explosion would signal the time to detonate the second explosion. The second detonation would ensure that the train's forward progress would end and that the tunnel would become air tight, capturing all 2,000 soldiers inside. The third explosion, actually a chain of detonations would collapse the three air vents in the tunnel after the detonation of White Phosphorous grenades strung at intervals the entire length of the tunnel.

Kaarle took up his position above the tunnel entrance with Yenegy at his side. He would command detonate the first explosion, setting the entire operation in play. 04:00 hours came and went and no train. Then 04:30 Hours and finally 05:00 Hours. Apparently the train had made an unscheduled stop, had mechanical problems, or worse, the Maquisard had been betrayed to the Gestapo and were themselves about to be attacked by the very troops they stalked in their own kill zone. Kaarle picked up the wire splice. He was on the verge of sending out a command to abort when suddenly the crank handled phone clicked to announce an incoming call. Kaarle pressed the button on the hand set. "Come in OP, over." "This is OP Forward. Train just passed. It is definitely our Troop train. Over." "Good OP forward. As soon as no one on the train can see you proceed as planned to the Rally point, Out!" The train abruptly appeared from around a curve one kilometer from the tunnel entrance. It slowed to a crawl speed.

"Damn it! If the train stops short of the tunnel it can only mean a foot patrol will be sent inside the tunnel to recon before the train commits to entering. We didn't have time to cover the wire and explosives. They will discover them. No matter how thorough the plan, bad luck was always the wild card." Kaarle thought. The train kept crawling forward and to Kaarle's relief, it didn't stop. 05:00 Hours was not a time when sentrys would be at their peak level of alertness and unless specifically tasked certainly no one would volunteer to dismount from the train and walk a kilometer ahead through a dark tunnel. Kaarle held his breath as the train continued on into the tunnel. When the last car passed into the tunnel Kaarle counted to ten backwards and cranked the handle on his electric detonator.

An enormous explosion shook the entire mountain as huge rocks and boulders and tons of earth and shale entombed the interior of the tunnel at the north end. Seconds later an equivalent explosion sealed the escape of the slow moving train at the other end. Kaarle switched his crank detonator to a second wire and the pop, pop, pop of white phosphorous grenades ignited at intervals along the entire length of the tunnel's interior. Kaarle let the white phosphorous cook, setting ablaze a mixture of kerosene and motor oil along the length of the tracks inside the tunnel before he switched his detonator to the third wire. Three explosions shut off the flow of outside air to the tunnels three air vents. Within seconds, the explosions and the stream of White Phosphorous and kerosene fire trails sucked all of the oxygen from the tunnel's interior. The white phosphorous continued to burn illuminating the ghastly scene inside the tunnel full of Nazi soldiers who were scratching along the tunnel walls in search of air as their flesh cooked from the intense heat.

"Why so silent, what are you thinking woman?" Kaarle asked Yenega as they counted their resistance team members filing by toward the farm truck. "Until now, it was Germans gassing helpless victims. Now we have just killed two thousand people in less than a minute. We're the same as the Germans!" She said. "If Germany had not invaded the rest of the world. If we were invading Germany instead of the other way around, if we had fire bombed their cities as they did yours for Franco, if we had herded their children and little grandmothers into ovens then yes, we would be the evil ones." Kaarle growled. Yenega looked down at her feet. Kaarle held her cheeks, forcing her face into his but she looked to the side and finally closed her eyes tightly. She couldn't look into his handsome face and his ice blue eyes again for fear she would lose her soul.

Neither knew it at that moment but she would probably never look into his eyes again. "You will never get me to admit, or understand that by becoming just as efficient in killing as their soldiers are that we have become just like them. This is a war that needs to be ended as soon as possible. It will drag on for decades if we don't make ourselves more fierce than the Germans have made themselves." Kaarle said with anger. Still looking away, Yenega tried to console Kaarle but her heart was no longer involved, only her logical mind, but that was the problem for her. War had finally cut the human heart completely out of the equation. Her entire life had been a struggle to reconcile the heart with the mind in the core of war's evil breast and she had now reached a thin line that divided her from Kaarle, the perfect warrior. He had already crossed the thin line but she simply couldn't cross it with him.

"Yes, I agree with everything you said, I just needed to hear it laid out for me. Thank you Kaarle, we are very grateful. I will never bring this up again." She said. It was too late. She had made herself a mirror for Kaarle to see inside his own darkened soul and it frightened him. What had he become? Exactly what his trainers had meant for him to become, an efficient assassin specialized in equalizing imbalances of force. The Nazis greatly outnumbered their conquered enemies and were well trained and well equipped to maintain the superior advantage. All Kaarle wanted was to bring some of the suffering and misery back to those who brought it to others in the first place, yet he had somehow crossed a line he didn't fully understand. He felt betrayed by Yenega. She of all people should understand. "Understand what?" He asked himself. "Understand that fighting and war was just business?

That killing two thousand people in their sleep on a train was any different than killing them with firebombs while they slept in Guernica and strafing those who tried to flee their burning village, until nearly two thousand civilians had died beneath the incendiary bombs of the Condor Legion? Not to mention the dozens of priests and nuns who were butchered by Franco's forces because they had dared speak out in support of the Republic. Albar told Kaarle of the hundreds of families taken in the night after Bilbao was leveled. "Women raped, or murdered, or sent off to the concentration camps and Yenega was worried about the morality of wiping out two German battalions on a f--cking train?" Kaarle wondered.He was wounded and he felt he could never forgive her for not standing with him when he was now beginning to question his own moral compass. His soul felt like a mirror fractured into a million splinters and the feelings he once had for Yenega could not be brought back, or pieced back together. She couldn't eat the guilt of mass killing and deflected and pushed it all on his shoulders. His heart was breaking because he really loved this woman and the pain of her taking back her love from him was his thin line. A line that was drawn between them without his ability to do a single thing to stop it, or change it.

He hoped the next night that she would come to him. He had to tell her how he felt and give her a chance to make things better but she didn't come. When Kaarle went to the house of Endika the next day she wasn't there. Endika saw his sadness. "Kaarle I would sell my soul to the devil to have just a squad of fighters half as good as you. You are a rare man. You are a deliberate man who cuts through fear as though it is just a distraction. Is there any way I can get you to stay?" "Thank you Sir but I was a fool to think I could join a larger force. For better, or worse, I was meant to fight alone.

Will you ever see her again?" Kaarle asked. "That is hard to say. She has left for the Maquisard in Normandy. She asked me to beg your forgiveness. She said she needed some time alone to sort herself out." Endika said softly. "She said that she hoped you would be here when she returns, but would understand if you are not." Endika said. Endika reached Kaarle a sub-machine gun and a shoulder pouch full of ammo clips. "Here are the keys to a new motorcycle we liberated from the Germans. The Nazis will be enraged about what we did to them in the tunnel. I am ordering a cessation of activity for at least a month. We will slip into the mountains in Spain before someone betrays our location here in the south of France. " Endika reasoned. "Go with God young Viking and return safe to your lands. Here is a contact near Paris if you travel that far north. A resistance fighter there may indeed still have contact with S.O.E. Branch in London who may yet arrange for your exfiltration. She can get you forged papers. Memorize her name and then destroy the paper." Endika said. Endika reached Kaarle a thick stack of Vichy French Francs. "Here you will need to eat. Kaarle embraced the old man who gently whispered; "I am so very proud of what you did to the Nazis my son."

Kaarle drove to Toulouse and hid his motorcycle in a small shack. He watched the German troops traveling about in jeeps and saw occasional troops on foot, but they traveled in groups of four. Finally he saw a German sergeant emerge from a woman's house kiss her good bye at the door and begin his walk to work. Kaarle shadowed him until at last the sergeant took a short cut through a heavily wooded park. Kaarle swiftly killed the sergeant by breaking his neck with a violent twist from behind. He then took his uniform and buried him in a shallow grave. He put his own civilian clothes with his ammo pouch for later use.

He returned to the motor cycle and began his trip to Paris. As Kaarle drove, he thought about his conversations with Albar, who gave him a general summary of Resistance in Nazi Occupied France. It seemed there were nine separate resistance organizations in France all symbolically under the command of Charles de Gaulle who issued orders from London in code over the BBC network. The Nazis had constructed a special concentration camp for resistance fighters in the Alsace called Natzweiler-Struthof. Thousands of captured resistance fighters were taken there who either died from deprivation, or were executed outright. This led to the resistance fighter's general policy of shooting all German prisoners on the spot. It was also impractical for guerillas who depended upon speed and freedom of movement to be tied down with guarding prisoners.

The missions ranged from targeted assassinations of German commanding officers and Gestapo agents, to derailing logistics trains, sabotaging food, vehicles, weaponry and munitions and even sending short wave code to S.O.E. Branch that provided intelligence to the RAF and the American Air Force for bombing German troop trains. "How had the resistance started?" Kaarle had asked. "It started when Germany cut through the Maginot line in 1940 like a sharp knife through butter." Albar had replied. The French relied so completely on this swath of tank traps and anti-infantry minefields they completely miscalculated the power of the Luftwaffe Bliztkrieg. Being over run as a country sent the socially elite and the French intelligentsia scurrying to England for protection. The Germans for their part were quite smug and self confident.

They relished finally taking back the historically disputed region of Alsace Lorraine and knew the French had been so completely defeated, they accepted the surrender of France in an armistice signed by Marshal Henri Philippe Petain which stated that all fighting would cease. It provided for a puppet French government in Vichy, France, where the Nazis graciously agreed not to station troops and the troops who occupied central and northern France were under strict orders not to abuse the citizenry. Instead soup lines were provided by the Germans and many French citizens began to accept peaceful nonresistance as the best path to follow. They accepted German rule so well in fact, that they collaborated with the Nazis in turning in their Jewish neighbors for transport to the Death Camps. Besides, in accordance with their treaty anyone involved in violence against German authority was considered an insurgent without protection from the Geneva Convention. As such, they could be shot as spies on the spot.

Kaarle knew his papers wouldn't get him past the first road block on the way to Paris so for now, he settled for finding a bombed out building and hiding his motor cycle beneath some destroyed planking. He neatly folded his German uniform, hiding it with the motor cycle. He put his peasant clothing on. Later he stole a bicycle and pedaled it into the town center. Suddenly a man darted out of an alleyway and motioned to Kaarle. Kaarle recognized the scar on his face. It was Gorka! One of Yevgeny's close followers. "Wolf! You must come with me. Yenega awaits you." "Yenega? But I thought she left for Normandy." Kaarle said. "She changed her mind about going there alone. She wants to either go there with you, or go with you to the mountains in Spain with Endika and the rest of us." Gorka explained. Gorka led the way down the alley until they reached an old warehouse.

Kaarle slid the heavy door open and saw her sitting alone at a table. "Run Kaarle! It's a trap!" She screamed. Suddenly, from behind a screen a man leaped out and hit her across the face with the barrel of his pistol. Gorka tried to pull a pistol out to shoot Kaarle but Kaarle shoved his Fiskar up through Gorka's tongue, on up through the roof of his mouth and virtually skewered his brain from bottom to top. Kaarle withdrew his Fiskar and threw it, striking the man with a pistol in his heart. He saw that Yenega was tied to the chair in which she was sitting. He ran to retrieve his knife and cut the ropes to set her free. "It's futile Kaarle. Gorka has betrayed all of us. They took me off the train and I heard Gorka giving them directions to Endika's camp." She said. "Did he describe our involvement with the tunnel?" Kaarle asked. "I don't believe so. I heard him tell the Gestapo who pulled me from the train that he would provide information about our operations later when he received an official pardon from the Reich, in writing, along with a paid position as a spy. I hate him. I'm glad you killed him." She said.

"Let's hurry. I have a motor cycle hidden nearby." Kaarle said. As soon as they slid open the door, they saw an entire company of Waffen SS soldiers filling the alley way and closing in from all sides as well as several well placed snipers on the nearby roof tops. As the heavily armed troops moved closer they began screaming with excitement that they had caught another terrorist. Kaarle quickly instructed Yenega. "Don't admit to anything Yenega. Tell them you were only involved with me romantically and had no idea what I was doing until you recently discovered I carried a pistol. That's why you were running away from me. I will tell the same story over and over until Hell freezes over. "I love you Kaarle!" Yenega said. As they dragged her away she stared into his loving eyes.

To humiliate him and inhibit his ability to escape Kaarle was stripped naked and marched down the streets of Toulouse to Gestapo headquarters where his intensive torture and interrogation routine would begin. One of the soldiers used a course steel brush that left lines of blood in streaks, carving a large "X" on the center of Kaarle's back as he was herded along to denote that he had been captured. Yenega was shipped off to the Natzweiler-Struthof concentration camp as a spy while Kaarle was toyed with for two gruesome weeks by Gestapo before being sent directly to Dachau. Neither Kaarle, or Yenega ever confessed to anything but a simple romance and false accusations by an obviously jealous Gorka.

Chapter Thirteen: Dachau, Doorway To Death.

Kaarle was separated as a Non-Jew Political Prisoner and escaped an immediate trip to the showers, but that possibility loomed if any prison guard, or German SS Officer determined by caprice that termination was called for. Kaarle had successfully convinced the Gestapo that he was a Sudetenland German who merely followed a French girl he had met back to her native France before the war broke out. He was still classified as an undesirable of the criminal element because after all, he had killed their informer, but they hadn't yet built a trust with Gorka who could have been lying out of jealousy as the pair had claimed separately.

Kaarle was miserable when he saw Dachau. High level Germans were beginning to worry about post-war recriminations and punishment should the Reich lose the war. It was far better just in case, to let the non-Jews die naturally of typhus and starvation. With the Jews, however, orders were orders and the showers followed by the Crematoria could not be stopped. After Kaarle was assigned to a building he fell asleep. A small group of men threw a blanket over his head and forced him to stand. "Please come with us! If you have nothing to be ashamed of you have nothing to fear. Resist and we will kill you." Their leader said.

They led Kaarle through the shadows until they reached another building that had a trap door beneath a grind stone machine. They took off the blanket and directed Kaarle down the steps to a hidden cellar. A man was sitting on an elevated platform that gave him the appearance of a judge. The man and several others in the room were frail and appeared to be walking skeletons. The men who had forced him to come, however appeared in good physical condition. Kaarle filed the information away, but remained silent.

"What you say now is not to the Gestapo. What you say now should be the God's sweet truth, or we may very well kill you if we think you are lying." The man said sternly. "How do I know you are not working for the Gestapo, or the prison Commander?" Kaarle asked. "You don't. But trust has to begin somewhere. Under the present circumstances, we are holding your life in our hands. I suggest trust is a good logical next step for you. Who are you?" The man spoke with the same American accent as EagleTen. "My name is Kaarle Tuuri. I am from Suomussalmi Finland. I am an agent for the S.O.E. Branch, Oslo and London." Kaarle said. "S.O.E.? London Oslo? O.K. What's your code name? ID number?" The American nearly shouted. "My code name is Wolf. My number is 1-6-6-8-6-9-8-6." "Sixes and Eights! he's legitimate." A man with a heavy French accent said. Those are Norwegian numbers!"

"So, you are Wolf. Information moves slowly here. More slowly out than in, but we have heard of you Wolf. Can you tell us, is it fact, or fiction, that you took out a Waffen SS train in a tunnel? How many kills?" The man asked. "Two thousand, give, or take." Kaarle said almost in a whisper. The room erupted. Everyone shook Kaarle's hand and slapped him on the shoulder.' "Who were you working with?" The American asked, still suspiciously. "I worked with some Basque Maquisard near the Spanish border. I reported to a man named Endika and worked together with a woman named Yenega." "How are they?" The American asked. " I heard the Gestapo in Toulouse say Yenega was sent to the Natzweiler Struthof prison in the Alsace. Endika was fine when I left him. He said he was going to hibernate in the mountains in Spain until the heat blew over in southern France after the train attack. I hope he made it.

Yenega and I were captured after a member of Endika's group named Gorka turned us both in to the Gestapo in Toulouse." Kaarle said. "A fellow Resistance fighter turned you in? I trained that group but I don't remember the name Gorka." The American said. "If you trained them then you must be Rene Guiraud." Kaarle said. "One in the same." Guiraud said. "Don't worry, this Gorka fellow has a short life line." Guiraud said. "I know. I shortened it all the way when I discovered what he'd done to us." Kaarle said. Looks of admiration, even from Guiraud, who was the most effective secret agent among the resistance during the war, were on all the faces. "This man is special. He is on my account. He fought with my Maquisard." Guiraud said to all in the room. "May I ask you a question?" "Sure." Rene replied. "Why are you and most of the others here so gaunt and these three fellows look like weight lifters in the circus?" Kaarle asked.

The room grew silent. "It's not their fault." Guiraud said almost apologetically. "They are forced to work in the Crematorium and they need extra food because of the constant lifting of bodies. Don't worry. In a few weeks you'll look just like us. There was a time that the Germans were roasting as many as 20,000 souls here a day. It's down to the low thousands. The over all camp is losing 200 people a day to typhus and starvation. I'm glad you brought that up. We are able to bribe a few of the guards for medicine. Where's your stash?" Guiraud asked. "My stash?" Kaarle asked. "Yeah. The money you hid from the Gestapo but couldn't keep with you here because they stripped you at the gate." Guiraud explained. "It's in the fake soles of my brown leather boots. I last saw them sitting atop a pile of foot wear in the processing area." Kaarle said. Guiraud sent a man immediately to look for them. He returned shortly with the boots.

Guiraud took out a home made knife and separated the soles of the boots. Several thousand French Francs fell out on the floor. "Monsieur Wolf, you are off to a good start with the Boys Of Dachau. Stay close and do as we say and we shall all survive this last test of the Teutonic Horde that you will often hear me refer to as Le Bosche. Take a few moments to get to know your fellow S.O.E. agents here. As for me I am OSS." Rene said with a smile. Kaarle spent a few minutes with each man and then made a general statement to the room. "If it is my fate to live then I am with brothers who have almost the same life as my own. If it is my fate to die, then I could never have chosen a more honorable group of brothers to die beside, with more innocence of purpose." Kaarle said sincerely. "Hear! Hear! " the men shouted aloud in response. Kaarle stayed as close as possible to Rene and followed his lead. Kaarle thought he had lost all hope as soon as he first encountered rat soup. After a few days of dry vomiting he became accustomed to it and pinched his nose each time he swallowed.

Just as Rene predicted, Kaarle soon lost extreme body weight and looked like any other prisoner. At night Kaarle cried out in his sleep for Laila, then Elina and often for Michelle. Kaarle had somehow separated Yenega from Michelle and let Yenega slip away. He still loved Michelle and suffered for her in places only his dreams could deliver him to but he felt no longer the same for Yenega. He dreamed one night that she had been hanged at Natzweiler Struthof. He ceased to dream of her. Six weeks to the day of his nightmare about her hanging, Rene called him aside to tell him that Yenega had been hanged by the Gestapo for treason.

The night after he was informed of her death, he awakened with chills and vomiting as his body struggled to survive in a place where death was far more natural than living. Kaarle became infected with typhus from the lice that no one in the camp was safe from and unless he received a miracle he would die from it. Typhus is caused essentially by two separate forms of bacteria. Rickettsia typhi, or Rikettsia Prowazekii. Rickettsia Typhi causes endemic, or murine Typhus. It is contracted by coming in contact with the lice of rats. This is what Kaarle was suffering from. He had abdominal pain and severe headaches and pain in his back and joints. He had peak temperatures of 106 degrees and a hacking cough, followed almost invariably with vomiting until the only product was blood.

Rene came to see him. "Kaarle, I don't know if you can hear, or understand me. You have a severe case of typhus old boy. We have a Jewish doctor here who we rescued from the ovens but he tells us there is no specific cure for what you have. It doesn't react predictably to penicillin. He tells us he knows how to prepare and administer a drug called PABA, I can barely pronounce it, it's called para-aminobenzoic acid. It sounds like a kill, or cure thing to me. If you want to give it a shot, squeeze my hand." Rene could barely feel the pressure but he did feel it. "Ok, my young apprentice, I felt the squeeze. The good news is we can use most of your stash to get and administer the stuff, the bad news is that it will probably kill you before the typhus does. Oh the last good news is that if you recover, you'll never get typhus again." Rene said. Kaarle was treated with PABA and he slipped into a coma for three days. Guiraud hid him from the Camp guards lest they order him burned with all of the other typhus victims. When he awoke he got up and walked toward the door, only to suddenly discover that he hadn't left the bed at all.

His mind played tricks with him. Finally he could wiggle his toes and eventually move his heavy legs. Within a few days after being fed potato soup Rene purchased with the last of Kaarle's stash, Kaarle was able to sit up on the side of the bed and then walk. He had his miracle but it came at a heavy price. His bone stretched skin caused his face to appear as a skeleton. It was jaundiced and his hands trembled. He was a shadow of who he once was physically and his once mighty edifice of self-confidence had all but vanished. They were killing him over time. Day by day, week by week it had become a slow race toward the same destination which was death almighty.

He had to do something. He talked to Rene. "Rene, can you get me on the Crematorium detail?" He asked. "Are you joking? You can barely walk, let alone carry the bodies of others. What about mentally? Can you stand feeling death in your arms? Skeletons of women and children?" Rene questioned. "Rene I am a walking dead person. What is there not to withstand?" Kaarle retorted. "Alright. But be forewarned if you fall behind the guards will shoot you." Rene said. "I won't fall behind." Kaarle assured him. Kaarle spent the rest of his time at Dachau carrying corpses to the ovens and he never once fell behind, or asked for special treatment. Even the guards developed a begrudged respect for the skeleton that could carry many other skeletons. With the added rations Kaarle regained most of his lost strength, but much of his degenerated muscle tissue had been lost forever. Kaarle loved gathering in secret at night to listen to Rene's intelligence briefings. Quite often there was nothing to report but Rene knew the men had only hope to preserve their self belief and he would at times use poetic license to connect the information.

Strangely his intelligence briefings predated actual events. By the time the news of the Allied advances reached the men at Dachau they had already been foretold by Rene and no one saw the anachronism as odd at all. His last briefing warned the eager listeners to expect to be liberated within months possibly weeks. This briefing was given on the night of April 26th. The morning of April 29th, 1945 was like every other morning to Kaarle. He walked to his post at the Crematorium to stack yesterday's delivery of corpses to be burned in the ovens. Halfway there, he noticed an absence of the usual contingent of guards. Then he saw Albert Guerisse, a Belgian who was an S.O.E. agent but who had convinced the Gestapo that his name was Patrick O'Leary. Guerisse was escorting two American soldiers around the camp, pointing toward the ovens and making gestures as he spoke. The camp was a ghost town. Kaarle sensed danger and ran back to the barracks. "American soldiers. That could only mean the Allies had finally reached the camp no doubt on their way to capture Muenchen. Kaarle bit his lip to control the anticipation. Could it be true? Or just some Gestapo trick to break us down even further?" Kaarle wondered.

Then a very strange sequence of events took place. A tall Waffen SS Leutnant gave a Heil Hitler salute to a man who had stepped down from a tank. Instead of a formal surrender ceremony the tall Leutnant was hustled away in a jeep. Moments later came the sound of a sub-machine gun. Then the jeep that carried the Leutnant away returned without him. With this the prisoners were convinced that the Americans had taken the camp by force and they all scrambled from the barracks, pushing forward toward the cement ditch and the electric fence. A few prisoners thinking that the Americans had cut off the electricity to the fence tried to climb over it. They were electrocuted instantly.

The events became even stranger. A small group of SS soldiers began shouting at the prisoners to go back inside the camp and began shooting prisoners who refused to withdraw from the fence. Suddenly a squad of Americans appeared and shot the Germans. Chaos ensued. Prisoners ran between the buildings along with German soldiers who weren't Totenkopfverbaende and had nothing to do with camp administration. More Americans arrived and bands of Americans stalked German soldiers shooting them on sight. Firing broke out in the nearby Waffen SS training facility. German guards began shooting at Americans from two of the watch towers and the Americans decimated them with dual fifty caliber machine guns. Guerisse came running back to the barracks without the Americans who were now closing the gates so no prisoners could escape. The Americans worried that the prisoners, if not quarantined, could cause an epidemic of typhus and other diseases if they were abruptly set loose upon neighboring towns and eventually Muenchen itself.

"Guerisse! What is happening?" Kaarle asked. "On their way to the camp the crazy Americans saw the Death Train from Buchenwald near the rail bridge. It has about two thousand dead and rotting bodies in open box cars." They're mad as Hell and they are shooting anyone they believe is a German. I had to beg them not to shoot the Red Cross bloke and he was carrying a f--cking white flag. Stay inside the barracks. The Americans are even shooting at each other." Guerisse said. "At each other? But why?" Kaarle asked. I think a strange coincidence has occurred. There are two divisons involved, the 45th and the 42d divisions and some tank outfit as well. Any one of these units could have taken over the camp, but because all three happened upon the camp at the same time it has created a breakdown in authority and coordination.

These aren't disciplined soldiers after what they have just seen at the rail head. It's quite dangerous. Soldiers who are now seeing the corpses at the Crematorium and some who viewed the train that came in from Buchenwald are hunting Germans to shoot for revenge. I saw them execute about thirty SS Germans from the training facility. They were without weapons. They had already surrendered. The American machine gunner yelled at an American Colonel that they were trying to get away. How in the f--ck could anyone against a wall get away? Where are you going Kaarle?" "I can't stand by and do nothing!" Kaarle said as he left the barracks. Kaarle ran outside. As he approached the main gate he saw three American soldiers preparing to fire on ten SS soldiers who were lying prostrate on the ground hands behind their heads begging for their lives. "Bitte nicht schiessen!" They pleaded. Kaarle leaped between the prisoners and the American soldiers and laid down on top of the Germans. "Don't fire! Can't you see they have no weapons?" Kaarle screamed. "One of the Americans was a sergeant. "What the f--ck? Look what they did to you man! Why do you want to protect them?" He cried out. "I'm not protecting them. I'M PROTECTING YOU! The evil of this war cannot get worse than killing helpless people. It makes you just like them can't you see?" "How in the f--ck do you know?" The sergeant yelled out. "I know because I killed two thousand Germans in their sleep inside a train, inside a tunnel and it devours me every second of my life. Go back from this. Tie their hands and let society judge them." Kaarle pleaded. The Sergeant and his two men looked at the gaunt, suffering face of Kaarle and lowered their weapons. The men quickly tied the hands of their prisoners and marched away with them leaving behind a ghost like cloud of steam from their breath on a very bitterly cold morning.

Rene Guiraud found Kaarle and told him to prepare to leave immediately. "How can we leave? The Americans have quarantined the camp." Kaarle said. "The ranking officer General Linden acted on my request to call his Corps Headquarters to establish my OSS credentials. I vouched for all of the S.O.E. members, especially you." "Especially me?" Kaarle asked. "Yes. You're a Finn. Even though your country broke their relations with the Nazis last year, if you don't come with me now it may take years for you to get home because of the bureaucracy." Rene said. "Thank you Rene." Kaarle said with tears in his eyes. "Don't mention it. You fought with Endika. Those are my people, that makes you my people too Kaarle." Rene said.

"You don't understand. I can't come with you. I'd appreciate getting through the gate with you though because I have some very important matters to attend to in Auschwitz." Kaarle said solemnly. "Are you sure?" Rene asked. "Quite sure." Kaarle replied. Alright then but our departure must look like it's against our will. We will be led away by an American security detail handcuffed as though we are to be interrogated or else the other prisoners will riot. We will ride with General Linden to Muenchen and an allied airplane will fly me to Paris. I have some scores to settle in France, I wish you could come with me. VJ day is going to be the biggest blast on earth. Wine and pussy like an endless sea. The war is over Kaarle! Can you believe it?" Rene smiled broadly. "So you have a score to settle in Auschwitz, eh? Let me see if Linden can get you flown there." Rene said. The security detail arrived and the OSS agent and S.O.E. agents were hand cuffed and marched out of the camp. Kaarle never looked back.

True to his word, Rene arranged with Linden for a plane to take Kaarle to Warsaw. They stayed in a gasthof nearby and had a hot shower and were given clean army fatigues without insignias and new shoes. The next day April 30, 1945, in the evening, just before they boarded separate aircraft, General Linden's Aide who had been left behind to ensure their safe departure announced the welcomed news that Adolf Hitler had committed suicide in his bunker in Berlin. Pandemonium broke out everywhere.

Chapter Fourteen: Lapin Solta, The Lapland War

Finland was never really an ally of Germany. They had a common enemy in the Soviet Union, but Finland made it clear to everyone that it never considered itself a part of WWII and it wasn't buying into the Master Race bollocks either. It had only one bitter enemy, the Russian Bear. It had its separate war with Russia which found certain circumstances where military cooperation with a host of countries that included Germany became necessary. The enemy of my enemy can at times be my friend. In Finland's case it had a friend that was temporarily a friend of its enemy.

That friend was America. It maintained diplomatic relations with the United States, who it never ceased to call a friend even in the darkest hours of its war with Russia. Churchill declared war on Finland mainly to appease Stalin. In the end however, Finland did declare war on Germany. Finland was attacked by the U.S.S.R. on June 25th 1941. Finland launched a counter-attack against Russia four days after Hitler launched Operation Barbarossa. Finland then signed the "Anti-Commintern Pact" along with several other countries that had alliances with the Reich, but Finland steadfastly refused to sign the "Tri-Partite Pact between Germany, Italy and Japan, in spite of frequent requests from Berlin. This stubbornness kept Finland from belonging to the Axis coalition. Finland had been fighting with the USSR since the Bolshevik Revolution and beyond, thus what the German's considered WWII the Finns recognized to be their "Continuation War" from their "Winter War" with Russia. When it was convenient for Finland they cooperated with the Reich against the U.S.S.R. but when offered a separate peace by the U.S.S.R. in 1944, they took it. The so called Moscow Armistice came at a heavy price.

The Finns were required to pay $300,000,000 million dollars in war reparations and cede Karelia Salla and Petsamo to the Soviet Union. This cost Finland its Nickel mines and more importantly, denied it an Atlantic port. Last but not least the U.S.S.R. compelled Finland to drastically reduce its military while at the same time drive out the German military. This became known as the "Lapland War." After bitter fighting by April, 1945 the Germans were driven from the north of Finland northwest into Norway. While Kaarle was struggling to stay alive in Dachau, Germany, his country was fighting Germans and making peace with Russia in order to continue its free democratic institutions.

The Sami people were Nomads. They moved freely across a vast region that included Northern Norway Northern Finland, Sweden and the northwestern most regions of Russia. The concept of fighting for land was totally alien to them, but as overwhelming invasion forces such as the German 20th Mountain division moved into their regions the Sami found themselves divided in accordance with which of the established nations they happened to be in at the time. This had the disastrous effect of causing Sami to fight Sami. Their animal husbandry with large herds of Reindeer as a way of life had influenced their culture to be quite peaceful. The Sami people are dark skinned and short in stature. Reindeer people. When the Quisling Nazi party became a puppet government for Germany a racist policy was instituted against them and they were used for forced labor along with European POW's to construct roads across Northern Norway and Finland to facilitate the movement of nickel and iron ore to German cargo ships.

When the Moscow Armistice was signed by Finland, a part of the agreement called for the forced removal of German troops from Finland however, the Germans had no intention of abandoning the nickel mines of Petsamo just east of Murmansk along the Atlantic coast. For a few weeks the Germans and Finns coordinated Germany's retreat toward Norway cooperatively. The Germans would move north and the Finns would fire weapons in the air and peacefully occupy the terrain in increments. The Soviets learned of this and threatened to re-invade Finland to help them remove the Germans. Finland had no desire for a major engagement between the U.S.S.R. across the northern half of its country so it made arrangements with the Nazis to allow a mass exodus of the Sami people to Sweden in preparation for an all out conflict. 129,000 Samis were relocated.

Finland made an amphibious invasion across the Gulf of Bothnia from Oulu to Tornio. The battle was waged heavily for a week until the Germans began a withdrawal. The Finns had taken about one hundred German soldiers as P.O.W.'s. For his part, the Nazi Commander General Rendulic ordered his troops to capture one hundred thirty two Finnish civilians in Kemi and one hundred twenty in Rovaniemi. He then sent a message to Lt. Colonel Wolf Halsti the Finn Invasion Commander that if the German P.O.W.s were not returned immediately the Finn civilians, including 24 women would all be shot and that the nearby Kemi Pulp Mill would be burned down. Lt. Colonel Halsti sent the message to Lt. General Hjalmar Siilasvuo, the "Hero of Suomussalmi" during the Winter War and Commander of the Finn 3d Army.

General Siilasvuo sent a terse reply: "No deals with Germans!" Lt. Colonel Halsti added his own reply: If any Finn civilians are harmed or if the Pulp mill is damaged all German P.O.W.s would be shot. Further that all staff and patients in the German military hospital would be gunned down. The Finnish hostages were released. This incident was thoroughly covered by Finland's media and created an immense anti-German attitude amongst the Finnish population. General Redulic reacted by declaring a "Scorched Earth" policy. As the Germans were driven toward Norway they burned every dwelling and structure in Lapland to the ground. Even cultural edifices that traced Sami culture for many centuries were lost and destroyed forever. The Samis had fought loyally for the host countries they happened to be in, but the way the Quisling Nazis treated Norwegian Samis and the way the retreating Nazis from Finland destroyed everything in their path made the Lapland War personal for Janne. He grieved for his old friend Ahti and missed Kaarle. He hoped with all of his heart Kaarle would return home with Laila someday.

His own beloved homeland was now completely destroyed. Janne had seen enough war for two lifetimes. He had fought hard in both the Winter War and the Continuation War and was at last reduced to fighting in his own sad homeland that would never again be the same. His family was a part of the movement of refugees to Sweden and he wondered at times if he would ever be able to find them again. For now his family was his ski soldiers and it would impoverish his soul to lose any of his team. His current mission was to harass and interdict the German retreat to Norway. Janne adjusted the windage on his white sniper rifle.

The German tank commander had ice formations on his chest but stubbornly refused to ride hatch down as he searched the landscape for signs of foot prints, or ski tracks that would suggest anti-tank mines had been recently planted. Janne slowly squeezed the trigger. The shock of the round in the German Colonel's chest caused the ice on his uniform to spray into tiny crystals that spewed with the redness of his blood. The Colonel's body slid back into the tank and the hatch was sealed. The tank was the lead in a column of twenty five tanks which responded by fanning out into a line formation. One by one the tanks hit mines that caused them to send pyramids of flames and black oily smoke up into the pristine blue and white Lapland sky.

Janne lay perfectly still in his snow blind as the tanks sent probing machine gun fire into the white snow banks nearby. One of Janne's ski soldiers took a direct hit in the stomach but he didn't yell out, or attempt to stand up. Instead he rolled over face down so his arterial blood would spray downward and not reveal his team's position. He bled to death within minutes without saying a word, or making a sound. Eight tanks made it through the mine field. Janne knew they would be back soon to close in on the attack site with infantry coming forward from the opposite direction. He quickly hustled his team. When his wounded man Jarl didn't respond he probed beneath the snow to to find a place to grip Jarl's parka. Janne pulled him up by the shoulders. The blood fell from the stomach wound in coagulated clots of snow and ice. Janne wailed at the loss. The others comforted Janne who quickly recovered and ordered the men to mount their skis. He smoothed snow over his fallen team member and was soon at the head of his men as they skied a downward slope that led to thick forest. Just before the team reached the forest Janne froze in his tracks.

The eight German tanks were lined up on the ridge. Each tank was adjusting its main gun in the direction of Janne's Long Range Reconnaissance Patrol. From nowhere eight JU-88 dive bombers of the Finnish 4th Flight Regiment screamed down from altitude dropping eight two hundred fifty pound bombs that slammed hard into the tanks before a single shot could be fired. "Ironic that we were just saved by German dive bombers manufactured by Junkers." Janne thought. The team yelled with relief as they slipped deep within the forest to hide and grieve their loss.

Janne's team fought on until the last German unit passed into Norway. They were disbanded with an outpouring of gratitude for exceptional service by General Siilasvuo. Janne's team split up and headed for Sweden. After several weeks Janne found his family. The children rejoiced to see their father again. Janne's children included two boys ages ten and twelve and his daughter Margrehtta who was strikingly beautiful and had just turned eighteen. "Where shall we go Janne? They have burned down our house." his wife lamented. "We shall travel south. God will take care of us. We shall stop by the house of Ahti to make sure it is in good condition for Kaarle and Laila if they have not already returned. If they have not we shall live there to protect their lands until they return." He said.

Chapter Fifteen: War Children

On May the 5th 1945, the same day that German forces surrendered in Denmark, General Eisenhower sent surrender instructions to Reichskommissar General Boehme in Norway and by May 11th an official surrender ceremony took place in Oslo at Akershus Fortress. The Royal family returned from London and order began to return to the devastated countryside. A total of 10,262 Norwegians were killed in the war. Of the approximately 30,000 children who were born into the Lebensborn experiment throughout Europe 12,000 were born in the Lebensborn clinics in Norway. Approximately 400,000 German troops occupied the country of only 3 million. 50,000 Norwegians had been arrested and tortured by the Reich, or their Norwegian puppet Quisling government so it isn't difficult to imagine that emotions ran high when the Reich finally collapsed, but the children that once wore the Reich badge of eugenic honor now wore the mark of Himmler.

They would be stigmatized in a bitter irony nearly as much as their eugenic opposite, the Jews. Hitler succeeded in creating a hatred based concept of a Master Race and once it failed the pendulum returned with a vengeance alas once again toward the innocent. Arin and Laila anxiously awaited their turn to board the RAF bomber bound from London to Oslo. The plane had been outfitted with extra webbing seats. Laila could barely speak and buried her face in Arins chest often, sobbing with anticipation and fear. They finally reached Oslo and fought their way through the crowds where people shrieked with excitement and happiness as soldiers came home, or political prisoners were re-united with family members thought to be dead. There was no such thing as available public transportation.

The streets were filled with people looking for other people. Occasionally, a Quisling traitor was identified and sent running for his life only to be beaten to death by an accusing crowd. Order had all but vanished as the pandemonium affected everyone. Arin bought two bicycles and they began the ride toward the Lebensborn clinic where Laila was once held prisoner. Trucks, buses, cars and bicycles made it nearly impossible to get anywhere. When they arrived they saw a large crowd of people gathering outside the clinic. "Kill the Monsters! Burn the evil place to the ground!" the people outside were shouting. The German guard was gone and only two volunteer security guards were standing between the crowd and the clinic.

Laila pushed her way through the crowd followed closely by Arin. Once inside they heard babies squealing from hunger and lack of care. The German staff had all gone leaving a half dozen recently delivered mothers to tend to about forty children. Laila moved to the children and called out Roland's name. "Excuse me Miss!" One of the mothers spoke to Laila. "There was a young boy here by that name once but he was taken to Germany by Doctor Mengele. Something about special genetics I believe." She said. "My God! How long ago?" Laila cried. "About two months ago, I think. Possibly three." She said. Laila fell to the floor crying. Arin came to her side. Just then a large rock flew through the window and hit a young mother on the arm. The children began to scream. Some men forced open the door. Armed with axe handles they headed for the children. "Kill the little bastards! Evil German spawn! They yelled. Arin pulled out a revolver and shot it into the ceiling. "Take another step you sons of bitches and I'll drill all of you." He shouted.

The men backed away and were pushed aside by a squad of Norwegian volunteer policemen. "Back away! Back off! They warned. They began taking the children to a large van outside. The mothers were holding their own children while the policemen pulled the frightened, screaming children outside. The children were motherless as their real mothers ran away leaving them behind as soon as the Germans began retreating and the angry mobs formed outside. Laila saw two small infants lying in a crib together. She approached a mother who was on her way out through a side exit. "Who do those two belong to?" She asked. "Their mother ran off and left them. They're twins." The mother replied. Laila ran to the crib and scooped up the twins. Arin took one and she the other. A boy and a girl. "What are you doing lady?" A policeman asked. "These two are mine! Where are you taking the others?" She asked.

"We have orders to deliver them to the city mental hospital for testing. No telling what the Germans have created here. Some believe they aren't human." He replied. Laila was shocked that Norwegians could be so ignorant. "Well, these are mine so I will be sure to have them tested." She said with sarcasm. She ran out through the side exit with Arin close behind. They walked the bikes with the infants in baskets all the way to the house Laila grew up in. There were documents strewn everywhere on the floors and a large photo of Adolf Hitler on the wall, but the house had been fairly well maintained. A policeman walked in through the front door. "Just who might you be?" He asked. "I am the owner of this house. Unless the Germans destroyed the Kings archives I can prove that the Nazis forcefully confiscated my home. I would kindly ask you to leave unless you'd like to help us clean up the mess." She said. The officer shook his head with a grin.

"Mrs. I don't doubt a single word but if I were you I would head for the city document office first thing in the morning lest someone else tries to claim your home away from you." He said. "I will officer. Have a pleasant afternoon." She said. Laila took the infants to her bed room upstairs. The bedding was surprisingly clean. She bordered the infants with pillows and tore down curtains in another room to make them into diapers. Arin started burning the German documents in the fireplace and soon the house was spotless. "I want only to re-paint the entire place inside and out to remove the stench of occupation." She hugged Arin for a long time. "I'm so glad you and I are on the same wave length." She said. "What other wave length is there?" He asked."I only wish we could have taken all of those poor kids. I'm so ashamed of my fellow Norwegians. After all the suffering we have all been through how could they take their frustrations and hatred for the Nazis out on poor children who never asked to be born?"she asked. "Let alone born in a eugenics laboratory." Arin said softly.

Arin found a position with the Kings administration as an economist. His work was a monumental challenge, to rebuild the country from absolute devastation. The media covered the famous and not so famous hangings especially of the likes of Quisling. Laila stayed home to care for the children and piece by piece their lives grew back together. The nightmare would last until they died they both knew that, but if they stayed busy at least other things occupied their thoughts. Arin became involved in helping rebuild Jakob Stein's Synagogue and Laila made plans to convert to Judaism. They attended Synagogue regularly with the twins. Arin swore he would never dismiss his people, ever again. Laila cried all afternoon one day when she found aunt Sani and Uncle Ole's wedding picture in a small chest in the attic.

She opened the chest and discovered both Kaarle and her birth certificates and marriage certificate as well as a picture of Laila's mother and father along with a living will signed by Aunt Sani which gave all of her property and wealth to Laila. As it turned out several claims had been made against their house and it was only these documents that matched what was left of Olso's pre-war housing registry that enabled Laila to defend her ownership. Bank records taken by the King when he escaped the Nazis restored many people's homes and property and helped prepare the transition to peace. Laila's inheritance revealed a hidden bank account of Uncle Ole for a very large sum that was transferred to Laila as the only living relative. Laila tried not to think of Kaarle. The memories were overwhelming and sad. He was considered by her to be a hero and a great deal of others revered him from her Husband Arin to the Norwegian and Finnish government as well. Laila fought the concept of holding a funeral for Kaarle. Arin wanted it just to pay homage to the hero who rescued both himself and his wife, but Laila said she wouldn't be able yet to bear the sadness.

Then one bright sunshine filled afternoon in August the hot sun caused Laila to leave the front door wide open. She sat on the living room floor folding laundry when suddenly the door was filled with a large shadow. She squinted her eyes against the haze and blur of the sun rays until the image came into focus. She screamed at the top of her lungs. Arin pulled his pistol out of his desk drawer. The city plans he was working on went flying everywhere. He rushed to the living room and his jaw dropped. Standing in the door frame was Kaarle, holding little Roland's hand. "Kaarle! My dear wonderful brother you've come back! And you brought my son with you." Laila gasped for air as Arin tripped over the coffee table to get to Laila to help her up from the floor.

He was so excited he didn't realize he was still waving his pistol around in the air. "I hope you don't intend to shoot us Arin." Kaarle smiled. "Oh my God! What? Oh this? Sorry! Arin bleated out as he pushed the pistol into his waist band. Laila smothered Kaarle with kisses on the cheek and she hugged Roland carrying him to the sofa.

"Come Kaarle sit down. I want to know everything. Where have you been since you didn't return with Arin? How did you find Roland? Why weren't you able to get word to us?" Laila sobbed and looked at Roland who seemed confused by the out pouring of emotion. "Roland loves Uncle Kaarle. Roland loves La La. Roland loves Tarja." He said as he pulled out a worn and wrinkled drawing Laila had sketched for him of her favorite Reindeer.

"I received word from S.O.E. Branch, that is British Intelligence that the Lebensborn eugenics laboratory was re-built in Northern Bavaria in a cave. I knew as long as the Nazis had the ability to create clones that you, myself and other Scandinavians who fit their Aryan profile would never be safe. With the help of S.O.E. I parachuted in and blew the place up. I was picked up by the Americans and then the plane we were in was shot down." Kaarle explained. "Kaarle, I regret to inform you that Elina fell in love with the American pilot who flew your plane. They were married in London and are now living in California somewhere." Laila said. Kaarle looked off into infinity for a moment and became misty eyed. "I wish her well." He said softly. "Where was I? Oh yes, after we were shot down I was rescued by these wonderful Basque Maquisards and taken from central France to a camp down near the Spanish border. I fought by their side against the German occupation until I was betrayed by a traitor in their midst.

The Gestapo arrested and interrogated me but they never guessed I was on Himmlers short "Most Wanted" list. Instead they discarded me by sending me off to Dachau." Kaarle said with a breaking voice. Only Arin knew what those last words really meant. Kaarle had regained his weight and was physically quite fit, but he had the lost deep expression in his eyes that only those who had suffered so much wore. Arin's tears fell as he hugged Kaarle. Laila thought she had no tears left but seeing Arin hug Kaarle released the pain she felt.

"Well, last April as you know Dachau was liberated by American troops who arranged a plane for me to anywhere and I chose Warsaw. I reasoned that after you escaped and after both of their eugenics labs had been destroyed, Mengele would have free reign on genetics experiments. As long as they had you and later when they discovered I was your twin brother and that I was running from them in Germany, Roland was safe. After the second lab was destroyed, however, Roland was all they had. I discovered that Auschwitz had been closed down in January 1945, while I was still in Dachau. Little Roland was transferred with Mengele to Gross Rosen in lower Silesia but that place was shut down as the Soviets drew near. I followed Mengele's trail to Bohemia where he had joined the Wehrmacht medical unit of his old friend and fellow eugenicist Hans Otto Kahler in May, 1945. Mengele was a very demented and strange man. He could perform abdominal surgery on children without administering anesthesia while afterward visiting his "special" children, giving them candy and assuring that they had all of the food they needed and clean warm clothes. Thank God Roland was in the latter category. Mengele was preserving Roland for his study of siblings of twins and was acutely aware of the importance Dr. von Verschuer had given to Roland's genetic composition.

I believe our Finnish DNA was the only thing that saved Roland from dying on the Butcher's table, as insane as that may seem." "Roland was liberated when Mengele's unit was captured by the Americans. The Americans established an orphanage just outside Prague and that was the only place children who were still alive and who had been with Mengele could have been sent to. Complicating matters was the fact that Mengele didn't use Christian names, but rather case numbers to identify his patients. Without a name, the Orphanage merely assigned one. I surveyed and interviewed many children and was about to give up when Roland pulled out his little sketch of a Reindeer named Tarja." Kaarle said his voice breaking again.

Laila jumped up from the sofa and gave Roland to Arin to hold. She returned soon tenderly carrying a picture frame. Inside the glass encased frame was an official document signed by King Haakon with a red, blue and white ribbon attached to a gold cross, Norway's highest medal for heroism, the coveted War Cross. "King Haakon learned about your actions in Norway and Germany Kaarle. In a small private ceremony he awarded you this. Because you were believed dead he presented the medal to me on your behalf." she said reaching it to Kaarle.

Kaarle accepted the medal from her and his eyes teared. This belongs to several people who risked their lives to help me get you and Arin back home. I saw impossible bravery in places of extreme desperation. Mothers who comforted their children on their way to be gassed deserve this more than me. Thank you Laila, now take this and keep it in a chest in your attic. It is too painful to look at. I never want to see it again." he said softly.

Kaarle stayed on with Laila and Arin until early fall. He read incessantly about the broader war, which he had not been privileged to understand, since he was fighting in it. He read about other countries and developed an obsession first for Spain and then Brazil. He became more knowledgeable about both places than citizens of those countries though he had traveled there only in his imagination. He reasoned that their people were probably like the Basque. He then became obsessed with Micronesia and South East Asia and actually began making plans to work his way there on a cargo ship. Then one day he suddenly announced he wanted to return to their house in Finland to visit their parent's graves. Laila wanted to accompany him, but her work with the children made it a bit too hard for her to do so.

Kaarle gathered up his skis and snow shoes and hugged and kissed his family as he departed for Finland. Kaarle left at first snow, insisting on skiing instead of taking the train. Kaarle finally skied near Erik's house and wondered in anticipation if the old boy still lived there. He knocked on the door and was jubilant when Erik met him again with his shot gun cradled over his arm. "My God man is it really you?" Erik exclaimed. "I followed your exploits until you were shot down and then I worried that you'd met an untimely death. We escaped to Sweden after you left us that day and then on to London. I still had enemies in Sweden so we felt it prudent to keep floating on through. That's why I was able to help for awhile as I accepted an analyst position with S.O.E." Erik reflected. "I have a wonderful grandson but I'm afraid we never saw our son again. He must have met a foul ending at the hands of the Quislings." Erik's eyes watered up. I've retired from the University you know. Not a great deal of interest in genetics at the moment." Both men chuckled. "What do you suppose the future holds for genetics?" Kaarle asked.

"It doesn't look bright." Erik said with a sad and distant expression. "It seems the quickest way to start a witch trial nowadays is to espouse some idea about culling the human society of genetic defects. People can't quite make the small step in understanding that genetic engineering does not have to imply racially directed eugenics. With all of this racist blarney the Nazis spewed about I'm afraid science has been set back at least by a century. I worry now that the entire war has placed far too much power in the hands of Stalin and the U.S.S.R. From the news it appears they are wasting precious little time in absorbing their border states.

Quite a shrewd and brave little thing your country pulled off by keeping their war with Russia separate from their cooperation with the Nazis. Even today political historians seem to have missed the fact that if Finland had resisted the Reich instead of join them, Germany would have Blitzkrieged Finland into oblivion. The Russians couldn't have helped, even if they had wanted to, which they didn't because they were too busy being pushed to Moscow and Stalingrad by the Nazis themselves. With the Winter War fresh in their memories they would have no doubt callously stood by with a tinge of satisfaction as Germany picked apart an old foe. Finally after Germany would have vanquished Finland, the Russians would have moved in after they defeated Germany to then turn a greatly weakened Finland into a Vassal state. They weren't able to do that because they themselves had been vastly weakened by their war with Germany. I believe the U.S.S.R. has developed a grudging respect for Finland's stubborn determination and skillful military prowess which makes you safe from the current Soviet expansion." Erik observed. You are the little fish, that if swallowed can give the whale an awesome belly ache." Erik said.

"Finland accurately surmised the Reich would fail as far back as early 1944 when the Russians pushed the Nazis out of Stalingrad. That's why they were willing to accept a treaty with heavy war reparations when it was finally offered." Erik concluded. They talked into the late night and Kaarle indulged in both the Professor's conversation and his very old scotch. Finally Kaarle walked outside and urinated the scotch away into the bushes. He was astonished to see two wolves frolicking in the snow obviously engaged in some mating ritual. Even the animals in the wilderness seemed to realize a new era had begun. An era of natural versus unnatural. He looked out across the vast expanse of the clear galaxy and stared at the Milky Way. It made him melancholy to think that it was the same Milky Way he had stared at as a child with Laila. He missed his father dearly and loved his mother's image even though he never had a chance to be held by her even once. "Damned scotch!" He said. He hated how it made him get all soft inside.

The next morning after a hearty breakfast Kaarle bade farewell. He knew he would probably never see Erik and his lovely wife again. They knew it too and each of them choked up so much they could barely whisper good bye. Their memories belonged to a moment in time that was fading fast from the present. The only way one who had experienced the insanity and bitterness of World War II could even bear to discuss it was to place it in a category of partitions. One didn't speak of the details graphically. That would have been morbid and not in good taste. One mentioned battles, or cities, even bridges and let selective memory decide just how deep one dared wander in precipitously dangerous shadows that hovered within each category in dreadful abundance.

Kaarle skied without urgency for the first time since childhood and stopped often to admire the breathtaking scenery of the Norwegian and Finnish countryside. After three days he began to recognize old mills and churches and small villages that told him he was drawing nearer to his father's farm. When he saw the grey smoke circling skyward from the chimney of his father's farm house, his heart skipped a beat. "Squatters!" He thought. He became angry that someone would just move into another's house without permission. Especially when the absentee was fighting for the country. He took off his skis and ran through the front door. Janne's wife recognized him from the time he stayed with them during his training rotation. "My God Kaarle you startled me!" She yelled. Kaarle began to laugh just as Janne came running down the stair.

"Kaarle and Janne embraced and danced up and down in a circle. Neither could stop laughing and celebrating their reunion."I'm sorry Kaarle. The damned Nazis burned us out in the North. My poor homeland. I thought you wouldn't mind if we moved in here to temporarily protect the place for you from squatters and it looks like we became the squatters." Janne explained. "Janne don't be ridiculous. I was planning to ski North and beg you to come and stay with me. This is just perfect. Just please never go. Laila is going to stay in Oslo and other than my aunt in Helsinki, if she is still living, I have no one." "I don't want to live alone." Kaarle said sincerely. "Well in that case you have convinced me that we have a responsibility to you to stay and take care of you." Janne said. Just then Margharetta walked in the door. She was stunning even in common clothes. Kaarle tried not to stare but he couldn't take his eyes off of her. Janne noticed and when Kaarle wasn't looking Janne raised his eyebrows and grinned at his wife who tried to pretend to be put off by the suggestion.

"You were just a small girl when I saw you last." Kaarle exclaimed. "Well I'm eighteen and a woman now!" She said without shyness. Kaarle bowed slightly and smiled as he acknowledged her new status. When spring arrived Kaarle and Janne used the lumber Ahti stored in the barn to build a larger house on the south forty hectares of the farm. Kaarle and Margharetta had fallen madly in love and this would be their starting house. They had a summer wedding. Laila, Arin and their beautiful children traveled to the farmhouse to attend. Everyone whispered how stunning Margharetta and Kaarle were as a couple with her bronze skin and dark shiny hair and beautiful brown eyes that sparkled when she looked at Kaarle's blue eyes and blonde hair. "How boring if everyone looked the same." Laila thought. Janne managed to collect an enormous herd of Reindeer. One little female reindeer that demonstrated gentleness was trained to give the children rides. Laila opened a string of successful dress shops and salons all over Scandinavia and became quite wealthy. Under protest, Kaarle finally caved in and accepted a wedding gift of cash from Laila that would mean his new family and himself would never want for anything. Laila very proudly showed off that she and Arin were expecting a baby by the fall. Its name would be Kaarle if a boy and Sani if a girl. The wedding party moved from the church to the farm and the festivities and celebration lasted all week.

Finally the day came when Laila and her family had to return to Norway. The farm hummed with excitement a few months later when Margharetta announced that she and Kaarle too were expecting their first baby. Kaarle took Margharetta out for a stroll through the snow and as they gazed up at the sky it began to pulsate with Northern Lights.

"This is good luck in the Sami culture Kaarle." Margharetta said gently. "Yes I know. Guovsahas. It means that the vast sky and the powerful lights are being sent down to you and me and our baby as all of natures Gods watch over us." He said. "Oh you know about our Shaman history." She said with surprise. "I was taught many more things by your father than just fighting." Kaarle said as they kissed beneath the clear, perfect arctic sky. Kaarle looked at the beautiful face of Margharetta and watched the colors of the sky dance across her eyes. His heart was filled with hope for the future. He would soon train Janne's sons to be ski soldiers and when his own sons were old enough Janne's sons would train Kaarle's sons and so it would continue for all time, for the future of Finland.

The End

Visit http://actionthrillers.net

Made in the USA
Charleston, SC
04 March 2014